ALIEN³

THE UNPRODUCED FIRST-DRAFT SCREENPLAY BY WILLIAM GIBSON

THE COMPLETE ALIEN™ LIBRARY FROM TITAN BOOKS

ALIEN³™

THE UNPRODUCED
FIRST-DRAFT
SCREENPLAY BY
WILLIAM GIBSON

A NOVEL BY HUGO-AWARD WINNING AUTHOR
PAT CADIGAN

TITAN BOOKS

ALIEN³™: THE UNPRODUCED SCREENPLAY BY WILLIAM GIBSON

Print edition ISBN: 9781803361130
E-book edition ISBN: 9781789097535

Published by Titan Books
A division of Titan Publishing Group Ltd
144 Southwark Street, London SE1 0UP
www.titanbooks.com

First hardback edition: August 2021
First paperback edition: November 2022
10 9 8 7 6 5 4 3 2

A CIP catalogue record for this title is available from
the British Library.

Printed and bound by CPI Group (UK) Ltd., Croydon, CR0 4YY.

This one is for William Gibson, of course,
a true friend, a brilliant mind
And the rest of the *Mirrorshades* crowd
(In order of appearance on the
Mirrorshades Table of Contents):

Bruce Sterling
Tom Maddox
Rudy Rucker
Marc Laidlaw
James Patrick Kelly
Greg Bear
Lewis Shiner
John Shirley
Paul DiFilippo

(Pro-tip: If you're looking for the only woman's
name, it's on the title page of *this* book)

Like everything else I do, this is also
for the Original Chris Fowler
Always the most interesting person in the room

1

Homo sapiens had been gazing up at the stars for about three hundred millennia before they finally managed to launch themselves off the planet of their origin toward those countless points of light. It was nowhere nearly as long before interstellar space travel became as matter-of-fact as the daily commute on the freeway had been for previous generations.

By that time, humanity had been through many changes but certain things were perennial: humanity's restless curiosity, competitive spirit, and stubborn territoriality, which had so often caused hostilities among themselves. Then humans made contact with other intelligent species and discovered to their uncomfortable surprise that as a civilization newly capable of space travel, they had an awful lot to learn, mostly about distance.

The standard for planet-dwellers was miles or kilometers. In space, however, the distances were so enormous they were measured in terms of light-speed, ranging from the light-year all the way down to the light-second. Humanity found that the old organizational models that had, in one form or another, guided the development of civilization on Earth didn't hold up at such a large scale.

One of the biggest adjustments for humankind was in the area of conflict-resolution. For most planet-based societies, it was business as usual—war, then peace, then war, then peace, interspersed with diplomacy or political chicanery, depending.

War in space, however, just wasn't possible. In the time it took for opposing forces to meet for combat, circumstances on their respective sides had changed and they had no reason to fight. This was due in part to the fact that although space travel had become easier, it still wasn't cheap. In general, no government could afford, much less condone, the expense of sending out a fleet of warships just to have them destroyed.

Nor did it make sense to fight over territory when there was more than enough to go around. Even in the remote arm of the Milky Way where Earth was located, there was a plethora of unclaimed worlds where humans could plant a flag. Many of the planets needed terraforming but there was no shortage of technology or volunteers for new colonies, either in search of adventure or simply because they wanted a fresh start on a new world.

The colonists on LV-426 were all first-wavers, i.e. terraformers who were in the process of turning a rock into a not-so-hard place. LV-426 was actually a planetoid in stable orbit around an equally stable star. But its wealth of natural resources was the real appeal for its co-financiers. Both the American Extrasolar Colonization Administration and the Weyland-Yutani Corporation agreed that it would be worth every penny of their respective investments. Weyland-Yutani had been so confident, they had requested the colony be named Hadley's Hope, in honor of their first administrator, Curtis Hadley.

Besides terraformers and environmentalists, the one hundred and fifty residents of Hadley's Hope also included research scientists, engineers, geologists, and warm bodies for manual labor, along with their families and a full complement of medics, nutritionists, educators, and other support personnel. Working continuously around the clock, they produced a breathable atmosphere in under forty years, breaking the previous record of fifty-nine years. Hadley's Hope became the prime example of how a partnership between a governmental body and a corporation in the private sector could yield a success that both could be proud of, a brilliant jewel in their two-headed crown.

Or it had been, until that awful woman suddenly popped up out of nowhere after being in cold-sleep for forty-seven years claiming there were monsters on LV-426. Some grotesque creature had supposedly killed all her crewmates on a freighter called the *Nostromo* where she'd been a warrant officer. With the rest of the crew dead, she'd been forced to abandon ship and blow it up, saving only the ship's cat.

The crew had been killed but she'd saved the *cat*? Yeah, that could happen to anyone.

The crazy cat-lady had to be trouble. Right after she showed up, Weyland-Yutani lost all contact with the colonists—as if she'd jinxed them! A rescue party of Marines was sent out, taking the crazy cat-lady with them, and that was the end of the matter. There was no further mention in the general news outlets and the details faded from public awareness. Had anyone given it even a brief thought, it was with the assumption that the Colonial Marines had taken care of everything. They always did.

Four years later, the Union of Progressive Peoples border protection crew received an alert that a spacecraft was heading straight for them. If it continued on its course, it would enter the UPP sector in blatant violation of a treaty the unprincipled capitalists had sworn they would honor unfailingly, above all things.

Breaking promises was typical of capitalists. The UPP governing council were only surprised that it had taken them so long.

The *Sulaco* had departed for LV-426 with a squad of twelve Colonial Marines and the synthetic assigned to them, plus two civilians: a Weyland-Yutani bureaucrat, and the crazy cat-lady. When it reappeared four years later, there were only four passengers aboard, all in sleep capsules: one Marine, the now-forgotten crazy cat-lady, a nine-year-old girl who was the sole survivor of the Hadley's Hope colony, and the Marines' synthetic—or rather, what was left of him.

A human couldn't have survived such catastrophic injuries; most synthetics wouldn't have made it, either. But this was a particularly robust model, built for adverse conditions, skilled in the use of many different kinds of equipment, including weapons.

Unfortunately, none of these things had protected him from an enraged queen Xenomorph. But then, all the Marines' skills, training, and weapons hadn't done them much good, either.

And to make matters worse, it wasn't over.

2

The plastic cocoon enveloping Bishop was more translucent than transparent, so even before milky-white condensation had occluded the inside of the sleep capsule, all he'd been able to see were vague shapes, and not even that much after the lights dimmed. He could barely discern the outline of the thing growing out of the ragged hole where his torso ended. But he didn't have to see it to know what it was. He just didn't know *how* it had come about.

This development didn't line up with anything they had learned about the Xenomorphs. Apparently there was far more to this particular horror than they had ever suspected. The intelligent beings that had engineered this species were highly complex and even more deadly than their creation.

There was no doubt in Bishop's mind that the Xenomorphs had been engineered. Humans had encountered plenty of aliens and the equally alien environments that had spawned them. On every world,

Nature was a merciless and unforgiving force that had produced some pretty startling lifeforms. But Nature was also well-ordered; even the most vicious predator had an ecological *raison d'être*. This species' behavior didn't fit any known system.

The Xenomorphs weren't territorial—they didn't seem to possess the concept. For all Bishop knew, they didn't even understand the idea of location, except in terms of a change in ambient conditions. No matter where they were, they were always in the same place: their killing ground.

Bishop filed that away for later study, although he had no idea if there would be a later for him. The *Sulaco* was so far off-course that by the time anyone found it, the growth sprouting from his innards might have already consumed the rest of him and adapted itself as necessary. It was the only known lifeform capable of such extreme, not to mention rapid, biological adaptation, all for the sake of its drive to kill.

As far as Bishop could tell, killing was the species' first and only purpose. The simplicity was deceptive, something humans had rarely—if ever—encountered in any lifeform larger than a virus. Humans tended to equate "simplicity" with "simple," which had caused them to underestimate the species' capabilities and overestimate their own chances against it. There was little data on them because few people survived an encounter long enough to make any detailed notes, and those who did escape with their lives had little insight to offer beyond, *Take off and nuke them from orbit, it's the only way to be sure.*

But the aliens weren't just simple—they were pure.

The sound of the alarm was slightly muffled by the sleep capsule, but it was no less discordant and unpleasant. Something else had gone wrong, but for the moment Bishop didn't know whether it was a few malfunctioning sensors on the cargo deck, or the hull starting to buckle from damage they hadn't detected before going into cold-sleep.

Or rather, *more* damage, he thought. If his unwanted bedfellow was any indication, a great deal had escaped their notice.

Abruptly, the console nearest his row of sleep capsules activated and began to transmit a copy of the message currently scrolling slowly upward on the monitor to the incident log in Bishop's neural net:

```
TROOP TRANSPORT SULACO
CMC 846A/BETA
STATUS RED
TREATY VIOLATION
REF # 99A655865
CAUSE: NAVIGATION ERROR
```

The alarm cut off and Bishop heard the bland, female

voice of the ship's security system addressing the empty air:

"Attention: this is a ship-wide notification. Due to a failure in the navigational system, the Sulaco has entered a sector claimed by the Union of Progressive Peoples. Auxiliary systems are now online and the course has been corrected. In the absence of Diplomatic Override, hardwired protocols prevent—repeat, prevent—arming of nuclear warheads. On the present, corrected course, the Sulaco will exit the UPP sector at 1900 hours, 58 minutes."

A glitch in the navigational system wasn't good news but it was preferable to imminent structural failure. Bishop was more concerned about the spoken announcement. With all of them in cold-sleep, there shouldn't have been one. It could have been another glitch—there was never just one of anything, especially glitches. Or someone was up and moving around. Someone or some*thing*.

Bishop knew it couldn't be any of the three humans. A capsule malfunction would have tripped a different alarm to wake all three of them, who wouldn't have just left him like this. No, the surprise guest had to be a Xenomorph. Despite their size and eagerness to kill, they were incredibly skilled at concealing themselves.

The queen from LV-426 had stowed away in the dropship's landing gear without triggering any alarms, then made its presence known by driving its tail through his chest and ripping him in two like a piece of paper. Now, in hindsight, he knew they'd been foolish to assume the queen had been alone, that Ripley's forcing it out the airlock meant it was all over. But then, they'd all been more concerned about Corporal Hicks. He'd still been in a great deal of pain from acid-blood burns and Ripley had kept him conscious only long enough to brief him.

She'd had a harder time getting Newt into the sleep capsule. When Ripley told her it was safe to dream again, the girl had looked at her with a mix of hope and uncertainty, as if wanting so much for Ripley to be right, but not quite believing it.

Ripley had tried to be as gentle as possible when she had wrapped him in plastic and placed him in the capsule, even as he had assured her she wasn't hurting him. Pain served the same purpose for a synthetic as for humans— i.e. a warning that something was wrong—but it wasn't the same kind of physical sensation. It wasn't a pleasant sensation but it wasn't debilitating in and of itself; he could damp it down to the equivalent of background noise while he continued to function.

Being torn in half by a furious alien, however, exceeded all parameters of sensation. The pain utility had overloaded and was now completely offline. What resources were left in the ruins of his body were mostly concentrated on maintaining coherent mentation. He was programmed to continue as best he could until he had completed his mission, or his power ran out.

Ripley didn't seem to understand this, probably because she wasn't familiar with artificial persons made for hazardous duty. Or maybe she had simply been demonstrating that she had forgiven him for being synthetic.

It was too bad he'd been physically unable to do her the favor of putting her into cold-sleep. As traumatized as she was, she'd needed gentleness a lot more than he did. Then again, if he *had* been able to put her into the capsule, maybe *she'd* have something growing out of her midsection. And for all he knew, she did—perhaps all three of them did. There was no way to tell, no way to know if the humans were safe.

The only thing he did know was, there was never just one of anything.

His vision started to dim as his systems put him into standby to conserve his remaining energy. His last observation was that the coating on the inside of the capsule lid was becoming thicker.

3

At Rodina Station, first and only interstellar capital city and home of the Union of Progressive Peoples, four shifts of border-watch crews tracked the approach of the wandering spacecraft while making bets as to whether the pilot would actually have the stones to unlawfully violate UPP territory, or turn aside at the last moment.

If it were the former, would they send an SOS begging for help because life-support was failing and they were almost out of air? Rodina Station would have to take them in, of course—all governments and nations were bound by the Benevolent Civilizations Treaty, which made it mandatory to rescue travelers in distress, or face universal embargo. The UPP preferred to have no contact with decadent capitalists, but an interstellar space station couldn't survive without trade.

Someone suggested the pilot might be one of those blustery libertarian-anarchist-sovereign persons who deliberately violated borders, refusing to recognize what they called bullshit authority because nations weren't real, and nobody could own empty space. A rather exciting prospect for sure, but also highly unlikely—there weren't many blustery libertarian-anarchist-sovereigns around anymore. Most of them were imprisoned by some bullshit authority that didn't know it wasn't real.

By contrast, the universe was absolutely *infested* with capitalists.

When the *Sulaco* finally entered UPP space, it did so without even a minimal hailing signal, as if no one aboard had any idea they were violating a treaty. It had been a hell of a long time since some entitled, money-worshipping, shopaholic capitalist had been so brazen. Maybe this was how they relieved their capitalist ennui—they went looking for trouble just to rouse themselves from the semi-conscious stupor brought on by compulsive consumerism.

The watch-crew on duty immediately hit the all-hands alert, effectively putting Rodina Station at DefCon 1 before they had any actual information on the errant spacecraft. Then the data came through, and the anticlimax was overwhelming. Worse, nobody won the pool.

Rodina's intelligence division didn't share their feelings. As an official Colonial Marines vessel, the *Sulaco* was a treasure trove of information that had drifted into their reach sheerly by chance. Shit happened, and sometimes it was *good* shit. Since it would only be accessible for limited period of time, they had to act fast.

* * *

The interceptor Rodina sent out to rendezvous with the *Sulaco* was an older model the manufacturer had replaced years ago, but it was hardly obsolete. The pilot made a perfect in-motion landing atop the *Sulaco*, directly above an airlock. He and his two-person crew had worked together before, gathering intelligence from sources not easily (or legally) accessible, under difficult circumstances.

This assignment wasn't especially hazardous but the pressure was on. The ruling council hadn't actually told them in so many words that they shouldn't bother coming back without something of unprecedented significance, but they all got the message.

The commando in charge was an old-school warhorse with the old-school name of Boris, who said he was a direct descendant of the Bolsheviks who had overthrown the Russian government in the early twentieth century. A bold claim, but questionable—most of the Progressive Peoples at Rodina were of uncertain parentage. As well, pedigree was for animals, not humans, and thus not progressive. Still, everybody had quirks; his was harmless.

The commando in the number two spot was a young Vietnamese woman who had fetched up at Rodina some years earlier on a transport filled with an assortment of the rootless, the stateless, and the hopeless. Everyone, even the non-English speakers, called her Lucky. Explaining her surname was Luc and her given name was Hai was a lost cause—Occidental name order was standard at Rodina Station like it was almost everywhere else. Nor did she try correcting anyone's pronunciation; the Progressive Peoples were as tone deaf as the capitalists they scorned.

In any case, she didn't mind the name—more often than not, she *was* lucky. Not in the superficial way involving money or material goods, but in the important way: survival. Early in her young life, Luc Hai had learned that the key to good fortune was being observant. Bad things always happened, to the good and the not-so-good, to the innocent and the guilty, the just and the unjust. It was simply how the universe worked. But no matter who you were, where you were, or what happened to you, chance *always* favored the prepared mind.

The third member of the team was Ashok, and Luc Hai didn't actually know very much about him beyond his name and his repertoire of skills. This wasn't really unusual. Most people who came to Rodina Station didn't share much about themselves. While chance favored the prepared mind, discretion was the better part of everything.

Even from a distance they could see that the vessel had sustained the sort of damage incurred in out-and-out warfare. The logo on its hull was scraped but still readable: Weyland-Yutani. It figured that the fascist military would fall under the aegis of the most corrupt operation in the galaxy.

Once the interceptor was securely attached to the

trespassing spacecraft, they suited up and Boris opened the floor hatch to let Luc Hai into the airlock, closing it behind her so she could expel the air before opening the outer door. She attached a couple of decryption units to the *Sulaco's* airlock, waiting with one hand pressed to the access so she could feel the vibrations as the units worked.

Nothing happened.

She looked up at Boris watching her through the small window of the inner door, and shook her head. He signaled Ashok, then gestured for her to wait. Fifteen seconds later, the airlock shuddered under her hand as it started to open. She gave Boris a thumbs-up, closed the interceptor's outer door, and waited for him and Ashok to come through the airlock so they could enter the *Sulaco* together.

The ship's gravity kicked in as the lights came up to reveal they were in the cargo hold. Luc Hai was first down the ladder to the deck. After a quick look around, she signaled Boris and Ashok that it was safe to follow. Radios would have made this so much easier, but the commanders-in-chief for field operations had decided no frequency could be made completely secure from eavesdroppers.

Luc Hai would have pointed out that sign language wasn't completely secure, either, but at her present rank, she wasn't qualified to offer criticism. All she could do was stay alert and hope she never got into a life-or-death situation with her hands full. At least the air was breathable so they could open their faceplates.

The commandos fanned out, weapons up and ready. With all the passengers in cold-sleep the place hadn't seen any activity for a long time, but Luc Hai couldn't shake the idea that something bad had happened here. The battered dropship secured to the deck a few meters away did nothing to allay her uneasiness.

Had there been some kind of armed conflict on LV-426? She couldn't remember hearing anything, but Boris might. He was looking the ship over with great interest while taking care not to get too close.

Luc Hai took a step toward him, then froze as she felt something strange under her boot. She looked down but what she saw didn't make sense.

The human legs lying twisted and broken on the deck were attached to a partial lower torso that appeared to have been torn from the rest of the body by sheer brute force. What was so powerful it could rip a person in two like flimsy cloth, and discarded the unwanted part like trash?

More importantly, was it still here?

Slightly less importantly, why was there powdered milk all over the remains? Or was it talcum powder?

No, she realized, it was dried-up robot-blood. There was an old joke about putting it in coffee, but she could never remember it because she didn't drink coffee, and it wouldn't be any funnier to her now—

Before her thoughts could pick up momentum, Boris and Ashok came over to see what she was looking at.

Boris made a disgusted face and reminded them that time was short, the council was expecting a hell of a lot more than broken robot legs, and they had to find a way out of here to the rest of the *Sulaco*. She and Ashok dutifully obeyed, Ashok looking as spooked as she felt.

"Attention, please. This is a ship-wide security announcement."

They all jumped. The female voice had no hint of urgency, nothing except a bland matter-of-factness.

"Breach detected," it continued. *"Security personnel are to proceed immediately, with full backup, to B Deck, Cargo Lock 3 to take appropriate action."*

The three of them stayed completely still, in case security personnel in the form of humans or robots actually showed up. After ten seconds of utter silence, the voice repeated the message. Luc Hai hoped they could figure out how to shut it off before it drove her crazy.

Boris beckoned to her and Ashok from the entrance to a dark passageway. He took a step in and waved one arm around, waking the motion sensors and turning on the light. That had to be a good sign, Luc Hai thought. If the motion sensors were still working, conditions aboard the ship couldn't be *too* bad, and it was unlikely they'd come across anything worse than broken robot legs.

The announcement repeated only once more as they moved cautiously along the passageway. Probably triggered by movement, Luc Hai thought, and now that the security system no longer detected anything moving around on the deck, it assumed the situation had been resolved. Capitalist security was such a joke.

The passageway took them to the cold-sleep chamber. As soon as they entered, lights flickered on but only at half-strength. Luc Hai wanted to believe the passengers probably knew the lower setting would be easier on the eyes when they woke up, but she'd never been any good at lying to herself.

Her misgivings intensified as she looked around at all the empty capsules; their open lids gaped like sterile beaks. All, that was, except the first four capsules in the row nearest to where she was standing.

Gesturing for Ashok to have a look around the rest of the chamber, Boris moved slowly to the first occupied capsule. Luc Hai followed him, keeping her weapon up and ready.

There was nothing out of the ordinary about the first three capsules: a woman, a little girl, and a Marine. Status lights on each one indicated they were functioning perfectly and the occupants all looked normal, although the Marine had sustained injuries to his face and upper body, burns of some sort. Bandages hid most of the damage, but he'd need treatment when he woke up.

The last capsule, however, was trouble. The condensation on the inside of the lid was the same milky-white as robot-blood, and Luc Hai didn't think it was a coincidence.

If the top half of the robot was in there, something had gone very, *very* wrong.

Luc Hai stood back as Boris attempted to pry the capsule open by forcing his gloved fingers under the edge of the lid. He wasn't having much luck, and despite the bulky vacuum suit, his body language clearly indicated he didn't want any help.

Fine with her, she didn't want to help him—she wanted to stop him. But she knew better than to try. Boris didn't react well to a subordinate questioning his actions. On the other hand, he'd react a lot less well if he had to leave his legs behind when they went home.

Letting out a frustrated growl, Boris punched the capsule. Luc Hai's jaw dropped; Boris was often gruff but he was calm-gruff, not given to displays of temper and not tolerant of those who were. The impact instantly jolted him out of his anger fugue and back to himself.

He turned to her and gave a faint, embarrassed laugh. "That's called 'percussive mode.' Learned it from an engineer."

Luc Hai barely heard him. She was staring at the capsule, now slightly off-kilter on its base. The red and green status lights on the end flickered for a couple of seconds before they went off. There was a soft *clunk* as a lock released, and then the whited-out lid slowly lifted away from the bed.

Dense white fog flowed over the edge of the capsule in graceful billows. Luc Hai tried to pull Boris away with her but he shook her off with an emphatic gesture to keep her distance. She took another step back, half-expecting the fog would turn to liquid when it hit the floor, but it only disintegrated. She started to say something to Boris about leaving, then saw that all the fog had cleared away to reveal some kind of egg-shaped thing sitting in the middle of the capsule.

Or, more precisely, growing, its roots indistinguishable from the ragged guts of the robot's upper torso.

The egg didn't have a hard shell—it looked rubbery and wet, like something a reptile would produce. Had the capitalists programmed their machines to reproduce like robot-lizards? Was it more economical to have robots grow their own? Unease increasing, Luc Hai moved around behind Boris to move up on his left.

Now she saw a few shreds of plastic under the robot's head, the remains of a medical catastrophic-injury cocoon. Wasting medical treatment on a machine was yet another example of capitalist stupidity but she couldn't work up much indignation about it. There were probably two dozen cocoons untouched in their supplies and none of the humans needed them, not even the Marine.

The robot's head rolled to one side and its eyes opened, staring directly into her own with an expression of *suffering* on its face.

Luc Hai felt an intense dropping sensation in the pit of her stomach. No machine could actually suffer, whether it was a centrifuge, a spacecraft, or a robot that looked like a human. Her gaze traveled from his face along what was left of his body to the egg growing out of his torso, which was also impossible. Nothing grew out of inanimate objects.

At the top of the egg, flaps suddenly unfolded with a moist, fleshy, smacking sound. Boris took a step back just as something sprang out of it, hitting his face with a splash of ugly, yellowish liquid. Luc Hai jerked back, avoiding a large blob that landed exactly where she had been standing only a moment before. To her horror, it began eating through the metal with a loud hiss, which was quickly drowned out by Boris's screams.

Luc Hai turned to see Boris was still on his feet even as the thing from the egg sank *through* his helmet and into his head. The creature looked like a three-way cross between a snake, a jellyfish, and a squid. His screams became muffled, then took on a strangled quality as he staggered backward, clawing at the creature with both hands as he turned and broke into a clumsy run.

Leaving Ashok to fend for himself, Luc Hai closed her faceplate and followed him into the passageway at what she hoped was a safe distance. Her helmet was filled with the sound of her own terrified breathing but she could still hear Boris's cries of pain as he headed for the cargo deck in an off-balance, stumbling run, sometimes hitting one wall and rebounding off the other.

She kept waiting for him to fall, wondering what she would do when he did, how she could possibly help him. Somehow he made it all the way to the cargo deck, and kept going for almost half a minute before he finally fell face-down three meters from an airlock marked EMERGENCY ONLY.

Luc Hai used the barrel of her rifle to roll Boris onto his back, hoping it was over. The creature's body was pulsing now as he clung to life, his hands making feeble swipes at the thing. Or maybe those were just spasms—he couldn't possibly be alive with a monster eating his head.

Slinging her rifle, she drew her sidearm, and then hesitated. Boris was past caring, but after all they'd been through together it felt disrespectful to shoot him in the face, even if he didn't really have one anymore.

On the other hand, he'd have ordered her to make sure the thing was dead no matter whose face it had landed on.

She moved out of range of blowback and took aim, then closed her eyes as she pulled the trigger.

The mess of bloody tissue, fragments of bone, and helmet were dissolving even more quickly than the metal deck underneath. Other, smaller holes were opening up all around wherever pieces of the creature had landed, and the hissing was so much louder here, practically thunderous. Luc Hai could barely hear her own grunts of effort as she dragged Boris by one leg toward the nearest airlock, desperate to get them there before he fell apart.

Muttering an apology to Boris for the unceremonious treatment, Luc Hai hit the OPEN button beside the hatch, shoved him into the airlock, and punched EMERGENCY

EXPEL. A red light overhead started flashing as the inner door snapped shut and a siren went off. Luc Hai closed her eyes, feeling the vibration as the airlock opened and spat Boris's body into the void.

The siren cut off as the outer hatch closed and the airlock was re-pressurized. Luc Hai remained still, counting her breaths and willing her pounding heart to slow down. Although her commando training wouldn't let her fall apart until she was back in her quarters, she needed a few seconds to pull her shit together.

It had just been a mission to gather intel—get in, get the data streaming, get out, and get gone, leaving no sign they'd displaced so much as a molecule of air. A simple mission, and about as safe as any espionage mission could be.

Was supposed to be safe. *Should* have been safe. *Would* have been safe if they had just set up a data transfer conduit from the cargo deck without investigating anything else on the ship. If they had, they would have been back on the interceptor, monitoring the big fat data stream from the *Sulaco.* Boris would have been telling them about their mistakes, in between bullshit fairy tales about his glorious Bolshevik ancestor, not flying headless through the void, and she'd have been a little bored, not traumatized. While Ashok—

Her heart began pounding faster again as she realized she was no longer alone. She'd been so stupefied, she hadn't sensed something creeping up behind her. Hell, she hadn't even noticed that the hiss of acid eating through metal was nowhere nearly as loud as it had been. Luc Hai swallowed hard as she straightened up and turned around.

The monster standing at the mouth of the passageway had multiple limbs sprouting at weird angles from an irregular bulk atop two legs. As she raised her weapon, the thing stepped forward and turned into Ashok, carrying half a robot in his arms. The *right* half.

Ashok was so smart, she thought. The robot would contain data that wasn't in the ship's computers and they were legally allowed to confiscate it as suspicious tech aboard a trespassing spacecraft. It would give the UPP an even greater advantage than they'd thought.

When they returned to the interceptor, Ashok locked the robot in the quarantine box. They put themselves through decontam three times during the return trip and twice more on arrival, just to be on the safe side. Still, Luc Hai couldn't scrub the image of the robot's face from her mind. She told herself not to anthropomorphize, but she couldn't forget how relieved she'd felt when they'd closed the quarantine box and the robot hadn't looked like it was suffering anymore.

4

Anchorpoint was one of many refueling and layover stops serving several interstellar shipping lanes. The size of a small moon, it was a hodgepodge of variously sized chunks that might have been stuck together at the shifting whims of a very inventive child using pieces from several different sets of toys. Construction was always in progress here, either to add new areas or to expand and modify existing ones to accommodate the needs of a changing population.

Not that turnover was especially rapid. Anchorpoint was home to a military installation and a small but substantial number of artificial persons assigned to the station's permanent staff. However, the vast majority of people in residence were employees on long-term contract with one of the many businesses leasing workspace.

Exactly how long any term of employment might be varied from company to company, but as nobody went into cold-sleep for a long weekend in the middle of interstellar nowhere, the scale was measured in years. Depending on the type of job, some people stayed for only three years, although five was the usual minimum. Over half the contractors would re-up for another five or even seven, most often to finish a project and to collect the increased remote-location bonus. Very few people stayed any longer.

Those who worked in the scientific and technological fields seldom renewed their contracts more than once. Places like Anchorpoint were resumé fodder—you paid your dues by taking whatever contract was available in the middle of nowhere so that later, you could get the position you really wanted in the middle of somewhere better.

This had been the grand plan that Tully, Charles A. had been working from when he'd signed a five-year contract as a tech in the Weyland-Yutani tissue laboratory. Now, six months into his second five, he'd realized to his great dismay that he wasn't looking as far ahead as he had when he'd first taken up residence in one of the many sleeping cubicles that housed the unmarried, the uncommitted, and the unfocused.

Everyone in Tully's neighborhood was under thirty and most, including Tully, were under twenty-five, which meant they were still young enough to tolerate dorm-style accommodations—i.e. one room, and not a very big room at that, more like a cell. But they all had doors that locked, unlike the Marines, who had to live in barracks without *any* privacy.

The decor in Tully's cubicle was what a behavioral psychologist might have called "new adult, immature fledgling": a chaotic nest of clothing interspersed with shiny bits of high-tech gadget/toys and tools. Shelving barely wide enough for a small water glass took up some of the wall space; Tully had covered the rest with photos of landscapes from worlds he'd probably never visit.

There *was* a window—the Whole-Person Wellbeing Act required that all space stations provide at least one in each discrete residence. Anchorpoint's were actually 10.19 square centimeters larger than the legal minimum. Regardless of how big the windows were, however, the scenery left a lot to be desired.

If you were new to life in space, the view was breathtaking... for all of three days. Then you realized you'd seen everything there was to see. The stars didn't actually *do* anything—they didn't move, didn't change, and out in space, they didn't even twinkle.

Nor would spaceships sail past your slightly larger-than-the-minimum window in stately silence. Spacecraft came and went from an area on the other side of the station so that any unfortunate incidents like explosions wouldn't endanger the residents (much). If you wanted to watch vessels come and go there was a viewing terrace, but arrivals and departures weren't that frequent, and if you'd seen one, you'd seen them all. So much for exciting adventures in outer space.

For Tully, however, the space *inside* Anchorpoint was

the more difficult adjustment. Even in the generously large common areas, he was always conscious of an absolute limit to the dimensions. When you went for a walk on a planet, you might come to a fence with a NO TRESPASSING sign, and either turn away or defy it at your own risk, depending on your mood.

But on a space station, you always came to a bulkhead and that was it, end of the line. You couldn't go on because there was nothing to go on to.

That feeling of being *contained*, inside a place with no outside, was always with him, a low but unceasing agitation rippling at the edge of his awareness. Anchorpoint seemed—well, not crowded, exactly, just a bit too small.

This was in spite of the fact that when he had lived on Earth, he'd never cared for long walks or climbing over fences and trespassing; even as a kid he'd opted to stay in and read. Apparently, having the choice to be inside or outside affected him on a level he wasn't even aware of.

After almost six years he was comfortable enough to function, but Anchorpoint would never feel completely normal to him. Except for his sleep cubicle—it was the one place where he actually felt at home. And like most techs, he was hardly ever there except to sleep.

The comm had been ringing for a while before Tully finally became aware of it. He slept like the dead, always had. Spence had helped him rig the lights to go on whenever he got a call. Otherwise the device would probably burn out before he heard it. Unless his neighbors, driven mad by the noise, broke in to slaughter him first. If they ever did, it would be Mandala Jackson's fault.

As Chief of Operations, Jackson could override anyone's voicemail whenever she felt it was necessary. Supposedly this was in compliance with the Whole-Person Wellbeing Act, so that anyone incapacitated by illness or injury while alone wouldn't spend hours suffering, possibly even dying, just because everyone else was respecting their privacy.

In reality, it meant no one could dodge work calls even when they were off duty.

Tully groaned as he sat up, reluctantly knuckling sleep out of his eyes with one hand and slapping the comm on the table beside the bed with the other. Jackson appeared on the screen, as usual wearing one of her stupid baseball caps with her stupid light-pen clipped to the bill, her stupid jerry-rigged version of "hands-free." Behind her, however, the activity in Operations looked practically frantic, and that wasn't usual.

"Morning, Tully," she said.

"'Morning'?" He winced. "Jesus, Jackson, I'm still on scheduled downtime. *My* morning's not for another day and a half."

"Cry me a river," she said. "*Later*. In Ops, we don't get luxuries like downtime. Sixteen hours ago, a Marine transport came in on automatic." Her head bobbed as she aimed the light-pen at the left side of the screen. "Ship's called the *Sulaco*. Four years ago it left Gateway with fifteen souls aboard—twelve Colonial Marines, an android, a rep from Weyland-Yutani, and some ex-warrant officer from a merchant vessel that blew up."

"So?" Tully asked sourly.

"So let me finish," Jackson said. "The bio scan readout says it now has *three* people aboard: the ex-warrant officer—" She nodded and the light-pen made a thick line at the bottom of his screen as she ticked them off. "—one—count 'em, *one*—Marine, a nine-year-old girl who happens to be the only surviving colonist from LV-426, and half an artificial person. The *bottom* half. Makes you wonder what the hell happened out there, doesn't it?"

"Ask *them*," Tully said. "Not me."

Jackson's sudden bright smile was bizarre as well as dismaying. "But that's the *good* news," she said, as if it really were. "Three hours before the *Sulaco* turned up, we docked a chartered, priority transport out of Gateway. The *Mona Lisa* had two passengers, both MiliSci." Her smile became even brighter. "Weapons Division."

Tully's heart sank, hard. Anything involving MiliSci's Weapons Division usually came with a body count. "Isn't that the *bad* news?" he asked, too dispirited to be wittier.

Jackson ignored him. "Our new MiliSci friends want us to grab the *Sulaco* in full biohazard mode by 0800 hours. Senior biotechs have priority for deck crew assignments, and the most senior of 'em all is the one and only *you*. Tully, Charles A."

He opened his mouth to protest but the screen went blank.

"Aw, *shit*," he said, meaning it with all his heart.

With a tremendous effort, he hauled himself to a sitting position and started sorting through the clothes immediately within reach for something wearable, smell being his primary criterion. Wrinkles didn't matter— people expected lab techs to be rumpled—but even the biggest slobs were squeamish about bodily aromas.

The clothing he tossed to one side on the bed stirred, then fell off as Spence sat up beside him, smearing her dark, unruly curls back from her sleepy brown face.

"What is it?" she asked through a yawn, watching him sniff at a shirt.

"'*It*' is something called 'the military industrial complex,'" he replied. "'*It*' is also called 'getting my ass out of bed too soon' and 'me being jerked around.' Whatever you call '*it*,' by any other name—" He sniffed another shirt, decided it could do one more shift. "—'*it*' is the same old bullshit." Spence nodded resignedly and got up to help him.

Five minutes later, Tully stepped into the hallway, still a little groggy but fully clothed, wearing—despite Spence's advice to the contrary—a battered flight jacket over his acceptable shirt and slightly stained trousers. The jacket's sleeves were festooned from shoulder to wrist with an assortment of embroidered patches bearing the logos of various products and companies. Anchorpoint strongly encouraged all residents to promote companies leasing space from them so they'd feel appreciated and thus inclined to do more business.

His gaze fell on the ID posted beside the door, displaying his name, photo, job description, and contact info. The photo had been taken the day he'd arrived, all bright-eyed and excited about getting a job on a space station yet apprehensive about measuring up, a feeling his grandmother had called *enthusianxious.*

Yeah, that described the guy in that photo perfectly—enthusianxious. Eager to please, clueless as a puppy.

So is it everything you hoped for? he asked the photo silently. That bright-eyed, fresh-faced rookie would probably have said yes.

"Sucker," he muttered, but a bit wistfully.

5

Deck 4Δ was Anchorpoint's largest single space in active use, and also one of the very, *very* few places that didn't feel cramped to Tully. Even with work crews scrambling around the chunky, slower-moving service heavy-loaders plodding or rolling or gliding over the metal deck, he didn't feel boxed in.

On the deck below the overhead portal, a work crew waited with scaffolding materials and floodlights; a short distance away from them was another group in full biohazard gear. Was that the boarding party? Tully frowned—more than half of them were Marines. He pulled his flexi screen out of his inside jacket pocket and found directions to the gear-up area as well as a note saying he was late. Damn Jackson.

A couple of medics sealed him into a biohazard suit, strapping his flexi to his forearm on the outside of his suit before shoving him toward the deck crew. Just as he took his place among them, the voice of the deck officer of the day came over the speakers in his helmet, on the general address channel.

"All personnel except the deck squad and support are to fall back to designated periphery. Deck squad, brace for a little indoor weather. The baby's in the cradle and she's coming in."

"Indoor weather—" Tully had always thought that sounded silly, even if it was the quickest way of saying anyone nearby would feel wind rushing either into or out of the airlock when it opened. It could be a gentle breeze or a hard gust, depending on the skill of the Deck Ops OD at the controls.

As the overhead door rolled back, air rushed upward, ruffling the plastic of Tully's biohazard suit. This OD was an under-cooker, opting to open the inner door while the air pressure in the lock was still lower than the deck's. Under the transparent canopy of the arrival dock, the *Sulaco's* silhouette blacked out part of the starry sky as it descended slowly, touching down on the deck with a surprisingly quiet metallic *tap*.

The work crew erected scaffolding with quick efficiency. Apparently even the general work crews had their best people on duty today. Tully supposed that indicated how highly Jackson thought of him, but he was still peeved about losing his last bit of downtime. He didn't see Jackson anywhere; maybe she was giving the under-cooker hell.

What the present moment lacked in Jackson, however,

it more than made up for with Marines. It wasn't unusual to have a few of Marines in a deck squad, but not this many. They were *big*, too, like Jackson had asked for the biggest guys they had. She hadn't mentioned anything about a heavy military presence, maybe because she'd thought he wouldn't show up. Right now, he was sorry he had.

According to his contract, he couldn't be forced to work in "unduly adverse, abnormal, or extreme conditions" that would cause him to fear for his life. He'd never thought about that clause till today. While he was pretty sure he couldn't make a legitimate claim that the presence of a bunch of big, well-armed Marines in the deck crew caused him to fear for his life, he was tempted to try.

The Marine looming over him on his left grinned down at him.

"It's go time," he said, his voice filtered over the comm. *"You know what 'go' means, right?"* His nametag said Skyre. He winked at Tully, then turned to look behind them. Tully followed his gaze to see a cherry picker rolling toward them.

Please keep me safe, Tully begged Skyre silently, *even if I mispronounce your name.*

To Tully's dismay, he was in the first group to ride up to the airlock. He watched one of the Marines use electronic lock-picks to open the outer door. After opening the inner one, he motioned to Skyre. Another Marine nametagged

Ocampo followed him. Tully stepped into the airlock then stopped, blinking into the darkness.

Someone poked him between his shoulder blades. *"Go ahead. Don't worry, I got your back."*

Tully turned to look up at him. His name was Nenge and the calm confidence in his face only gave Tully a premonitory chill as he shuffled forward, waiting for the lighting system to wake up. Nothing happened.

"What's the matter with the lights?" he asked shakily.

"Relax, brother," Ocampo said, and Tully did, for all of half a second. Then the beam from the torch on Ocampo's pulse-rifle landed on a bulkhead; the metal was scorched black, with long, deep furrows in the metal, like claw marks. Made by *really big* claws.

"Look at that, will ya. Been some action in here." Ocampo sounded sorry to have missed it.

"Action?" Tully said in a faint voice. *"Did I mention I'm allergic?"*

"Oh, yeah?" Ocampo turned to shine the torch into Tully's face. *"Then maybe you want to remind us what the fuck you're supposed to be doing here,"* he said, sounding like every gym teacher Tully had ever met.

Taking a breath, Tully drew himself up with all the dignity he could muster. *"Forging a new home for all mankind in the depths of space,"* he replied in the tone that usually made bullies homicidal. If the Marine killed him, he could go back to bed.

Ocampo wasn't impressed.

Tully detached the absorption unit from his belt and held it up. *"Also taking air samples,"* he added, *less defiantly. "For testing."* He thumbed the button, producing a sound like his grandmother kissing him, only much louder. *Great,* he thought. *Why does serious scientific equipment have to make stupid noises?* This was why techies got so many beat-downs.

Strangely, Ocampo seemed to be on the verge of cracking a smile. *"Okay, professor, you just keep on suckin'."* He turned away to sweep his torch through the darkness. Nenge's strong hand landed on Tully's shoulder again, steering him farther into the *Sulaco* while the rest of the boarding crew came in.

Tully sighed. You could never get a beat-down when you needed one.

Weapons up and ready, the Marines fanned out. The torches clipped to their rifles had little effect on the darkness. Nenge's strong hand kept Tully moving farther into the ship, not really pushing him but not giving him a choice, either.

It wasn't until they reached the sleep chamber that any lights finally came on, but only at half-strength, some of them flickering. Tully considered asking someone to find the chamber's utility console so he could try goosing the lights past the lounge-lizard setting to noon-plus-500-watts. Not Ocampo, though—he'd just tell Tully to shut up and suck. He looked at the sampler, and vowed he'd invent a silencer for it.

The sound of the OD's voice on the squad channel made him jump. *"Technician Tully to the cold-sleep chamber, if you're not there already, for air sampling. Technician Tully to sample the cold-sleep chamber air, stat."*

Skyre turned his torch on Tully. *"That's your cue, professor—hit it!"*

What the hell, maybe it would jerk a laugh out of Ocampo. He pressed the sampler button again. This time it sounded like a recording of a whoopee cushion played backward, but Ocampo didn't even glance at him. His attention was on one of the sleep capsules.

"We got one Marine here in need of serious medical attention." He beckoned to the two nearest Marines. *"Get him to sickbay.* Stat."

Immediately, the soldiers lifted the capsule off its base and unfolded a metal framework from the underside so they could wheel it out. Tully stared after them for a moment, wondering how they were going to get that into the cherry picker, then turned back to see Skyre standing over a capsule with a little girl inside, his expression unexpectedly tender. Tully averted his eyes, feeling like he was intruding.

Ocampo found the third passenger, a woman almost as white as a biohazard suit. His expression was concerned as he glanced around the room, and Tully knew he was trying to decide whether he could spare two more Marines to take her to sickbay immediately, or wait till they were all ready to leave.

Skyre started to say something, then cut off with a terrible choking sound, his whole body shaking. Reflexively Tully took a step forward, wanting to help him, then froze.

A vivid red blotch suddenly blossomed in the center of Skyre's chest, just before a long black *thing*, frighteningly sharp and shiny with blood, broke through his torso.

Tully's jaw dropped. The terrible black *thing* protruding from Skyre's chest was too curved for a machete or a sword and too wide for a scythe, nor was it metal. It actually looked more like a thorn, except thorns weren't curved and they weren't large enough to go all the way through a big, well-muscled Marine and come out the other side dripping with blood and tissue and something more awful. Meanwhile, someone was screaming, "*Oh my God, oh my God, oh my God!*" over and over, like that would help.

Then, as Skyre twisted and writhed and cried out in agony, he began to *levitate*.

Tully had a clear moment to notice how Skyre's biohazard suit went on collecting his blood before all coherent thought ceased. Everything else should have ceased as well but the Marine continued to rise upward like the subject of a sadistic magic trick.

Abruptly, a long black whip flew down from the ceiling and lashed through the air to wrap itself around Ocampo's neck several times. Ocampo yanked desperately at the coils as he, too, began to levitate.

Someone shoved Tully roughly to the floor as the room filled with the sound of weapons-fire and people shouting, yelling, screaming in terror. He cried out, but his throat was so raw he could only produce a hoarse croak. *He'd* been the one screaming, he realized as he struggled to his knees and looked up to see a black shape directly overhead, reaching a hand down to him.

Only the hand wasn't right—it had too many fingers that were too long, with too many joints, ending in shiny talons dripping with some kind of thick, clear substance. Tully heard himself cry out hoarsely just as a familiar heavy-strong hand grabbed the back of his biohazard suit and yanked him roughly out from under it. The creature made to leap away, back toward the sleep capsules, and Nenge fired at it. Pale yellow liquid burst from its side, splashed on the deck, and began eating through it like carborane acid.

"What the fuck?" Tully croaked. Instinct screamed at him to run. Instead, he crawled toward the sleep capsules on his hands and knees, thinking of the little girl and the woman and monsters that bled acid.

Nenge planted a leg in front of him to block him, shouting orders to get the civilians out, get 'em out NOW, dammit. Tully looked around, wondering if they were going to get him out, too.

Well, if any conditions were unduly adverse, abnormal, and extreme enough to cause him to fear for his life, these were them and his contract couldn't help him now.

Which could only mean one thing: there had been some mistake, and not just an ordinary mistake—someone had fucked up so royally, it would make the history books.

Not him, of course—Tully, Charles A. didn't make this kind of mistake. He worked in the tissue lab, where everything was double- and triple- and quadruple-checked because precision and accuracy ruled over everything. There was no "kinda" or "sorta" or "maybe" on the macro scale.

Tully shook his head, trying to make his brain stop babbling so he could think. He got to his knees again and saw that Ocampo had gone limp with the whip still tightly coiled around his neck. Or maybe it was a very long black python? His gaze traveled along its length from Ocampo's broken neck to the hole in the ceiling where panels had been torn out.

The creature hanging from metal beams was black and shiny, with a misshapen, grotesquely long head, hard-muscled limbs, and the same long claws that had reached for him, made for cruelty and pain.

Tully's inner biologist filed all this away for later theorizing as to whether the creature was a GMO. It had all the earmarks of a weapons-developer's genetically-engineered wet dream—the worst characteristics of various reptiles crossed with a Freudian nightmare. And just so it was even deadlier, acid for blood, making it dangerous, dead or alive.

He saw another creature drop down from the ceiling

to land on the woman's sleep capsule, jarring it out of position. The status lights blinked off and the woman woke immediately.

She tried to sit up, then screamed and banged her fists against the capsule lid. The monster bared its steely teeth at her in a predatory grin that widened as it opened its jaws. Suddenly something shot out of its mouth like a striking cobra and hit the lid right over her face.

For a moment, Tully thought it *was* a cobra and his inner biologist started to correct his original impressions. Then the monster raised its misshapen head and he saw a second set of teeth telescoping from its jaws, snapping at the air. Tully decided his first impression of the creature had been too lighthearted.

"There's been a terrible fuck-up," he said hoarsely.

The alien on the sleep capsule whipped its head around to face him. Tully flinched, raising his arms defensively. The woman in the capsule was still screaming and yelling and trying to punch through the capsule lid. The monster *couldn't* have heard him, Tully thought, *couldn't* have been looking at him.

Nenge slapped the side of his head, hard. *"Get outta here!"* he bellowed.

As Tully tried to obey, he saw the alien that had impaled Skyre give its tail a twitch, flicking the Marine away with a seemingly casual movement. Its misshapen eyeless head turned toward him and Nenge and its second set of teeth snapped at the air.

It's telling us we're next, Tully thought, unable to move.

The monster crouched on its thick hind legs, preparing to spring. If Nenge fired now, Tully thought, its acid-blood would drench the woman's sleep capsule, and if he caught it mid-leap, everyone in a two-meter radius would get an acid shower, with the two of them taking the worst of it. Tully's panic was about to reach critical mass when a long, thick stream of fire roared out over his head and engulfed the monster in flames.

The creature let loose with a terrible howling shriek, and Nenge gave it another blast from the flamethrower. The alien, the sleep capsule, and the screaming woman inside all disappeared in a ball of fire. Tully clapped both hands over his eyes.

In the next moment the smell of diesel oil, scorched metal, and burning alien flesh hit Tully in the face like a physical blow, and his stomach spontaneously emptied itself.

Oh, Jesus, he thought, as his stomach clenched again. *My first firefight, and all I can do is puke.*

He was barely aware of Nenge dragging him away.

6

Corporal Dwayne Hicks of the Colonial Marines sat on the edge of his hospital bed. He'd had damned little to do since coming out of cold-sleep and there was no sign of that changing any time soon. Maybe Boredom Therapy was the latest trend in medicine. Today, however, he'd decided to defy the rules by smoking a cigarette, just for kicks. What the hell, it was his last one anyway.

It wasn't a premeditated offense. Smoking had been the farthest thing from his mind when the medic had come in earlier, too cheerful for the time of day as usual. He'd removed the old dressing, checked his dermis with a hand-scanner, before reapplying the topical medication with fresh dressing.

"You've got *great* skin, Corporal Hicks," he'd chirped. "The scar tissue's fading already. Your vitals are good, too, even your renals. Problems with kidney function are pretty common after prolonged cold-sleep but you're peeing like a champ. Keep up the good work and I'll be back in a couple of hours."

That had been three hours ago. Well, at least the painkillers were working. They were good ones, too—worked on the pain while leaving his head clear, something he felt was far more important than erasing scar tissue.

At present, he was halfway through a five-year re-up that he had very nearly passed on (time in cold-sleep wasn't included until a person left the military). Hicks was a veteran of eleven official combat missions, six peacekeeping actions that had turned out to be bug hunts, and four humanitarian rescue operations. The most recent of those had turned into a bug hunt and FUBARed him into a brief stint as CO before the rest of his squad were wiped out by hostile alien creatures.

Xenomorphs, they called them. The *Xenomorphs* had left him responsible for the evacuation of two severely traumatized civilians, one of them a child, and the synthetic assigned as technical support to his squad, all of whom had had to fend for themselves when he'd been incapacitated by acid burns.

FUBAR, however, had continued just fine without him. Before she'd put them all in cold-sleep, Ripley had awakened him just long enough to brief him on how an alien queen had boarded the *Sulaco*, dismembered Bishop, and very nearly slaughtered her and the girl before she'd blown the thing out the airlock.

Things certainly were a lot quieter around here but Hicks knew better than to assume it was all over. At best, this was intermission. There was never just one of anything, and even if there were, it wouldn't be FUBAR.

Every FUBAR was a disaster unique unto itself, but most, if not all, started the same way: someone in authority gave orders and expected the entire universe to obey them. Well, fuck that shit. As of now, Hicks decided, he was done with authority—all authority, of any kind, any place, any time, in general or in particular. He was going outlaw; hasta la pasta, baby.

All the same, he was still weak from extended time in cold-sleep as well as his injuries. If someone came in to make him stop smoking, he wasn't up to much more than harsh language.

His gaze fell on the pillows at the slightly elevated head of his hospital bed and he smiled to himself. Next week he was going to rip the tags off those suckers with his bare hands.

And if he couldn't, then he'd take off and nuke them from orbit. It was the only way to be sure.

He blew a stream of smoke at the ceiling light and waited. Nothing happened, not even a scolding over the PA system. Jesus, had everyone in surveillance fallen asleep?

Hudson appeared in his mind's eye, goofy and smug. *That all you got, Corporal Badass?* Hicks stubbed out his cigarette on the metal bedframe and dropped it on the floor.

Still nothing, not even crickets. Either it was shift change and nobody was paying attention, or the whole goddam universe was broken. Correction: *more* broken.

He looked over at the open doorway and it occurred to him that he hadn't seen anyone even just walk past in the hall for quite some time. According to his watch, it was now three and a half hours since the medic's visit and longer than that since he'd seen anyone else.

Fuck this. If someone didn't tell him about Newt, Ripley, and Bishop by dinner time, he'd go full-on outlaw, and find out for himself.

"Uh… you know there's no smoking in here, right?"

The woman in the doorway looked from him to the cigarette butt on the floor and back again in obvious disapproval, although she didn't look anything like an authority, not even a hall monitor. It was probably her biohazard suit.

"Won't happen again, ma'am." He covered his disappointment by sweeping the butt under the bed with one slippered foot.

That seemed to throw her off-balance. The good boys and girls always got a little flustered by a polite outlaw. Or maybe it was the first time anyone had ever called her *ma'am*.

"I'm Spence," she said. "I'm not a medic. I'm from the tissue culture lab. I have to get a sample." Pause. "Of tissue." Shorter pause. "From you."

He was tempted to thank her for making that clear, in case he was too tobacco-addled to understand. "How?"

She took a case out of her lab coat, removed a metal cylinder from it, and held it out to him.

"Stick your thumb in there. Please," she added.

Outlaws had to pick their battles, Hicks thought, doing as she asked. Something nipped him and he automatically jerked back. There was a tiny pink mark in the fleshiest part of his thumb.

"Sorry." Her expression was a bit sheepish. "It's better if you don't expect it."

"Better for who?" he asked darkly.

"Both of us." She returned the cylinder to her pocket. "You're the last one."

That sounded vaguely ominous, Hicks thought. She turned to leave and he grabbed her wrist.

"Hold it right there, *Spence*," he growled. "What about the others—Ripley and Newt. Did they come through okay?"

The woman looked warily at his hand around her wrist. "Who's 'Newt'?"

"The kid. The little girl," he added.

"Oh, you mean *Rebecca*." She tried to pull away but Outlaw Hicks's heart of gold was in the laundry. "Rebecca's fine. Really, she's just *fine*."

"What about Ripley?" he asked.

The woman hesitated, which made him tighten his grip a little more. Her wary expression intensified; he was really starting to scare her now. His conscience jabbed at him for mistreating someone weaker than himself, but he told himself to feel guilty later. This woman could have been anything from a shady synthetic spy to an undercover storm-trooper gauging his physical condition for a round of torture.

Oh, sure. Lots of stormtroopers worked undercover taking tissue samples. Nonetheless, he was still responsible for Newt and Ripley, and as of right now, he didn't even know where they were.

"And what about Bishop?" he demanded, giving her wrist a little shake. "Where's Bishop?"

The woman blinked at him, so surprised that she seemingly forgot she was scared. "What kind? Episcopal, Orthodox Catholic, or Roman Reformed?"

That was almost funny. "The artificial person assigned to my squad. His *name* was Bishop."

"The *Sulaco* arrived with only you three aboard," she said, speaking slowly and carefully, like a shrink trying to persuade a suicide bomber to put down the detonator. "That's what they said, anyway. They don't usually tell me *that* much." She took a breath. "Listen, maybe you just need a little more rest. You want me to call someone? I can get someone in here, they'll give you something—"

Hicks pulled her closer and spoke directly into her face.

"Why haven't I been debriefed yet?" he demanded. "What's going on? Did something happen to Newt and Ripley?"

She tried to twist free and he tightened his grip even more, knowing he was hurting her and hating himself for stooping to cruelty. But he couldn't let her go without getting a straight answer.

"*I. Don't. Know,*" she said through gritted teeth. "I told you, I'm from the tissue lab. I'm just a tech. Nobody tells techs anything. If my chronograph broke, they wouldn't even tell me the *time*. All I know besides what I just told you is, everybody's been sleeping short hours ever since you got here."

Before he could respond to that, there was a loud crash of metal and glass in the corridor followed by a cry of pain. Hicks let go of the woman, who immediately moved out of his reach, rubbing her wrist and glaring at him. He paid no attention as Newt raced in, wearing a bright green hospital gown and fuzzy socks to match.

The girl slid across the polished floor like it was ice, looked around wildly, realized there was no way out, and backed into the nearest corner, pale and wild-eyed. She'd looked the same way the first time Hicks had ever seen her on LV-426. Somehow she'd survived on her own for weeks before his squad had arrived on their would-be rescue mission.

Some rescue. Without Newt, he and Ripley never could have survived.

"God*dam*mit!" The orderly in the doorway was wearing the same biohazard gear as the tissue-lab tech, except one glove was torn. "She *bit* me!" he huffed and started toward her.

Instantly, Hicks was off the bed and standing directly in front of the orderly in a combat stance. The man backed away, holding both hands up. Not an interrogator in sheep's clothing, then, Hicks thought, just clueless about kids, probably because he'd never been one himself.

"Where's Ripley?" Newt demanded from behind him. She sounded a little less wild but not yet inclined to behave. Hicks didn't blame her. "Where is she? I want her! I want *Ripley* right *now,* where *is* she?" she shouted.

"She asked you a question," Hicks told the orderly, in case he was too addled by Newt's bite to understand.

The other man straightened up like he thought he was an authority. "Are you looking to get yourself sedated, soldier?"

Clueless about kids *and* too stupid to live, Hicks thought unhappily. Maybe *he* should bite the guy, too.

"*Where is she?*" Newt said again, shouting even louder.

"And now *I'm* asking you," Hicks added, dangerously quiet.

Abruptly the lab tech stepped forward, pulling down her mask. "Hey, Rebecca—" She glanced at Hicks. "—Newt—honey—Ripley's okay, I promise. She's resting so she can get better." She inched toward the girl, glancing at Hicks to see if it was okay with him. He gave a barely perceptible nod. "Ripley's going to be just fine," she continued. "We're taking real good care of her, honest."

Newt's breathing began to calm. The kid had better instincts for danger than anyone Hicks had ever met. If she thought this woman was okay, then she was. But that didn't mean *he* could relax.

"I know where Ripley is," the woman said, holding out her hand as she took another step toward Newt. "I can take you to see her. That's what you want, right? To see for yourself that she's all right?"

"Hey, Spence, what the hell?" The orderly had the sour tone of a habitual complainer. "You know there's *no way*—" He took a step toward her and Hicks blocked him again, pointing at a far corner. The orderly went without protest.

Newt eyed the tech's outstretched hand, then tucked both of her own under her armpits. The woman didn't push, only moved toward the door. Newt made sure that Hicks was coming, too, before she followed.

As they rode up on the elevator with Spence, Hicks began to wonder if he was doing the right thing. He hadn't been able to find out exactly what had happened when the *Sulaco* had arrived at Anchorpoint, and all he knew about Ripley was what the lab tech had told Newt: *She's fine, just fine.*

He wanted to believe that Ripley was unharmed simply because Newt was all right. Sleep capsules were remarkably sturdy, fire-resistant, waterproof, and airtight, and could even provide extra protection from radiation. But nothing could stand up to the aliens' acid-blood.

When they got to the right floor, Spence gave Newt the room number and the girl ran ahead before Hicks could tell her to wait. He braced himself for hysterics but there were no screams, no tears, and it finally came to him that Spence would never expose the kid to anything really bad. Feeling a little foolish, he followed her in and was relieved to see that Ripley hadn't been injured during the boarding party fiasco.

At the same time, however, she was not *just fine*, not with all that high-tech equipment surrounding her. Even the bed was high-tech. Ripley was practically in a cocoon of hardware.

No, not *cocoon*, that wasn't a good word. *Nest* was better. Ripley was in a *nest* of hardware, looking like she was peacefully asleep but in no way *just fine*.

The hardware wasn't a problem for Newt. She didn't even blink at the line of wireless electrodes across Ripley's forehead. There were two more electrodes at her temples and others hidden in her thick dark hair.

"See?" Spence said. "She's resting. Sleeping." Then she looked at Hicks, as if to make sure he was okay with that. He made an awkward movement that was part nod and part shrug. Hicks thought Ripley's condition was probably closer to coma than sleep, but Newt didn't need to know that.

Or maybe she *did* know—the kid was pretty sharp. At the moment, she was looking from Ripley's serene face to the overhead monitor and back again. It seemed to be a highly elaborate EEG, more complex than anything Hicks had ever seen. Not that he had seen a whole lot of them. But Newt seemed to be familiar with it.

The memory of the biolab on LV-426 came back to him. At the time, he'd thought it was awfully elaborate for a colony of first-wave shake-and-bakers, but circumstances hadn't allowed further consideration. Otherwise, it might have occurred to him how strange it was for terraformers to be doing in-depth research on the alien specimens, instead of shipping them off to a Company facility specializing in xenobiology.

"That's a good thing, that she's asleep," Spence was saying. "Sometimes people need a lot of sleep. To get over things."

Newt studied Ripley's face for a few moments, then checked the EEG again. "Is she dreaming?"

"Well…" The tech looked at Hicks nervously. "I don't know, honey. Are her eyes moving?"

"Ripley said it was okay to dream." Newt's voice was heavy with sadness "But it's always better not to. *Always.*"

7

Rodina Station was a lot smaller than Anchorpoint, and so was its population. Unlike Anchorpoint's, however, it was permanent. The governing council were proud of Rodina Station as a genuine home to its Progressive Persons, not a gold farm that made fat capitalists fatter.

There were no ugly corporate logos defacing bulkheads or clothing—everything on Rodina was homegrown and homemade, developed by the people, for the people, to use at no cost (beyond necessary contributions toward upkeep).

Occasionally, there were rumors that some of the Progressive Peoples wouldn't have minded a little commercialization if it meant getting up-to-date tech that much sooner. But the council knew these so-called "rumors" were planted by capitalist agents attempting to sow dissension, hoping to get their foot in the door. Progressive Peoples were too smart to fall for such tricks— let those bastards in and the next thing you knew, you were under new management with corporate logos tattooed on your ass.

Any fools who felt enslavement to commercial interests was worth getting faster delivery on video screens with resolution 0.5% higher than last year's model were free to leave and sell their souls. Of course, they wouldn't have time to watch their fancy new screens because they'd be working sixteen hours a day just to make rent on a single windowless room, air not included—it never was with capitalists. Pretty soon, they'd have to choose between breathing and eating, with both bills past due.

Fortunately, Progressive Peoples were too intelligent, too enlightened, and too ideologically informed to be seduced by the superficial gloss of consumerism. They knew things didn't have to be shiny to perform properly, and even if something wasn't the absolute latest, it still worked.

Take the cybernetics lab, for example. Chrome and designer labels had nothing to do with function. Rodina's computers were maybe a hundredth of a second slower than the ones at Anchorpoint but they got the job done with the same accuracy and precision. Most humans couldn't perceive even a fiftieth of a second, so what was the big goddam deal anyway?

The matter of capitalist accomplishments loomed especially large in the mind of Colonel-Doctor Timur Suslov. At the moment, he was studying the upper half of the robot recovered from the spacecraft that had violated UPP space. It hung in a stereotactic frame while the station's best, quickest, and most precise data gathering system sucked out every bit of its information it had, without erasing it or leaving any sign it had been touched, even in its raw activity log.

There were whispers that this marvelous software had been pirated from Anchorpoint on a fly-by, then customized to burn off all traces of its origin. A serious charge, but Suslov was less interested in gossip than he was with results.

What really fascinated him, however, was the insane amount of effort the capitalists put into making robots look like people, uncanny valley be damned. This one was quite exceptional, the most human-like he had ever seen, even with its mouth twitching every few seconds (probably a software incompatibility).

Suslov had always believed none of the capitalists' talking dolls could fool him. No matter how well-rendered they were, they inevitably gave themselves away because they couldn't smile, not the way *real* people did. They couldn't laugh convincingly, either.

But more than anything else, it was facial lines—which was to say, there weren't enough of them. Human faces moved in concert with their thoughts, even when they were alone, but robot faces never did. Consequently, their synthetic skin, while virtually identical to the real thing, never developed character lines, which gave them a dispassionate, even aloof appearance. It reminded him of those silly capitalist celebrities who paid for poison injections to paralyze their facial muscles, preventing wrinkles by making their faces more robot-like.

Robots were made to look like people while people made themselves look like robots. The valley didn't get more uncanny that that.

This robot was different—it had more facial lines than other robots he'd seen. Maybe some overfunded capitalist lab had programmed it to practice expressions in a mirror. That sounded pretty silly, but capitalists *were* silly. Most people Suslov knew didn't care, but he did. Not being able to tell the difference between a robot and a person was a secret fear he didn't actually want to admit to, even to himself. Nor did he want to admit that the only thing he was more afraid of was war against machines indistinguishable from humans.

Maybe that war had already started, he thought suddenly—the war to end all wars, the one between people and machines passing for people. It had been coming ever since the damned capitalists made the preposterous claim that their machines were "smart." They'd slid willingly down the slippery slope, merrily calling robots "artificial persons" that possessed "artificial intelligence," giving them human names, treating them like citizens, while they treated real people worse than animals.

That was capitalist society in a nutshell—upside-down and backward.

At least this robot was useful, not to mention valuable. The information streaming from it was as rich as anything they'd pulled out of the *Sulaco*'s memory banks, and it was all thanks to human beings, Suslov thought, turning to Luc Hai.

"Lucky," everyone called her, and she certainly had been—another big difference between humans and their human-looking robots. There were plenty of things machines could do better than humans, but only humans could be lucky. Losing Boris had been very bad luck indeed, but the robot was an unprecedented windfall, and that counted as more good luck than bad.

The diagram Lucky was currently watching take shape on the lab's largest high-res monitor looked like a partially deflated balloon with a snakelike tail and a cluster of too-long fingers on either side. When the diagram was complete, she nodded emphatically.

"*Đúng,*" she said. *Yes.* Meaning this was the creature that had killed Boris. Suslov was glad he hadn't seen it himself. She tapped the "print" symbol in the bottom right corner of the screen, then looked at Suslov again to see if he had any objection to her using up paper for a hardcopy printout. He didn't.

The finished diagram vanished and a new one began to appear, something far more complex. Suslov stood beside Lucky in silence, sneaking glances at her now and then. She rubbed her left arm, absently touching this or that tattoo. These were personal, he knew—good luck symbols, lotus flowers, a village flag. The tattoos on her right arm were regimental: the standard symbol indicating she was a commando, hashmarks showing her rank, five ideograms she had received for exceptional service or bravery, and on the inside of her forearm, her UPP identity barcode.

As the new diagram on the screen filled in with more detail, Suslov could see that it was the front and side views of a creature even stranger than the previous one. They seemed to be related although he wasn't sure how—larval stage and adult form, maybe? If so, he couldn't imagine how the transition occurred.

He paused the screen before it finished rendering.

"Cái này thì sao? Bạn có nhìn thấy sinh vật này không?" he asked her. *What about this? Did you see this creature?*

Luc Hai shook her head. *"Không."* No.

He tapped the "resume" icon. She and Ashok had been damned lucky not to have seen that organism. Unlike machines, he thought, turning to look at the robot hanging in the stereotactic frame. Machines had no luck at all.

The corner of the robot's mouth was still going twitch-twitch-twitch as data continued pouring into the feeder cable attached to the base of its skull. According to the readout on the frame, they had accessed barely half the content in its machine brain. *Dammit*, how could such a decadent, corrupt society produce such excellent compression algorithms? When the computer techs saw this, they might defect en masse.

His gaze went from the robot's fake face to the ragged end of its torso and all the exposed cables and tubes. With so much of its body missing, part of the robot's nervous system was dormant, while the rest supported its brain function, or tried to. It was hooked up to an auxiliary system that worked just as well as any flashy, over-chromed capitalist model at keeping its "blood" purified and circulating. According to the readouts, the robot's neural net and cognition were well within optimal parameters. If there was any damage in that area, it had happened before Rodina's brave commandos had recovered the robot. Who knew what the alien growth might have done to it—*after* its body had been ripped in two?

Suslov turned back to the high-res screen, thinking again how extremely lucky the commandos had been not to have met the creature strong enough to do such a thing.

The problem with good luck, however, was that it never lasted quite long enough. Plus, it was inevitably followed by bad luck; the universe always balanced the scales.

The last thought replayed in his mind and he shook his head. That was complete foolishness, not worthy of a colonel-doctor in the UPP who lived solidly in the real world. He knew better than to indulge in superstitious dread like some downtrodden refugee fresh off a lifeboat.

8

All her life, people had told Talisa Nkosi that her extraordinary manual dexterity meant she had a bright future. She'd go far, they said, do fascinating things, and meet lots of interesting people.

To date, her bright future had come about in the darkness of space. Anchorpoint was the farthest she'd ever been from home, although discovering it wasn't much different than any other space station had been kind of a letdown. The fascinating jobs were always some kind of detail work done under a microscope, using tools she had to operate by remote control because, even with her dexterity, anything too small to see with the naked eye was also too small to feel, let alone manipulate.

Not that she was unhappy to be the first one called in to connect microscopic objects A and B, or to detach the extremely minuscule C from D, or to graft foreign microbe X onto molecular chain Y to catalyze process Z.

For her birthday, her co-workers had given her a complex chain of molecules she could use to sign her handiwork whenever she was permitted to do so, which, sadly, was never.

Nkosi had indeed met plenty of interesting people, although the vast majority were assistants from a rota of "jacks"—as in jack-of-all-trades, workers with a broad range of work experience but without a degree or certification in any particular field. Most were newly adult, trying out different kinds of work in search of a career.

There were also a good number of people not so new to adulthood, like Nkosi's current jack du jour. Miller was older than she was, sharp-witted and more easygoing than his slightly craggy features made him appear. Nkosi thought he was far too knowledgeable to be a jack-of-all-trades when he could have mastered any of them.

As curious as Nkosi was about his status, however, she didn't ask. If she offended him, he might refuse to work with her, and she didn't want to lose him. He was quick on the uptake, not given to pointless chatter, and able to assist her and manage the data without falling into a boredom fugue, even when the work was so tedious that she could have dozed off herself.

That wouldn't be a problem with today's job.

The lab hadn't told her much, just that a general scan had picked up the presence of a previously unknown alien contaminant in an unprecedented state. Translation: "We found some weird shit that's acting strange and it's making us nervous."

A lot of the weird shit that acted strange turned out

to be a spill by an inexperienced lab tech who'd forgotten to wear gloves to clean it up. Other times, it was a case of mistaken identity (by an inexperienced lab tech), and even, on occasion, the odd practical joke (inexperienced lab techs made irresistible targets). She'd showed up expecting a variation on the same disappointment until they told her the weird shit was acting strange on the *Sulaco*'s cargo deck. Then she hadn't been able to get her biohazard suit on fast enough.

She'd been so eager to get her gloved hands on the stuff, it didn't occur to her until much later that they hadn't asked if she and Miller had any questions or concerns beforehand.They arrived at the *Sulaco* to find the cargo deck fully enclosed in a transparent quarantine bubble with airlock-style entry. The weird shit in question was located in the bottom half of a synthetic; its top half was officially missing and would remain so until there was hard evidence that it had been destroyed.

The legs were twisted and broken but, interestingly—to Nkosi, at least—they contained a fair amount of still-liquid artificial blood. If the unknown alien contaminant had kept it from drying out into powder, she had no idea how. For once, "unprecedented" hadn't been laboratory hyperbole for the sake of getting priority status for the investigation.

This was quite the plum assignment and Nkosi was surprised they'd tapped her for it—steady hands or not, she didn't have as much seniority as Tully or Spence or the

Castevet twins. Just before they entered the cargo deck, her supervisor Tatsumi let it drop that she was the only tech on Anchorpoint who had experience with an unknown alien contaminant outside the controlled conditions of the laboratory.

Tatsumi had said it casually, as if it were no big deal, but it made Nkosi uneasy. There wasn't supposed to be just one of anybody or anything on a space station. When she asked how this could have happened, he had just shrugged it off as chance. Or, in the vernacular, *shit happens*.

Which left her holding the bag. Or rather, the legs. Either way, it made her nervous.

By contrast, Miller was his usual unflappable self. He went about his work with characteristic efficiency, setting up monitors and recording equipment, cleaning her micro-goggles before she asked, and then fitting them to her head in exactly the right place so they wouldn't slide around every time she raised her eyebrows. He even cleaned tools for her as they worked, simply because he knew it was her preferred routine. Small courtesies were so underrated, Nkosi thought, and made a mental note to put a gold star in his file as he cut away the synth's trousers for her.

Miller had also laid out the specialized scalpels she used for artificial tissue and arranged them by size. She was about to take the smallest, then decided to go up two sizes. Synthetics attached to active-duty military had denser muscles than those in less physically demanding positions. Judging by how hard it was to slice his thigh, this one had been due for flexibility therapy. Instead, he'd been dismembered by who-the-fuck-knew-what.

She wondered what had become of the rest of him. The grapevine had offered little information, which was *really* strange. People on space stations craved gossip more than chocolate. The shipping lanes Anchorpoint served were for long-haul travel. Since there was no such thing as a good surprise in interstellar space, a schedule had to be laid out in advance and adhered to without deviation, as a matter of life and death.

The unscheduled arrival of *any* spacecraft was the kind of capital-E Event that should have sent the Anchorpoint rumor mill into high gear. The air itself should have been crackling with wild speculation.

Instead, no one had a word to say. That was also some pretty weird shit acting strangely, Nkosi thought as she worked the scalpel through the tough artificial thigh muscle. She managed to cut out five samples before her hand started cramping.

Flexing her fingers, she sat back on her heels and pushed her goggles up on her forehead. "Everything coming through okay?" she asked Miller.

He looked at the flexi screen strapped to his wrist, then at the larger one beside him on the deck. "Perfect, no noise whatsoever."

"Great." She wiggled her fingers. "This synthetic's really tough. Like a hundred-year-old racehorse in peak condition."

"Yeah, the military ones get downright gamy." Miller startled her by taking her hand, turning it palm down, and massaging the area between her thumb and forefinger, moving inward from the edge for about ten seconds.

"How's that?" he asked her.

"Damn." Nkosi flexed her fingers. "It doesn't work that well when *I* do it."

"That's because *you* can't use both hands." Miller looked pleased with himself.

"You're right. Who knew?" Laughing a little, Nkosi lowered her goggles and bent over the synthetic's legs again. She increased the magnification, then took it up another two levels.

"You see this, right?" she asked Miller.

"The screen is showing smooth black globules that seem to be rooted in android blood," Miller replied. "If that's what you see, then yes, I see it too."

"Okay, good," she said. "I just hope anyone else who sees this doesn't ask me to explain it."

Synthetic blood had been designed not to interact or combine with anything organic, to prevent undesirable substances from damaging artificial persons, or even just hitching a ride to a human host. Common wisdom said human and alien biology would be incompatible, but as humans had discovered, most biological systems had some degree of kinship, even if the owners didn't breathe air, or for that matter, anything.

Nkosi had been trained to treat any alien material as a source of contamination until proven otherwise. She hadn't expected to find anything like that at Anchorpoint; the biolab inventory contained no exotic substances, just organics familiar to everyone. Even the diseases were ordinary, with well-established procedures to follow in case of exposure.

Unlike the weird shit she was looking at now.

Studying the smooth, shiny surface of the globules, Nkosi saw it wasn't an illusion—they really were rooted in the synthetic blood, which was supposed to be impossible for organic material. Quite often, alien material found in or out of a lab appeared inorganic to human eyes. In some cases, it required a great deal of testing to identify it as organic, which was crucial. The field of xenobiology was full of stories about the sharp-eyed lab tech who spotted something everyone else had missed, and narrowly averted a genocide, or even an extinction.

Like her colleagues, Nkosi still secretly hoped to do something that heroic. What she didn't want to do was discover that a substance was lethal by leaving it out in a jar with the lid off.

Increasing the magnification another five levels gave the surfaces an uneven, bumpy texture. It wasn't enough to let her see any molecular bonding but she could almost visualize it now. All she had to do was go to maximum magnification and she'd be the first person ever to see something previously thought to be impossible.

If she could bring herself to do it, that was—she wasn't sure this was something she wanted to look at.

Which was not how the scientific method worked. Taking a breath, she jumped the magnification all the way. The smooth globules were now all jagged edges. She was about to extend the micro-probe from her glove when something caught her attention.

"Hey, Miller, we're recording, right?" she asked, blinking at the globules.

"You know it. Nothing on the clock is off the record."

"Good thing," she said, a bit shakily. "Because I swear I saw a piece of this weird shit move by itself."

"That's weird even for the weirdest weird shit," Miller said.

Nkosi had a sudden urge to drop everything, run for the airlock, and spend the next twenty-four hours submerged in a decontamination bath. If weird shit could bond to artificial blood, it could grab onto anything and all bets were off. Nothing was safe from it, nothing and no one.

Despite that, despite everything, her hands were still steady. She told Miller she was taking a sample as she extended the probe and prodded until she found the point of bonding. It took a lot of careful pushing and poking while she made sure her probe hadn't drifted from the target, but she finally pried a sample of the alien material free of the blood.

"Incoming," she said as she withdrew the probe. Miller had a sterile tube ready and she ejected the sample from the tip of the probe. "Bull's-eye." She exhaled in a rush, sitting back on her heels and pushing her goggles up on her forehead again.

Miller sealed the tube, tucked it into a metal canister, then wrote a number on the side with a red grease pencil. Nkosi couldn't help smiling; it was such a retro thing to do. All the jacks had little quirks.

"So," he said as he put the canister into an open case beside him. "Since when do androids get infections?"

"Dunno." Nkosi dipped her head noncommittally. "Something real bad got to this poor bastard."

"How many more samples does the lab want?"

"As many as possible," she told him. "They wouldn't be any more specific."

Miller gave a short, humorless laugh. "I reckon it'll be six more than whatever we give them."

"That's their problem." Nkosi sighed. "Might as well finish up while we're young."

"While *you're* young," Miller said. "Too late for me."

9

The monitor set into the surface of the imitation rosewood desk was angled so that only the man who sat there could see the screen, and he had not looked away from it since the incident report on the *Sulaco* had come in. He intended to review the file, text and video, until he had memorized every written word and every second of footage.

This was something he'd done before, whenever shit happened. Shit always happened, but in all his years as an officer, shit like this had never happened on his watch. Not in peacetime, anyway.

He had been in the Colonial Marines for his entire adult life, but even before he'd enlisted, most people had assumed he was military. As a child, his bearing gave people the impression that he was a student at a military prep school. Recently, he had overheard a civilian ask his secretary, Sergeant Feng Mei, what his first name was.

"*Colonel*," Sergeant Feng had replied archly.

Colonel Pasquale Vincenzo Rosetti had showed his appreciation by putting her in for promotion to master-sergeant on the officer track, despite knowing he'd lose her to Officer Candidate School before the year was out. That was simply how things went. You never got to keep a good right arm. By contrast, dumbshits stuck to you worse than Martian goosegrass.

Currently, he took pride in knowing that the installation at Anchorpoint was one hundred percent dumbshit-free. No mean feat—it had taken a great deal of care and attention, along with a little horse-trading with COs at other space stations. But it had been worth the effort to have personnel he could count on. They didn't have a lot of experience, but that only meant they had fewer bad habits to unlearn. Rosetti made sure they stayed in peak condition, body and mind, partly because peacetime wasn't a permanent state, but mostly because a complete lack of morons provided no protection against the vagaries of chance—as in, dumb bad luck. E.g. what had happened on the *Sulaco*.

Corporal Uzoma Nenge's written account was clearer than any of the body-cam videos. Rosetti had never heard of such a FUBAR on a space station, and worse, it had come right after Corporal Hicks's debrief. While the incident on LV-426 had occurred four years earlier, that wasn't really a whole lot of time out here, where distances could put travelers in cold-sleep for eight weeks, or eight months, sometimes more.

Rosetti had seen plenty in his nearly forty years with the Marines, and some of it had been awful enough that it still made him shudder. But this gave him a bad feeling like he hadn't had since the Sector Seven War. That had been the longest, most fucked-up bughunt on record, run by a committee of the dumbest dumbshits since the legendary Three Stooges. The only good thing about it had been the change in regulations limiting the distance between personnel and their commanding officer; anyone giving orders now had to do it in person.

While the *Sulaco* events hadn't been nearly as disastrous, they had been bad enough. Nenge was still hospitalized, undergoing post-trauma rehab along with the other surviving Marines and civilians. Most of Rosetti's generation had been treated by practitioners of the suck-it-up-tough-it-out school of therapy. But after watching the first third of Nenge's video, Rosetti had sent mental health sick-leave approvals to the hospital before the doc-in-the-box had the chance to request them.

Sergeant Feng's coded knock at the door jarred him out of his thoughts: one-two-three, pause, then a much quicker one-two, which meant someone had arrived sans appointment and was too important to throw out. She came in at a near-run, smart and professional as always in her dress blues, but looking apologetic as she held out a large red plastic envelope.

"Susan Welles and Kevin Fox from Military Sciences," she apologized.

He grunted in acknowledgement, using his index finger to scrawl his signature on the envelope before he dumped the contents out onto his desk.

"Weapons Division," she added ruefully.

He glared down at the two photo IDs and a three-sheet printout labeled AGENDA. In his experience, an agenda was usually a to-do list he was expected to have finished the day before he'd received it, a trick no one had tried to pull on him since he'd made colonel. One of the privileges of rank was the sharp decrease in communiques from entitled bureaucrats. Unfortunately, the Weapons Division shitheads could slip through any filter.

"Send 'em in," he growled. A violent encounter with an alien species, followed by a visit from a MiliSci power couple, Weaponized Barbie and Ken. The timing indicated they must have been on the way to Anchorpoint even before the *Sulaco* had strayed into UPP space. A retired four-star general had once told him that no matter how unusual, unlikely, or unexpected something might be, somebody somewhere had seen it coming.

"Colonel Rosetti? I'm Kevin Fox."

The smiling man holding out his hand looked exactly like his photo—overly tanned with yellow-gold hair and teeth that were too white and even. Classic Weyland-Yutani stock—overconfident, overtrained, overpaid, and now, over here. Rosetti suppressed the urge to twist his hand until it broke off his arm. Fox stepped aside to let Barbie take his place.

"Susan Welles," she said and offered her hand exactly as Fox had. Rosetti didn't break her hand off, either.

"Welcome to Anchorpoint," he said flatly. They sat

down in the chairs on the other side of his desk without waiting to be invited.

"I have to tell you, Colonel, we're im*pressed*," Fox said with official Company heartiness. "I mean that, *truly*. Susan and I could *not* be *more* impressed, and we're *not* the only ones."

"I'm sure the videos don't convey the actual scale, do they?" Welles enthused.

"We're *particularly* impressed with *your* handling of the situation," Fox went on. "The situation so far, that is. And of *course*, we're *really* impressed with your cooperation."

Shit—Fox was another ex-mouthpiece from newscasting. The vocal cadence was unmistakable. The Company pulled half their PR staff from all-news channels, and this one sounded like he'd fallen off the anchor desk yesterday. Welles had probably come out of teaching so they complemented each other. Company Ken gave the headlines, and Company Barbie filled in the details— Human Resources engineering at its finest.

"That's absolutely true," Welles was saying. "We couldn't get a single thing done without the cooperation of good people like yourself, Colonel."

Rosetti realized he was still holding their ID cards. They were ridiculously complete, giving blood type, fingerprints, retina scans, even genomes. He tossed them down on the desk.

"Around here, we call that 'following orders,'" he said, stone-faced.

"Yes, and it certainly would simplify things if everyone had your attitude." Welles's smile was practically blinding. "Especially the civilians who boarded the *Sulaco* with your men." She shifted position, leaning forward a little. "Pardon my frankness, but I think there's a very real possibility of serious problems there—"

"It's not *just* a *feeling*, Colonel," Fox added. Rosetti suppressed the urge to laugh. Alpha male Ken couldn't resist taking the conversation away from Barbie. "We've been going over *psych profiles* and the *picture* couldn't be any more *clear*."

Clearer, Rosetti corrected him silently.

"Anchorpoint has a population that's quite—oh, call it *variegated*," he went on while Welles nodded her emphatic agreement. "Which is only to be expected, considering how many *different fields* are represented here. But it also seems to attract people of a *certain type*—" He paused and made an exaggerated thinking-hard face. "Ah, let's call them *idealists*."

Rosetti gave a short, humorless laugh. "Or liberals."

Welles's perfect face puckered slightly with concern. "This has nothing to do with politics, Colonel. It's just that we've noticed a certain antipathy to the Company's Military Sciences. Among a good percentage of highly placed civilians, there's a *definite* lack of sympathy for the goals of Weapons Division."

"Anchorpoint is under the Colonial Administration Authority," Rosetti said before Fox could tag in again.

"This isn't a military operation. We don't run things here. Interfering with a civilian government would be a violation of the Strategic Arms Reduction Treaty. Our remit is to *solve* problems, not *create* them." Dammit, the newsreader speech pattern was contagious. Rosetti wanted to wash Fox's mouth out with soap.

"All of which looks *damned good* on paper," Fox told him, with approval so intense that Rosetti could practically feel the man patting his head. "But it *doesn't* always work very well in *reality*. We want all the civilians who boarded the *Sulaco* sewn up tight. *Very* tight."

Rosetti's eyebrows went up. "How do you suggest we do that?"

"Forfeiture of shares, for starters," Welles replied, looking pleased that he'd asked. "The threat of forfeiture's the one sure way to get their attention. Tell them anyone who talks will lose their shares immediately, no appeal. We've found this approach quite effective in the past."

"But *that's* a *simple* matter." Fox took a small flexi from his inside jacket pocket and passed it to him. "This *isn't*. The *Sulaco* logged a three-person boarding party during its time in the UPP sector."

Rosetti wasn't surprised. He had imagined UPP teams swarming over the *Sulaco* like locusts, frantically streaming all the data they could get within two hours. Nor was he surprised that Fox and Welles had gotten hold of the *Sulaco*'s incident log before he'd seen it himself. But Fox's rubbing his nose in it pissed him off.

Instead of punching him, Rosetti said, "Why wasn't I informed when you obtained this information?"

"We're informing you right now," Welles told him brightly. "We're also informing you that you seem to have lost an android. Or 'artificial person,' which I believe is currently their preferred term. This one was a Bishop model. To be more precise, you've lost only *half* of the artificial person, but it's the upper half—the one with the brain—so it might as well be the whole thing."

Rosetti set his face in an impassive mask while he considered his next move. Sending Marines into the UPP's *apparatchik* utopia to reclaim stolen property was out of the question. The UPP was a collective of wannabe Bolsheviks who thought misquoting Karl Marx made them socialists. They were amateurs, lacking the Marines' training or focus, not to mention hardware. On the face of it, the Marines could eat them for lunch without working up a sweat.

But any group whose members put their ideology above their own lives were extremely dangerous. A lot of good Marines could get maimed or worse before the amateurs either ran out of ammunition or changed their minds about their lives *vis-à-vis* their ideology. To Rosetti, that didn't justify losing a single life on either side, especially not in peacetime.

His gaze fell on the desktop screen, where his calendar popped up a reminder for yet another meeting, scheduled to begin as soon as these two stereotypes could put up a privacy bubble in Conference Room 8B. Because in MiliSci: Weapons Division, nothing, not even life itself, progressed before there was a meeting to discuss it.

No doubt this was how he would die, Rosetti thought. Not in a blaze of combat glory nor quietly in his sleep, but in a meeting, where his heart would give out from bureaucratic tedium. He might not even fall off the chair, just face-plant on a conference table. Come Judgment Day, he'd need a nose-job.

1 0

Two very young Marines escorted Hicks to the meeting room, where he was surprised to see that anti-bugging security hadn't changed at all in the years he'd been gone. The large, mirrored bubble dominating the bare chamber was exactly like the last one he'd been in, back when his squad received the assignment to LV-426.

"Just go on in, Corporal Hicks." The Marine on his left opened the outer door of the airlock-style entrance for him. Her nametag said *Beauchamps.* Her squad probably called her *Bee-champs.* Or maybe *Byoo-champs.*

"Everyone's waiting for you, Corporal," the other Marine added. He was a tall, beefy guy labeled Volkov. They probably called him *Volvo.*

Let 'em wait. The words were on the tip of his tongue, but Hicks knew if he made trouble, these two would answer for it. God, they were so young. Beechamps looked about twelve and, despite his size, so did Volvo.

"Copy that," Hicks said, then he hesitated outside the airlock-style door. "You two watch your six, okay?"

"Soon as we see yours get inside, Corporal," Beauchamps said cheerfully, which made him laugh in spite of himself.

The first door closed with a whispered *shhh*. Hicks stood in the area between the doors with his feet apart and his hands clasped over his head as a scanner checked him for spyware and whatever else was currently on Anchorpoint's Bad-Shit List. It took longer than he'd expected—either they didn't trust him, or he had underestimated their level of paranoia. Probably both.

The door in front of him finally blinked green—the whole door, not just a light. Pretty showy, he thought.

Five people were seated at an enormous round table, but Colonel Rosetti was the only one Hicks recognized, and only from a photo. The colonel had sent an artificial person to handle his debrief and Hicks had been waiting for some kind of response ever since. The people on Rosetti's right were probably high up in the civilian government, while the two on his left were pure Company, through and through. The body language was unmistakable; Mr. and Ms. Smiley Q. Cheerful, of the perfectly-tanned and dentally-gifted Cheerful dynasty.

Not that they'd be married, or even just good friends—off duty, they probably couldn't stand each other. But they were good little worker bees, doing their job as the Company's public face, all shiny and confident. Because at the end of the day, Weyland-Yutani always called the shots and these two were here to make sure everybody toed the line.

Hicks snapped to attention and saluted.

The colonel stood to return the salute. "At ease, Corporal Hicks." He gestured toward the single chair placed ninety degrees to the right of his own. Hicks obeyed. "My name is Rosetti. Station's military attaché."

Hudson's goofy, insubordinate face suddenly appeared in his mind. The ghosts in his head were showing up more often since he'd visited Ripley, ambushing him in such vivid detail it was like seeing them in person.

"This is Dr. Adele Trent, chief of our Exobiology Division," the colonel told Hicks, glancing at the woman on his immediate right. She nodded politely. Hicks thought she looked more like a Ramirez. Or a Vasquez—and there she was, looking him right in his mind's eye. *Not mi familia, vato.*

"And Werner Shuman, of the Diplomatic Corps," Rosetti added.

Shuman didn't so much nod as twitch a little without smiling. Some diplomat, Hicks thought. Maybe he was new at this.

Rosetti turned to the over-tanned couple on his left side. "And this is—"

"Kevin Fox, Corporal," Mr. Fake-Tan said. His expensive clothes apparently made him too good to be polite to military rabble, even if the rabble was a colonel.

Right on cue, Lieutenant Gorman's too-serious baby-face was there in his brain. The CO had had a corncob up his ass and his combat experience had all been simulated. The image was accompanied by the faint echo of Vasquez's last words as they had come to Hicks via the crazy acoustics in the airduct. *You always were an asshole, Gorman.* Too good to eat with his squad but good enough to die with Vasquez.

"My associate, Susan Welles, and I are with the Company," Fox went on, as if it weren't obvious. "We'd like to congratulate you on a successful mission."

"*Successful?*" Hicks gave a single, harsh laugh. "I lost my entire squad!" He glanced at Rosetti to see how he was taking this. The colonel was stone-faced.

So why should he care how Rosetti felt, Hicks thought, remembering that he was done with authority, although this was definitely not the time to announce his new approach to life. It would just inspire the Company stooges to spout hours of corporate bullshit. No one would thank him for that; Rosetti might even shoot him.

Sergeant Apone popped up in his mind, glared at him for a moment, then disappeared.

"But *you* returned," the Welles stooge gushed at him. "*And* you rescued the colony's sole survivor. No small thing, by any measure."

Rosetti picked up a flexi screen on the table in front of him. "We've all read the transcript of your debriefing, Corporal—"

"Then maybe *you* can answer my question," Hicks said before he could stop himself. "Where's Bishop?" Pause. "Sir."

Rosetti's commanding officer mask slipped for a second, revealing his wariness, before he recovered his stone-face. "We've tabled that for now."

The colonel made it sound like it was an order, but Hicks saw him flick a glance at the Company stooges. Why would he care how they felt? Hicks's opinion of Rosetti fell a few notches.

"After reading the transcript, I've got some questions for the corporal," Dr. Trent piped up. "Are you absolutely *certain* you have nothing more to tell us about the alien's life-cycle? We need as much detail as possible. Detail is *crucial*."

"I've just told you, that subject is classified," Rosetti said before Hicks could reply. "The corporal's security rating would have to be upped considerably before we can discuss this with him."

Hicks blinked. Had the old man *really* just said that? "I've already told you everything I know, Dr. Trent. Every *crucial* detail."

"Corporal Hicks—" Rosetti started, a warning in his tone.

"*No*, let him *speak*," Fox said. "After all, he *is* the *only* one in the room who's actually *seen* these creatures in *action*." There was something weird about the way he talked, Hicks thought; like he was reading news headlines.

"*You* ordered that the subject be classified," Rosetti said, almost snapping. "Or does 'maximum security' mean something different now?"

Dr. Trent shook her head. "I'm sorry, but I really don't think Corporal Hicks is being completely truthful when he says he doesn't know anything more than what he's already told us. But perhaps not deliberately," she added to Hicks, looking apologetic. "In any situation, human observers overlook things without realizing it. On the other hand, the synthetic, Bishop, was designed for meticulous scientific observation. The Hyperdyne A/5 model is, in effect, a walking archive."

"Corporal Hicks has been asking the right questions from the beginning," Welles put in. She looked Company-smug, a characteristic Company expression, what Hicks's mother had referred to as a *house-face*.

Rosetti's stony look became a glower. "To answer your previous question, Corporal Hicks," he said stiffly, "we aren't certain."

Translation: *Nobody's got a fucking clue and it's so classified you're not supposed to know even that much.*

Sergeant Al Apone's face reappeared to Hicks's inner eye, complete with cigar. *Another glorious day in the corps! Every paycheck a fortune, every meal a banquet! I love the corps!*

Welles leaned forward, her Company smile even brighter. "Uncertainty doesn't mean we can't guess, does it, Colonel."

Hicks's chuckle was humorless. Bust someone's balls for violating maximum security and then keep talking around the big secret—*that* was chutzpah in the first degree. Unless the Company's meat puppets really *didn't* know what maximum security meant. Or maybe since LV-426 all bets were off.

"So don't stop now—go ahead and guess," Hicks said in a simple tone that was actually his normal speaking voice. It always made shifty characters like these two assume he knew less than he did. "You go first, I'm dying to hear it. By the way, where's Bishop?"

Welles and Fox looked at each other. Her nod was barely perceptible.

"Bishop is currently being held at Rodina Station," Fox said, looking around to see everyone else's reaction to this information.

Hicks needed a couple of seconds to get it. "You mean the UPP?" He laughed a little in disbelief. "What the hell have *they* got to do with this?"

"The *Sulaco*'s navigation system glitched." Rosetti's weary tone had an edge in it. "You were in UPP territory for one hundred nineteen minutes. Ordinarily, the UPP would have responded to this with threats, accusing us of a treaty violation, but for some reason they didn't." He paused, and Hicks knew he didn't want to talk about this with the Company power couple in the room. "The *Sulaco*'s event log shows that during this time, it was boarded covertly. But still we've heard nothing from Rodina—nihil, nada, zilch."

Werner Shuman cleared his throat loudly, as if reminding everyone he was in the room. "In diplomatic terms, Corporal Hicks, the UPP have our diplomatic ass in a diplomatic sling. If—no, *when* they respond to the *Sulaco*'s breach of their borders as a hostile act—and let me assure *you*, Colonel Rosetti, they'll do so at a time as inconvenient as possible for us—it will seriously compromise our position in negotiations for arms reduction. The communications time-lag to and from Earth is a week each way, meaning we'd have a two-week wait for policy clarification—not helpful in the middle of a major crisis. There will be grave consequences for all sides."

Hicks blinked, incredulous. Did Shuman really think telling everyone what they already knew displayed his diplomatic acumen?

"Fortunately, *we've* arrived with a policy brief, Ambassador," Welles said in a breezy tone. "I believe you've already seen it. My partner and I are here to implement it."

Rosetti stared into the middle distance somewhere over Hicks's shoulder. "The UPP incident predates your orders. This change in circumstances—"

"—doesn't change the job we were sent here to do," Fox said confidently. "And we *will* do it."

"Do you really *not understand* the situation?" Shuman threw up both hands in exasperation, and for a moment Hicks thought he was going to start tearing his hair out. "'Doing your job' involves a very strong potential for interstellar war—starting *here*, between us and Rodina Station!"

Fox started to say something, but Rosetti was already talking over him.

"Any further questions for Corporal Hicks?" The colonel didn't wait for an answer. "No? In that case, Corporal, you're dismissed."

Hicks jumped to his feet and saluted, then made a perfect about-face and all but ran for the door.

1 1

What is this life if, full of care,
we have no time to sit and stare...
... at stainless-steel mermaids.

Not the right words, but for the last twenty-four hours, Tully, Charles A. hadn't had *any* words. He'd left them behind when Corporal Nenge had dragged him out of the *Sulaco*. Or so he thought. Or would have thought if he'd had the words.

But only minutes after he'd wandered into the mall and plumped down on this bench by the stainless-steel mermaid fountain, his vocabulary had grown back, or maybe just come out of hiding. *All clear! Olly-olly-oxen-free, it's safe now!*

Sure it was. The biggest, most egregious lie ever perpetrated on the human race was that any place in the universe was, at any time, by any stretch of the imagination, *safe*. Worse, Tully had a terrible feeling that this was the one and only secret of life.

The stainless-steel mermaids in the center of the fountain were oblivious, untouched by human concerns. They posed prettily on artfully arranged stacks of stainless-steel rocks, combing their stainless-steel hair, playing with stainless-steel starfish, or scanning a distant horizon that only their stainless-steel eyes could see.

If it *was* stainless steel—metals had never been Tully's strong suit. It could have been an alloy, or even a *trompe l'œil* plastic coating. Tech was so advanced these days it could *trompe* anyone's *l'œil*. Except for Spence's. She was never fooled. He'd always envied her clarity, but not today. Today he was okay with being susceptible to illusion, he didn't want to know better. There was nothing *better* about what he knew, and every time he turned around, it got worse. But not in here in the mall. Not yet. Anchorpoint had malls like this on every level, all with restaurants, bars, stores, theaters, and cinemas both vintage and regular immersive, and in the larger ones, gyms and playing fields. The design was based on the twentieth-century iteration of the village marketplace, located mostly in suburban areas of North America and some parts of Europe.

Tully had always found it amazing that the quintessence of ordinary space station life was something that had been just as ordinary in the days before Earth had achieved space travel. It made him think of the old cosmic fairy tale about time travelers sneaking the concept of malls into the past, to prepare humans for a future in space.

Some people actually believed that was a reasonable hypothesis.

The concept of *reasonable* no longer meant anything to him. He had wandered wordlessly into the mall because it was an ordinary place where only ordinary things could happen—drinking and eating, shopping, maybe a pick-up game of basketball or soccer. Ordinary *in extremis*, where monsters *never* dropped down from the ceiling—

Tully looked up. Fifty feet overhead there was a fake skylight showing a holo-looped fake blue sky, with fake fluffy clouds. There was also a rainy sky, and sometimes snow, just for variety, all very authentic fakes. Anyone bored with fake sky could opt for the reality of a black void and unchanging stars, visible from the scenic outlook on the mezzanine level. They could also toss wish-tokens down at the mermaids.

His gaze fell on a mermaid who seemed to be staring at something over his left shoulder. Suddenly unsettled, Tully got up and walked quickly to the nearest transit access spot. When the train arrived, he planted himself in the doorway and took a careful look around the small carriage, especially at the ceiling, before he sat down.

The handful of other passengers ignored him, and he felt an intense surge of envy. They were so lucky. None of them had any idea that they lived in a universe where savage creatures could come out of nowhere to kill them in unimaginably horrible ways.

Well, he wasn't about to tell them, they'd just think he

was crazy. And they wouldn't like him any better when they found out he wasn't.

He found Spence alone in the tissue lab, handling something in a Petri dish within the confines of a safety tank. Her face was a mix of deep concentration tinged with annoyance. She hated tanks, said the glove mountings were badly positioned and had too little freedom of movement.

She looked up when she heard the door open, and her jaw dropped.

"Hey," Tully said faintly.

"Jesus, Charlie, you look like homemade shit," she said. "*Godawful* homemade shit. That went bad a month ago." She covered the Petri dish, put it down, and wriggled out of the rubbery white gloves with some effort; as usual, she'd forgotten to powder. "What the fuck happened down there in the *Sulaco*? There's this security blackout—"

"Yeah, there is," he said, feeling heavy with fatigue now. "Me included. I had to sign a whole new set of forms. I can't tell you shit. Not even godawful homemade shit." His smile was brief. "Talk to anybody and I lose my shares—*all* my shares, instantly, no appeal. I'm just *out*."

"You're joking." Her eyes widened, making her look very young. Then again, she *was* very young, Tully thought, a lot younger than he was now, after the *Sulaco*. Compared to him, she was a baby. "Right?"

"Wish I were," he said unhappily. Spence started to say something else but he talked over her. "So, what's Dr. Trent got for me to dick around with this shift?"

She hesitated, then led him to a nearby workbench and a larger, more elaborate safety tank equipped with waldos instead of gloves.

"Here you go," she said as she plucked something from the inbox beside it. She started to give it to him, then hesitated again. "Are you sure you're up to a shift?" she asked, with very real concern. "You really *do* look like homemade shit gone bad."

Tully beckoned and she handed over a small item wrapped in a printout with a rubber band around it. He removed the rubber band, ignored the printout, and held up a small, metal canister. There were marks on it that looked like red crayon.

"All yours, whatever it is," Spence told him. "Orders are, you use the waldo tank. Or we all have to suit up in full biohazard gear and seal the lab. No unprotected exposure."

That made him frown, but Tully slipped the canister into the insertion chamber and waited for it to be dumped into the tank, airlock-style. Airlocks were supposed to be good protection but the *Sulaco*'s hadn't worked very well.

"*Dammit*, Tully." Spence grabbed his arm, hard.

He turned to her, wondering how he could have upset her already.

"What *did* happen on the *Sulaco*?" Her fingers dug into

his bicep. "How come they're ordering so many biopsies on the three survivors? And where'd the sudden backlog of autopsies come from? That's why nobody else is here, in case you hadn't noticed. Pathology requisitioned most of our people and locked them down in ultra-clean rooms."

Tully drew back a little, wishing he could just tell her he had no idea what she was talking about. Unfortunately, he'd already said too much, and even if he hadn't, she'd never let him off the hook that easily.

"And why the hell is everything triple-X classified?" she went on, practically yelling now. "Two spooks from Gateway come in today, and they're walking around like they just *bought* the place. What's *that* about? Come on, Tully, what the *fuck*?"

"Okay, *okay*." Tully pried her fingers off his arm, rubbing the muscle and wincing. He wasn't sure what scared him more—getting busted by Company fascists, or a long, black tail swooping down either to impale him or strangle him. "Not now, all right? *Later*. And *not here*."

When Charlie didn't want to talk about something, Spence knew he was either scared or embarrassed. Either way, a full-on interrogation wouldn't work. What she had to do was peck at him little by little, preferably while he was busy with a complicated assignment. Eventually, she'd wear him down and he'd spill.

This time, however, she'd have to work a lot harder to reach him.

It wasn't just that he'd been gone for more than twenty-four hours, that happened to everyone. Every so often a couple of higher-ups started obsessing over a specimen or a process or a system and requested a full, unabridged work-up. If you got tapped for one of those, you could end up sequestered for days or even weeks, grinding away on the project, logging every detail in real time—minus any mention of the meds that kept you going—until either there was no more data to grind out, or the higher-ups saw a new shiny thing to obsess about and they let you go home.

Spence had been through several of those, although Tully had done more. It was one of the disadvantages of being the senior tech. He was also the best, although Spence was trying hard to catch up with him. Seeing him like this, however, made her wonder if she wanted to.

Jackson wouldn't have pulled him out of downtime early just for a routine assignment, but why Ops had needed the top tech to collect air samples was beyond her. A 'bot could have done it. Then she'd heard there'd been more Marines than civilians in the deck crew. That usually happened when the Marines had to impress some VIP.

She'd planned to squeeze every detail out of Charlie the moment he came back. But then he hadn't come back, and she couldn't find out why. The *Sulaco* had fallen into a high-security black hole from which nothing could escape, not even a single paranoid rumor. And just as two spooks had arrived from MiliSci's Weapons Division. Coincidence? Not fucking likely.

Instead of going back to her own assignment, Spence grabbed the last clean mug from the shelf under the workbench and went to the coffee machine on the counter against the back wall. The machine made single cups, as well as tea and hot chocolate and even broth, although anyone who tried that last knew by the smell that they'd made a terrible mistake.

The coffee machine stood next to a small sink, usually crowded with unwashed coffee cups. Under the counter was a half-height fridge filled with soft drinks nobody liked. Spence rooted around in the basket of coffee capsules, found a variety she didn't hate, and popped it into the machine, sneaking glances over her shoulder at Tully while she waited.

He didn't react to the sound of the machine or ask her to make one for him. If he was that preoccupied, maybe she could catch him off-guard. Cup in hand, she parked herself on a stool a short distance behind him and to the right, which put her just beyond his peripheral vision while giving her a good view of the monitor on the shelf above the tank.

The feed from the electron microscope was high-res, but she wasn't sure what she was seeing. It looked like android blood cells, but they were bonded to some kind of black substance—which everyone knew was impossible.

"Hey, Spence," he said suddenly, "you got any idea what this shit is? Or where it came from?"

Should have known better than to try sneaking up on him, Spence thought. "Didn't you look at the printout?" She got up and took it off the desk, scanned it quickly, then read it over more carefully. "The stuff's from the *Sulaco* and it's—" She cut off as he increased the magnification. The black blobs looked more porous and lumpy, but the lumps were oddly regular, like something inorganic disguised as biological material. "God, Charlie, what the fuck *is* that?" Spence tossed the printout aside; it glanced off the workbench and fell to the floor.

"I asked you first," he said absently, increasing the magnification. The blob contained a system of tunnels or channels, and the texture made Spence think of insect secretions. Plenty of insect species on many different worlds built homes from matter produced by their own bodies. But there was no visible evidence of any actual bugs here, no spoor or frass. The Marines could call off their bug hunt.

Unless the bug hunt had already happened, and this was all that was left. This, and Tully.

Spence shifted uncomfortably. "Can you up the res?" she asked.

Charlie cranked it to maximum without increasing the magnification.

"Yeah." She picked up the printout lying on the floor near her feet. "It says this was taken from what was left of a dismembered artificial person," she said. "From still-liquid artificial blood inside the thigh tissue."

"Did they find the rest of the body?"

She read more. "No, just the legs." Spence put the print-out on the workbench; a puff of air from the ventilation system sent it to the floor again. "Am I crazy, or is that black crap bonded to the artificial blood cells?"

"At the molecular level," he confirmed. "Whether you're crazy or not."

"But that's impossible," Spence said. "Synth blood is inert."

Charlie gave a single, humorless laugh. "Looks like somebody found a work-around for that one. Probably shoulda seen it coming."

The Madagascar eco-pocket was beautiful, one of a dozen eco-pockets in Anchorpoint. According to the assistant director of Green Spaces, all were perfectly maintained versions of their respective originals. Spence had suggested it to Hicks because it was closest to both his and Newt's quarters. Hicks liked it simply because it was nothing like LV-426.

Since they'd first visited Ripley, Hicks had brought Newt here almost every day. She loved to sit in the tall grass, enjoying the authentic but fake breezes that carried a hint of the fake ocean and feeling the fake sunshine on her face. He liked that himself—it felt good on the new skin coming in on his face and arm. Sometimes it got a little itchy—or a lot itchy—but that meant he was healing. Itchy was better than painful. He just had to remember not to scratch.

Right now, he was doing his best not to scratch by watching Newt reach one hand out to a ring-tailed lemur. The pocket was home to a small colony of the little primates, which were the main attraction for Newt. The kid had listened attentively as the pocket's lead caretaker explained in a friendly-but-serious way that just because the lemurs had been bred in captivity and were accustomed to people, they weren't simply free-range pets. "In captivity" didn't mean domesticated. The lemurs didn't mind humans visiting, but this was *their* turf.

Hicks had marveled at the way Newt had shown no signs of impatience or restlessness. Apparently her off-the-chart survival instincts also worked in environments *without* monsters—although the kid was smart enough to know that not all monsters looked like aliens.

Or as Ripley had put it, *At least you don't see them fucking each over for a share.*

"Have you ever been to Africa, Hicks?" Newt asked softly.

The lemur stiffened at the sound of her voice.

"Yeah, I have," he replied, just as softly, hoping he wouldn't startle the animal. No such luck—he caught a glimpse of its ringed tail as it vanished into the grass. "I was in the Atlas Mountains in Morocco for four weeks of high-altitude basic. Nothing like Madagascar."

Newt wrapped her arms around her folded legs and rested her cheek on her knees, looking at him wistfully. "I'd like to go there."

"Shouldn't be a problem," he said, smiling. "You'll go to Gateway on a transport a lot like the *Sulaco*. Once you get there, you catch the long-haul ship to Earth and the next thing you know, you're in Oregon with your gramma and grandpa. After that, it's simple—jump over one big puddle, then another, smaller one, and there you are, on the island of Madagascar."

Newt's brow furrowed, as if she had the weight of the universe on her shoulders. Hicks wanted her to believe everything was all right, that she would never again face anything like what she'd gone through on LV-426. But belief could be tricky. He and the rest of the squad had believed they were going to LV-426 on a rescue mission. Instead, they'd screwed the pooch, then had to take off and nuke it from orbit, because it was the only way to be sure.

If only Ripley had been right about that.

"Oregon," Newt sighed. "I don't even remember it. Or my grandparents."

Hicks chuckled. "That's okay, they remember you."

She raised her head with a pointedly skeptical expression and he knew better than to try bullshitting her. Besides, he owed her his life. She deserved the truth.

"Trust me, kid, grandparents *always* remember their grandchildren," he said. "It's what they do. It's what they're *for*."

Her smile was fleeting. "But what about Ripley? She'll wake up and I won't be there. Can't I wait?"

"Ripley's pretty smart." He grinned. "She'll find you. She always does, right?"

The kid nodded, looking no less troubled.

"Look, after the transport leaves for Gateway, there won't be another for months," he told her. "That's too long for you to wait. But hey, if you want to make double-sure Ripley'll know where you are, leave her a note and tell her. I'll help you work out the precise coordinates if you want. Sound good to you?"

Newt hesitated for a couple of seconds, then smiled. "Affirmative," she said. "You just better make sure she gets it, okay?"

"Affirmative," he said feeling his heart break.

From the doorway of Ripley's room, Hicks watched Newt sitting at a fold-down desk, working hard on an elaborate star map. A water glass held felt-tip pens in a dozen different colors, and Hicks was pretty sure she had used all of them. Despite the circumstances, it was the closest she had ever come to childlike behavior. Maybe she'd have a chance at a real childhood, or something like it.

Her grandparents were going to have their hands full with her. Hicks hoped they would know enough to keep her busy. He made a mental note to send them a copy of this star chart, so they could see how meticulous she was, right down to the tiniest details.

Details are crucial, Corporal.

Oh, fuck off... he wished he'd said.

Hicks would never regret helping Newt lie about

not remembering what had happened on LV-426. He'd coached her on how cold-sleep exacerbated traumatic memory loss to help her come across like the real deal. Maybe he should have felt bad—protecting her was one thing, but showing her how to lie wasn't exactly ethical, even if it was the Company.

On the other hand, the Company hadn't sent any trauma specialists along with their weaponized power couple. Neither of them had broached the possibility of neurological procedures to restore Newt's memory, and Hicks wanted to get her safely out of their reach before they did. The kid needed to go home to her family, not to a black ops lab.

Newt printed her new address in the bottom right corner of the map in careful, very legible block letters, then showed it to Hicks.

NEWT JORDAN
c/o
MR. & MRS. RICHARD JORDAN
34877 GREENLEAF AVE. #582
NEW PORTLAND, OREGON AB994J2

He gave her a thumbs-up and she flashed him a brief grin before she went over to Ripley, pushing the monitors and consoles aside so she could get in close.

For a few moments, she just stood, leaning against the side rail and gazing at Ripley's pale, silent face with the row of electrodes on her forehead. Hicks could practically see the little wheels turning in Newt's mind. She was wavering about leaving again, wanting to stay until Ripley woke up, even if Ripley yelled at her for it.

Hicks doubted Ripley would yell at her for anything, but she wouldn't have let the kid stay at Anchorpoint, either. In the absence of scheduled transport, Ripley would have put a pistol to somebody's head and commandeered any spacecraft available.

"Ripley?" She waited a few moments, and Hicks knew she was hoping Ripley would finally hear her and wake up. "Ripley, it's me. Newt."

Still no reaction. Hicks felt his heart breaking again.

When Ripley had helped him into his sleep capsule, he'd heard Newt calling her *Mommy*. He hadn't assumed that automatically made him *Daddy*, but he would have thrown himself between the kid and anything that could hurt her, whether it was a hundred screaming, acid-bleeding aliens or a couple of Company goons, and not solely because it was his job. If that made him Newt's daddy, then he was everybody's daddy, at least sometimes.

"I'm sorry, Ripley, but I gotta go now," Newt said finally. Hicks could see how she was refusing to let herself cry. "I'm gonna go live with my gramma and grampa in Oregon. Hicks says that's a good place." She looked over at him and he nodded at her, hoping his smile looked encouraging.

"But I'm leaving you a map of how to get to where I'll be," she went on. "You can come and stay with me after you wake up, okay? I want you to. You *have* to. *Please.*"

Newt's eyes welled up. She silently mouthed the words, *Bye, Mommy*, before turning away and going quickly to Hicks. He was about to help her with the backpack, but she grabbed his hand and pulled him out of the room.

"Crew Only Beyond This Point," Newt said, pointing to the sign over the entrance to the departure deck. "Only I'm not crew, am I? Not *really.*" She looked up at Hicks with a solemnity so disquieting that he made a business out of helping her put on her backpack, just so he could compose himself.

"The *Mona Lisa* isn't primarily a passenger vessel, but it's fully licensed for them," Hicks said, keeping his voice light. "One of the medics will be serving as your temporary guardian." She started to say something, and he cut her off. "Don't argue. All unaccompanied minors have to have one in transit, it's the law. You'll have access to recreational areas, but only at certain times, as determined by the skipper. Stick to those and don't bite your guardian—" Newt looked up at him, and he winked at her. "—and everyone on the crew will be your friend, okay? Which is a very good thing. Anything else isn't so good."

"I know what to do," she said as he turned her around and lifted her chin with one finger. "You and Ripley trained me real good." Her smile was sad. "But I'd really rather stick with my old crew."

Hicks chuckled. "Well, now you've got a new crew and a new mission," he said. "Good luck in Oregon. Affirmative?"

"Affirmative." Newt started down the long, narrow hallway to the departure deck, then stopped and looked back to give him a thumbs-up.

He gave her one in return and watched as she continued up the corridor, her bright red backpack bobbing with her movements. At the far end, she stopped again, waved, then disappeared around a corner before he could wave back.

Hicks had planned to go straight to the gym to take his feelings out on the heavy bag. Instead, he ended up on the observation platform, watching Newt's transport depart; what the hell, a little more torture wouldn't kill him. For thirty seconds the *Mona Lisa* moved slowly out of the docking bay, until it was completely clear of the station. Then it zoomed off into the black. Phase one of torture complete—now he could start missing her.

If they hadn't found any surviving relatives, Hicks would have petitioned for his sister to get custody—Zelda would have loved the kid—but this was better. Newt had been through enough. Sending her to her family was the right thing to do.

And it was the only way to be sure.

Wasn't it?

1 3

"Obviously, Colonel-Doctor, their mission was to obtain specimens of this lifeform," Lara Braun said. She was the chief of Research and Development at Rodina Station, and not given to speaking unless she had something to say, which was why Suslov was paying close attention to her.

Or trying to. There were too many other people squeezed in around the table, and the room's ventilation system was struggling to counter the carbon dioxide build-up. If this meeting went on too long, they'd start passing out.

"The robot dissected a specimen while they were still on LV-426, a planetoid they were in the process of terraforming. There's a description labeled 'the pre-larval form,' which is apparently the form that killed Boris Lenko." Braun paused to consult one of several long yellow sheets of paper on the table in front of her. She was a throwback, unable and unwilling to go paperless. It made her an oddity—most people her age barely knew what paper was.

"Personally, I think it's more correct to call it an

'ovipositor,'" she went on. "Albeit a very unusual one. It functions not only independently of the lifeform's anatomy but aggressively—something we've never encountered before. It's—well, *alien*."

One of the military officers sitting opposite Braun leaned forward.

"You call the thing an *ovipositor*?" he said, his tone overtly challenging. "It came out of an *egg*. Eggs are *laid by* ovipositors, ovipositors don't hatch out of eggs, and they don't spray *acid*."

Braun was unperturbed. "That one was defective, Captain Strelnikov. If you remember, it had grown in the robot's sleep capsule, where its only resources were inorganic materials. The robot itself was severely damaged, which I'm sure contributed to the creature's defects."

Strelnikov eyed her skeptically. "Now you're just guessing."

"No, I'm *hypothesizing* from known facts," Braun said with a faint smile. Strelnikov was about to respond when Major Olga Georgivna, sitting on his left, spoke up.

"And do you *hypothesize* that these creatures could be of military importance?" The major was another one like Braun, who didn't chatter needlessly. She was the best strategic thinker Suslov had ever met, which was why he had made her Head of Logistics and Planning, a position Strelnikov had coveted for years.

"I can prove they are, Major," Braun replied. "All I have to do is clone the alien cells."

An apprehensive murmur went around the table. Cloning had been universally proscribed for almost a century under the Benevolent Civilizations Treaty. Just the mention had jerked them all out of imminent CO_2 stupor. Suslov beckoned to his assistant sitting behind him and told him to step out and notify climate control to triple both the oxygen feed and the ventilation. *Now.*

He turned back to the meeting. "Dr. Braun," he said loudly over the not-so-dull roar of aggrieved bureaucrats, and was relieved when they all shut up. "Could it be that these creatures were *already* weaponized? That they were *created as* weapons?"

Braun looked pleased with him. "That's *exactly* what I think, Colonel-Doctor," she said. "Video extracted from the robot shows the mature form is an extraordinary killing machine, as strong and relentless as it is savage. The individual creatures don't display normal animal behavior—they don't mate or compete for food or territory, nor do they form groups. All they do is kill, with no concern for their own safety. They don't even *try* to protect themselves.

"According to information the robot acquired from the colony laboratory, despite the size of the head, there's nothing that would correspond to the cortex or the cerebrum. They show no sign of what we'd call intelligence—no mental activity that is remotely like conscious thought. They seem to be governed solely by instinct, and in a way that's closer to programming than any natural phenomenon."

Novo Ismail, recently appointed as Head of Intelligence, put up their hand. "Our covert sources in Weyland-Yutani have already told us of an ongoing Weapons Division project. However—" Their expression turned a bit sour. "—we have yet to penetrate the Company's security measures to acquire more substantial intel."

"Could their project be connected to this alien?" Suslov asked. "Are they trying to develop a living weapon?" He was definitely more alert now, and so was everyone else. He had to wrap this up before they regained the will to argue.

"Excuse me." The head of the Diplomacy Bureau raised her voice, as well as her hand. She was new in the position, appointed by someone else on the governing council, and Suslov couldn't remember her name. "I'd like to remind the Colonel-Doctor—and everyone else, of course—that cloning experiments on living tissue from *any* species violate the Benevolent Civilizations Treaty. And conducting those experiments as part of military research contravenes the primary restrictions on chemical and biological weapons, as agreed to in the Strategic Arms Reduction Treaty. Are we *really* prepared to do that?" she continued. "Moreover, can we justify it—not only privately to each other, but also to the other signatories to the Treaty—when our activities become known?"

She paused to look at each person around the table. "And I promise all of you, they *will* become known," she added. "Things like this always get out. *Always.*"

Lara Braun shook her head. "Nonetheless, *I'd* like to inform Chief Diplomatic Officer Duchamps that Weyland-Yutani is prepared to do exactly that. I promise you, Irina, that our capitalist cousins are well under way with this project." She scanned the group, mimicking Duchamps. "We're all painfully aware of how our technology has lagged behind that of the capitalist cartels," she said. "Thanks to a stroke of good luck, we have the opportunity to catch up with them—but only if we push ahead *now*."

"I agree," Suslov said. "We must proceed." He pretended not to notice how delighted Braun was, so she wouldn't think he wanted to forge an alliance.

By contrast, the head of the Diplomatic Bureau was anything but delighted. Suslov hoped she was better at hiding her feelings when dealing with the capitalists. He made a mental note to send her an anonymous message suggesting she have Freez™ injections. Certain jobs really did call for a faceful of poison.

"With all due respect," Duchamps said stiffly, "what we have no choice about is the fate of the robot. I go on the record as strongly advising that it be sent to Anchorpoint. Before we do so, however, we should restore it to full function. Are our technicians capable of repairing the thing?"

Braun's confident composure disappeared; she stared at the other woman in disbelief. "Why would *we* waste resources doing *that*?"

"When it comes to diplomacy, courtesies are *never*

wasted," Duchamps said, gazing at Suslov now. "Today's gesture of goodwill, no matter how small, might be crucial in resolving tomorrow's crisis. If we return the robot to them as is, they could claim we damaged it while we were looting its data."

"All right, say we *do* repair it," Suslov said, slightly amused. "They'll still think we squeezed it for every last drop of data."

"Of course they will." Duchamps seemed equally amused. "But accusing us publicly would make them look very bad—so ungrateful. It would also leave them open to accusations concerning the so-called *accidental* violation of our territory." Her smile widened. "The enemy can't fire on us if we don't give them ammunition."

A murmur of agreement went around the table. Even Strelnikov seemed mollified.

"Our technicians will repair the robot," Suslov said with a tone of finality. "We'll restore its motor functions and other capabilities using our highest-quality components. The technicians must do their very best work and clean it thoroughly to remove any contaminants that might impair its function, allowing us to return it to them in better condition than we found it." He paused, holding up a hand to forestall any comments or questions.

"And then," he continued, "using the alien cells recovered from the robot, we proceed with a program of scientific research. We will clone the alien… *not* to explore its potential as a weapon, but to discover the properties of a substance previously unknown to us. Is this clear?"

They all nodded dutifully.

"Then the matter is settled, *with* prejudice," he told them. "We're adjourned."

His wasn't the only sigh of relief.

14

"Initially, this was a routine test for organic-biological compatibility," Dr. Trent said while a tech she had introduced as Tully set up for the holographic display. Rosetti recognized him as one of the civilians who had been on the *Sulaco*, and he looked like he hadn't gotten over it yet.

If he'd been a Marine, Rosetti would have insisted he remain in the clinic for further observation. He wondered what Adele Trent was thinking. Maybe she was showing off for Company Ken. *See how fast my people recover?* Company Barbie, however, was conspicuous by her absence, which surprised him. He'd thought Fox and Welles were electronically stapled together.

As if he'd caught the gist of Rosetti's thoughts, Fox turned to him, his smile professionally cordial. "Ms. Welles is catching up on file work we didn't have a chance to finish yesterday, thanks to, ah, some sudden developments. She should be joining us later."

Rosetti nodded. A JAG officer had once told him that

any time people volunteered answers to questions you hadn't asked, it was misdirection, like a stage magician.

"I should clarify that Ms. Welles isn't my assistant, nor am I hers," Fox went on. "We're colleagues." He shifted impatiently in his chair as he watched the tech, who seemed to be having trouble with the hardware. Tully looked up from the projector, first at Trent, who made a small, hurry-up motion, and then at Rosetti.

"Is there some problem?" Rosetti asked.

"Sometimes it has trouble connecting with the nebula," Tully told him.

"The nebula?" Fox sat up straight, looking to Trent, then to Rosetti. "What nebula?"

"On a planet, it's called the cloud," Trent said, "but a cloud in space is a nebula."

Fox's expression turned wary, as if he thought Tully were trying to put something over on him. "If a nebula is a cloud, why not stick with the original term? Everyone knows what a cloud is. 'Nebula' sounds like something different."

Tully paused to face him. "It *is* something different. On a planet, clouds are water or ice crystals. Out here, a nebula is made of dust and ionized gases."

"Tully." Trent looked a warning at him.

"Sorry," the tech said, sounding a bit sulky. "It's been tough going lately. You ever have one of those lifetimes?"

Rosetti gave a short spontaneous laugh that surprised all of them, including himself. "I hear you, Mr. Tully," he said, ignoring Fox's disdainful look. "Take your time. We'll wait."

Trent's expression said she didn't know what had gotten into him. Rosetti would have told her to relax, but he knew how she felt. Nobody could relax with Company goons on the premises. Fox was staring hard at the tech as if he were trying to will him to work faster. The son of a bitch was probably trying to think up some way to penalize Tully for lecturing him on clouds and nebulae. Maybe he'd issue a fiat saying anyone using the word "nebula" would forfeit their shares.

That would give Rosetti a great reason to shove his boot up Fox's ass sideways. Or maybe he should retire before that began to sound like a reasonable response.

"Okay, we're in business," Tully announced. "Sorry about the delay. I don't know why it was so hard to get the connection. It's supposed to be brand-new equipment— the Company sent it less than a month ago." Rosetti grimaced inwardly, and imagined Fox adding "criticism of Company hardware" to the list of Tully's high crimes and misdemeanors.

The lights dimmed and a large silvery cube blurred into existence in midair, seemingly balanced on one corner. Its edges went from fuzzy to hard and bright as it grew to twice its original size. A second later, the image of a familiar double helix, complete with red and green beads, appeared in the center of the cube.

"As I was saying," Dr. Trent began, "this was a

compatibility test, checking for any markers in common." Her tone became more confident as she warmed to her subject. "The theory that terrestrial life has an extra-terrestrial origin may be out of fashion these days but it still hasn't been disproven. The building blocks of terrestrial life have been discovered on a multitude of other worlds, countless meteors and asteroids. To dismiss it—"

"We're all familiar with the theory, Dr. Trent," Fox said impatiently. "So let's get to the point. What kind of DNA were you looking for?"

"Human, of course," Trent said archly. "What we found—well, see for yourselves."

A new image appeared inside the cube. It looked like a cubist's interpretation of an Art Deco staircase, some of its lines in glowing neon purple, others in bright chartreuse. The image was clear, yet Rosetti had trouble focusing on it, as if it were somehow resisting his sight, refusing to be seen.

"Are you sure that's a biological structure?" Rosetti turned to Trent, glad to give his eyes a break; they were starting to hurt. "It doesn't look organic to me—more like a machine."

Trent chuckled grimly. "Wait till we get to the good part."

He turned back to see the weird shape in the cube moving toward the double helix. Rosetti expected them to bounce off each other. Instead, the weird one pounced on the double helix; its glowing lines broke, became entangled with it, incorporated some of the beads while others melted into the lines of the new shape. Any remaining red and green beads from the helix had been transformed into polygons, their colors no longer solid but distributed here and there on the various sides, making a random mosaic. The new form was easier to look at, although Rosetti was pretty sure that wasn't a good thing.

"The only things I've seen behave like that are viral cells," Fox said. "*Never* genetic material. *Never.*" He sounded awestruck. "How long does this process take in real time, Trent?"

"You just saw it." Trent seemed revolted, either by what they'd just seen or by Fox's enthusiasm, or both. The long-suffering tech looked as if he was about to throw up.

"It's a Darwinian ideal that *exceeds* Darwin," Fox continued. "Nature offers all living things just two alternatives: adapt or die. These creatures are the ultimate survivors—no matter what, they adapt. *Immediately.*" His enthusiasm was starting to piss Rosetti off. "We could learn so much from them. I want a preliminary report—"

"I can tell you everything you need to know, right now," Tully said.

Everyone turned to look at him in surprise.

He jerked his chin at the cube. "*They* adapt—*we* die."

1 5

Workshop 11 was a cavernous space filled with big machines in various stages of disassembly or reassembly and the heavy smell of oily metal. Hicks had been told he could pick up some paid shift work on the civilian side, if he didn't mind manual labor, and he didn't. The shrink who'd signed him off as fit for a routine employment furlough told him his wanting to keep busy was a good sign, and he'd be interested in hearing about it afterward.

The shrink's response had given Hicks pause; it made him sound like a neurotic who'd been running around inside his own head for so long that he couldn't get out. But then, prolonged periods of isolation could do that to a person.

Cold-sleep was supposed to ameliorate the disrupting effects caused by extreme dislocations in space and time, but it wasn't completely foolproof. Even asleep, those three little pounds of fatty tissue called the brain could somehow sense that long periods of time had passed and it processed the experience in the whacked-out funhouse of the subconscious mind.

Still, the shrink had okayed him for real work rather than booking him into a hobby lodge for needlepoint or bridge, so Hicks figured he knew what he was doing.

According to the woman on the assignment kiosk in the nearest Operations node, W-11 was the big machine shop on this level—it was all loaders, construction equipment, big engine parts for spacecraft, terraformers, and large-scale life-support.

"It's all things they need for waystations the size of Anchorpoint or bigger," she explained. "We need to keep them running at top efficiency. Sound like something you could do?" She looked at him with a glimmer of curiosity. Instantly, Hicks was back on the *Sulaco* with Sgt. Apone, prepping for the drop at LV-426, with Ripley saying she felt like a fifth wheel and asking was there anything she could do.

Standard military protocol was to treat all civilians like the highest-ranking officers, but Hicks knew Apone had been strongly tempted to tell Snow White to get the hell out of everyone's way. Instead, he'd removed the cigar from his mouth and said, *I don't know. Is there anything you can do?*

Hicks had figured she'd back down, but instead of slinking off in embarrassment, Ripley told him she could drive a loader. *I've got a Class Two rating.* Then she showed him it wasn't an empty boast by expertly picking up a crate of weapons.

Where do you want it? she'd asked with a smile, almost glamorous amid all that heavy machinery. Apone had looked from her to Hicks and back again before bursting into hearty, good-natured laughter.

The memory vanished and Hicks realized the woman at the kiosk was still waiting for an answer. He tapped the edge of his flexi against the tablet on the counter to accept the job and told her the same thing Ripley had said to him later on, after Apone wasn't around to be impressed.

"I can handle myself."

The map on Hicks's flexi had made finding the workshop easy enough. The schematic for the workshop itself, however, was less helpful, as it couldn't convey how much the interior landscape shifted as machinery came in for maintenance and repair. Worse, the lighting was terrible—Anchorpoint was pretty stingy with the candlepower. It was standard practice on the larger space stations, but Hicks had never liked it, especially in a place like this. It was like trying to find his way around shadowy rock formations in a canyon at nightfall.

He made his way through the clusters of machinery and finally found a workstation surrounded by piles of metal components, bits of framework, and machines in various stages of assembly. A small round housekeeping 'bot was scrubbing at grease stains on the floor. Pink foam bubbled up from its brushes as it spun around and around. The spiral design on the 'bot's flat surface was too scratched and faded to be even vaguely hypnotic.

"You Hicks?"

A husky man with dark brown skin and a full head of short dreads, some of them beaded, peered at him from a perch on a tall stool at the workbench. There was a rack of high-intensity light hanging just above his head. Only one was turned up to full power, its beam aimed directly at the complicated jumble of hardware in his hands. Various other parts were scattered over the ersatz-wood surface, along with wires, bits of circuit boards, and other things Hicks had no clue about. Off to one side was an angle-poise magnifier-lamp with extra lenses. It looked like a genuine antique.

"None other," Hicks said, glancing at his flexi. "If you're Walker, I'm here on a temporary duty assignment."

The man nodded. "Glad you didn't get lost—I can really use you." Under his nimble fingers, the jumble he was holding turned into a joystick controller. Walker touched a fingertip to it and Hicks heard the harsh metallic growl of a power-loader coming to life behind him. He stepped to one side as it lumbered forward, thumping to a heavy-footed stop fifteen centimeters to Walker's right. *Exactly* fifteen centimeters, Hicks knew, no less and no more. Engineers like Walker lived and breathed precision.

"We got some throwbacks around here that have to have a joystick," Walker said. "Won't use voice commands or gestures or a touch-pad. Won't even *try* to learn." He slid off the stool and gestured for Hicks to follow him. "So, tell me, you ever blow out the hydraulic lines on a force-feedback system?"

"No," Hicks said.

"Never too late to learn," Walker assured him. "And it's a lot more fun than it sounds."

Hicks followed him past several large wire bins filled with metal pipes. The odor of oily metal became stronger and acquired a surprising undertone of citrus.

"If you smell lemons, you're not going crazy," Walker told him.

"You guys use lemon oil?"

"We use whatever works. Sometimes it's coconut." Walker chuckled. "We tried baby oil but we kept running out of babies." He glanced over his shoulder at Hicks. "Heard that one, huh?"

Hicks nodded. "In boot camp."

"Well, I wasn't kidding about the lemon and coconut," Walker said, sounding slightly disappointed. "Ever since they put olfactory in the AIs, it's been hardware potpourri around here."

"Maybe it's so AIs can tell the difference between what smells and what stinks," Hicks said.

Walker surprised him by bursting into hearty laughter. "Damn, that's a good one," he said. "I gotta remember it." Then he looked curiously at his new charge. "You're off the mystery ship, right?"

The sudden shift gave Hicks mental whiplash. "The

Sulaco's a mystery ship?" he said, surprised. "What's the mystery?"

"That's what we'd all like to know," Walker said as they went down a short flight of stairs to the hydraulics area. He had to raise his voice now to make himself heard as the sound of pressurized liquid rushing through all the channels became louder. "Whole thing's triple-classified, but there's a rumor that two of the Marines in the deck crew never came out."

"Don't ask me, I was still in cold storage." Hicks looked around, hoping Walker would take the hint that he felt more like working than talking, but the man only stood there with his arms folded, staring at him. "Hey, I'm just a jarhead," Hicks added finally, "and nobody tells jarheads nothin'. Hell, if I got hit on the head and forgot my own name, they wouldn't tell me that, either."

Walker's smile was perfunctory. Hicks couldn't blame him. Civilians didn't realize that the brass treated jarheads like mushrooms: they kept them in the dark and fed them shit.

"So this force-feedback system you want blown out," Hicks said. "Do I need an air compressor, or do I just take a deep breath?"

Walker laughed again as he led Hicks to the far end of the platform. "I gotta remember *that* one, too."

16

For once, all of Jackson's monitors were giving her ultra-def without any pixilation or noise. Even the feeds from the work crews out on the hull were strong. She got to enjoy it for almost half a minute before a buzzer sent ripples through almost all the images, and made one roll like an antique cathode-ray tube. So much for taking time to smell the res-es, she thought.

The screen directly in front of her went black, and large orange block capital letters scrolled up from the bottom:

```
UPP RODINA
DIPLOMATIC ENCRYPT>>>
>>>DIPLCORPS WSHUMAN
```

Jackson turned to the monitor beside it, bobbing her head so the light-pen clipped to her cap would wake it up. A moment later her assistant Lulu appeared onscreen, looking sleepy and put-out. That would teach her to sneak off for a nap.

"Buzz Werner Shuman and tell him we've got another call from Rodina, coded standard diplomatic," Jackson said. "I guess his opposite number at the UPP decided it's time for another bullshit session. And make sure you tell him that, yes, it came directly to me here in Operations—*again*—and no, I don't know why."

Lulu yawned. "You ask me, I think they just like pissing him off."

Werner Shuman sat alone in the anti-bug bubble, gazing into the flatscreen-and-camera setup on the table in front of him. Irina Duchamps always kept him waiting. This time it was twenty minutes before she appeared on the monitor, with her camera angled so she was looking down on him, as usual. Her predecessors had all played the same silly semiotic game and Shuman wondered if any of them would ever realize it was too obvious to take seriously.

Today, Duchamps' black hair was cropped very close to her skull, a drastic change from the last time he'd seen her, when she'd had it braided in tight, complicated patterns. Perhaps Rodina's council were on another anti-vanity crusade, and officials had restricted personal grooming time to five minutes a day. In Shuman's opinion, the Progressive Peoples had far too many hang-ups.

He let her speak first before giving the customary formal greeting. Duchamps' response was a diatribe about their violating the UPP's sovereign borders, and with a military transport, no less. The UPP could have taken it as an act of war and, fearing for the lives of their citizens and for their very existence as a nation, responded with force.

Shuman bided his time while she lectured him about how lucky Anchorpoint was that the UPP had exercised caution and patience by waiting to see if the *Sulaco* would fire on them. When it hadn't, they had decided not to blast the ship into atoms, thus saving the lives of the three people aboard.

"Nor did we seize it as an object abandoned in space, and thus officially ownerless," Duchamps continued loftily. "Which we had every right to do. However—"

"*However*—" Shuman said the word in unison with her, but louder. It startled her enough that she hesitated, and he jumped in. "You detected the specific destination in the still-active navigational system, as well as the glitch that had caused it to *accidentally* breach your borders. This proved the *Sulaco* wasn't abandoned, nor was its presence an act of aggression. Its weapons system is for defense only, which I'm sure was obvious to you."

To his surprise, Duchamps didn't take the bait about inspecting the weapons system. Instead she smiled, cordially but without warmth.

"The UPP *does* understand your claim that there was no malign intent," she said. "So, in the spirit of goodwill, we are returning your lost property to you. And, I might add, in *much* better condition than it was when we found it."

Shuman stared at her. Had she actually just admitted outright that they'd confiscated the other half of the synthetic from the *Sulaco*?

"We *do* have the right to board any vessel that crosses the border into our nation-space even by accident," she added. "In accordance with the Benevolent Civilizations Treaty, we were obligated to check on the welfare of the passengers. If they were injured, or if their sleep capsules had malfunctioned, we couldn't just leave them to die. Which was how we discovered the robot. At first, we thought it was beyond repair. Fortunately, we have brilliant engineers who were able to fix it, restoring its motor functions and providing it with new legs."

Shuman almost laughed. "You realize, of course," he said, speaking quickly so she couldn't interrupt, "that under our laws, androids are afforded the status of citizens. They have rights."

"Under *your* system," Duchamps said, oozing disapproval. "The UPP affords them the status of what they *are*: machines. Robots. Tools." Pause. "Inanimate objects."

A wave of ennui passed through Shuman. He'd had this discussion with every single one of her predecessors, more than once.

"But under our *equally valid* legal system," he said, "you're holding one of our citizens captive, without cause. The *Sulaco* entered UPP space purely by accident. You, however, are doing this deliberately."

Two pink spots appeared on Duchamps' cheekbones.

"Perhaps you didn't hear me. We provided your 'citizen' with *new legs*. Would *you* make such extensive repairs to one of *our* machines? And this so-called *citizen*—" She all but spat the word. "—this *robot*, this *object* named Bishop was removed during a treaty violation by one of your armed military vessels."

"The *Sulaco* was homing in on Anchorpoint," Shuman said patiently. "You've already acknowledged this 'violation' was just a malfunction in the navigation system, not an intentional hostile act."

"We've acknowledged your *claim* to that effect," Duchamps said stiffly.

Shuman didn't hesitate. "While holding one of our citizens without cause."

"The incident is being investigated as a possible violation of the Strategic Arms Reduction Treaty," Duchamps added.

Shuman's jaw dropped. "I'm sorry, I don't think I heard you correctly," he said with a small, incredulous laugh. "The *Sulaco*'s weapons systems comply with all regulations—"

"Another wrong answer," Duchamps said with a small, dismissive gesture. "I refer to those sections of the treaty concerned with biological warfare."

And there it was. The times were about to get interesting, just like the old Earth curse.

He could retire, Shuman thought. He had enough years in for a full pension, but he was still young enough for another career if he wanted.

"That allegation has absolutely no basis—" he began.

"What allegation?" Duchamps was wide-eyed and slightly hurt. "*We* make no allegations at this time. I was simply discussing an ongoing investigation. In any case, the robot you call Bishop is of no further use to us in our inquiries, so we're returning *it* to you—fully repaired and functioning—to demonstrate our goodwill. With, as I said, new legs."

Shuman remained silent.

"You're welcome," she added finally, and broke the connection.

Bishop stood back while the Vietnamese commando opened the hatch, not moving until she gestured for him to go out ahead of her. She had been uncommunicative for the entire duration of the trip from Rodina Station. He had attempted to ask her about her tattoos, then given up after seeing how uncomfortable it made her.

He'd already known how the Union of Progressive Peoples regarded artificial persons, but simply knowing about something was very different from engaging with the reality, even for him. He had never been among people who didn't regard him as an intelligent entity. It gave the humans on Rodina Station a degree of strangeness that to him was practically alien.

At the same time, he could tell that not all of them were as certain about him as the UPP had told them they should be. The Vietnamese commando, for instance—he had sensed a great deal of curiosity from her as well as some apprehension, which was only normal for people who had little or no experience with APs. The strict orders she'd been given not to interact with him beyond the necessary minimum hadn't killed her curiosity, although it had increased her anxiety—and not just about him—turning a simple assignment into an ordeal.

From what he gleaned of life in the UPP during his short stay, their brand of "progressive intellect" was supposed to be realistic—they didn't play with dolls and pretend they were human. The UPP had designated artificial intelligence as something confined to a computer. It was machinery, strictly some*thing*, not some*one*. In their world view, only the deluded, the decadent, or the willfully blind would treat things like people.

Bishop had hoped the commando's curiosity would impel her to talk to him, so that even if she decided he was less than human, she might be able to understand him as more than an inanimate object.

After giving it more thought, however, Bishop realized that was actually a very bad idea. The UPP had no intermediate level between human and machine, between organic or inorganic. Seeing him as anything more than a robot would put her in direct conflict with her own government, which was not a safe place to be. She was better off obeying the order not to engage.

It was too bad. Even a single conversation would have

given Bishop a fair amount of useful information, although nowhere nearly as much as what they'd taken from him. He knew the Company would already be frantic about that. But stolen data was a minor issue compared to the threat posed by the Xenomorphs.

He had yet to find out what had happened when the *Sulaco* had arrived at Anchorpoint, what they had found when they'd opened the airlock. To his knowledge, the UPP hadn't even tried to warn the station about the *Sulaco*'s dangerous stowaways. If Hicks, Ripley, and Newt had been compromised, too, the space station might already be under siege.

But he'd heard nothing in Anchorpoint's communications with the commando that indicated anything was wrong, and now, as he stood with her at the top of the interceptor's debarkation ramp, he didn't see anything unusual. The half dozen Marines waiting on the arrival platform were in full armor and carrying weapons, but the military display would be for the commando's benefit, so she would go home and tell the UPP Anchorpoint was well-armed, well-protected, and well-prepared for visitors.

If there had been any Xenomorphs aboard the *Sulaco*, they weren't loose in the station. Not yet, anyway.

Bishop wasn't obligated to wait for the commando to dismiss him, but it seemed as if for courtesy's sake he should. At the moment, she was distracted by the decor. Rodina Station was plain and spare, and mostly shabby. By contrast, Anchorpoint's arrival bay was designed to be welcoming, with warm lighting, a display of flags from a multitude of nations, states, and colonies, along with banners from various sports teams and logos of the various corporations currently in residence. But there was still enough wall space for large, colorful murals of planetary systems and alien landscapes.

Color-coded lines on the padded flooring directed new arrivals to the customs and immigration kiosks. Even the power-loaders, corralled a safe distance from where passengers disembarked, were brightly colored and festooned with designs.

After goggling for several minutes, the commando shook her head slightly as if she were coming out of a daze. Then she gestured for him to go.

"Cảm ơn bạn," Bishop said. *Thank you*.

She didn't react. In her world, there was no such thing as a polite machine. He headed down the ramp to where the Marines waited with a formally dressed man wearing the purple sash of the Diplomatic Corps. That would be Werner Shuman, according to Bishop's database; he looked very disappointed, as if he'd expected someone more important than an interceptor pilot.

Bishop paused at the bottom to look back. The commando darted back into the shuttle. Maybe she'd only wanted to make sure he got all the way down the ramp without falling. His replacement legs weren't nearly as sophisticated as the originals. Sensation and range of motion were drastically reduced, which made it difficult to adjust to them. Even his proprioception was off.

The Rodina technicians who had worked on him had made sure he knew the UPP didn't waste top-of-the-line inventory on robots—not when there were disabled *people* in need of prosthetic limbs. However, Bishop's quick and very discreet scan of the robotics lab had told him that anyone in need of prosthetics would be no better off than he was.

"Artificial person Bishop, welcome to Anchorpoint," Shuman said in a stiff, formal tone. "You're under quarantine, effective immediately. These Marines will escort you to the Medical Laboratory. There you will be examined and, if necessary, decontaminated, after which we will complete your repatriation."

The soldiers kept their weapons holstered as they took him to an electric cart but the tension Bishop could feel among them told the truth: they *had* found more aboard the *Sulaco* than three people in cold-sleep, and it probably wasn't the now-dead egg in his sleep capsule. There was never just one of anything.

And it wasn't over yet.

1 7

Blowing out the hydraulic lines on a force-feedback system wasn't intellectually demanding work, but it had been exactly what Hicks needed. There was one set of unambiguous procedures to follow and one desired outcome. When he finished, there were no repercussions to argue, no pros and cons to debate. Doing the job correctly was good, screwing it up wasn't.

Everybody needed to do that kind of work sometimes. Even Gandhi and Einstein must have dug a hole once in a while, Hicks thought, just to smell the dirt. Maybe they'd even gone out for a drink afterward, although not in a mall.

According to Walker, this was the largest mall "upstairs" —above Anchorpoint's equator—although Hicks had seen bigger. Malls didn't vary much from place to place—one was pretty much like every other one. This was deliberate, the idea being that familiar surroundings would make people feel more at home, and less like exiles, in far-flung regions of space.

From Walker's description, Hicks had expected to find a lot more people on the main thoroughfare, but the place was practically deserted. There were some bored-looking window-shoppers and a few more people sitting on benches by this or that fountain, tossing tokens at centerpieces. Maybe there was some kind of exclusive, members-only VIP party somewhere that he hadn't been invited to?

Or maybe Spence and Walker hadn't been exaggerating when they'd told him the *Sulaco*'s arrival had sent everyone working round-the-clock. In which case, the Anchorpoint workforce needed more backup from their unions, not more places to shop.

Right now, however, he'd settle for a beer and a shot of decent whiskey. It wasn't long before he came to a sign that sounded promising:

Stosh's Bigger Jigger

The name was scrawled across the red-brick facade in fake neon tubes bent into graceful script. Below it were two windows with brightly lit signs. One advertised Schlitz, Budweiser, and Black Label; the other boasted Zubrowka, Boodles, and Blue Sapphire. Hicks couldn't remember if any of those brands still existed, or had ever existed at all. "Boodles" sounded a bit suspect. Maybe the signs were supposed to be ironic.

Every time he woke from cold-sleep, he'd hear irony

was making a comeback, and somehow he always went back into a sleep capsule before it did. So far, irony seemed to be running late.

He went in to find the place was mostly empty. Across the room, two pool tables, one with screaming neon-orange felt, the other with the traditional green, stood idle, ignored by the three or four patrons. Each sat alone, engrossed in something on the monitor built into the tabletop. The back wall was a floor-to-ceiling screen where a football game went unappreciated by everyone except the bartender watching it from the far end of the bar.

After a minute or so, Hicks realized it was a rerun of a first-round playoff game from five or six years back, Brazil vs. Haiti. He'd lost money on it but, oddly enough, he couldn't remember which team had won. It hadn't been much money, so what the hell.

Only one person was sitting at the bar and he'd obviously been there a while. Hicks took the stool on the guy's left and the bartender came over immediately. She was in the vague territory between mid-forties and early sixties, with short, curly, snow-white hair, dark brown eyes, and the dignified bearing of someone who didn't take any shit. Maybe she was the owner, although she certainly didn't look like a "Stosh." More like Ripley thirty years older.

"Stout or the closest thing to it, please," Hicks said, fishing the chain with his dog-tags out from under his shirt.

"Got Nightside on tap," she told him. "The real thing, not a fax."

"Works for me." He detached one of the dog-tags and handed it to her. She inserted it into the pay slot on the bar, then picked up a glass.

"Run a tab or PAYG?" she asked, pulling the Nightside with an expert movement that made her bicep bulge in her shirtsleeve.

"I'll pay as I go," Hicks said. "Keeps things neat."

The guy on the stool beside him roused and turned to look at him through heavy-lidded, bloodshot eyes. There was half a glass of red-gold ale on the bar in front of him, no doubt the latest over several hours, Hicks thought, unless he was an even cheaper drunk than Wierzbowski.

For a second, he saw Wierzbowski's face, drunkenly indignant at the insult and too trashed to complain.

"You're Hicks," the guy said, his voice thick and slow. "Off the *Sulaco*. Right?"

"Who's asking?" Hicks said, keeping his tone light as the bartender gave back his dog-tag.

"Tully, Charles A. Tech 5 of the ye old tissue lab. D-fuckin'-NA." He shook his head and gave a short laugh. "Goddam, the *Sulaco*. Lucky."

Hicks paused in the act of clipping his dog-tag back onto the chain. "Who's lucky? You?"

Tully laughed again. "*You*," he said. "You're lucky. You're one lucky son of a bitch, man."

"How do you figure *that*?" Hicks took a sip from his

glass. It had been a long time since his last Nightside, and the taste was a rush.

"Travel all that way from LV-whatever with those fucking *things*." His hangdog face turned mournful. "All those fucking things on board, and they didn't touch you."

"You know something about it?" Hicks asked sharply. *"Tell me."*

Tully, Charles A. gave him a drunken side-eye. *"Uh*-uh. Ain't talking. Had to sign NDAs, Non-Disclosure Agreements. Every single one of us signed. *Had to.* Or lose *all* our fucking shares. Tell *anybody*, the same thing—lose everything."

"They *were* on the ship with us." Hicks felt the hair on the back of his neck stand up. The synthetic who had done his debrief had said they'd just found a little biological matter on the cargo deck and they'd taken care of it. But of course, they *hadn't* taken care of it and now he couldn't imagine what had made him believe they would. He looked at the bartender, who was down at the far end again, watching larger-than-life-sized players scrambling around on a grass field, oblivious to the existence of Xenomorphs. *Must be nice*, he thought. *Everyone should be like that, all the time.*

"They sure were," Tully was saying. "I saw 'em. Now I can't *un*see 'em—but I'm trying. I'm trying. Maybe this'll do it." He finished the rest of his ale in one long swallow.

Hicks leaned closer to him, lowering his voice. *"When* did you see them? Where were they? How many?"

"Hey, I, uh—" Tully blinked at Hicks like he'd suddenly awakened while talking in his sleep. He looked over at the bartender, at the few other customers, then up at the ceiling. "This's a bad place to talk. And I gotta go—" He tried to slip off the stool but Hicks grabbed his arm.

"You're not going anywhere," he said in a low, dangerous voice. "Not until you—"

Wincing, Tully tried to twist out of his grip. "Hey, I didn't sign up for this shit. I came out here to build designer *ecosystems*, not designer *weapons*. You want Madagascar? I'm your man. I did that, you know. You can see it, it's on this level—I *think*. Where are we?" He looked around again.

"We're right here." Hicks tightened his grip, knowing that he was hurting the guy. He was doing a lot of that lately. "*Talk*."

"Okay, *okay*," Tully said. "But *not* here. You want an earful? Shift after next, DP-54, Level 7." He jerked his chin at Hicks's flexi. "It's on the map."

Hicks let go of him. Tully backed into a stool, begged its pardon, and fled out the door just as a group of people were coming in. They called after him by name, but he didn't stop.

"End-of-shift Happy Hour," the bartender said, moving to the center of the bar, waving cheerfully as more customers came in. "Just letting you know, it's gonna get pretty drunk and crowded in here."

Hicks thanked her for the warning and finished his Nightside. A couple of waiters came out of the back as he got up to leave. On his way out, he glanced at the back wall-screen. Half-time score, 4–1 Haiti.

It wasn't over yet. He wondered if it ever would be.

"And Bishop has agreed to undergo complete physical and chemical analysis?" Welles said, repeating what Adele Trent had just told her.

This must have been how the legendary Spartan boy felt with the stolen fox under his shirt, gnawing on his guts, he thought. Except the boy had gotten off easy, with a mere garden-variety fox. Rosetti had *Kevin* Fox, who was now demanding to know Bishop's test results.

"He's clean," Dr. Trent told him. "No irregularities have been detected, and no trace of any alien cellular material."

"Any signs he's been tampered with?" Welles asked. "Or reprogrammed? Did our UPP friends add anything new, besides the legs? It would be just like them."

Dr. Trent shook her head. "He's still being examined, but so far we've found nothing."

"*So far.*" Fox leaned forward. "What about the data on the Xenomorphs? Is it all there, intact and undamaged?"

Adele Trent hesitated, giving Rosetti a troubled glance. "It *seems* to be," she replied. "We can't tell if they copied his memory, but we should assume they did." She glanced at the colonel again. "It's what we'd have done. Tampering is very hard to detect, due to the nature of the neural net. Even Bishop himself wouldn't know."

"The UPP's tech isn't as up-to-date as ours," Welles said, "so we can only hope that in the process of copying, the UPP didn't damage anything, inadvertently or not." She looked pointedly at Rosetti, as if she believed this wouldn't have occurred to him.

"Just get on with your brief," Rosetti said, sick of listening to the weaponized Barbie and Ken goons lecture them on how to suck weaponized eggs. "You want Dr. Trent to clone the cultures. Which is why you didn't want Shuman here."

"This has *nothing* to do with diplomacy." Fox's voice was quietly grave.

"Doesn't it?" Rosetti replied. "You mean we *aren't* discussing a violation of the Strategic Arms Reduction Treaty?"

"Excuse me, Colonel?" Fox was the portrait of dignified innocence. "I didn't hear *anyone* mention military applications. Did *you*, Dr. Trent?"

The exobiologist hesitated again. "Well... *technically*, no. A case might be made for this as research into applied exobiology." She gave Rosetti an apologetic look. "In fact, we have a standing mandate to study *all* alien life-forms, wherever we encounter them, under any and all circumstances. Our preliminary analysis of the material from the *Sulaco* reveals the potential for remarkable adaptive and healing properties. The therapeutic possibilities for degenerative conditions, for cancer research—" She spread her hands. "As risky as it is, this *might* lead to our biggest medical breakthrough in a hundred years or more."

"Imagine it, Colonel." Beaming, Welles picked up the ball and ran with it. "If biological material can be programmed, not only to kill malignancies, but to prevent even the very *beginning* of abnormal cell growth—"

"So what are you proposing, Dr. Trent?" Rosetti said, looking only at her, his back to the other two. Dr. Trent started to answer, but Fox was too fast.

"That's obvious, Colonel," he said. "We nourish the cells in stasis tubes and keep them under constant observation, maintaining a human presence at all times. We terminate any developing embryos before they become viable, unless or until we receive authorization for additional procedures." He sat back, adding, "To further cancer research, of course."

"Of course," Rosetti said. "Cancer research. Our motives are purely humanitarian. Is that all for now? Or is there more?"

"Ambassador Shuman will be hearing from Earth shortly." Welles looked exasperated at having to spell this out for him. "As soon as he does, priority *will* be given to military development of the alien. Let's be honest, we know that because we know where our orders come from. The decision has already been made. Waiting for the go-ahead is simply a formality."

"The prospect that the UPP may be weaponizing the alien makes the matter that much more urgent," Fox added. "They're several years behind us scientifically, but they *do* have some bright minds over there. This could put them well ahead of where they were—to where they're breathing down our necks. We *can't* wait." Fox sounded less like a news mouthpiece today; Welles must have been coaching him.

"Any decision that concerns the military here is mine," Rosetti said, in a tone of finality. "Whether it has to do with personnel, a course of action, or weapons."

Welles frowned at him. "I don't think you understand, Rosetti—"

"*Colonel* Rosetti," he corrected her.

"They're not fooling around, *Colonel*," Fox said, impatient now. "They won't just *break* you. When they get through with you, it'll be like your *career* never happened—like *you* never happened. These are the *real* shot-callers, the ones who are *really* in charge. They can make you disappear, erase you like you never existed, and you know it."

Rosetti decided he had reached his daily limit of Company bullshit. "Shuman must be informed," he said coldly. "In case he has to answer any inquiries concerning our new direction in 'cancer research.'"

"Of course," Fox said. "Although it's best not to make *any* public announcement, or to be *too* optimistic, too *early*. Giving people false hope about cancer is *so* cruel."

1 8

Bishop lay on the scanner bed in the opaque body stocking customary for situations requiring artificial persons to undress. APs didn't have the nudity taboo, but most humans preferred them to behave as if they did.

Since his initial activation, Bishop had experienced all kinds of humans, and had developed workarounds for a good many of their idiosyncrasies. All of his assignments had been with the Marines, whose catalog of quirks was unique to the military. For the most part, Bishop found them straightforward in a way that many civilians mistook for simple.

Then again, a surprising number of humans misunderstood the whole concept of simple. They believed simple things could become complex, but complexity couldn't yield simple things. Bishop theorized it was because most humans lived in three dimensions, or four, if you counted time; he didn't.

The hum of the doughnut-shaped scanner became louder as it glided up past his hips and over his torso.

He couldn't see the life-sized output screen on the wall behind him, but he didn't have to—he was receiving the data directly via the strategically placed nano-sensors under his skin. The UPP techs had missed those, because he'd kept their intake functions fully encrypted.

If they *had* examined him more carefully after attaching the new legs, they'd have discovered the nanos multiplying and spreading into the dermis below his waist. Then they would have dissected him completely, eager to understand how the nanos worked. They'd have learned plenty, enough to advance their fields of robotics and nanotech by several years, but *not* enough to put him back together, which would leave him as the inanimate object they claimed he was.

The doughnut finished its latest pass upward and came back the other way now. It glided down his torso, moved over his thighs to the shins, where it stopped and moved back to his knees.

"Look at that," the junior tech said. The microphone was off, but Bishop could pick up the vibrations on the booth walls and translate them into words. "Just *look* at those knees."

"I know," the senior tech said, "but we're not set up to do that kind of extensive restoration." The microphone clicked on. "How about it, Bishop?" she asked. "Your knees feel okay?"

Bishop rolled his head to the right and looked at her through the radiation-proof window in the booth. "So far."

She thanked him and clicked off.

"But that's *polycarbon*," the junior tech said. "I can't believe they used *polycarbon* for his goddam *knees*. They won't hold up worth a damn."

"Not much we can do except shore him up until he can have those cheap-assed substitutes replaced at Gateway." The senior tech chuckled a little. "I doubt he'll be doing anything too strenuous around here."

The doughnut began to move again. Bishop resumed staring at the ceiling, then heard the microphone click on again.

"We want to make a few more passes," the senior tech told him. "Just to get as much detail as possible. That okay with you, Bishop?"

"I've cleared my calendar," he replied.

Both techs laughed, the junior one sounding slightly surprised that an artificial person could be funny. He must have been a new hire, Bishop thought, and remembered hearing Hudson say the best thing about newbies was that they hadn't already heard his one-liners.

Rodina Station's biolab also had a scanner, an older model that was larger, worked more slowly, and made more noise. At the moment, it stood unused while Lara Braun and the two assistants she had chosen as much for their discretion as for their ability huddled around a stasis tube placed in a cradle on a workbench.

The stasis tube was also older, not as compact as the latest model so it used a lot more nutrient. But Braun had always preferred the larger size simply because it was easier to see the contents.

A day earlier, the grayish-pink organism in the tube had borne some resemblance to a human embryo, but it had doubled in size overnight. Now it was slightly larger than Braun's thumb. She hadn't expected it to develop so quickly and her apprehension was growing along with it.

In another couple of days, she would know whether she had coaxed the alien material into viability, or just pumped up a clutch of cells that would dead-end in a blob of goo.

Braun was privately hoping for the latter.

According to Hicks's flexi map, DP-54, Level 7 was a construction area, which meant it would not only be abandoned in the off-hours but unmonitored as well, making it the perfect place for a secret meeting. Hicks just hoped it wasn't full of people having affairs.

Feeling the need for exercise, Hicks decided to jog to his meeting with Tully, Charles A. Of all various-sized passageways in the station, the ones nearest construction areas made the best running tracks. They were brightly lit, cooler than average, and had some give to the paving. He didn't see many other people—apparently this wasn't jogging rush hour—and there was no reason for anybody to wonder about him. All the people on a space station were accounted for and identified; they might not know each other personally but they weren't total strangers.

Except for Company spooks, Hicks thought. They didn't come any stranger than that.

The last person he saw before he got to the construction site was another Marine, a young woman almost as tall as he was, well-muscled, hair thickening in after a baldy cut. There were stripes on her bicep, one of them new and still red. Above it on the curve of her shoulder was a screaming neon-blue devil brandishing a gold pitchfork. Hicks gave her a friendly wave, and she surprised him with a soft punch on the arm, as if they had served together.

Maybe she'd been among the deck crew sent into the *Sulaco*.

He almost turned around to run after her and ask what had happened. Maybe she'd tell him, but probably not. Her focused expression reminded him of Ferro, who obligingly popped into his head.

Hey, Hicks, sometimes a sock on the arm is just a sock on the arm. Maybe she was making sure you didn't hit her new stripe.

Ahead of him, he could see where the tunnel forked. According to the map, both routes would let out in the same place, about fifty meters apart. He just hoped the status update was current, and neither had been sealed off for bad air. Or no air.

* * *

There was air, but the map was wrong. The tunnel outlets were twenty meters apart, and only one of them was open; luckily, it was the one he'd taken. The other had a length of flimsy chicken wire glued across the opening at a haphazard slant. *Somebody's last day on the job*, Hicks thought.

The construction site itself was gigantic, far wider than the map made it out to be. Two football stadiums could have fit side by side, with just enough room for hotdog vendors to walk the perimeter. He couldn't estimate the length; the unpartitioned space ahead disappeared into shadows. The map was no help, saying only *Exact Dimensions TBD*.

Hicks looked around, letting his eyes adjust to the darkness. The deeper shadows around him resolved into sections of metal plating for bulkheads, some of it in neat stacks, some seemingly scattered around at random. He moved a few more meters into the site, feeling slightly annoyed. How the hell was he supposed to find Tully, Charles A. he thought—yell, *Tully, Tully oxen free?* Would the guy even know what that meant?

"Hicks."

He turned around. A shadow next to a stack of metal plating was moving toward him. Not Tully, but the woman who had taken him and Newt to see Ripley. What was her name?

"What are you doing here?" he asked her. "I'm supposed to meet a lab tech. Know where he is?"

"We work in the same lab," she said. "He, uh…couldn't make it."

Spence, that was it. "Hung over, is he?" he said.

"Scared," she told him, her tone serious. "Loose lips lose shares."

"And that doesn't scare *you*?"

"I didn't sign anything," she said. "Not yet, anyway. The only people who know what happened were there, on the *Sulaco*. *They* signed."

"Okay," he said, after a moment. "So, for the second time, why are *you* here?"

"Tully and I are close." Spence lifted her chin defensively, reminding him of Newt. "Nobody knows him better than I do. He's not Mr. Testosterone, but he doesn't scare easy. He told me what happened, what was on that ship. What he saw." She paused, then added, "*You* know what it is, too. Don't you."

Hicks took a breath, let it out. "I don't think *anyone* knows what it is."

Spence's expression said she knew an evasive answer when she heard it. "Fine, have it your way. Whatever it is, they've got the lab growing it in stasis tubes. We've been running recombinant DNA processes on some of the samples, using human genetic material—"

"You're doing *what*?"

"You heard me," Spence said. "They claim it's cancer research, 'all for the benefit of humanity.' Tully says that's pure bullshit and he's right. It would be like killing cancer cells with a shotgun. There are a couple of spooks from MiliSci here—"

"Fox and Welles," Hicks said, more to himself.

Spence nodded. "From Weapons Division, no less, which isn't supposed to exist these days—not officially, anyway. Not in these enlightened times of the Strategic Arms Reduction Treaty." She gave a short, humorless laugh.

"So why are you telling *me* all this?" Hicks asked.

"To be brutally honest, I'm not sure." She shrugged, looking a bit embarrassed. "Maybe just because someone else ought to know the weird shit that's happening. There's a rumor about someone coming in on a UPP shuttle, too, someone who was supposedly with you on the *Sulaco*—"

"Bishop," Hicks said. "The synthetic they sent with us to LV-426." He paused, frowning. "You think the UPP are growing their own, ah, 'cancer research'?"

"Shit. We all better hope not," Spence said unhappily. "Their tech's at least five years behind ours. They'd *never* be able to control it."

"And the Company spooks think *we* can?"

Spence gave another single, mirthless laugh. "Nobody asked *me*."

1 9

Everything in the lab was out of whack today and Tully's hangover wasn't helping.

Spence had tidied up his work area again even though he'd told her over and over and *over* not to, because now he couldn't find anything, and what equipment he could find was glitchy, if it worked at all. The workbench monitor was totally dead, forcing him to use a spare tablet. Several times he'd nearly knocked it onto the floor before he finally wedged it between a partly disassembled centrifuge and a box full of stray parts on a shelf above the worksurface, where it was safe but at an awkward angle.

It was his own fault. Everybody knew that when you woke up face-down on the floor, you should stay there. He was about to call time on the whole day when the tablet lit up with Jackson's face.

"*What now?*" he snapped.

"And good morning to you, too, sunshine," Jackson said. "What's *your* problem?"

Had she really just asked him that? "Get some goddam maintenance people down here right goddam now, will ya?" Tully said testily. "I need them to run a diagnostic on the stasis system. The pressure differential's off and the reads keep fluctuating. I'm goin' outta my mind here. Punch it to Priority One request—Trent'll okay it. Right now, I'm her Fair-haired Progeny. Or I'd better be," he added darkly.

"Your wish, my command." Jackson's head bobbed as she used the light-pen clipped to her hat on her screen. "I live to serve, alla that. Hey, you want in on the Super Bowl?"

"Is *that* why you couldn't call me back till now—because you're making interstellar book?" Tully said. "Pass."

"Sure about that?" Jackson wiggled her eyebrows, making the light-pen bounce. "You don't want Denver?"

"God, no." He rolled his eyes. "Gimme a tenth on Chicago."

"Chicago?" Her expression said he had to be crazy. "Okay, but it's your funeral."

"And my maintenance," he growled. "Right goddam *now.*"

A day went by. Maintenance visited and things progressed.

Another day passed.

* * *

"There's an irony in this," Suslov said, gazing at the alien embryo.

It floated in its own private world of nutrient contained in a stasis tube about half a meter long and thirty centimeters in diameter, an older model that took up most of the worksurface. While there was no discernible movement, Suslov was sure he could actually see it growing before his eyes.

"Irony, Colonel-Doctor?" Lara Braun was completely focused on the computer where she was entering data and adding notations. She was the only other person in the tissue lab and they'd each been so engrossed in their respective concerns, they might as well have been alone. The tone in Braun's voice indicated she would have preferred it that way.

"The readiness with which this organism lends itself to genetic manipulation," Suslov said. "The way its cells multiply so quickly."

"I'd call that remarkable, not ironic," she said absently. As busy as she was, Suslov had expected more enthusiasm from her, given that this was a landmark moment. Perhaps this was her way of displaying a professional attitude.

"It's as if the gene structure had been deliberately designed for ease of manipulation," he went on. "As well as what seems to be a universal compatibility with other plasms."

Braun finally turned to look at him. "And this is ironic to you, Colonel-Doctor? How?"

"Ironic that we're attempting to weaponize tissue that combines so easily with other organic material."

"I'm afraid I still don't know what you mean."

"I think this alien is the fruit of an experiment begun a very long time ago—perhaps so long ago as to be ancient by our reckoning," Suslov replied. "A living artifact, genetically engineered to be, first and foremost, a weapon that ends war by ending the *enemy*. To vanquish a foe— any foe, *all* foes—permanently. This species could be the product of an arms race that escalated while we were still learning to paint on cave walls."

Braun's expression was dubious. "Since we don't know where this organism came from, we can't know what kind of forces shaped its development," she said, her tone stiff and formal. "What we *do* know is that this project will strengthen the position of the UPP among other sovereign nations. I truly believe this. Otherwise, I wouldn't commit my time and effort to it, not even if I were ordered to."

Translation: she wanted to get back to work with no further interruptions for philosophy or speculation about weapons developed by some ancient alien intelligence. Suslov nodded and she turned back to the computer— Braun did love her data—while he went back to studying the creature in the stasis tube, which to his eye resembled an eyeless fetal dolphin.

Perhaps cloning these things would help them understand the creatures' methods of reproduction. What kind of natural biology could produce a creature that laid eggs containing an organism with a lifespan of hours and existed only to forcibly deposit a larva in a living host, which would provide sustenance until its explosive, fatal emergence?

Once it was out, it somehow grew from the size of a large rodent to a monster that towered over humans and had no other purpose or drive except to kill, for as long as it lived—however long that was. Nowhere in any of the data gleaned from the robot or the *Sulaco* was there any indication of the species' natural lifespan, or even a vague estimate. Perhaps these creatures *didn't* die, unless they were killed.

The robot's data was surprisingly rich in detail, more so than Suslov had expected from a machine.

They are organic and alive, but that's all. They have no culture, no history, no attachments, no sense of self-preservation, no fear of injury or death. In fact, they seem to lack any concept of life and death, which would suggest that they also lack consciousness. Yet they have the capacity for planning. They can be cunning—they hunt, they set traps, and they have displayed what looks like rage, often as a reaction to injury, so we can infer that they feel pain.

Which made Suslov more certain than ever that the species had been constructed. Its contradictory biology made no sense in the context of natural evolution, and its terrifying, nightmarish characteristics made it a superb weapon. Even the most aggressive, empire-building civilization based on coercion and conquest might have a collective existential crisis after meeting a few face-huggers.

This wasn't a weapon for warfare. It was an instrument of extermination.

"That's quite a piece of machinery, Corporal Hicks."

Hicks looked up from the circuit board he was reconfiguring to see Bishop standing in the doorway of the workroom.

"We used to say the same thing about you," he replied, grinning. "Heard you got snatched up by the UPP. What's it like in the socialist paradise of Progressive Peoples?"

Bishop tilted his head noncommittally. "The best thing I can say about them is, they sent me home. But only because they had no further use for me." He moved around the room, having a look at the open boxes, crates of spare parts, and the shelves full of hardware in need of fixing. Hicks was about to explain this was all busy work to keep him out of everyone else's way when Bishop added, "It appears Weyland-Yutani's Weapons Division intends to develop the alien. To fulfil its weapon potential, so to speak."

Reflexively, Hicks looked at the camera in the corner nearest the doorway but not at the one he wasn't supposed to know about, in the opposite corner.

"And where'd the bastards get that material?" he asked in a low voice.

"I assume you know about the alien that stowed away on the dropship and got aboard the *Sulaco*," Bishop said, speaking just as softly. "It was much bigger than all the others. Ripley called it the queen. She killed it."

"Yeah." Hicks's smile was grim.

"Somehow the queen deposited genetic material on the ship," Bishop went on, "and Weapons Division plan to make the most of it."

"Then they're stone crazy," Hicks said. "They just want to stay ahead of the UPP, who'll be trying to do the same thing. So much for the arms reduction treaty."

"Treaties can't stop an arms race when there's a new kind of weapon in play," Bishop said. "I'm programmed to protect human life. It's what I was made to do." Pause. "Everything I am, everything I know, everything I've seen and learned tells me whatever experiments they're doing with the alien *must* be aborted."

"I hear *that*," Hicks said.

"But there's a problem." Bishop hesitated, looking at him with a strange expression, especially for a synthetic. "I can't be entirely sure you can trust me."

"You can't—" Hicks shook his head slightly. "Say again?"

"We have no way of knowing if the UPP tampered with me," Bishop said in the calm, matter-of-fact voice that could by maddening or reassuring by turns. "I've undergone thorough examination, of course, and the most troublesome thing anyone has found is the quality of my knees. But my neural net is all fuzzy logic, so there's no way to be sure."

Unless we take off and nuke it from orbit, Hicks thought. Something else occurred to him. "Wouldn't *you* know?" he asked Bishop. "I mean, wouldn't you feel different?"

Bishop shook his head. "I wish it were that easy but it isn't. If they buried an encrypted routine deeply enough, I won't know it's there till it activates."

"And they let you out of the lab anyway?"

Now Bishop almost looked sheepish. "Since they couldn't find anything, they couldn't justify my taking up space. They think they'll learn more if they let me wander around, see if there's a trigger."

Hicks shrugged. "Either way, we have to kill this thing, this alien. Right?"

"I *have* to try," Bishop said, "whether you're with me or not."

"You know I am," Hicks said, "and I think I know where we can find us a little help. Maybe even a lot."

2 0

"I *said—do* you—*want* some—*coffee?"* Spence asked, almost shouting.

Tully finally looked up from the six stasis tubes in the cradle on the workbench. "Sorry?" he said blankly.

Spence was amused but no less exasperated. Tully's depth of concentration made him great at research, but sometimes hard to work with. "Last time: do you want some coffee? I'm going to the lounge with the better machine."

"Uh…" Tully hesitated for so long that Spence was afraid he'd forgotten the question. "No," he said finally, turning back to the tubes. "Thanks."

Spence decided to bring him a cup anyway—he'd probably change his mind when he smelled hers. Instead of leaving, though, she lingered beside him, the way she did on those mornings when he was likely to go back to sleep between one sock and the next.

"Hey, did Maintenance ever cure your pressure differential problem?"

Tully shook his head slowly. "They said it was just a transitory glitch."

"Meaning they didn't feel like working for a living, huh?" She chuckled sympathetically. Getting Maintenance to make a call could be harder than getting an audience with the Pope—the old pre-Schism Pope.

"It straightened itself out," he said distantly, "so I guess they were right." He was back down the rabbit hole with tube #6 and Spence left him to it.

Tully, Charles A. sat with his elbows on the lab table and his chin cupped in his hands, gazing at the alien tissue growing in the nutrient mix. Each stasis tube was twenty centimeters long, with a diameter of six centimeters— big enough that he could see the contents easily, small enough not to take up too much room on the workbench.

Of the six, half of the growths were embryos, while the other three were egg-shaped. The eggs would grow up to hatch something he was calling a remote ovipositor, which implanted an alien larva in the nearest available lifeform. For the unlucky recipient, gestation was brief, and birth was fatal.

But there was still no answer to the perennial question: which came first, the alien or the egg?

Sighing, he took a light-pen from his pocket and backlit the egg in tube #6. Sure enough, there was a shadow in the tiny translucent area at the larger end.

"Hey, little guy," Tully said softly. "How ya doin' in there? Nutrient solution agreeing with you? Guess so. We're looking *lots* bigger today, aren't we? You bet. Terrific. Just abso-fucking-lutely *wonderful*. By the end of the week, we'll have to move you to a bigger condo. The week after that, you'll be beating up cancer cells for their lunch money. Then you'll get out the shotgun—"

The lab doors whispered open. Was Spence back already? He hoped she'd ignored him and brought him a coffee anyway.

"Communing with nature, Tully, Charles A.?"

His heart sank. It was the lady spook from Weyland-Yutani. Someone had said Rosetti called her Weaponized Barbie. Tully couldn't imagine why she was there; she didn't have any coffee.

"Where's Dr. Trent?" she said breezily and looked around.

"At lunch." It was Tully's standard answer. He had a fifty-fifty chance of being right and it usually made the person who'd asked go away. Instead of leaving, however, the spook swanned over to the workbench and stood too close to him.

Tully drew back, momentarily at a loss before inspiration struck. "You're not wearing a badge." He tapped the ID clipped to his lab coat. "The white strip registers contamination, turns red if you've been exposed to a pathogen. Come back later, after you get yours."

Unperturbed, she peered into tube #6. "So how's our little friend?"

"*Friends*," Tully corrected her. He stood up and moved a few steps away, repositioning the cradle of stasis tubes with one hand and dragging the stool with the other. "Our little *friends*, plural. They're growing."

The woman grabbed the stool from him, sat down, and pulled the cradle closer to herself. Tully had a sudden premonition that this wasn't going to end well.

"Get me hardcopy data for the past six hours," she said, the fake warmth gone from her tone.

"Sorry, no." Tully moved to the computer console on the desk behind her. "You'll have to ask Dr. Trent. Did I mention she's at lunch?"

The woman swiveled around to look at him. "I don't think you understand the situation, Technician Tully, Charles A., so let me break it down for you." She got off the stool to stand too close to him again. "You're going to—"

Tully heard a hiss from the workbench. Weaponized Barbie missed it because she was running her mouth but she heard the loud *crack* that followed.

"Oh, Jesus," he said, looking at the fine spray of nutrient coming out of the hairline fissure in tube #6. Tube #2 was trembling. He took a step toward the workbench just as both tubes exploded.

Nutrient and stasis tube fragments blew into Tully's face and he fell backward, landing on something hard and lumpy. The alarm went off, a harsh rhythmic buzz that kept time with flashing red lights in the ceiling.

Wiping nutrient out of his eyes with his sleeves, he realized he'd landed right on top of Weaponized Barbie and she wasn't happy about it. He rolled off her, struggled to his knees, and reached out blindly for something he could use to pull himself upright. His fingers closed on a desk drawer handle and he managed to get all the way into a crouch just as the woman leaned her full weight on his back. His feet skidded out from under him and they both went down in a pool of nutrient, this time with her on top of him.

Tully shoved her away and tried grabbing the edge of the desktop to pull himself up, but his wet hands were too slippery and he went down again on his front. He felt the woman clutching at his legs and kicked out at her hands. Breathless and bruised, he raised his head and found the egg from tube #6 sitting only centimeters from the end of his nose.

It was definitely bigger than it had been before Spook Barbie had barged in uninvited. Which made this fuck-up *her* fault.

"Okay," he whispered, or thought he did. He couldn't hear anything but that damned buzzer. Carefully, he reached up and felt around on the desktop, hoping he really *had* seen a pair of tongs in a tray that Spence hadn't put away yet.

He could have cried with relief if that awful woman

hadn't been there. Holding the tray close to his chest, he got to his knees. Behind him, he heard Weaponized Barbie trying to stand up. She'd fall on her ass again, of course, and Tully hoped with all his heart she'd fall the other way.

She didn't, but by some miracle, Tully avoided falling on the egg. He heaved her off again and moved closer to the egg, tongs ready.

A ripple went through its surface and four tiny flaps at the smaller end folded back. He froze, unable to imagine what could possibly hatch from it, but all he saw was a dark sparkle, a little cloud that was gone as quickly as it had appeared. With a desperate now-or-never feeling, Tully used the tongs and managed to grab it up without crushing it.

A speaker in the ceiling directly over his head crackled suddenly and, despite the deafening buzzer, he heard Spence's voice.

"Tully! Goddammit, Tully, what the fuck *happened in there? Are you okay?"*

"Decontam!" he shouted, hoping she could hear him. He glanced at his badge; the white strip was now the deep red of arterial blood. "We need decontamination! Get them down here *now!"* Weaponized Barbie's hand landed heavily on his shoulder as she fell down again.

"You might as well stay down," he told her. "Decontam's sending a team." She glared at him as if she thought he was lying, and he didn't say anything else. He knew what was coming next and she was really going to hate it.

Of course, if she'd listened to him about the badge, this could all have been avoided. Her jerking the cradle around on the workbench had probably fucked everything up. You had to handle things carefully in the lab, a lesson she was about to learn the hard way. Which, now that Tully thought of it, was probably the only way she'd ever learned anything.

Standing under the hard sprays of near-scalding water from multiple nozzles and the even harder scrubbing by three orderlies in protective suits, Tully caught an occasional glimpse through billows of steam of the spook undergoing the same treatment in the stall opposite. He wasn't trying to, but in decontam, modesty got scrubbed off along with the outer layers of your skin.

It wasn't pleasant or easy, but at least he had known what to expect. Welles hadn't, and like all first-timers, she couldn't help resisting, pulling away simply by reflex, which meant the orderlies had to manhandle her to get the job done. For a moment he actually felt sorry for her.

Then they hit him with the disinfectant again and he forgot all about her. The damned stuff was so strong it stung even if you hadn't been scoured with wire brushes. It was like getting sandpapered with red hot chili peppers.

Later, as they sat in the recovery chamber in balm-lined pajamas, Tully almost told her what Spence had said after an accident had sent the whole staff to decontam en masse: *Look at it this way—we won't have to exfoliate for years.*

He turned to her and saw she was glowering at him like it really was all his fault.

Nah.

2 1

"Every space station has emergency system access points that aren't on any published blueprints," Bishop told Hicks. "Only a few people in Ops know about them."

"Makes sense." Hicks followed him through a long, narrow passageway that Bishop had referred to as one of the corridors less traveled. Since they generally had little traffic, surveillance activated only when sensors registered unusual activity, unauthorized weaponry, or anyone tagged with an arrest warrant. Unquote.

"The Company only spends when it absolutely has to," Bishop continued, "and this being a civilian station, even Colonel Rosetti might not know where the surveillance is spotty."

"Or he's just not saying," Hicks replied. In his experience, most high-ranking Marine officers didn't tell as much as they knew.

At the end of the corridor, Bishop turned left into a shorter passageway cluttered with stepladders, toolboxes, and a few crates of light fixtures. It came out directly opposite the entrance to the tissue lab where the contamination incident had occurred.

Bishop put a surveillance feed on Hicks's flexi and told him to keep watch. "Let me know if you observe anyone coming our way. If they see you—when they see you—tap this—" He pointed at a white circle at the left edge of the screen. "—and start laughing."

"*Laughing?*" Hicks asked, bewildered.

For answer, Bishop touched the circle and the surveillance feed was replaced by an animated cartoon of a weird little duck having a temper tantrum.

"It's a classic. You can't beat the classics," Bishop said with a hint of a smile. "Or so they tell me."

"Very clever," Hicks said, chuckling. "What do I say if they ask me why I'm hanging around here, watching a cartoon duck with no paint?"

"Tell them you're working Maintenance, and you're waiting for someone to bring you the right parts," Bishop said.

Hicks frowned. "You think they'll buy that?"

"They will if you're holding this." Bishop handed him a power-screwdriver then tapped the flexi again to bring up the surveillance feed.

"And if someone comes along from your side?" Hicks wanted to know.

"I'll tell them I'm assisting Maintenance—namely, you—by checking on the connections in a lesser-used area," Bishop said.

Hicks couldn't resist. "What if it's someone *from* Maintenance?"

Bishop was unperturbed. "Then I'm updating my structural engineering database. Or I brought you the wrong part because you weren't clear about what you needed, and now I'm making you wait while I double-check everything. Now go stand watch and don't forget to laugh."

Four and a half meters from Hicks's position at the end of the corridor, Bishop scanned the wall with a flexi borrowed from Operations. The flexi was a good piece of tech—better than what they usually had available. It gave him a true-res image of the interior hardware.

When he found the access point, he swiped upward on the flexi for the keypad and tapped in the code he'd found buried in the Maintenance database, then ran a fingertip down the center of the screen, splitting the display and adding the surveillance feed for Operations HQ.

Chief Jackson appeared at a U-shaped console where a multitude of flatscreens displayed either readouts scrolling slowly upward or surveillance feeds from various places around the space station. Every so often she bobbed her head to use the laser-pen clipped to her baseball cap.

Bishop wondered why the motion didn't make her dizzy. Human engineers were a quirky breed, and the best ones were the quirkiest; it had something to do with their compulsion to customize interfaces.

He had to tap into four of Jackson's screens before he found the feed from the tissue lab, which included sub-feeds from four different cameras and shifted every five seconds. Fortunately, they were all running on a single template so he didn't have to coordinate each one separately, but it took several tries to roll back the time-stamp on the tissue lab. It wouldn't hold past 190 seconds but that would be long enough for them to do what they had to do, although probably not long enough to get away with it.

He and Hicks would be facing serious consequences for what they were about to do. But what they'd face if they did nothing was so much worse.

"We have three minutes to do this," Bishop said. "I managed to push it an extra ten seconds on the off-chance it's all we'd need to get away with it."

Hicks nodded as Bishop entered an override code into the flexi strapped to his forearm. The lab doors slid open and the smell of industrial-strength disinfectant hit him in the face, making him wince.

"Word is, only a couple of tubes burst." Hicks looked around nervously, following Bishop to the workbench. "What do you think they did with the other four?"

"Locked them down." Bishop pointed at a safe under

the workbench. It was the kind of small, dense thing that looked as if it could withstand a supernova. "And yes," he added as he tapped more numbers into his flexi, "I can open it."

Hicks stood aside and watched Bishop remove the cradle with four remaining tubes and set it on the workbench. Then he opened a panel on the surface and pulled out a bundle of color-coded cables. Feeling very out of place, Hicks took a close look at the four remaining stasis tubes, hoping he wouldn't see what he was sure would be there. Tubes #1 and #3 contained miniature face-hugger eggs, and #4 and #5 held embryos.

If there was even the tiniest shred of justice in the universe, Hicks thought, there would be a very special punishment for the Company spooks who'd forced this "experiment" on the lab techs.

"You ever figure these things out?" he asked Bishop. "I mean, their biology? Because I don't get them at all."

Bishop didn't answer. He had separated a yellow cable from the bundle and plugged it into the cradle, then looked from the flexi on his wrist to the stasis tubes.

"Is that it?" Hicks asked him. "Will that kill them?"

Bishop nodded without looking away from the tubes.

"Then do it! *Now.*"

The synthetic raised his arm slowly, as if he was underwater or in a hypnotic trance.

"I said, *do it!*" Hicks yelled. "That's an order!"

"I can't," Bishop said. "You'll have to destroy them."

Hicks gaped at him. "Why? Because the UPP tampered with you?"

"No." Bishop's usual calm expression turned apologetic. "My sensors have detected the presence of human material in the organisms. It's not much, just enough that I'm unable to harm them directly."

Hicks shoved Bishop aside and had a look at the setup. In the panel compartment, he spotted a large, serious-looking red button beside the bundle of cables, and just above it a metal plate with the words:

STASIS SYSTEM MICROWAVE STERILIZATION

Below it were smaller letters:

EMERGENCY ONLY

Hicks slammed his fist down on the button. As the nutrient inside the tubes began to boil, he stepped back from the workbench, dragging Bishop with him. Seconds later, the material in each tube blew apart, leaving ragged fragments that disintegrated in the still-bubbling liquid.

Alien goose overcooked—mission accomplished, Hicks thought, although he wasn't completely relieved. Just plugging in a cable couldn't possibly be enough to kill these things. He was wondering how much time they had left when the alarm went off.

"Guess we're done." Hicks turned to Bishop, who

absurdly still had one arm raised. "You might as well put your other arm up," he said as the lab doors slid open and three Marines burst into the room, weapons raised.

"Don't you fucking *move*, Jack!" yelled the one on point.

Hicks had a sudden image of how they looked, standing at the workbench with four stasis tubes of boiling liquid like the Marines had come in while they were making tea, and Bishop holding his hand up, like he wanted permission to explain what the fuck was going on.

This was funnier than the cartoon duck. Hicks burst out laughing.

The Marines marched them double-time to the brig, in white medical restraints rather than the standard felony straps. Hicks was sure that had been the spooks' idea. Normal procedure would have been to transfer him and Bishop to the custody of the Colonial Marines' criminal investigation unit for court-martial, where a guilty verdict would send him to a military prison, probably for life.

But as a mentally-ill prisoner, he could be held indefinitely and forced to undergo any kind of "treatment" deemed necessary—drugs, neurological conditioning, surgery—and administered by the Company.

The Company might persuade the Marines' central command that sabotaging "cancer research" deliberately and with malice aforethought robbed innocent people of the chance to benefit from new and better treatments and, in effect, caused their deaths. This was nothing less than mass murder on a planetary scale—on multiple planets—a crime so heinous, he had forfeited the right to due process. They could skip the court-martial and send him directly to a Company facility, where he'd be too drugged-up to talk about "weaponizing alien lifeforms."

They took him and Bishop to separate cells so they couldn't conspire to escape, and although they removed the restraints, they left the white wrist-cuffs in place so everyone would assume he and Bishop were criminally insane. All Hicks could think as he watched the Marines march away was how damned *young* they were, how untried, unseasoned, unscarred.

They had no clue.

2 2

It was goddam crowded in the bubble today; Rosetti knew that couldn't mean anything good, especially with Weaponized Barbie and Ken on hand. Of the people there, some were part of Anchorpoint's civilian governing body—department heads, residential area admins, intra-station commerce and entertainment execs (God only knew why)—others were representatives from the Department of Safety and Wellbeing (what they called "law enforcement" on Earth).

Plus one very pissed-off Chief of Operations, who currently had the floor.

"They knew where to find that emergency access point." The light-pen clipped to Jackson's cap made fleeting streaks in the air as she spoke. "*No one's* supposed to know where those access points are. We don't even put them on deep-detail schematics, to prevent anyone using them to hack the surveillance system. Which is *exactly* what they did. They ran a loop from earlier in the day—" Jackson cut off, making an exasperated noise as she looked around. "Oh, sorry, I *forgot*. Talking about anything that *actually matters* makes everybody's eyes glaze over."

"Did you ever consider that keeping these access points secret would make them attractive to hackers and thus *more* vulnerable?" one of the administrators asked. "There are software safeguards—"

"Yeah? Who's gonna pay for them—you?" Jackson glared at him from beneath the bill of her baseball cap, shining the light-pen directly into his eyes. "The Company's full of cheap bastards who won't even give us full-strength lighting." The beam swept across the room and landed on Welles, then Fox. "Am I right?"

To Rosetti's relief, neither of them said anything.

"After hacking the security feed, getting the lock-up code for the tissue lab was—" Jackson snapped her fingers. "Somebody probably wrote it on a candy wrapper and taped it to the door. Or scrawled it on a bathroom wall."

Fox leaned forward. "They also knew where to find the inventory and how to poach our eggs. Who do you suppose gave them *that* information—maybe one of yours, Chief?"

Jackson didn't miss a beat. "You're a true-blue Grade A Company prick, aintcha?"

Welles stood up and turned to Rosetti, wearing the kind of expression he could imagine on a hanging judge with indigestion. "Let me make something clear for you—

all of you," she said, looking down on the room from the Company's Mt. Olympus or wherever she thought she was. "The Anchorpoint phase of this project is now terminated, Rosetti, you—"

"*Colonel* Rosetti," he corrected her.

She raised her voice. "—*you* will keep Hicks and the rogue synthetic in solitary until they can return with us to Gateway, where they will both stand trial for treason."

To Rosetti's surprise, it was Adele Trent who spoke up, matching Welles's volume. "What do you mean, 'the Anchorpoint phase?' You know as well as I do that there's no more alien tissue to work with."

"No, *you* have no more alien tissue," Fox informed her, practically gleeful. He gestured for Welles to sit down, but she remained standing. "And it wouldn't matter if you did. You and your technicians are *woefully* inadequate for this job. Luckily, we foresaw this and took the precaution of obtaining our *own* samples, which are currently in transit to Gateway."

Welles turned to Adele Trent and Rosetti saw her tan had faded visibly. Some trick of the light? "Everything *you've* done—you and your sadly deficient team of clowns— will be subject to review," Weaponized Barbie told her, and Rosetti realized it wasn't the light. The woman's skin really was grayish; something was very wrong with her, and it was more than indigestion.

He pressed the emergency button under the table, neutralizing the bubble's privacy field and summoning medical help. Welles paused, suddenly breathless. Rosetti inched his chair back. "Gone over with a fine-toothed co-co-co-co-c-c-c-c-c-c-c—"

The woman started to fall forward, then caught herself on her hands, still going, "—c-c-c-c-c-c-c-c-c-c." Her head drooped and thick strings of blood-tinged saliva dripped onto the polished tabletop. Now everyone was pushing back in their chairs as the *c-c-c-c-c-c-c* sound became an insect-like chittering.

Was she having a seizure? Rosetti felt a flash of irritation. She should have told them, they'd have made environmental adjustments to avoid her triggers. Maybe she'd thought she'd look weak—but how did she think she looked now?

Welles raised her head. Blood was running down her cheeks, dribbling from her mouth. This *wasn't* a seizure or anything else Rosetti had ever seen. Apparently Fox didn't know what it was, either; he was already down at the other end of the room, cowering behind a chair.

Welles straightened up and began clawing at her arms. Her flesh rippled and writhed as if something under her skin was desperate to get out. Abruptly, there was a loud, sickening *ripping* noise as the skin on her hands and fingers split.

Rosetti's stomach did a slow forward roll as people cried out in horror and revulsion.

Her hands clawed at each other, tearing off skin and muscle tissue, blood vessels and finally the finger bones themselves, leaving long, black talons shiny with blood. The woman stared at them in amazement, then let out an inhuman scream. Someone demanded that Rosetti call for help, which set off a chorus of panicky cries for the Marines and Jesus by turns. Rosetti glanced at the door. Where was the goddam emergency crew, why hadn't they already popped the lock and come in?

Welles gave another, much louder scream that shut them all up. Then she raised those shiny wet talons and tore her own face off.

Now the air was heavy with the copper smell of blood as the claws ripped away the rest of Welles's flesh and, when only grinning skull remained, the talons took hold of it and squeezed until it broke into pieces.

Sirens finally went off and Rosetti wondered why it had taken so long. People were screaming and crying as they crowded into the part of the bubble farthest away from the monster that had been Welles. A couple of brave souls tried to force the door open but it wouldn't budge. *That's topnotch security*, Rosetti thought, a little dazed; *we can die and take our secrets with us.*

Alien Barbie shook the remaining bits of human detritus off her shiny, lethal talons, sending blood and tissue in all directions, some of it hitting the walls where it stuck briefly, then slid down, leaving bloody trails. *Jackson Pollock, eat your heart out*, Rosetti thought, feeling surreal as the level of hysteria in the room increased.

He looked down at himself to see if he was wearing

any of the late Weaponized Barbie on his uniform and discovered Adele Trent was still beside him. Giving him a quick glance, she executed a perfect about-face and, with her back to the creature, vomited forcefully enough to hit the wall.

No one would mistake that for a Pollock, Rosetti thought, catching a fleeting whiff of bile before the dense coppery miasma of human blood overwhelmed it. Reflexively, he pushed the doctor behind him as the alien's misshapen head turned in their direction.

No eyes. Apparently it didn't need any.

Maybe it also knew everything that poor, dead Weaponized Barbie had known, including which terrified human was Kevin Fox, still cowering behind a chair. He'd tried to cram in among the others but they'd pushed him away; no doubt they thought he was about to turn into a monster too, and Rosetti didn't blame them. It made sense—*if* Alien Barbie, *then* Alien Ken.

Fox picked up the chair and held it in front of himself, shaking visibly as his partner—ex-partner, Rosetti corrected himself, while everyone else screamed at him to get them *outta here right now!*—bared what looked like thousands of teeth, all made of gleaming metal.

"No," Fox said in a trembling, hopeless voice somehow audible under the screams.

The alien's jaws opened wider and a second set of teeth telescoped slowly out of its mouth. It was smaller but nastier, and coated in thick saliva. They snapped at the empty air over and over, the alien grinning at Fox in what seemed like sadistic delight.

Fox whimpered as it took a step toward him. "Please don't. Susan?"

The room went quiet, watching the long, tube-shaped head tilt to one side, as if the name had given it pause.

"You know that name, don't you?" Fox began to cry. "It's *your* name—Susan Welles. You're still in there, aren't you, Susan? Yeah, you're still you, I know you are. And I'm Kevin, your friend. We're friends—*best* friends."

The alien's misshapen head tilted to the other side, like a curious dog's. Fox went on babbling about always working together and being best friends, although he was crying so much that Rosetti could barely understand him. Did the guy really think there was still something of Welles inside that monster?

The alien retracted the smaller set of teeth and gave a long, wet-sounding hiss that made Fox cringe and raise the chair. Then he began apologizing, saying he wasn't threatening her with the chair, he was just scared, he didn't want to be but he couldn't help it and that was on him, not her—

In a movement almost too fast to see, the alien batted the chair away and grabbed Fox up in both taloned hands. He continued to yammer as the creature pulled him into a crushing embrace against its armored body.

For a few moments, it held the gibbering Fox in a travesty of an embrace. Then it pulled his head back and the second set of teeth punched into one eye, going all the way through his skull and out the other side in a burst of blood, bone, and brains.

The room erupted in screams again, jarring Rosetti out of his semi-daze. This was happening on *his* watch. It didn't matter if Fox and Welles had caused it, *he* was responsible for the safety of everyone on Anchorpoint.

Beside him, Adele Trent turned away and threw up again. Damn it, the emergency crew should have been here by now, Rosetti thought, looking toward the door—

Rosetti came to flat on his back, looking up at the ceiling and gasping for breath. Someone had sucker-punched him and knocked the wind right out of him. Then he turned his head to find Adele Trent on the floor beside him, facing away so he couldn't tell if she were dead or merely unconscious.

A hand touched his lower leg and he raised his head to see someone else on the floor at his feet, feeling around blindly. The air was filled with dust and he couldn't hear anything except a continuous high-pitched tone.

It took a couple of seconds before he understood the emergency crew had finally blasted their way in.

Rosetti lowered his head and lay still, waiting for the initial shock to wear off. It had been ages since he'd been anywhere near a blast radius, much less inside one. Once he'd left the field for Anchorpoint, he hadn't had to worry about blast injuries. For the safety of all concerned, the rescue team would have been careful not to use more explosive than absolutely necessary but Rosetti knew he'd still have to see that everyone, himself included, were thoroughly examined by doctors with combat training. Most civilians were unaware that internal injuries didn't always show right away, particularly contrecoup. No civilian was going to drop dead of a brain bleed on *his* watch.

He took a deep breath and winced. Dammit, when the shock wore off, he was going to hurt *everywhere*—

All at once, he was upright, sagging between two Marines with his arms around their shoulders. Their faces were set in the hardcore calm expression of trained emergency responders, and although their lips were moving, he still heard nothing but that high-pitched tone. Didn't matter; he knew they were probably apologizing for the rough handling as they helped him toward the ragged hole where the airlock had been.

There was a flurry of activity all around him as Marines hurried to evacuate everyone, getting them away from the thing that had been Welles. Company Barbie was now as weaponized as she could possibly be. Where was it, anyway? Had it been caught in the blast? He tried to look around for it but his rescuers wouldn't stop.

Just as they reached the ruin of the entrance, another Marine appeared, carrying a flamethrower. She stepped past him and he craned his neck to see where she was going. He finally spotted the former Susan Welles, still clutching Kevin Fox's very dead body to itself. Then the Marine opened up on it full-strength and turned Alien Barbie into a column of flame.

It must have been screaming but Rosetti still heard nothing. His rescuers had dragged him out into the hallway now, and they refused to stop and take him back, even just to the blown-out entrance, so he could oversee the monster's destruction.

He wanted to make them understand that as the CO, he was responsible for everything that happened, even the clean-up afterward, but he was too weak even to try digging in his heels. They handed him off easily to two other Marines who put him on a gurney.

They were gently strapping him down and he saw Mandala Jackson half-carrying, half-dragging Adele Trent into the hallway, slapping at the Marines trying to help her. Someone needed to tell her she was in shock, he thought, and noted absently that his hearing had begun to come back; he could hear Jackson swearing, faintly as yet but clearly.

The daze was definitely wearing off, his head clearing. Good thing, because he had a number of high-priority matters that needed immediate attention.

First on the list were those samples of alien material currently in transit to Gateway, courtesy of the late Company power couple. Normally, tissue samples didn't activate themselves and develop into fully mature life-forms, but these weren't normal tissue samples. He had to send warnings to both Gateway and the *Mona Lisa*, with video of what had just happened to make sure they took it seriously.

Traveling at light-speed, the message would reach Gateway well ahead of the spacecraft carrying the alien samples, so even if it was already too late for the *Mona Lisa*, the Marines there would be ready to defend the station against hostile organisms.

Unless, Rosetti thought with a sudden, terrible dread, MiliSci intercepted the message before it reached the station.

2 3

"Hey, Tully—you awake in there?" Spence thumped Tully's door with the heel of one hand. "Get up and let me in, I've got food."

She thumped the door again and held the bag of takeout in front of the door-cam. "Got your favorite—Pad Thai, onion rings, and fusion quesadillas. It's the chef's special—salmon with lemongrass and coriander. Come on, let me in already. You *love* fusion quesadillas."

Spence put her ear to the door. Nothing.

Tully was probably sleeping like the *cremated* dead. Decontamination was hell—after her last experience, she'd slept for eighteen hours and seriously considered changing to a career where no one was ever forcibly parboiled and scoured by people in hazard suits. Even her *hair* had hurt.

"Tully, Charles A., are you alive?" she said again, still with her ear to the door. "Check your pulse and tell me, will ya?"

More nothing. Spence touched the small square screen beside the door and it lit up with a graphic of a keypad.

She and Tully had exchanged entry codes, but she'd said she didn't want them routinely going in and out of each other's private quarters without asking first, and he had respected her feelings.

Only this *wasn't* routine. She hadn't seen Tully since he'd stumbled out of decontam, red and raw in medicated white pajamas, saying he wanted to sleep for a year. He hadn't answered her calls or replied to texts or emails. There was no way she was going to leave without making sure he was okay in there. If he *was* in there.

"So help me, Tully," she muttered as she tapped in the entry code, "if you're dead on the floor, I'll make them bring you back—" The door slid open. "—so I can kill you again…"

Her voice trailed off as she felt for the light switch on the wall, put it on maximum brightness, and waited for the pile of clothing on the bed to erupt with sleepy profanity. Seconds passed; yet more nothing. Tully wasn't there, and the room was more chaotic than she had ever seen it, everything thrown around like someone had tossed the place. A desperate search for clean underwear?

Not hardly—nobody wore *any* underwear after decontam. You got a couple of days off to recover and most people spent the time lying naked on memory foam with an extra-large jar of skin balm. If Tully was doing that, it wasn't here.

Spence set the bag of takeout on a shelf and picked her way over to the bed. Maybe something there would give her a hint as to where he was. If it didn't, she could try asking someone in Ops to locate him by his implant. Normally, Ops refused, saying they weren't a stalking service, come back with a warrant. Occasionally, though, a tech who knew you would trade favors. Not that her job in the tissue lab gave her much to barter with.

Hey, one crisis at a time—jump off that bridge when you come to it. Tully's voice in her head was so clear, he might have been standing beside her. Only he wasn't.

She had barely started sorting through the mess on the bed when she found his wadded-up lab coat. All her alarm bells went off. You *never* took your lab coat home—you were supposed to drop it down the dirty linens chute at the end of your shift. Anyone who forgot would get a reminder every five minutes on comms until they brought it back. Hardly anyone ever forgot, least of all Tully. It was one less item of laundry to put off doing.

Something flapped as she shook out the coat—his lab ID badge, clipped to the lapel. Spence blinked at it. This was his new badge, the one they'd given him after decontamination because the indicator strip on his old badge had turned bloody red from end to end. She'd watched them drop it into the disposal bin for incineration and expulsion.

So how could the strip on *this* badge be hard bloody red all the way across? It couldn't have been a mix-up with the badges, that just wasn't possible.

Therefore, someone had screwed the pooch in a big way.

It was Murphy's Law, as absolute as the speed of light: *Any pooch that* can *get screwed,* will *get screwed.*

And she knew which pooch had been screwed this time; she was holding his ID.

The door to the cell opened, and Hicks looked up. At last, someone had come to give him hell—the Company power couple, he hoped. He was dying to take them on.

Instead, it was one of the Marines from the arresting team, wearing full combat armor.

"Guess I've got a better rep than I realized," Hicks said, laughing a little as he stood up. "Hope you brought grenades—" He cut off as the Marine stood aside and Rosetti came in. Hicks immediately snapped to attention, mostly by reflex but also to cover his shock at how haggard the colonel looked, like he'd just come straight out of combat.

Rosetti nodded at the Marine. She slung her weapon so she could remove Hicks's white cuffs and toss them aside.

"Colonel Rosetti?" Hicks asked, still at attention.

"As you were, Corporal Hicks." The man's voice was heavy. "We need you in Ops."

Hicks felt the same terrible plummeting sensation in the pit of his stomach he'd had back on LV-426, when Ripley and Newt had been trapped in a dark lab with two face-huggers.

"We didn't kill it," he said.

"No, you didn't," Rosetti said. "*It* killed Fox and Welles. And now it's loose."

It looked like his life sentence in a Company black spot was canceled; he should have known, Hicks thought. He wasn't getting off that easy. Never had, never would.

"We need Bishop, too—" he started.

"We know, we've got him," Rosetti said. "Now, for God's sake, Corporal, *haul ass!*"

2 4

The electric jeep had looked more like an over-built go-kart to Hicks. He'd thought the rollbars were especially absurd. Why put them on a vehicle that probably had a top speed of 65kph? Then Walker had gotten behind the wheel.

Now Hicks had one arm wrapped tightly around a rollbar so he wouldn't go flying out of the elevated seat behind Walker whenever he made a high-speed turn. The pulse-rifle slung across his chest was an M41. He would have preferred the M56 smart gun, but it was too bulky for the jeep, and Jackson had insisted a flamethrower was out of the question in a construction area. Well, he could improvise weapons from whatever was lying around—he'd done it before—and they could put it on his tab with the illegal alien clones he'd destroyed.

Ripley, back on LV-426, laughing: *They can* bill *me.* Hicks suspected they had.

He blinked to wake the lens over his left eye; the feed from Ops showed Jackson, Rosetti, and Bishop gathered around a console, with Spence peering over Jackson's shoulder, her brown face ashen and pinched with worry.

"Someone gimme a read, will ya?" he said into the mic.

"*You're getting close. Twenty feet, hang a left,*" Jackson replied. Hicks glanced at Walker, who made the okay sign with one hand to show he'd heard. Walker had sound only, saying he couldn't watch TV and drive. They'd probably be okay as long as Jackson didn't announce any turns at the last second, Hicks thought, almost losing his grip on the rollbar as Walker swung the jeep left.

"Is Tully moving?" Hicks asked.

"*No, not for a couple of minutes,*" Jackson replied.

This tunnel was a lot narrower than the one they'd just come out of. If Walker lost control, they'd get wedged between the walls instead of rolling over.

Abruptly, the jeep bounced out of the tunnel and into the cavernous construction area. Was this near where he'd met Spence? He couldn't tell. All construction areas were remarkably alike, especially in the dark.

Walker let up on the accelerator. "Is he still here? Is he moving?" he asked.

"*Ten o'clock,*" said Rosetti.

Walker stamped on the accelerator again and then had to veer around a stack of bulkhead connectors, narrowly missing several dozen barrels stacked up in a complex arrangement. Plenty of room here to roll the jeep, maybe into a fifteen-foot pile of unpainted metal plating.

"*Are you sure that's Tully?*" Spence asked, her voice

high and tight. Hicks blinked to wake the lens again. She and Bishop had switched places.

"*Of* course *I'm sure!*" Jackson snapped. She pushed Spence back from the console, making her and Bishop switch back. "*That's* his *locator frequency, can't be anyone else! Or didn't they tell you how implants work?*"

"*It's just that he's still not moving,*" Spence said unhappily.

Jackson rolled her eyes.

"*I don't understand why he'd go* there, *of all places,*" Rosetti said.

"*No mystery, really,*" Bishop said, sounding oddly apologetic. "*When he saw his badge and realized decontam hadn't worked, he got as far away from everyone else as possible. That area is all bulkhead—nothing on the other side but vacuum. If we can't get him into an airlock, blowing a hole in the bulkhead won't threaten the entire sta—*" He saw Spence's stricken expression and cut off. "*He's very brave,*" Bishop went on after a moment. "*And honorable, to think of other lives.*"

"*He's* scared." Spence's bleak voice had an undertone of anger. "*Scared and alone.*"

"*You're getting real close, Hicks,*" Jackson said, talking over her. "*You should see him soon if you don't already.*"

"It's a goddam obstacle course here," Hicks said. "All this construction crap doesn't show up for you, does it?" He gave Walker a soft nudge with the toe of his boot. "Put on the screen."

Walker slapped the dashboard and a screen lit up, showing a basic grid, white lines on black, and two dots, one large, stationary red one and a smaller green one moving along a circuitous route. "Okay, but I told you, I don't like to watch TV and drive."

"*I'll* watch, you just don't hit anything," Hicks said.

"*Do you see him yet?*" asked Jackson just as Spence said, "*You're practically on top of him!*"

The screen said Spence was right. "Stop!" Hicks ordered.

Walker stood on the brakes and Hicks barely managed not to fly over his head into another large collection of barrels. He turned on the torch clipped to his rifle and climbed out of the jeep, looking for anything that could be human.

All he saw here were barrels and more barrels. Some were stacked three, even four high, but most of them were gathered into groups of half a dozen. As Hicks moved around them, he saw several more lying open on their sides, the lids scattered like forgotten Frisbees™.

"Tully!" he called. "Tully, yo!"

A short distance away, something about six meters tall and covered with a tarp loomed over him. Hicks raised his rifle and swept the torch beam over it. Nothing; he turned away and caught a flash from something on the deck. Keeping the light on it, he inched forward and saw it was sitting in the middle of a pool of thick, dark sludge. At first he thought it had spilled out of the overturned barrels, but his torch showed that the overturned barrels were dry.

As he got closer, he saw lumps of various sizes in it, maybe tools or other things left behind by the construction workers. The morning shift wouldn't be too happy when they saw this; the shop steward would call management to remind them unidentified sludge wasn't part of the deal.

Hicks wished he could have said the same. Where the *hell* had this shit come from?

The answer came to him unbidden: the aliens. Of course; if it was weird, completely unfamiliar, and appeared without warning or explanation, the aliens were behind it, which meant you could assume it was also lethal. Except he'd never seen sludge before.

Or had he? Maybe this was a cruder form of what they used to cocoon humans for their chest-bursters. Or it was an alien version of a tar-pit, and those lumps in it were only asleep. If so, he didn't want to wake them.

As he got closer, however, he saw one of the larger lumps near the edge of the pool was just partially covered and he didn't have to worry about waking it. Flight jackets didn't sleep.

Using the end of the rifle, he lifted it out of the pool. One sleeve had been torn off; the sludge on the one remaining didn't completely obscure the Company logo badges running from shoulder to wrist.

Hicks let it drop and told Walker to roll forward three meters with headlights set to maximum. Now he could make out the scattered fragments of bone on the surface as well as a flap of scalp with hair attached.

"*Any sign of him?*" Jackson's voice in his ear made him jump. He'd practically forgotten about her and the others back in Ops.

"Uh, yeah," he said. "A few."

"*What's* that *supposed to mean?*" Spence demanded. Jackson shushed her.

"You gotta be looking straight at him," Walker called from the jeep. "The screen shows you're standing right next to him—"

The reading says they're in the room!

It's not reading right!

Or you're not reading it right!

For all of a second, Hicks was back in the laboratory on LV-426 with his greatly reduced squad, bracing for the aliens' attack, all of them baffled by the sensor readings until they had finally thought to look *up*. As he did now, not at a low ceiling in a dimly lit room, but at the top of a shadow five meters tall.

Movement flickered, a shadow in the bigger shadow. Or was it just his eyes? Then a shape broke free of the larger darkness, hissing as it flew over his head and landed on the jeep's rollbars.

Walker's bellow of surprise became a scream.

2 5

Hicks heard the sound of metallic teeth snapping and a long tail lashing the air like a whip. It was all happening fast but he felt like he was moving in slow-motion. Raising the pulse-rifle to his shoulder seemed to take a very long time, like *he* was submerged in the sludge eating Tully's flight jacket.

Walker bellowed again as the end of the alien's tail missed his face and struck one of the rollbars, leaving a deep groove. He tried to get a bead on the alien without hitting Walker but they were both moving around too quickly, while he was still mired in slow-motion.

All at once, Walker was gone.

Hicks yelled his name. No answer but a hand appeared from under the dashboard, reaching for the controls. The electric motor whined sharply and the jeep pulled two three-sixties in rapid succession, sending the former Tully, Charles A. flying off into the sludge. It was back on its feet in an instant, turning its ugly, eyeless face toward Hicks.

Shoulda warned you about Walker's driving, Hicks thought.

The creature leaped for him and he fired, catching it in midair so it dropped back into the sludge. The hiss of acid-blood eating through the deck and the foul, poisonous smell made Hicks give ground in a hurry. The jeep's high-beams swept through the darkness and he had a quick glimpse of the alien crouching to leap at him again, unbothered by the acid-blood pouring out of the hole in its chest.

"Get the fuck in!" Walker roared as Hicks launched himself at the vehicle. He snagged a rollbar with one hand, swung himself around, and landed in the backward-facing seat just as Walker stamped on the accelerator. The rear wheels threw up a spray of sludge; Hicks heard more hissing but the sound faded quickly as they sped away, back into the tunnel. Hicks clung to the rollbar, keeping the pulse-rifle up and ready, but the thing didn't chase them.

Walker's driving was even crazier on the way back but Hicks didn't feel critical. After a while he became aware of Jackson's voice in his earpiece, calling his name over and over, and demanding to know what happened.

He adjusted the lens and blinked to wake it. Jackson's red face appeared, her expression a mix of fear and anger. Beside her, Rosetti stared blankly, like someone had just hit him with a brick and he was too stunned to fall down. Spence had both hands over her nose and mouth, crying soundlessly.

And there was Bishop on Jackson's right, looking calm and composed, as if he knew exactly what to do next.

Hicks hoped he did, because he was sure as shit that nobody else would.

This must have been what it was like when Saigon fell, Luc Hai thought, standing back from the entrance to the dining commons with Ashok, while the last surviving Progressive Peoples crashed through the place, overturning tables and chairs, scattering dishes and utensils in a mad rush toward the far end of the room. Through the ragged hole where the door had been, she could see people swarming up the angled ladder normally used by maintenance crews to move between levels.

She and Ashok would have to get up the ladder before the last of them went through and locked the hatch. Otherwise, they'd never be able to get through, even with grenades. The metal alloy was blast-proof—although probably not monster-proof. So far, nothing could stand up to the horrors that had escaped from the biolab, but this might slow them down just long enough to let most of them reach the lifeboats. Or many of them.

Or *any* of them.

Then they could drift through space, huddling together and hoping rescue arrived before the air ran out. In interstellar space, surviving in a lifeboat long enough to be rescued was always an iffy proposition. Not like staying on Rodina, where dying was a sure thing.

And they owed it all to that towering genius, Colonel-

Doctor Suslov, Luc Hai thought bitterly. Thanks to his brilliant notion that they get a step ahead of the capitalists by stealing their bioweapon, most of the Progressive Peoples had been slaughtered in ways more terrible than any of them could have imagined.

Lara Braun, the chief of Research and Development, had died first. Her reward for working so diligently on Suslov's great idea had been to spend the last hours of her life wrapped in some kind of alien cocoon, until the monster forcibly implanted in her body was done feeding on her. Then it had burst—no, *exploded*—from her chest and gone in search of living things to kill.

When Ashok had showed her Braun's ruined corpse on the laboratory surveillance, Luc Hai's horrified pity had been dwarfed by her outrage at Suslov cocooned beside her, unconscious and still intact. His head hung to one side, showing the too-fast pulse in his neck. She would have gone in and shot him in the face, except that would have spared him what Braun had suffered.

"I hope it's *twins*," she'd said in English, the language so popular with capitalists—or at least all the ones she'd met. There was no time to stay and watch; the creatures rampaging through Rodina were getting closer. She had to settle just for knowing Suslov would die in agony.

Too bad it wouldn't last very long.

Ashok nudged her—everyone was out of the dining commons. Luc Hai called to the last people on the ladder, reminding them not to lock the hatch yet, then turned toward the passageway. As soon as the aliens appeared at the other end, she and Ashok fired several short bursts then hurried to push the big double doors shut. The doors wouldn't stop the monsters, but they activated all the locks anyway and rolled a heavy metal cabinet in front of them before they ran for the ladder.

It took the aliens only a few seconds to crash through the doors, barely noticing the cabinet as they flipped it aside. They reached the bottom of the ladder just as Ashok came through the hatch. Luc Hai fired down at them while he rigged the lock to jam it. She could hear their acid-blood hissing and the inhuman screams of pain and rage. Or maybe only rage—Luc Hai wasn't sure they felt pain any more than they felt fear. Ashok pushed her aside and slammed the hatch shut.

A second later, something rammed it from below. Luc Hai felt the deck under her vibrate and she bit her lips together to keep from crying out. Her gaze met Ashok's; he was as terrified as she was. The alien rammed the hatch again, making the whole deck shake harder. Under the nerve-shattering, inhuman screams of fury, she heard the sound of very dense, blast-proof steel starting to buckle.

When Hicks finally got back to Operations with Walker, he saw that the diplomat, Shuman, had joined the group, Spence was conspicuous by her absence, and the argument about what to do next was in high gear.

Jackson looked ready to come to blows with Rosetti, either because she had something against him personally or the military as a whole, or just because she was losing her shit and Rosetti was the lightning rod for her demons.

Rosetti himself wasn't having an easy time, popping pills when he thought no one was looking. Hicks recognized them; every combat vet knew what painkillers looked like. No doubt the colonel was still feeling the effects of the blast when the Marines had breached the privacy bubble. Hicks hoped he was well-stocked, with enough to let him keep it together even if he had to share. The last thing they needed was another Gorman.

Which was to say, the Gorman who had fallen apart and lost half the squad in the first hour on LV-426, as opposed to the one who had died with Vasquez and left him responsible for keeping everyone alive and getting them to safety while he ran out of ammunition, options, ideas, and time—everything except aliens.

Hudson's pained face appeared in his mind. *And I was getting short! Four more weeks and out. Now I'm gonna buy it on this rock. It ain't fair, man!* His expression changed to that goofy-smug grin. *Damn, Hicks, you never learn, do ya?*

No kidding; Hicks moved toward Jackson and Rosetti, intending to cut them off before shit got real. But then Walker spoke up.

"Hey, I don't know about any of you guys," he said with an edge in his voice. "But I know what *I'm* gonna do."

"Which is?" Jackson asked, caught off-guard.

"I'm an engineer. Gimme some hardware, I can make a weapon outta anything. Then I'm going hunting."

"Alone?" Rosetti shook his head. "That's suicide. You can't—"

"I don't take orders from *you*," Walker said, talking over him. "I'm gonna take a look around, see what's what. If I can get all the comms working, I'll report in. You can find me anywhere by my implant."

"But you're not trained for this," Rosetti said. "You're not ready."

Walker laughed in his face. "After what I just went through? I'm readier than *you* are."

"They'll kill you," Jackson said.

"Maybe." Walker shrugged. "Okay, probably. But I'm not gonna sit here and wait for my number to be up. Don't gimme a hard time, okay? I'm *going*."

"Wait." Rosetti went over to a bright red cabinet marked EMERGENCY ONLY. He pressed his palm against the door and it slid open to reveal a cache of weapons, including pulse-rifles, grenades, and ammunition.

Jackson's jaw dropped. "Holy *shit*. I thought that was medical stuff, defibrillators, whatever."

"Over there," Rosetti said, gesturing at another cabinet offhandedly. He pulled out a pulse-rifle and some cartridges, and gave them to Walker.

"Shoulda known." Jackson frowned as the engineer slung the rifle over one shoulder and stashed cartridges in the various pockets of his overalls. "You guys'd stash weapons under your grandma's bed—hell, under *my* grandma's bed. But here? In *Ops*?"

"The Marines will send you a formal apology," Rosetti said.

"Thanks a lot." Jackson made a face. "I don't get it. You guys hardly ever come to civilian Ops. Why would you hide weapons here?"

Rosetti spared her an arch glance. "In case of emergency. *Any* emergency," he added as she started to respond.

"Excuse me." Bishop's calm-serious voice made them all turn to look at him. "We should contact Rodina Station. In light of their encounter with the *Sulaco*, they're probably in a similar situation."

"You think *they* could help us?" Rosetti's short laugh was scornful. "More likely they'll beg *us* to save *them*."

"Either way, it would be useful to know their status," Bishop replied.

"You're right." Rosetti looked unsettled, possibly because he'd never agreed with an artificial person before, Hicks thought. "Contact them. *Now*."

2 6

Twenty minutes later Jackson straightened up from the comms console. "Sorry, Colonel, can't raise them."

"Try the diplomatic codes," Shuman suggested from a chair in the far corner. Hicks had forgotten he was in the room.

Jackson glanced at him, annoyed. "If they aren't responding to Mayday Interplanetary-Interstellar, I doubt diplomacy'll work." She studied the data scrolling on one of her screens. "Could be a hardware problem, bad transponders or—" She broke off, tapped a button below the screen. "Whoa. Found an outgoing transmission. Military encryption, not diplomatic—" She glanced at Shuman again. "—and full of noise. Let me try filtering."

Her hands moved quickly over the console while she aimed the light-pen on her cap at a screen on her left.

"They have anyone in the area to receive?" Rosetti asked tensely.

Jackson turned the light-pen on a screen to her right. "Not much that I can see. Automated mining unit on

NC-313—" She paused. "—and a test module for a terraforming op on MV-43, but they're not transmitting directly to either one." She turned back to the first screen. "Okay, guys, who are you talking to?" she murmured. "*Aha!* Battle cruiser *Nikolai Stoiko*, about four and a half hours out from Rodina. Four if they push it."

Shuman got up and went over to her. "Can we listen in?" he asked.

"Still running it though the detangler," Jackson replied. "I swear, their transmission standards get worse all the time. Right now, it's still more mess than message. Gimme a minute."

"What about us? Have *we* got anything in the area?" Shuman said, sounding a bit plaintive.

Jackson chuckled drily. "Not a lot, this being the off-season, as it were. There's the *Kansas City*—it's a colonial admin transport. Just sent her a mayday. They'll get it in ten hours, give or take. Best I can do, folks."

"Then we'll just have to hang on for ten hours," Rosetti said. "When the *Kansas City* gets here, we'll abandon the station."

"No, we'll *destroy* the station," Hicks said. "We've got nukes, don't we?"

Rosetti shook his head. "No nukes. It would be a violation of the Strategic Arms Reduction Treaty. Our cooperation with the treaty is greatly appreciated by all concerned," he added sourly.

"No nukes, no problem." Jackson's tone was bizarrely

cheerful. "We can override the safeguards on the fusion package. Baby nova, big finish, hasta la pasta and that's all, folks."

Rosetti's expression said he didn't like that idea. Hicks could all but see his mind working on arguments against it.

"If you're worried about the cost, they can bill us," Hicks chuckled.

"And it really *is* the only way to be sure," Bishop added. "This version of the alien isn't the same as the one on LV-426. It's added a whole new method of reproduction. Maybe more than one. There's no telling how many people at Anchorpoint are already infected."

Rosetti frowned. "What do you suggest?" he asked Bishop.

Bishop looked at them solemnly. "The only way to stop this thing before it takes the next transport out and spreads to every inhabited planet is if we blow the fusion package *now*."

Seconds passed in utter silence. Then Jackson cleared her throat. "Did you just say 'now'?" she asked warily.

"I thought you were programmed to protect human life," Hicks said.

"I am," Bishop said, as Zen as ever. "I'm taking the long view."

The long view? Hicks was trying to wrap his mind around that when Jackson's console chimed, making him jump. One of the screens displayed an array of ID photos.

"What's that?" Hicks asked.

"Missing persons—specifically missing Ops staff," Jackson said, aiming her light-pen at an onscreen control. The photos shrank to make room for text. "I've been keeping track."

"People go missing here?" Hicks said, looking from her to Rosetti and back again. "I thought everyone had locator implants."

"Yeah, they do. Once in a while a locator'll malfunction, or some goofball shorts theirs out just for fun. Tully's signal disappeared while you were on your way back here. I don't think it's a prank." Jackson's voice was grim. "We just lost three more—two of them had been on cleanup in the tissue lab, the third lives with one of them. None of them were the merry prankster type. Makes a grand total of twenty-five and counting."

"Weren't the cleaners in hazmat suits?" Shuman asked.

"Of course," Jackson snapped, giving him another annoyed glance.

"But it was already too late," Hicks said, more to himself. "Tully and Welles had been discharged from decontam as clear. Who knows how many people each of them came into contact with before—" He turned to Rosetti. "Dammit, Colonel, it's contagious."

Rosetti didn't look at him. "Send a mayday to the *Kansas City*," he told Jackson.

"What about the *Mona Lisa*?" Hicks said. He was trying not to think about what Newt might wake up to on arrival at Gateway.

The light-pen drew a zigzag in the air as Jackson shook her head. "The *Mona Lisa's* still in overdrive—it's got another two days before it reaches maximum acceleration, and it'll take about that long for a message to reach them. By then, they'll have passed the halfway point, so they won't have enough fuel to come back."

"Would we even want them to?" Shuman said. "They're carrying tissue samples—"

"If they even know that shit's on board," Hicks added, his voice bitter.

"They know," Rosetti said sharply. "I sent warnings to them and to Gateway. *With* video."

"If Weapons Division didn't intercept them," Shuman said darkly, looking an accusation at Rosetti.

"*Finally!*" Jackson shouted. "I've got the Rodina transmission. Our socialist space brothers speak at last!" Her head made quick little movements as she used the pen on one of the console monitors. A large screen descended from a slot in the ceiling above the console, displaying multicolored static. "Like I said, their transmission standards get worse all the time. They never settle for mere excellence when crappy will do—"

The static cleared, revealing a young woman reading from a tablet in Russian. Her features were a mix of Slavic and Mongol and she was disheveled, with a dark smear on one high cheekbone and stains on her overalls, not all of them dry. Her voice was calm and matter-of-fact, but the way she clutched the tablet in both hands with her arms pressed tightly to her sides failed to hide her trembling.

"Can we get this in English?" Shuman asked.

"Working on it." Jackson bent over the console, her head moving back and forth.

Abruptly, a female voice-over cut in.

"... of Progressive Peoples. I repeat, I am Technician First Class Tatjana Lewchuk. We regret that we must inform you of an unfortunate development in our laboratory. We have undertaken an experiment with genetic material harvested from a foreign military vessel traveling on a course that took it briefly within our borders, which made it subject to seizure and inspection." She looked up for a moment with an expression that was both apologetic and defensive.

"We attempted to clone cells from a Xenomorph found aboard this spacecraft within the safety of a stasis unit to avoid contamination. Unfortunately, the stasis unit failed in the fifteenth hour. Modifications of the genetic structure have resulted in a subspecies variant to the original found aboard the Sulaco. This subspecies replicates more rapidly—much more rapidly. Due to circumstances beyond our control, we have been unable to sequence the genome, and so cannot say whether these modifications were those intended as part of the experiment or are spontaneous adaptations of the organism to a new environment. It has—"

She paused and looked up, directly into the camera.

"—it has... taken... most of us," she said. "We few who remain will not last long, but we wish to warn you—we urge *you, with utmost desperation, to terminate any experiments with this material* now." She took a shaky breath. *"You* must *destroy it,* all *of it,* completely. *It is impossible to contain or control. There is no protection, no immunity. Infection is absolute with a mortality rate of one hundred percent—"*

The voice cut off as the image began to slide sideways, and then went dark.

For some unmeasured time, they were all silent. Then Jackson said, "That's our show for tonight, folks." She looked around. "Anybody want to see it again to get the full effect of the cinematography?"

Rosetti's face had lost all color. Hicks grabbed the nearest chair and placed it behind the man, in case he collapsed.

"She was just a tech," Jackson said. "Hell, she looked like a schoolkid and she had nobody backing her up."

"I doubt there was anyone else left," Bishop said mildly.

The memory came to Hicks as vividly as a video, Newt running ahead of him through the airducts on LV-426. The setting morphed into the *Mona Lisa*, with Newt crawling through maintenance access channels and airducts, searching for a hiding place where the monsters couldn't get at her—

"*Hicks!*" He came back to the present to see Jackson glaring at him. "I *said*, look at this."

She pointed at the hanging screen, now divided into four quadrants, all of them black. Hicks shook his head, bewildered.

"These feeds are from the tunnels around the air-scrubbers," she told him. "There's something covering the surveillance cams." Jackson did something with the controls and the sections lightened a little. Hicks could make out the curve of the tunnel walls and something with an irregular texture covering the tiles. "That's as good as I can get it," she said.

Hicks moved closer to the screen. Jackson was talking about how she'd never seen anything like the stuff on the walls. Instead of telling her he had, he grabbed his rifle and a couple of cartridges out of the cache and left, barely aware of Jackson calling after him, wanting to know where the hell he was going.

2 7

It was morning in pocket-Madagascar.

Normally this was Spence's favorite time of the eco-module's artificial day, but without Tully, the magic was gone. Now the sunshine was only simulated daylight on a dimmer switch; the blue sky, the clouds, the tiny daytime half-moon were all just elements in a simple holographic projection any six-year-old could produce.

One of the ring-tailed lemurs approached her in the tall grass, hesitating every half-meter or so until it finally reached her. It waited briefly, then climbed into her lap and hugged her. The affection completely undid her. She broke down in tears as she cuddled the little primate, feeling how fast its heart was beating. Tully had engineered the lemurs just for her, because he knew she liked them.

Tully, you stupid asshole. You stupid, stupid *asshole.*

The cool morning air touched the back of her neck, sending a chill down her spine and along her arms. Her grandmother had said it meant a goose walked over your grave. Back then, the expression had sent Spence into a fit of giggles.

It wasn't funny anymore.

On Rodina Station, Luc Hai was having the same sensation. Her foster sister Zara had referred to it as the Devil tapping you on the shoulder. Zara had been a devout believer in all things occult, which Luc Hai took as absolute proof that capitalist society didn't know the difference between culture and a brain disorder.

Well, Ashok had said the mind came up with some pretty crazy shit at the weirdest times. She gazed at his body on the deck beside her, wishing she could have told him he was right. A shower of acid-blood had burned through his armor in only seconds. It would have landed on her except he had stepped in front of her.

It was the first time she had screamed in her adult life and it hadn't drowned out the hissing of the acid doing its work. She hoped Ashok hadn't lived long enough to hear her.

Now it was on her to make sure he hadn't died for nothing, but she wasn't sure that was possible. Life had no meaning to these creatures except as something to be wiped out.

For all she knew, it was why they were here.

* * *

Unlike Ops, Medlab didn't seem to be short-staffed, Hicks noted absently as he stalked through the Outpatient Ward on his way to Ripley's room in Critical Care. Only one person made a move to approach him, a young, anxious-looking guy in nursing scrubs. One of the other nurses caught his arm and pulled him back. Hicks didn't hear what she said to him. Probably explaining that you didn't tell a Marine in battle armor to come back during regular visiting hours.

He found Ripley alone in her room. According to the tablet at the foot of her bed, her condition was something deeper than delta sleep, but not a coma or a persistent vegetative state. Leave it to Ripley to find her own unique level of unconsciousness. The notes said there was no telling when or if she would find her way back from wherever she was, but Hicks knew the longer someone remained unconscious, the less likely they were to come out of it.

Ripley didn't stir as he pushed the machines aside and plucked the electrodes from her forehead and out of her hair. He removed the IV carefully, making sure there was no blood leaking from the back of her hand. Her medical record would be on her locator chip, and the information would be accessible no matter where she ended up.

There was no gurney in the room but the bed had wheels. Hicks released the brakes and started to push it out into the hall, then caught sight of Newt's map.

"Not to scale but close enough for government work," he muttered as he peeled it off the wall. "Correction: *too good* for government," he added as he folded it carefully and tucked it under the neckline of Ripley's hospital gown.

All space stations placed hospitals close to lifeboat bays, so Hicks didn't have far to go with Ripley. He half-expected someone to call Security on him, maybe even send a negotiator to talk him into releasing his hostage. But the most anyone did was stare and move out of his way.

From her desktop console, the receptionist opened the door to the departure hall without raising an eyebrow, as if Marines hurried past her with unconscious people in hospital beds all the time. At the very end of the hallway, Hicks saw the small rectangular screen on the entry hatch light up; the receptionist had prepped it for him remotely, and he ran for it.

Just below the screen was a six-centimeter vertical slot. He fished his dog-tags out of his shirt and inserted one without removing it from the chain around his neck. A sine wave appeared on the display while the hatch thought things over.

Seconds later his dog-tag slid out and he heard a rapid series of clicks as the locks disengaged. The door swung open and Hicks crossed a short walkway to the lifeboat airlock, which was already open for boarding.

The vessel was a six-pack, the smallest model available in this bay. Its sleep capsules were laid out in an asterisk, with food supplies in transparent cabinets so passengers would see them on waking. At the far end was the open-plan cockpit and the controls for navigation, comms, and life-support. The economical space would be a snug fit for half a dozen passengers even if only half of them were awake at a time, but it would probably feel pretty empty to Ripley. Still, she'd be safe.

"Sorry, Ripley, I'm not taking liberties," he said softly, picking her up in his arms. "But you can't make this trip in a hospital bed."

Her head lolled against his shoulder like a sleepy child's and Hicks froze, afraid he'd woken her. But there was no change in her breathing or her face, no sign of returning awareness.

Relieved, Hicks carried her into the lifeboat and placed her gently in the capsule facing the airlock. Before closing the lid, he waited another half minute or so in case she woke up. And then lingered a few minutes longer, telling himself he was making sure there were no malfunctions while the capsule scanned her.

Eventually, he ran out of excuses. Ripley had paid her dues… *twice*. The first time, it had cost her the life she should have lived, with her daughter and her grandchildren. The second time, it had stolen her second chance to be a mother and raise Newt in a world where you woke up *from* nightmares, not *to* them. He was damned if he'd let her face something worse than the chest-burster.

And as much as he wanted to talk himself into going with her, he knew he'd never be able to justify it.

"*Corporal Hicks?*" Bishop said politely in his ear.

"Yeah, hang on." Someone had gotten station-wide comms working again, Hicks thought, probably Bishop. He sealed the lifeboat and the entry hatch, then initiated the launch sequence. The countdown was a full minute and Hicks watched every second displayed on the small screen.

The deck under his feet vibrated as the lifeboat disengaged and the screen flickered, changing from confirmation of the launch to a real-time video feed of the lifeboat slowly moving back from the berth. As soon as it was clear, it executed an almost dignified one-eighty and began to accelerate away from Anchorpoint, into the starry black.

"Okay, go ahead," he told Bishop.

"*I take it Ripley's hospital scans were clear?*" Bishop asked.

"You take it correctly," Hicks said. "She was never directly exposed to the new, improved model of those bastards, and now she never will be. She deserves to sit this one out." Pause. "I owe her that much."

2 8

The five Marines Rosetti sent to pick Hicks up outside the lifeboat bay were well-equipped and brought him better combat armor, as well as extra weapons. They arrived in a six-wheeled personnel carrier rather than a flimsy electric jeep and the guy behind the wheel, Private Zedong Wu, didn't drive like an engineer with a death wish.

Rosetti's brief message said they were among his best, the best trained with the quickest reaction times and the highest test scores. Hicks didn't doubt it. What worried him was how utterly green they were, untried and unseasoned, with no real combat experience. And yeah, some simulations could be crazy-tough, but no matter how deeply immersed you were, you always knew that if you made mistakes, you'd get graded, not killed.

Unlike the shitstorm they were barreling into now.

This whole thing is a mistake, Hicks thought. Instead of rushing to find out what was blocking the cameras around the air-scrubbers, they should have been engineering a mass evacuation, getting every single person off the station and into the lifeboats so they could blow Anchorpoint to atoms, obliterating the goddam aliens before they spread any further.

He almost told Wu the mission was canceled and they were returning to Operations, but the argument he'd have with Rosetti about that might end with him back in restraints, while the aliens overran Anchorpoint and left a space station full of monsters lying in wait for new arrivals.

And there *would* be new arrivals; Gateway would send in squads of Marines who'd have no idea what they were up against, and maybe even a few diplomats who believed they could initiate peace negotiations. Some might survive long enough to escape only to discover they had stowaways—

Hicks shook the thought away. One crisis at a time, and the crisis du jour was his being in command of five very green Marines who had no idea what they were getting into.

Vasquez popped into his head, tough, fearless, ready for anything: *I only need to know one thing: where they are.* Then she looked out of the memory at him. *Nobody* ever *knows what they're getting into, vato. You didn't. You still don't.*

That was probably true, Hicks thought. Maybe *he* was the one with the death wish, and Walker was just a lousy driver.

"*Next junction, hang a right.*" Jackson's voice in his earpiece gave him a start. "*Then at the fork, bear left and slow it right down. You'll see one of the larger traffic-security rigs overhead. All those cams are dead. Whatever's going on down there starts just past that point."*

"Copy that." Hicks glanced at Wu, who nodded to confirm he'd heard it, too. "Can't you make it brighter down here? We can hardly see a thing."

"Told you, something's blocking the lights," she said. *"That area doesn't usually need much candlepower anyway."*

Hicks gave a short laugh. "Your staff are all gonna turn into mole-people."

"Light eats energy. Portable lights and night-vision goggles are cheaper and why the hell *am I telling you this?"* Jackson gave a long-suffering sigh. *"Just stop at the dead cams and, you know, proceed with caution or whatever Marines do."*

"We brought a flood," someone said behind Hicks, speaking with a French-Canadian accent.

Hicks replied with a thumbs-up. He made a mental note to tell Jackson it was more important to save lives than candlepower. If he lived long enough.

When they heard the plodding *thump-thump-thump* of the air-scrubber, Wu slowed the carrier down and brought it to a rolling stop. The sound was oddly dampened—never a good sign, especially with life-support tech.

Hicks twisted around in his seat and looked at the four Marines behind him. The husky guy directly behind him with the French-Canadian accent was Private Joe

Beauvais; beside him was Corporal Binsa Gharti, a dark-skinned, muscled woman who had cheerfully informed him that Binsa meant "fearless" in Nepali. Hicks didn't tell her that wasn't always a good thing.

The two in the rear-facing seat were Private Sundown Brice, a tall, wiry guy, and Corporal Zeta Costello, a red-haired non-binary with facial tattoos Hicks recognized as tribal, although the motifs were unfamiliar.

"Okay, listen up," Hicks said and they all put on their best paying-attention expressions; it didn't reassure him. "*Really listen.* This isn't like anything you've faced before. *Don't* be Rosetti's best jarheads, be *here* and do *exactly* as I say."

He paused. So far they were with him, but they hadn't heard the good part yet. Or was it the punchline?

"We *don't* do this by the book. We *don't* pair off," he went on, watching their faces closely, looking for some hint that might tell him who was most likely to follow orders, who would revert to training, and who would freak out and die first. "We stay together and keep the group tight. Beauvais, keep the flood handy. Gharti, you're up front with me—you keep that flamethrower primed and ready. If it moves, torch it.

"The same for rest of you—if it moves, you *kill* it," he continued. "Don't think, don't wonder, just *kill*. You gotta get these fuckers before they get close. You know their blood's acid, you know they don't show up on infrared, and you know you *don't* let them take you alive. You don't let them take *anyone* alive—that's an order. If somebody needs help with that, you help them—me included. Got it?"

They nodded, their smooth, untried faces solemn.

"We're ready," Gharti said.

The hell they were, Hicks thought unhappily. No one ever was, not for this.

"All right," he said. "Move out."

They climbed out of the carrier and clustered up quickly. For all their inexperience they did well at moving together and keeping the group tight. Best-trained had to count for something; with any luck, it would keep them alive.

Hicks picked up the pace a little as they approached the next bend in the tunnel and he was glad to see they kept their weapons up without his having to remind them. Gharti held her flashlight in her free hand, sweeping the beam back and forth ahead of them. The thump of the air-scrubber grew louder but it still had a muffled quality.

"You're almost there, Hicks," Jackson's voice said. *"Right around the next corner."*

"Affirmative." Hicks spoke just above a whisper. "You getting anything from our body cams?"

"Too dark."

"Well, you're the one who can't spare the candlepower."

"I got an idea," Beauvais said suddenly. "We could move our cams nearer the torches—"

"No," Hicks said sharply. "Nobody lowers their weapon to mess with their cam. Got it?" There was a soft chorus

of affirmatives as they rounded the next bend and then came to a stop.

Even in the lousy light, they could all see it. *Should've tried to warn them*, Hicks thought.

"*What. The fuck. Is that.*" Gharti's tone suggested he'd better not bullshit her.

Hicks let out a long breath as his gaze traveled over the alien resin covering the walls and the upper part of the air-scrubber. The textures were uneven, some of them smooth, some rough with ribs and craters casting strange shadows.

"It's how they make themselves at home," he replied.

"Yeah?" Costello gave a nervous laugh. "I hate what they've done with the place."

"Should we try and blast some of that shit away?" Brice aimed his torch at a giant lump at the top of the scrubber.

"Not yet," Hicks told him. "Everybody hold your positions."

"Wouldn't take but a couple seconds," Brice said reasonably.

Hicks winced. Brice was one of *those*—he'd been helpful once and now he couldn't stop. "*Listen up*," Hicks said in a low, dangerous voice. "On three, we move forward slow and easy, and we keep the group tight. *Nothing else till I tell you.* Got it?"

There was a whispered chorus of affirmatives. He gave them the count and they inched toward the air-scrubber.

A few seconds later, Wu said, "Corporal Hicks?"

Hicks gave the signal to stop. "What is it?"

"Three o'clock, there's some kind of thick black—I dunno, *gunk* or something all over the floor," Wu told him nervously.

"Nine o'clock, too," Costello piped up. "I'm not sure but it might be spreading."

"I've seen it before," Hicks said. "It's not acid but don't get any on you."

"Copy that," Costello said. "It looks like there're pieces of bone in it."

"You want me to take a sample?" Beauvais offered helpfully.

"No," Hicks said, almost snapping at him. "Wu, scan it. *Twice.*"

Activating the flexi on his forearm, Wu turned in two complete circles, going a bit more slowly the second time. "No movement, Corporal."

"Nothing?" Hicks felt his heart beat faster. "You sure?"

"Not a twitch. Just air currents from the vents."

A cold spot started to form in the pit of Hicks's stomach. "Beauvais, gimme the flood."

Beauvais did so and he thumbed it on. The sudden brightness was momentarily blinding. *Talk about candlepower*, Hicks thought, eyes watering. He could feel the warmth of the beam as he swept it over the sludge before turning it on the air-scrubber. The mother-of-pearl sheen was especially pronounced.

Beauvais cleared his throat. "You sure you don't want me to take a sample of—"

"*No.*" The cold spot in Hicks's stomach had become a hard icy lump. "Everybody *hold your positions*—that's an order," he growled. "Don't *move*, don't *shoot*, don't nobody touch *nothing*—"

Like that, he was back in the LV-426 terraforming facility, in the area under the primary heat exchangers where all the colonists had gathered for some reason (… *a damned town meeting*). The stuff they'd found there had been lighter in color and the way it had covered everything had made Hicks think briefly of Pompeii. Except in Pompeii, the dead hadn't had chest cavities torn open from the inside.

And then they'd found someone still alive.

Dietrich had tried to reassure the woman but she'd just kept saying, *Kill me*, over and over until it was too late and the creature inside had burst out of her. Someone blasted it with a flamethrower, but by then it was too late for all of them. Amid the heat of the flames, the sickening stink of burning flesh, and the strange chemical smell of burning alien resin, Hicks had heard the sound of a multitude of aliens unfolding their limbs, coming out of hiding—

"Movement!" Wu was yelling. "Everywhere! They're *everywhere*—"

In the flood's harsh light, the walls had come alive with squirming aliens emerging from craters and shadows in the resin, their eyeless, elongated heads turned to the light as they crawled along uneven surfaces toward the top of the air-scrubber. They were hissing now, baring their steely teeth, extending the second inner set and snapping at the air.

Hicks couldn't move, couldn't speak, could only stand and watch as two creatures, one on either side at the top of the scrubber, moved toward the center, where resin had flowed down from the ceiling and hardened into an enormous, misshapen bulge like a tumor.

Should've known, Hicks thought as the aliens slashed at the bulge, tearing it away to reveal the creature within.

"And what the fuck is *that*?" Costello demanded.

"It's a queen," Hicks replied. "You can tell by the size." His voice sounded absurdly calm, almost like Bishop's. Discovering he could move again, he reached blindly for the nearest Marine and came nose-to-nose with Wu.

Hicks shoved the floodlight into his hands, told him to keep it on the queen, and knelt to open the bag with the mortar, only to find it still in pieces. It should have been assembled already. Someone had screwed up, but he wasn't going to bother kicking their ass. The aliens would do that.

He tried to work quickly, looking back and forth from what he was doing to the creature in the bright circle of light. The mortar was a different model than the ones he'd used, and if it was supposed to be an upgrade someone had screwed up there, too, because it seemed to have too many parts, all of them in weird shapes.

The queen was a different model, too, with a grotesquely

small head; perhaps the resin around it had restricted its growth. The rest of the creature was queen-sized, positioned with arms and legs splayed wide. Its most disturbing new feature, however, was the swollen abdomen in the center of its body, like an immense blister ready to burst.

"Hey, Gharti!" Hicks yelled. She stood transfixed, gripping her flamethrower. "Got a light?"

Gharti sent a stream of fire toward the queen. It fell short by a few meters but hit some lesser targets. The aliens screamed in fury. Hicks saw Gharti cringe as she shuffled forward a few steps and gave them another blast, this time panning the stream of fire in a wide arc from left to right. More aliens burst into flames and the poison-chemical stench of burning alien flesh and resin filled the air.

She glanced at him as she moved closer to the scrubber and its grotesque ornament and raised the flamethrower nozzle. This time, it produced a large fireball that lasted all of a second before it vanished, followed by nothing.

Hicks pushed the last component into the mortar; it jammed halfway.

Shit, said a calm little voice in his brain.

Two aliens clinging to the front of the air-scrubber turned their ugly, eyeless heads toward Gharti and leaped. She screamed and the Marines scattered in all directions.

"Fire, dammit! *Fire!*" Hicks yelled. "*Kill* the motherfuckers! Wu, where's the light? *I need the light!*"

Gharti's screams stopped as the aliens finished her off

and threw her body aside. Wu fired on them and Hicks heard the roaring hiss of acid burning through metal and cement, body armor and flesh. The godawful stench intensified and Hicks saw a hole open up on the deck barely half a meter from the toe of his boot just as the last mortar component unjammed and slid into place.

"Wu, the light—the fucking *light*!" Hicks shouted.

The mutant queen bared its teeth, hissing loudly, and then, impossibly, its swollen belly began to float away from the rest of its body. Because it wasn't a belly, Hicks realized. It was the bulbous tip of a very long, nasty tail. His stomach rose threateningly toward his throat as the queen's tail undulated in a slow, sinuous air-dance.

Keep your eye on the ball, said that calm little voice in Hicks's mind as he grabbed the mortar shell. There was an ugly wet ripping noise. *Too late*, the voice added as the fat tip of the queen's tail popped like a bubble, releasing an enormous black cloud.

"Bishop! Shut down the fans!" Hicks shouted.

"*Got it*," Bishop replied, unruffled.

No, he didn't, Hicks thought as the black mist disappeared into the fans a fraction of a second before they shut down.

Too late, as usual, the voice in his head said.

"The vents!" Hicks bellowed. "Seal the vents!" He dropped the mortar shell into the tube and turned away from it.

"*Done*," Bishop replied. "*You had better*—" The explosion

drowned out the rest, shook the floor, and sent rubble and acid flying in all directions.

Should've run, the voice in Hicks's brain chided. *Too late* again.

He raised his head slowly. Most of the scrubber had been demolished, including the queen. The poison-chemical stink became even stronger, making his eyes sting and his throat burn. For a fraction of a second he imagined breathing an aerosol of acid-blood from vaporized aliens, then shut it down. It wasn't time to imagine shit, it was time to bug the fuck out.

He turned to tell Wu they were leaving but the Marine was down on the deck, his body shaking wildly, arms flailing, legs kicking. Hicks backed up a step, lifted his rifle, and blew Wu's head off, then looked around for the rest of the squad.

Costello was face-down in the sludge, body twitching; Beauvais and Brice had been torn apart. His squad had been wiped out. Again.

Too late, said the voice in his head. *You're* always *too late*.

Hicks used his pulse-rifle on all of them anyway.

2 9

Perhaps checking Rodina Station's hub for survivors hadn't been such a good idea, Luc Hai thought.

In the conference rooms off the main hallway she found only bloodstains and damage from the creatures' claws and acid-blood. Oddly, the door to the meeting room across from Suslov's private office was completely unmarred; even its OCCUPIED sign was still in place. The prospect of finding someone else alive made her heart beat faster.

Then she opened the door to find that acid had eaten an enormous hole through the center of the floor, leaving a jagged perimeter barely two feet wide. She wondered how many decks the alien acid-blood had burned through before it petered out, but she didn't move in for a closer look. What remained of the floor might not hold her weight.

And yet she couldn't make herself step back and close the door, either. Probably shock—it nibbled at the edges of her mind, trying to get in, but she'd managed to keep it at bay. Shock wasn't a luxury she could afford right now. Collapsing and letting the trauma head-bugs run wild had to wait till later. Whenever that was.

It took a little time but she finally got herself moving again. As she closed the door and turned away, her gaze fell on the gold-colored nameplate across the hall.

Colonel-Doctor Timur Suslov

Luc Hai had thought the Gothic lettering was a silly affectation that showed Suslov wasn't as committed to Progressive principles as he claimed. She still thought so—not that it mattered anymore.

Her gaze moved to the framed prints on the walls. They were a fairly recent addition; someone had convinced Suslov that Rodina Station needed more in the way of visual interest. Nothing frivolous or silly like capitalists, things that would elevate the spirit and remind the Progressive Peoples they were part of a long, gloriously high-minded tradition conceived before humans had gone into space.

Luc Hai found the artwork bewildering—most of the prints were stylized images of groups, seemingly all men, brandishing tools like weapons, some with captions in Russian, others in Spanish. The more recent pieces showed oddly designed robot-like machines, while in others, people wore machines like clothes, in configurations so bizarre she couldn't imagine what they were for. The blood and tissue splattered on them didn't help.

There was more blood splashed on the walls, along with blobs of black sludge that stuck to whatever it landed on, then dried to become as hard as stone. Luc Hai avoided touching it, even with gloves.

Now she headed toward the partly open door to the control room, careful not to make a sound. The hub was supposed to run itself in the event that all the humans were incapacitated. She hoped she'd be able to see which systems were still functioning in good order, which ones were faltering, and which had quit. In particular, she wanted to know how much longer life-support would hold up. So far it was still online but there was a funny smell in the air, something like melting rubber mixed with burned-out electronics, and it was getting stronger.

She passed a print showing Karl Marx and Vladimir Lenin as giants with their arms around each other's shoulders, looking benignly down at a multitude of noble workers marching nobly off to their noble jobs; all men, not a woman among them. Well, Stalin *had* wiped out ten million of his own people, and as a man of his time he'd probably gone by that old rule-of-thumb: women and children first.

Luc Hai shook the thought away. In school, she'd never distinguished herself in the study of history, Russian or otherwise. But here she was with Rodina Station falling apart around her and a life expectancy that might be hours at best, and what was she thinking about? Fucking *Stalin*.

The rustling sound of many legs came to her suddenly

and she froze, not even breathing. Face-huggers; the noise was unmistakable. They were approaching from the corridor that crossed her own, three meters ahead. Both passageways were the same size, making it less likely the little bastards would change course, although she couldn't depend on that.

If they spotted her, they'd go right for her and she'd never shake them. They'd chase her until one of them got her, or she managed to kill all of them. Like the other forms, face-huggers didn't seem to know they could be killed, or even injured. It should have been a weakness. Instead, it made them relentless.

The rustling grew louder. Once they hatched, face-huggers didn't live nearly as long as fully mature aliens, nor were their senses as keen. She flattened herself against the wall, holding the butt of the rifle in front of her face and kept completely still, not even breathing. After an extremely long moment, three face-huggers raced by on skeletal-finger legs, tails whipping the air behind them.

We're late, we're late… for a very important date…

Luc Hai had to bite her lips together to keep from laughing. She gave it a count of ten and then dashed across the intersection, looking straight ahead at the control center. It was safer not to look in their direction, not even a quick glance to see how far away they were; they seemed to feel it.

At least there were no more junctions. When she got to the control center, she could lock herself in and have a breakdown of epic proportions, cry until her eyes ran down her cheeks along with her tears. All she had to do was get there.

The walls just outside the hub were clean, untouched by blood, black sludge, or acid, but the last print on the left was missing. The empty space gaped. Why anyone fleeing a painful and ghastly death would feel an overwhelming need for a souvenir from Socialism's halcyon days was beyond her. Maybe just art for art's sake, she thought as she pushed the door all the way open and stepped inside.

When her mind started working again she found herself sitting on the floor, and immediately got to her feet.

Just as she'd expected, the control room was abandoned. *Long* abandoned—she could tell she was the first human to set foot in the place since the crew had bailed, and she would certainly be the last. But she had to give up on the idea of restoring the comms or checking on life-support or anything else. All of the equipment was completely inaccessible, buried under a thick layer of hardened black alien crap.

Having a hysterical crying fit was out, too. All around her, the walls were covered with people in cocoons, people of all colors, all sizes—adults, adolescents, children. Some were intact, still gestating, while others had served their purpose, the ruins of their bodies crusted with blood dried black, or still wet and shiny. When the aliens had run out of wall space, they had simply covered the old cocoons with newer ones.

Luc Hai had no idea how long she had been sitting on the floor gaping at the grotesque gallery before her head cleared. Now she found herself wondering why the aliens had put cocoons on top of others when there was still plenty of space all over Rodina.

The answer came to her unbidden: art for art's sake.

She started toward a door on the other side of the room, then caught herself and decided to go back the way she had come in. There was no telling what the other door led to—maybe a hallway where cocoons hung between more framed prints celebrating the noble ideals of the noble past, when everyone thought the future would be even more noble, not full of cocoons. Art for art's—

Screw caution, she thought and fled.

Jackson was now pacing between various consoles, checking the monitors and muttering curses under her breath. It would have driven Rosetti crazy, except he understood how she felt. There had been no word from Hicks since his frantic call about the vents.

As if she had caught the drift of Rosetti's thoughts, she tried to contact the squad again, then Walker, and then anyone else, with no success.

"Whatever happened at the air-scrubber must've screwed up the comms for the whole area," Jackson said. She plumped down on a well-worn office chair on wheels.

"Then we'll just have to wait till they make contact."

Rosetti glanced at the two Marines he'd called in on guard duty security before comms had gone down. "I'm not sending anyone else out until we have some idea of what's going on."

Jackson made a pained face. "I wish you wouldn't say things I agree with. It makes me nervous."

Likewise, Rosetti said silently, turning away to take another painkiller. As he turned back, he caught sight of Bishop, who met his gaze with his usual android inscrutability. On impulse, he asked, "What do *you* think?"

"We could try sending a drone—" Bishop started.

Jackson made a frustrated noise. "Goddammit, I just said the comms are *screwed up*. There's no reliable—" The console chimed suddenly. "Hey, Rodina's got company."

The larger screen now displayed the UPP headquarters as seen from one of several spy micro-satellites; Rosetti couldn't remember if it was military or one of the Company private eyes he wasn't supposed to know about. The vessel approaching the space station was about a mile long and bristling with armaments; it was also the last thing Rosetti wanted to see.

"Jesus," Jackson said. "That doesn't look like a rescue ship."

"It isn't," Rosetti replied, as the spacecraft went into a very wide orbit around Rodina. "It's the *Nikolai Stoiko*, and it's early."

* * *

Luc Hai covered two large toolboxes with flight jackets, strapped them into the front seat of the flimsy electronic jeep, and set it to run driverless around the far end of the maintenance deck. It wouldn't fool the alien chasing her for more than a few seconds, but with any luck she could put a lot more distance between herself and it—

"With any luck"? Not anymore—her nickname had worn out. Maybe she should have gone with, "Hey, look," after all.

The alien gave another long, inhuman scream. It was very close now. She sprinted into the storeroom, locked the door, and piled several crates in front of it before climbing the corner shelf unit to a loose panel in the ceiling. Only a few people knew about this particular crawlspace; the configuration of airducts, pipes, and metal framework blocked locator signals, making it a good place for unscheduled downtime. It was one of half a dozen dead spots scattered around the station, and those who knew about them were careful not to use them too often, so the authorities wouldn't find out and fix them.

Unfortunately, aliens weren't as easy to fool.

But they *could* be distracted, which slowed them down, albeit only briefly. The jeep decoy wouldn't draw its attention for more than a few seconds but that might give her just enough time for what she needed to do. Because time was relative; Einstein had said so. Spending an hour with a lover could feel like a few seconds, while a few seconds of being torn apart by an alien would seem like forever. That was the theory of relativity, she thought, crawling through the dark space above the ceiling, and it explained how everything else she had ever done was just *gone* and running from a monster was now her whole life.

She heard the distant sound of a crash followed by another raw, enraged scream. That would be the alien discovering the jeep was a ruse. It would hit the storeroom next. The creature seemed to have no trouble homing in on her. Maybe her being the only human left on Rodina made it easy to pick up her spoor.

Luc Hai hadn't seen another living human for hours. Or had it been years since that encounter? The woman had been convulsing on the floor, writhing as blood poured from her eyes and mouth. Then the skin on her hands had split open with an awful ripping sound. When the talons emerged, the woman had begged Luc Hai to kill her.

She had made it as quick as possible. Red blood merged with acid-blood and vanished while holes appeared in the floor around the body and widened. Luc Hai had burst into tears.

Right after that, the alien had found her. Maybe, as in that old song, it could follow the tracks of her tears, even though she wasn't crying anymore. Or she hadn't thought she was, except every time she touched her face, it was wet. Like now.

Irritated, she wiped her cheeks roughly on her sleeves. This wasn't like her, she'd never been the weepy type. She tightened the strap on the rifle and slung it crosswise on her back so it wouldn't slide when she moved, and shone her flashlight around the dark crawl space.

Up ahead, something glinted in the darkness—a narrow metal ladder in a maintenance conduit. Luc Hai dropped her torch down the front of her shirt and crawled toward it as fast as she could, reaching the ladder just as she heard the alien break into the storeroom, hissing and screaming. The sounds followed her up the ladder. They always followed her.

At least she was getting closer to the departure deck. If the flight crew on duty had maintained their schedule before Rodina had gone to hell, she'd find an interceptor fueled-up and ready to go. Of course, there was a chance she'd find a welcoming committee of aliens had already trashed it, but she'd have to burn that bridge when she came to it.

Below her, she heard the scuttle of large claws, then another ear-splitting scream. Looking down, she saw the creature snapping its extra set of teeth at her in furious frustration. The conduit was too small, it couldn't follow her. The ladder vibrated in her grip as the monster slammed itself against it, but the metal didn't budge, didn't bend or buckle… yet. Luc Hai climbed faster.

The creature screamed up at her again, and for the first time she thought she detected the faint echo of a human voice. What if this one had been someone she had known personally—someone who she'd shared meals with, worked with, talked with, laughed with? A friend, now transformed into a monster, all for the greater glory of that preening fool Suslov.

The alien screamed once more and scrabbled back into the crawlspace, retracing its previous route. Not because it had given up, she knew, but to look for some other way to get at her. She kept climbing, going up another two levels before stopping at another crawlspace. No pillows here, just boards to floor it over for work crews doing maintenance. The boards weren't nailed or glued, but they were sized to fit snugly. It took almost half a minute to find one loose enough to pry up.

She kicked out the ceiling panel and poked her head through for a look. Oh, yeah, this was the right place. As she slipped through the opening, she felt her throat tighten. Oh, great—she'd turned into one of those fragile types who cried when they were *happy*.

Grow up, Luc Hai told herself. She eased herself down, dangled briefly by her hands, and dropped onto a small table directly below. It tipped over and she automatically tucked and rolled, bouncing to her feet right at the door. She opened it a crack.

The departure deck was empty. There was no welcoming committee and nothing had been trashed. The interceptor was untouched, undamaged, fully prepped and good to go. Pretending there weren't tears running down her face, she ran for it.

Right on cue, she heard inhuman screams just outside the deck, already too close.

Ignoring the aches in her strained leg muscles, Luc Hai flung herself at the boarding ladder, tumbled through the airlock into the cabin, and hit the emergency lockdown button. The outer hatch slammed shut half a second before something big smashed against it, screaming with fury.

Was that "her" alien or a different one? She couldn't tell. Didn't matter; she wouldn't mind if she never heard that sound again for the rest of her life. Except, of course, in her nightmares.

But if she didn't move her ass and get the fuck out of here, she wouldn't live long enough to have *one* nightmare.

The moment she was in the pilot's seat, training kicked in and put her in flight mode. She reached under the control board, found the handle every pilot had been told never to touch, and yanked it hard. There was a jarring *thump* she felt more than heard as the departure deck began the Exigent Launch procedure, which could not be paused or canceled.

Bright red lights flashed and sirens blared, warning anyone still on the deck that they had five seconds to be elsewhere before the bay doors opened. It was more like three seconds, Luc Hai noted, watching through the forward viewport as the sliver of starry space appeared and grew wider. Under the sirens, she heard claws skittering the length of the craft, and waited to see one or more of the monsters sucked out into the vacuum ahead of her, along with everything that hadn't been nailed to the deck.

Nothing happened. *What the fuck?* she wondered as fragments of an electronic jeep tumbled past. *What the fucking f—*

And all at once it *was* there in front of her, the hideous, eyeless face grinning viciously at her on the other side of the viewport. Its second set of teeth shot out and slammed against the vacuum-proof glass, making Luc Hai jump. For one terrible moment, she was afraid cracks would appear and spread outward from the point of impact, but the viewport wasn't even scratched. She decided not to find out if the glass would stand up to another hit and checked the launch status.

The bay doors were about halfway open. If her aim was true, that was wide enough; if not, all her troubles were over. She yanked the cover off the turbo control, set it to maximum, and hit launch.

The sudden acceleration threw her back against the pilot's seat, hard enough to knock the wind out of her. The alien clawed frantically at the viewport as it started to slide away. Luc Hai closed her eyes and braced herself, hoping that if she scraped the side of the interceptor on one of the bay doors, it wouldn't damage the hull so badly that it buckled before she found safety.

For a few seconds, she heard claws dragging along the length of the interceptor, and then nothing—no scrabbling, no skittering, nothing at all. Limp with relief, she let her eyes close.

Good-bye, you demon bastards.

* * *

Minutes later, the g-force started to ease up and Luc Hai opened her eyes. There was nothing to see through the viewport except tiny dots of light against black nothing. She was trembling again but she didn't care. Shifting position to strap herself in properly, she caught sight of a reading on the control panel. The proximity detector said she had missed the door on the right by centimeters. If she'd done that in training, her instructor would have made her clean grease traps for a week.

The interceptor's trajectory was changing to a wide curve as the autopilot prepared to slingshot around Rodina when Luc Hai saw another spacecraft in orbit around the space station. She had just enough time to register the name *Nikolai Stoiko* before there was a bright flash from one of its cannons and something streaked through the black, straight to Rodina.

The universe became a blinding white blank.

3 0

"Son of a *bitch*!" Jackson shouted as they all gaped at the screen. "They *nuked* them! They fucking *nuked* them!"

Rosetti spotted the tiny black shape of an interceptor tumbling away from the enormous white star that had been Rodina Station, out of control but still in one piece as it disappeared. While Jackson and everyone else was focused on the screen, he helped himself to another pill. These were supposed to be the longer-lasting dosage but he was burning through them in half the usual time thanks to elevated adrenaline. Well, that and the uppers in the timed-release patches under his shirt, but he needed those to counter drowsiness from the painkillers.

"I don't believe it! I don't *believe* it!" Jackson was saying. Her voice had gone up half an octave and the beam of her light-pen was sweeping around the room like a hysterical searchlight. "They called for help, and their own people *nuked* them—*their own people!*"

"I suspect Rodina told them to," Bishop said.

Rosetti had been thinking the same thing himself, but the civilians looked horrified by the idea.

"Oh, yeah?" Jackson turned to him looking ready to panic. "What if we're next? What if they nuke us, too?"

"They won't," Bishop told her. "They're leaving." He gestured toward the screen, where the ship was already leaving orbit around the white star that had been Rodina Station. Even on the screen it was still almost too bright to look at.

"Poor bastards," Rosetti muttered.

"No shit." Jackson's voice took on a bitter quality. "And to add insult to injury, they violated the fucking arms treaty with that nuke."

Rosetti resisted the urge to explain that the moment Weapons Division had gotten hold of the alien cells, the treaty had become the punchline to a very unfunny joke. At a time like this, civilians didn't need the truth, they needed something to do.

"Send the *Kansas City* another mayday," he told Jackson. "Unencrypted."

"*Unencrypted?*" Jackson said. "What the fuck *for?*"

"In case nobody heard us the first time. Just *do* it," he added as she started to answer.

Jackson wasn't deterred. "And what if the *Nikolai Stoiko* intercepts it?" she said. "They might come back and 'rescue' us, too."

Rosetti shook his head. "The UPP would never waste ammo on us."

Jackson hadn't noticed the interceptor, and Rosetti decided not to mention it. The spacecraft would still be intact—interceptors were sturdy—but exposure to that much radiation was a death sentence for anyone in it. They might not last long enough to reach Anchorpoint, and even if they did, the interceptor wasn't big enough for everyone just in this room.

"Send the mayday," he told Jackson. "That's an order."

Rosetti could practically see her mind working while she decided whether to continue arguing with him. Then she turned back to the console.

Now that the mall was empty, Walker couldn't help thinking how banal the place was—not just merely banal, but really most sincerely banal.

He drifted past a jewelry shop. The window display was undisturbed, but inside he could see at least one case had been tipped over and smashed, leaving shiny bits scattered all over the floor.

"The high cost of banal living," Walker said aloud, then frowned. He *really* wasn't himself today.

As an engineer, he'd always thought in terms of applied knowledge—if it wasn't useful, it wasn't knowledge, it was clutter. His job was figuring out what to do and how to do it, not wondering what it meant. Engineering wasn't fuzzy or vague, it had clearly defined parameters.

Some things were possible, some were not possible, or, in some cases, not possible yet, all based on matters of *fact*, not opinions or feelings. Or, worse, politics.

One very significant fact Walker had learned in the past twenty-four hours was that some kind of weird alien infection had turned a lab tech into a monster hellbent on killing anyone it met.

Fact number two: no one seemed to know exactly how it spread.

Fact number three: no one knew what to do about it, because they hadn't defined the problem clearly enough, despite their witnessing the results of infection.

And that brought him to fact number four, which would determine the outcome: no help could reach them quickly—unless what had happened to Rodina Station qualified as "help."

Walker had managed to pick up a spy-drone feed on his flexi, just long enough to see a warship obliterate Rodina Station. The video had been grainy but no less horrific; he could only imagine how the bunch in Ops had reacted to it on a larger screen in true-def. Even Rosetti must have blanched, and Jackson was probably still going bugfuck. But then, she'd been halfway there already, ever since he and Hicks returned from the construction area.

He hadn't liked seeing Jackson like that, which was partly why he hadn't checked in with Ops after saying he would. Even if he'd wanted to, though, comms were spotty all over Anchorpoint. Old-school radio would work, but only over short distances; Ops was well out of range. Video was also down just about everywhere. But that wasn't the worst of it.

According to the last status update on his flexi, one of the air-scrubbers was completely offline after "catastrophic damage," although the update hadn't specified what that was.

And it didn't matter anyway because the clock was ticking. The other scrubbers could carry the extra load for only so long before they broke down. Lack of oxygen would make everyone too stupid to realize anything was wrong until they started passing out, and by then they'd also be too stupid to care. Would that be fact number five, or fact four-point-one? He would decide later, if he was still around.

Still, this rather grim outlook hadn't kept him from using his time constructively. His first stop after leaving Ops had been the Large Machine Workshop. The place was deserted but there were plenty of heavy-loaders recently overhauled and in good working order.

Walker had tweaked their programming, given them new assignments, and paired each one to a remote control before turning them loose. He'd logged a lot of hours working on heavy-loaders, making them stronger and more durable, improving their joints for better range of motion. As far as he was concerned, there was no such thing as too many heavy-loaders. Although he was pretty tired of all the remotes hanging around his neck clacking against the pulse grenades stashed in his vest. No help for it; he'd run out of pockets.

And speaking of a place for everything, he was standing in front of a bar.

It wasn't the first one he'd seen since leaving Ops, but now his energy was starting to flag. After a day like this, he could use a drink or six and, as everyone knew, it was always Happy Hour somewhere in the universe.

He recognized the football game running silently on the back wall—Brazil vs. Haiti in the playoffs, whatever year that had been. It seemed like every sports bar at Anchorpoint ran that one on infinite repeat, but nobody ever seemed to give a shit. Now there was nobody but him, and under the circumstances, he didn't give a shit, either.

Turning away from the soundlessly cheering crowds, he put his rifle on the bar and went behind it to survey the available stock. The remotes hanging around his neck dangled heavily as he bent over to open a refrigerated case. Annoyed, he was about to take them off when he spotted a two-liter jug marked *Margarita Mix*.

"Gotcha!" Grinning broadly, he set it on the bar and found an unopened bottle of his favorite premium tequila sitting on a shelf in front of the mirror. He poured it into the jug, shook it vigorously, then sampled the results. Damned good for an amateur mixologist, he thought, and raised the jug to toast his reflection. Drink enough of this, and he might watch the whole game and see who won before he passed out.

The level in the jug was four centimeters lower by the time he wandered over to the pool tables. One of them had the standard green felt; the other was bright tangerine.

"What the *fuck*," he said, revolted, and had another long pull from the jug to reinforce his amiable buzz. Pool tables were supposed to be *green*. Only a sick son of a bitch would think of making one *bright ora—*

Behind him, something shattered on the floor.

Walker stared at the perverted tangerine felt, hoping it was just a clumsy new customer, but even after this much tequila he knew better. Then he heard the crunch of broken glass and a long, obscenely wet *hiss* as he turned to see the thing blocking the entrance. Light from the soccer game glinted off its hard black skin as it turned its eyeless, misshapen head from him to his pulse-rifle on the bar and back again. The steely jaws parted to let the second set of teeth emerge, dripping with thick saliva.

"So who did *you* used to be?" Walker asked, sidling a few steps toward the bar. The alien shifted with him, snapping those extra teeth at the air. All right, so the creature *wasn't* as dumb as a box of hammers. He drew himself up, one hand on the corner of the tangerine pool table.

"My sainted mother, God rest her sweet soul, always said, 'Have a Plan B,'" he informed the alien, looking down at the remotes hanging around his neck. The one he wanted was right on top of the others. What a beautiful pain in the ass, he thought, holding it up.

"Here's looking at *you*, motherfucker," he chuckled and thumbed the largest button.

The power-loader crashed through the bar's flimsy, painted facade, shattering the windows and the ersatz neon signs and making the floor shake as it stomped toward the alien. The creature lunged at it with an enraged scream. Walker didn't have to look at the control to make the loader grab the alien and slam it to the floor, which shook again under the impact.

Still screaming, the alien lashed its long tail around, clawing at the loader, leaving long scratches in the metal. Walker made the machine keep one heavy square foot on the thing's lower body while it took hold of its neck and pulled.

He beamed with tequila-enhanced pleasure as the alien's screams cut off. "As my sainted mother also used to say: *Fuck. You.*"

The loud hiss of acid-blood eating through the carpeting and the floor filled the air. Jesus, that stuff really *was* murder, Walker thought, watching the loader's foot melt away into the dead alien's guts. Holes appeared everywhere the acid-blood had splashed on the metal body, and grew larger with unsettling swiftness. Seconds later, the machine broke into pieces, and a sharp poison-chemical stench filled the air, growing stronger and more unpleasant by the moment.

Walker decided the atmosphere in the bar had definitely gone to hell; it was time to drink up and get the hell out. He would radio Ops as soon as he was in range and tell them all about the new use he'd found for heavy-loaders.

As he turned away and raised the jug for another hearty pull, his arm gave a sudden violent jerk. The jug flew out of his grip and landed on the tangerine pool table, spilling the best margaritas he'd ever had all over that obscene felt.

He tried to reach for the jug and couldn't; the muscles in his arm were *squirming*, like he had a bunch of snakes under his skin, trying get out. Walker opened his mouth to scream, and instead heard himself whoop loudly, trying to take a breath.

The pain hit like an electric shock and refused to let go. His mouth opened wider and wider until he felt his jawbone dislocating but he couldn't make it stop, couldn't stop shaking, twisting, jerking. On the back wall, the soccer fans were going crazy, screaming, hugging each other, delirious with joy as if they'd witnessed a miracle before they suddenly slid out of sight. Walker barely felt the impact when he hit the floor, tried to reach for a chair to pull himself up but his arm was flailing crazily, almost as if he were waving back at the ecstatic crowd.

Abruptly, he felt himself stiffen and another bolt of pain hit him as the skin on his hands split open, revealing something black and shiny with blood underneath.

And to quote my sainted mother's last *words*, Walker thought, *fuck* me.

* * *

It was dusk in pocket-Madagascar when Spence finally pulled herself together enough to think about feeding the lemurs.

No one else had come in while she'd been there, which was highly unusual. Anchorpoint's eco-pockets were as popular as the malls. They relieved the homesickness for planetary life, which was an inevitable part of living in space. Sooner or later, even the nerdiest lab rats got a yen to go outside and play, and virtual reality was no substitute. Of all the pockets on Anchorpoint, pocket-Madagascar was the perennial favorite. It had to be the lemurs, Spence thought, although she knew she was biased. Tully had made them for her.

She went to the food storage area, feeling guilty. Not that the little primates would be starving—they foraged for flowers, leaves, tree bark, and sap. The largest part of their diet, however, was fruit, which had to be supplemented from the hydroponic gardens. There wasn't enough room here for cultivation.

Normally the caretakers would have already put out a few baskets for the troops (it amused her no end that a group of lemurs was called a troop), but none of them had come in today, either. That was even more disturbing—they'd never have just abandoned the little primates.

The storage bins in the largest shed were still close to full. She filled two wire baskets, then left the bins closed but not locked and the shed door open so the lemurs could feed themselves, just in case. But if no one came back before the bins were empty—

Spence shut down that line of thought before she fell apart again, telling herself to get functional *now*. Feeding the lemurs would help, and it was the right thing to do, better than just hiding in here from aliens that took over people's bodies, or wrapped them up in cocoons—

No. She wasn't thinking about *that*, either; she was feeding the troops.

Carrying a basket of fruit in either hand, Spence marched across the meadow in the last light of the pocket-sunset. The forest was already dark, but she had been there many times at night. She paused to take the flashlight from her pocket and turn it on, angled the head at ninety degrees, then stuck it in her waistband. Not because she was nervous, but to avoid tripping over a root or a stone, she told herself as she kept going, albeit more slowly, making a *tk-tk-tk* noise to tell the lemurs she'd brought food.

She stopped again beside a large tree, listening for sounds of movement, but there was nothing—no branches creaking or leaves rustling, not even insect noises.

Maybe the wildlife could sense something was wrong out there in Peopleville. Placing one basket at the foot of the tree, she made the *tk-tk-tk* noise again. Still silence. These lemurs had been tweaked to be less nocturnal than their Earth cousins, but they didn't go to sleep this early.

The woods should have been alive with the sounds of them chattering and calling to one another.

There was a cold, hard knot in her chest as she took the torch from her waistband and shone the beam around the trees, looking for a low branch where she could hang the other basket. The lemurs would have fun with that. They should have been having fun *now*. Maybe she'd spooked them.

Yeah, sure, that was it. Primates were sensitive to humans and they'd be especially sensitive to her because she came here so often. It would be completely normal for them to pick up on her emotions. Here in pocket-Madagascar, there was nothing but normal. Nothing like the thick black blob on that tree a few meters to her left.

Or the pearlescent black cocoon above it.

Or the one on the tree behind that, or any of the others she now saw all around her. All those lemur-sized cocoons made to leave those little lemur chests uncovered so as not to impede the lemur-sized aliens that would burst out of their bodies.

Maybe they'd come out with cute little rings on those vicious, snakelike tails—

Something gave a high-pitched shriek and dropped down on her, hissing furiously and trying to claw her face.

"*No!*" Spence wailed and batted the thing away, adrenaline giving her strength enough to hurl it several meters away into the underbrush. The creature popped up immediately, hissing louder. The grotesque, long head was covered with patches of gray and white fur, and the second set of teeth extending from its jaws were all fangs. It raised its furry arms, showing its talons and whipping its long tail around, shredding the flora to pieces as it prepared to leap.

"*No!*" she wailed again, hurled the basket of fruit at it, and ran for her life. The beam from her flashlight swept around crazily as she tore out of the forest and across the field of tall grass under the rising fake moon.

At the exit, she caught a glimpse of several long tails scything through the grass, a glint of steely teeth, and deformed, eyeless heads covered with fur, only seconds behind her. Then she slammed the door.

She cried as she used the credentials on her dog-tags to enable the permanent emergency lock, but not because she was afraid. This time her tears were for her own foolishness, for running away from Ops, for believing nothing could be worse than what had happened to Tully.

The creatures had rings on their tails.

3 1

Wu, we hardly knew ye. And that's my *fault.*

Hicks had a hard time keeping the carrier centered as he sped through the tunnels. Every time he took a corner, he sideswiped the wall. By the time he got back to Ops, he'd have left most of the paint job in the tunnels, like a trail of breadcrumbs. The scrape of metal was a real nerve-jangler, as well, but it didn't drown out Wu and Gharti and all the others in his head.

He had to get on top of that, bury it deep and beat himself up later. Right now he had to concentrate on all the red dots that were pulsing on the grid. What a primitive setup. When he'd said as much, Jackson had responded with a rant about economizing resources, and not everything needed life-quality audio-video.

He'd almost made a crack about the info dump, then realized it was her way of steadying herself so her head wouldn't explode. Plus, there was one good thing about blinking lights on a black grid: they just went out, *sans* the gory details you'd never be able to unsee.

Hicks heard less scraping as he whipped the six-wheeler around the next turn. Maybe he was starting to get the hang of this, he thought. Half a second later he found himself trying to drive through a barrage of brightly colored plastic crates. They rebounded off the jeep, flew into his face, bounced off his head. The six-wheeler made a valiant effort but finally stalled out with its nose in the air at a forty-five-degree angle, trapped in all the happy colors of the circus.

Cursing, Hicks grabbed his pulse-rifle and climbed out of the jeep, kicked away a yellow crate nearby, and looked back at the turn. Two large mirrors high on the wall were angled to show people approaching from either direction any oncoming traffic, but he'd been too preoccupied to see he was about to drive into a secret stash of crates.

And what a goddam enormous stash it was. Crates were stacked floor to ceiling and three deep, taking up almost half the floor space, leaving no room for even the smallest vehicles to pass each other.

He was about to try pushing the jeep free from the crates when he heard a chime and looked up to see a blinking amber light on the ceiling ahead of him. *Gotta love those blinking lights*, he thought as he ran toward it, *especially when they lead to a freight elevator.* The metal, jaw-style doors were open as if it had been waiting for him.

"Don't mind if I do," Hicks said, stepping inside. He yanked the strap dangling from the upper door and the doors came together with a bang, reminding him too much of jaws. He hit the top button on the control panel.

The top level turned out to be the mall; he stepped out of the elevator and found he was close to where he'd come in the first time. It seemed like a hundred years since he'd found Tully, Charles A. in an ersatz sports bar, getting loaded and trying to decide if a bioweapon was scarier than losing all his shares. Hicks doubted the poor guy had lived long enough to fully regret it.

The bar itself was also a casualty. The floor was cratered with ragged holes, with the worst damage in the middle; Hicks decided not to see whether it would hold his weight. Machine fragments were scattered all around—the remains of a heavy-loader, Hicks saw and smiled grimly. A heavy-loader would make a good weapon against an alien. Ripley had used a different model, but Anchorpoint didn't have any of those. Probably too expensive.

His smile vanished as he spotted several remote controls in the debris. Some were in pieces, some were only cracked; a couple he remembered seeing on Walker's workbench, where they *hadn't* been crusted with blood.

He turned to look at the bar, which, in spite of everything, was still standing. The undamaged pulse-rifle sitting on it was the one Rosetti had given Walker back in Ops. Over by the pool tables were other, worse things, chunks of flesh and bone along with more bloodstains and shreds of the overalls Walker had been wearing.

Forgot to warn him not to put his weapon down, Hicks

thought, *in case he had to use it on himself.* They shouldn't have let Walker go off alone in the first place.

And then again, it would have been worse if he'd gone bugfuck in Ops. A *lot* worse.

Skirting the most damaged part of the floor, he grabbed the pulse-rifle off the bar and, as he slung it over his shoulder, he saw the same Haiti vs. Brazil playoff game running on the back wall. They probably made the playoffs every year, and always would—this year and next year, and so forth and so on, world without end, amen.

He went back out into the mall, which probably hadn't been this quiet since the day before Anchorpoint had opened for business. It was strange but at least he didn't hear any sounds that might have been aliens moving around, only faint background music and the soft splashing of the artificial waterfall farther up the concourse. This would be humankind's great legacy: fake waterfalls, reruns of Brazil vs. Haiti in the playoffs, and music to shop by.

Just ahead of him on the left was a shop with no exterior damage that he could see. The intact front window was startlingly clean, with large, old-fashioned gilt letters:

Nostalgia!

And below it, in smaller type:

... where the past is alive.

This week's special had been the early twenty-first century. Instead of holo-projections, there were three actual mannequins on display. One was posed so it looked fascinated by a small, handheld device, another wore a pair of oversized black goggles and a T-shirt that read "VR + AR = U"; a mirror-ball threw off tiny flashes as it rotated slowly above the third figure, which was decked out in a silvery jacket with a ridiculous amount of shoulder padding, black patent-leather trousers, and a shirt proclaiming, in glittery silver letters, "DISCO SUCKS!!!" The mixed message was amusing and, if Hicks remembered rightly, about thirty years wide of the mark. Still, it must have been nice while it lasted.

Inside, the shop had been demolished. Everything— merchandise, display cases, shelves, clothing racks—had been reduced to utter wreckage. Half the lights were either out or flickering on and off, but without a sound—no humming, no buzzing, just flickering. This annoyed Hicks for no reason he could think of, and he went in with the intention of finding the control box and shutting it down. It would be somewhere at the rear of the store—

Then he saw them.

They were up high on the back wall near the ceiling: two adults and three kids, one of them a toddler, all unconscious in pearlescent black cocoons that left their chests uncovered—their *intact* chests.

Hicks hoped they really were unconscious as he raised the pulse-rifle Walker had never had a chance to use.

He took care of them with seven quick bursts and got out of there as fast as he could, flickering lights forgotten. Although he did pause for a brief last look at the front window display. If he hadn't been in the middle of an alien apocalypse, he'd have taken a photo and sent it to Newt.

As he moved on, he felt something like a faint trembling deep inside himself. *No*, he told himself firmly, he couldn't react now. Later he could lock himself in the john and shudder and shake with LV-426 flashbacks till his bones rattled like maracas. But not now.

Abruptly, he caught sight of a transit-point sign. The light above the double doors blinked yellow, announcing the imminent arrival of a car. Hicks went over and pressed the call button. Seconds later, the doors opened to reveal Spence clutching a commuter strap with both hands, standing in the middle of an abattoir; every centimeter of the walls, the floor, and the ceiling was painted with blood and things he tried not to look at.

As if on cue, one of those things he didn't want to see dropped from the ceiling and landed beside Spence's foot with a terrible wet *smack!*

"Spence," Hicks said softly. He reached for her, to pull her out of the car.

She blinked at him with no sign of recognition, and screamed.

3 2

Two more of Rosetti's best Marines, one nametagged Martinez, the other O'Brien, were on guard at Ops when Hicks returned. Neither challenged him as he walked in carrying Spence over his shoulder. Martinez helped him ease her down into a chair and performed a quick field-assessment of the dazed lab tech. Hicks wondered if Rosetti had told her or O'Brien what had happened to their buddies at the air-scrubber. Probably not, he thought; they didn't look nervous enough.

Jackson glanced over her shoulder at him from where she stood at the main console. "Revised ETA for the *Kansas City* is another seven and a half hours from now," she told him. "Plus or minus the usual fifteen minutes." Hicks supposed that was good news. He strode over to where Rosetti sat staring at something on his flexi.

"Reporting from the field, sir." He yanked the man's swivel chair around so they faced each other. The colonel looked up at him with no expression on his face. "Right now, things ain't too shit-hot around here, they're just plain

shit," he continued. "We've got to rig the fusion package
and blow this joint as soon as possible." Rosetti gazed up
at him silently, his face still expressionless, then looked
around him to Jackson.

"Sound the general alert," he told her. "But make it a
routine lifeboat drill."

For a moment, Hicks thought his brain had exploded.
"A general fucking *alert*?" he said. "*A lifeboat drill?!* Who
the hell do you think's gonna be left for the *Kansas City* to
pick up? I say we blow the fusion package *now!*"

"*Hicks.*" Jackson turned away from the console to glare
at him. "You took out the main air-scrubber. Pretty soon,
there'll be nothing left to breathe in here. We'd've been
okay for five days, except you also started an electrical
fire, which is spreading because the fire suppression
system is fucked. And most of my Ops crew are dead
or missing."

Hicks wasn't really surprised but hearing it out loud
made him feel sick. "And you *still* haven't rigged this place
to blow?"

"Yeah, I was getting to that." Jackson straightened up,
her light-pen landing on Rosetti. "No."

"Corporal Hicks, you'll lead the group from this sector,"
Rosetti said matter-of-factly, as if he really were organizing
a lifeboat drill. "At the alert they'll meet up at the blue
assembly point, then proceed to the nearest lifeboat bay."
His neutral face took on a hard, stony expression. "And
we're calling it a drill because it'll make people more

cooperative," he added. "They want to get it over with, so they move faster."

Abruptly, Bishop stepped between him and Rosetti. "Colonel, I've sent you my analysis." He pointed at the flexi on his forearm. "It estimates that at this point, between thirty-five and forty percent of Anchorpoint's remaining population are already incubating—"

Rosetti's face turned an alarming shade of red. "Listen to me, you soulless, motherless zombie, those are *people*, not numbers! We have to get them out—"

"Understood, Colonel," Bishop said, unperturbed. "However—"

"And *you*—" Rosetti jabbed a finger at Hicks. "*You* have your orders, Marine!"

"And I'm not doing shit until Jackson sets Anchorpoint to blow," Hicks told him, going full-on outlaw. Out of the corner of his eye, he could see Martinez and O'Brien gaping. *You ain't seen nothin' yet*, he promised them silently.

"Look, Colonel," he went on, "by the time the *Kansas City* shows up, there'll be nobody to rescue. You know what they'll do—send in a boarding party. Can you guess what happens next, or do you need a video?"

"Dammit, Hicks, will you just *shut up and listen*?" Jackson yelled angrily.

He turned to look at her in surprise.

"I'm right there with you, all the way," Jackson went on. "But the fusion package chamber is directly under the main air-scrubber. You know, the one you took out with a mortar, and started a fire? That fire triggered the fusion package emergency safeguards. The package is completely sealed off. And because full comms are down, I can't *unseal* it remotely with an override signal, there's not enough bandwidth for the codes. That leaves the fusion package all wrapped up so it can't hurt anybody."

"I can go down there and set it manually," Bishop said, as if he were volunteering to go out for coffee.

"I'll go with you," Hicks said.

Bishop shook his head. "You need to assist with the… the 'drill.'" He glanced at Rosetti. "And evacuation."

"Yeah, the *evacuation*," Jackson said, glowering at Rosetti. "You just want to get your own ass outta here, don't you, Colonel, while you figure out how to cover it. Weapons Division couldn't have done any of this shit without your okay. Right?"

Despite his sympathy for Jackson, Hicks suppressed a groan. Even in the middle of the worst disasters, civilians always found time to lay blame.

"*Hicks!*" Spence yelled in a terrible panicky voice.

He turned to see O'Brien stumbling clumsily into the middle of the room, the strap of his pulse-rifle slipping off his shoulder. He shrugged it away and tore off his armor, letting everything drop to the floor as he doubled over and cried out in pain. Martinez took a step toward him and Hicks waved her back as they all heard something rip, loudly, horribly. O'Brien straightened up and pulled his shirt open; Hicks saw several red blotches on his white undershirt. The Marine looked down at himself in agony and horror, and then at everyone else.

"*Please*," he begged, blood dribbling out of his eyes and nose. He coughed, spraying more blood into the air, and Hicks gestured for everyone to move farther back. "I... I don't know what—"

He staggered toward Jackson, who sidled away from him in a hurry. The beam from her light-pen scribbled over his body as he fell face-down across the console. Hicks heard another ripping sound along with the crack of breaking bones. O'Brien let out a strangled cry that cut off sharply. He flipped over onto his back and blood exploded from his chest, along with half a dozen mutant chest-bursters.

"*Everybody out!*" Hicks bellowed, yanking Spence to her feet. A small, calm part of his mind took note of the fact that multiple aliens could now gestate in a single host, *sans* cocoons. God only knew what else was different. Not that he really wanted to find out.

The last thing he saw as he got everyone out of the room was a trail of tiny, clawed footprints rendered perfectly in blood running diagonally across one of the monitors.

Martinez took point as they hurried through the corridors, with Hicks and Bishop bringing up the rear. Rosetti had had the presence of mind to grab both Hicks's weapon and the dead Marine's pulse-rifle. He stayed right behind

Martinez, although it wasn't long before he was panting like a dog. He also looked like he was still in pain despite the pills he was popping on the sly. Probably hadn't moved this fast in years, Hicks thought, feeling a little sorry for him. A cushy desk job was supposed to lead to retirement, not a death-match with aliens.

Vasquez made a fleeting appearance in his brain. *Hey, I didn't volunteer for that, either. Did you?*

As they approached a junction of five passageways, Martinez signaled for them to slow down and stay behind her. Normally, there was plenty of traffic—on foot and on wheels—but now the place was deserted.

What would the aliens do if they *did* kill everyone on Anchorpoint, Hicks wondered suddenly. Would they turn on each other until their acid-blood destroyed the whole station? Somehow he didn't think so. They were unrelentingly savage but they practically ignored each other. Maybe they'd hibernate, put themselves on standby to wait for prey.

Which was, apparently, a pretty damned long time— Ripley's report on her first encounter with them had described the corpse they'd found amid thousands of eggs as *fossilized*. With a big, ragged hole in the torso where something had torn its way out from inside, maybe while it was sending out the warning the *Nostromo* had misinterpreted as a distress signal.

Weyland-Yutani, however, had known what it really was, and deliberately steered them to the planetoid. The

Company never missed an opportunity to make a profit. Unfortunately, they had failed to consider the drawbacks of this particular ultra-deadly bioweapon: the aliens didn't kill on command, or for a nation, or a cause, or any reason at all—they just killed. They were animals that behaved like a disease, one that had no vaccine, no treatment, and no cure.

The hand on his shoulder made Hicks jump. He turned to find Bishop beside him.

"Overload at 2200," he said. "That should be enough time. If we aren't off Anchorpoint by then—"

Hicks moved them both away from the others. "Just blow it—that's all that matters." He shoved the flexi up on his forearm so he could set the alarm on his watch. When time was of the essence, there was nothing better than a good old mechanical watch you wound by hand, one that didn't crash and couldn't be hacked. "There can't be *anything* left of these bastards when the *Kansas City* shows up. Got that?"

"Understood, Corporal," Bishop replied. He left quickly but without hurrying; Hicks stared after him. Only Bishop could plan to blow up a space station with such equanimity, he thought, sorry that he couldn't send someone else. Bishop's *sangfroid* was like a safety net.

Get over it, he told himself, and turned back to the group to see Martinez looking a question at him. Hicks gave her the get-moving signal. She pointed at the second corridor on their right, then turned to the rest of the group, snapping her fingers to get their attention.

"See that passageway at two o'clock?" She waited for everyone to nod yes. "Good. On my mark. Ready?"

They all nodded again.

"Three… two… one—*mark*."

Rosetti's lifeboat drill expectations had been wildly optimistic.

There were only half a dozen people waiting for them at the assembly point and they knew this was no drill. Hicks made a mental note to rub Rosetti's nose in that later as he used the flexi's facial recognition to identify them.

The woman with short dark hair and a religious tattoo framing her left eye was named Halliday, and Hicks knew immediately she'd be trouble. She fluctuated between confusion and imminent collapse, a condition that would only get worse. Eventually, they'd have to carry her. Until they couldn't.

The older man, Tatsumi, was steadier, a lab manager with the slightly wary look of someone whose world had suddenly mutated into something unrecognizable. The other four were his staff and still deferred to him. The two guys, Abellera and Vito, had a strong bond that reminded him of Vasquez and Drake, who had grown up together in a Brazilian favela. It left the other two, a tall, dark-skinned woman named Talisa and a curly-haired non-binary called Quill, as buddies by default.

Talisa had been on Anchorpoint for almost two years,

but the other three were new hires who'd arrived only a few months ago. As green as they were, however, Hicks was pretty sure the fake lifeboat drill hadn't fooled them for a second. It was almost funny. *So how's that fabulous career in space working out? Met anyone fascinating? Be careful—if you catch an alien from them, you're screwed.*

"Is this all?" Rosetti said, looking around. "There should be at least thirty people here."

"I can't find Tom," Halliday said, full of concern. "What's going on? What happened? Tom was just here. I mean, there. But then—"

"Forget it," Jackson said, patting her shoulder. "He's probably waiting for you on the lifeboat. Good old Tom, that's just like him, isn't it?" She glanced at Hicks and shrugged. "If this is everybody, I guess we can go, right?"

As the group gathered together, Hicks caught Jackson's sleeve and slipped her his service automatic. "Help me keep an eye on them, okay, Ops?"

Jackson stuck the weapon in the back of her waistband and covered it with her shirt. "Listen up, everybody!" she ordered. "You all know I'm Jackson, Chief of Ops, right? Great. So you all know the goddam drill, we've only done it a million times, even you rookies. We stick together and take route A-52 to Blue Concourse, where we'll meet up with two other groups at Bay 5 and proceed to board—"

"Excuse me," Tatsumi said politely, raising one hand. "What is happening here, please?"

Hicks winced; maybe the guy wasn't steady after all.

Jackson took it in stride. "Don't interrupt, please," she said. "We're on our way to board a lifeboat and we'll be following emergency procedures until we either get the all-clear or we launch, whichever comes first. *Then* I'll be taking questions, and not before. Everybody clear on that?" She glanced at Hicks and he gave her the go-ahead.

"Great!" she said. "Let's move it!"

3 3

Most of the lights in the mall were out, with the rest starting to dim; even the background music was offline.

Bishop looked down the length of the concourse while he adjusted his eyesight and fine-tuned his hearing. That he'd managed to get this far without running into any aliens was almost enough to make him reconsider the idea that luck was real. On the other hand, if it were, his had just run out.

The freight elevator he needed was at the other end of the mall and the movement he could detect between the lift and his current location didn't belong to humans. His cheap, polycarbon knees weren't up to the stress of crawling through the airducts under the floor or in the walls. Running was also out of the question—there was no give to this surface. It was either a brisk walk or levitation, and the latter wasn't one of his factory-installed features.

The artificial waterfall just up ahead was now surrounded by a lake about seven and a half centimeters deep. If the drain were blocked, it should have shut down before overflowing. He reached it and was surprised to see a little water still trickling down the ersatz rock formation despite the body floating face-down in the pool. Under the circumstances, his core programming didn't command him to investigate or identify the deceased but it did log the corpse as another failure within the grid of his responsibilities. He'd racked up a lot of those lately. The official count included the entire colony on LV-426, which just by itself exceeded the total of all his previous failures combined.

A human doing the accounting might have excluded them since almost all the colonists had died while the Marines were still in transit. But artificial persons were programmed to a different standard that called for complete and utter service. The human architects behind artificial intelligence had done this to prevent the emergence of a rogue, megalomaniac AI hellbent on enslaving or wiping out *Homo sapiens*. Even centuries after the dawn of AI development, the nightmare of a robot uprising refused to die.

Humans had been so worried about their intelligent machines turning against them, they hadn't given as much consideration to the nightmares that might be waiting as they spread throughout the galaxy. Well, except to bring weapons, in case of hostilities. Weapons had always worked before, as long as there were enough of them, although even just one weapon was better than nothing— which was, at the moment, what Bishop had.

Not that he'd have taken one even if Hicks had offered. The group needed weapons more than he did. After he had set the fusion package to self-destruct, maybe he could look for something.

Once he was through the impromptu lagoon, Bishop took a moment to shake water from his boots. He didn't see any more water hazards ahead, just plenty of broken glass and other detritus scattered over the floor from the various shops where creatures had smashed their way in or out.

Several meters farther on, he stopped again in front of a place where a sphere covered in a mosaic of tiny mirrors lay among dismembered mannequin parts and glass from the smashed display window. It was listed in his database as catering to nostalgia fantasies. How humans could be nostalgic for times they'd never experienced seemed improbable to Bishop, but humanity was an improbable species.

The crunch of broken glass under heavy steps made him freeze in place. It was coming from the wreckage of a sports bar. Bishop's database said it had been well-stocked with a wide variety of potables while the sports part had been more of an afterthought—it ran one recording of one soccer game continuously on the rear wall-screen. The shifting light told him it was running even now.

He moved toward it for a closer look, staying behind one of the few bits of the facade that was still standing just as a large blob of black sludge hit the wall-screen with a wet *smack!* It stuck there for a second before an inhuman hand with long talons started spreading it around as it slowly began to harden, acquiring a pearlescent sheen.

There were four of the creatures in the bar, the last one emerging from the large, ragged gap where acid-blood had eaten away part of the floor. They were of the older generation, the ones that cocooned their victims. One had just finished wrapping up an unconscious older man Bishop recognized as Werner Shuman. He'd left Ops saying he was going to try contacting the diplomatic network from his office and hadn't made it. No one, including Bishop, had thought he would.

The alien mashed Shuman's cocoon roughly against the screen, pushing it upward until the back of his drooping head touched the ceiling, then stood back and hissed loudly at the man. It made Bishop think of big-game hunters from a less enlightened age, hanging animal heads on the wall as brutal trophies. This species took brutality to a much higher level.

The alien bent to take a fistful of black sludge from a pool on the floor and added more layers to the cocoon, careful to leave Shuman's chest clear. It paused every few seconds to thrust its eyeless face close to Shuman's and hiss, spraying him with thick saliva. Shuman remained unresponsive; either he had nerves of steel or he was comatose and all but dead. Bishop hoped it was the latter.

The other three aliens were busy cocooning other unconscious victims, one using the sludge on the floor, the other two extruding the same material from under armored plates in their torsos. Producing sludge from their bodies was something Bishop hadn't seen before; he added it to his store of existing data, careful to get every detail.

He was still watching when it occurred to him that he had been so focused on the activity in front of him that he had failed to register the subtle ambient changes in his surroundings. His left knee signaled strain as he straightened up from his hunched-over position and turned around.

The enormous queen had undergone some mutations. The framework around its head was larger and more elaborate and a sort of coxcomb with razor-sharp edges ran the length of its elongated skull, although the head itself was noticeably smaller, and still eyeless.

Its perception, however, was undiminished, although at the same time he had the impression it didn't know what to make of him. Thick saliva dripped from its jaws as its head tilted from one side to the other. Given the circumstances, Bishop was certain it had never encountered an artificial person before. He was also certain that whatever it decided to do next wasn't going to end well for him. The last queen he'd met hadn't liked him much, either.

Then, from the bar, he heard bones cracking and flesh ripping, and a choked cry of pain as an alien emerged from one of the cocooned humans. The queen looked up to see what all the fuss was about and Bishop didn't hesitate. He dashed for the freight elevator and found it waiting with its doors open.

The queen let out an infuriated scream. Leaping into the elevator, he grabbed the strap dangling from the upper door while he was still airborne, and yanked it hard as he landed, shutting both doors barely half a second before the queen rammed into them.

The impact shook the car and made Bishop's knees wobble. The queen continued to scream and throw itself against the elevator until the top door bent inward, making a gap wide enough to thrust its tail through. Bishop squeezed into the corner by the control panel, barely out of reach as it whipped from side to side, and hit the down button.

The machinery growled, and the queen answered it with an even louder scream Bishop felt clear through to his skeleton, both original and cheap polycarbon. The car shuddered, sank a few meters, and stopped. Bishop hit the down button again. Metal scraped and squealed as the motor strained, and then quit with a very final *thunk*.

The tail withdrew and the enraged queen tried to shove its head through the gap but it was too small. It pulled at the lower door in an effort to widen the opening. The metal bent a little, just enough to keep the elevator jammed in the shaft.

Bishop flattened himself on the floor and felt around carefully. What he wanted would be near the center of the car, although the schematic in his database wasn't quite to scale—

There it was.

Hicks wasn't there to smile so Bishop did it in his place as he started prying up tiles.

The burning smell was pretty strong by the time Martinez and Hicks got the group to the Blue Concourse entrance. Jackson unlocked the hatch with her ID, and was about to step through it when Martinez pulled her back and went in ahead of her. Jackson's light-pen drew momentary zigzags in the air as she shifted impatiently from one foot to the other, waiting for Martinez to signal it was safe to go through.

Hicks stood guard as Rosetti followed Jackson. Spence had to help Halliday to keep her from tripping—she was getting worse, and so was the air. If both continued to deteriorate, the group would have to make some hard decisions.

Or rather, *he* would.

It should have been Rosetti's call—Rosetti's *burden*—but it was clear to Hicks that the group didn't trust the colonel enough to take orders from him. Part of that was due to the bad feeling Jackson had fomented, although in Hicks's view, Rosetti was more to blame than she was. Jackson was only a civilian. Rosetti had let his peacetime desk job turn him into a hothouse flower. He was no better than Gorman, who hadn't stepped up until the whole squad had been wiped out.

This was worse than LV-426. Not just because there were more monsters and more civilians, but because he didn't have Ripley and Newt to help him out. At least he had Bishop, and if they came out of this alive, they would have him to thank.

And if they didn't live through it, at least they'd be taking the goddam aliens with them. Assuming Bishop made it to the fusion package, that was. He would. He had to. The alternative was unthinkable.

A distant crash followed by an inhuman shriek jarred Hicks out of his thoughts. Quill had frozen halfway through the hatch with Talisa's hand on their shoulder; both looked terrified. Hicks gave both of them a rough push to get them going again, and signaled Martinez to pick up the pace.

There was another long, high-pitched cry, brutal and full of rage. Hicks patted himself down, found the chunk of plastique he wanted in his top-right vest pocket, and stuck it in the center of the door. When he was sure it would stay put, he wedged a time-delay grenade into the center of the explosive, molding it like clay to make sure it held fast.

Time-delay grenades had improved in the last four years. This one was more compact yet more powerful, and the maximum delay was two minutes—twice as long as before. Judging by the shriek he'd just heard, he thought ninety seconds would do it. He stepped through the hatch, pulled it closed, and locked it, then ran to catch up with the group.

Jackson had taken his place at the rear. As soon as she heard his footsteps, she whirled, aiming his own service weapon at him.

"Easy there, tiger." Hicks gestured for her to keep moving. None of them were especially athletic, but he was pretty sure they could manage a hundred-and-fifty-yard dash in a minute and a half.

"Where *were* you?" Jackson demanded.

The explosion answered for him. The group was well out of range but the blast was powerful enough to shake the deck. Vito lost his balance and fell over, mostly from surprise. Hicks yanked him back up on his feet and pushed him forward, making him turn around when he tried to look back.

"What *was* that?" Vito asked, wide-eyed with fear.

"Tell you later," Hicks said as he got them going again. There was a lot of damage in this section. Small vehicles, scooters and two-seaters, had skidded out of control to collide with each other or crash into the tunnel walls, leaving wreckage, torn-up rags that had once been clothing, and plenty of blood, some dry, some less so, as well as fragments of bone and flesh. The odor of decomposition mingled with the smell of smoke; it wasn't an improvement.

He and Martinez did their best to move them along too

quickly to get a close look at anything especially ghastly, in spite of the worsening air quality. What they needed, Hicks thought, was a transport like the six-wheeler he'd had to abandon. It would be easier on them if they didn't have to plod past the remains of what might have been their co-workers. If someone recognized a rag as a friend's shirt—or worse, a tattoo on a patch of skin—

Hicks killed that line of thought and focused on the group's condition as a whole. Despite her youth and inexperience, Martinez was a damned good Marine, and she had a great poker face. But Rosetti should have retired years ago, taken up residence in some Veterans Administration outpost or even gone back to Earth, to spend his days trading exaggerations with other warhorses.

Spence was all right for the time being, mostly because she'd been tending to Halliday, trying to keep her too distracted to fall apart again. Hicks knew she blamed herself for poor old Tully, Charles A., and she was trying to make up for it by saving someone else. He'd known plenty of other people like her; they were called "Mom," or "Sarge," or even "CO," Rosetti being a particularly glaring exception.

Big talk for a guy whose life is repeating on him like bad chili. In his mind's eye, Apone blew cigar smoke at him, then vanished.

Jackson, Chief of Ops: he could probably depend on her to dig deep and come through without losing her shit. Although he'd never imagined working with anyone named "Mandala." Unless he was way off about how old she was, her parents would have been the right age for the last resurgence of hippie culture. She probably had siblings or cousins named "Steelpike" or "Frodo" or "Starsong."

The others—

"Come on, Hicks, what was that, *really*?"

Jackson had materialized on his left; damn it, she just wasn't going to leave it alone. "Some of those things are following us," Hicks told her in a low voice. "I left them something to slow them down."

"Fine with me," she said. "Just don't blow up another air-scrubber. Or worse, blast a hole in the outer hull."

Hicks nodded, then saw that Vito and Abellera had slowed down, obviously wanting to listen in. "Hey, I didn't say 'rest'!" he said loudly. "Get the lead out! ¡*Andale! Vite, vite! Bistro!*"

"There's a bistro? Where?" Vito said, looking around.

"Just move it already!" Jackson gave him and Abellera a push. "And in case you don't know, that's not London fog, it's *smoke*, so either haul ass or lay down and die!"

In spite of everything, Hicks allowed himself a momentary grin. If he couldn't get these people to safety with Jackson and Martinez helping him, he probably wouldn't make it himself.

3 4

It wasn't long—twelve minutes, by Bishop's internal timer—before the queen's attacks on the elevator began to taper off. It would slam itself against the doors for a while, then stop for minutes on end. Bishop suspected it had sensed other prey approaching, and when it didn't come within easy reach, the queen returned to continue pounding away at the elevator. Each time, the metal complained and bent a little more, but still wouldn't give way enough to let the thing in.

In fact, the doors shouldn't have buckled at all. As he went on pulling up tiles, Bishop wondered who was going to break it to Weyland-Yutani that their "impervious" alloy, currently *the* standard material for space stations everywhere, wasn't alien-proof.

Or maybe an enterprising administrator had swapped out the alloy for something cheaper, then cooked the books to pocket the difference. Admin sleight-of-hand had fooled a number of savvy contractors in the past.

He had a sudden memory of something Sergeant Apone

had said to Hicks: *Make something foolproof and nature'll make a better fool.* Bishop didn't know if Apone was right, but he did know that something—maybe nature, maybe a better fool—had somehow created a species more dangerous than *Homo sapiens.* Any fool who couldn't see *that* wasn't the better kind.

The last floor tile came away, exposing the trapdoor. Long strings of industrial glue hung from the underside of the tile, showing it was a recent installation. Why Maintenance would floor over the emergency exit was yet another vagary of human behavior Bishop didn't even try to account for.

There was no lock on the door, which opened out and down—assuming it wasn't boarded up on the other side. Newt would have crossed her fingers; as she wasn't there to do the honors, he did it for her. Then he pressed the latch and the door dropped open. Lucky again. At this rate, he might become the first superstitious artificial person.

Bishop lowered himself through the hole and dangled by his hands while he checked things out. All four shaft walls had service ladders tucked into recesses, presumably for the safety of maintenance crews, although Bishop thought they could have been deeper. Husky types risked having their clothes torn off.

At the bottom of the shaft he saw the flickering orange glow of an ongoing fire; judging by the unpleasant, pungent smell, it was something illegal to burn in any environment that was home to air-breathers. He could tolerate polluted air better than humans could but his olfactory function told him that for the sake of his more delicate components, he would be wise not to prolong his exposure.

And that was going to be trickier than he had anticipated—the trapdoor's position put him a meter short of the nearest ladder.

Can't hang around here all day. Filing the thought under accidental humor to share with Hicks later, Bishop put his feet together and worked at making his body swing back and forth. He increased the arc, despite the car shuddering in his grip as the queen continued its assault on the doors. In only a few seconds, he managed to build up to the right amount of momentum. One somersault would be enough, he thought, and used the human trick of counting down while he double-checked his calculations.

"Three… two… one… *mark,*" he said aloud, putting extra force into the forward swing before he let go. The cheap polycarbon knees twinged as he curled into a tight ball and twinged again when he straightened out and reached for the ladder.

His hands closed on empty air.

Rungs flashed past him like frames of an antique filmstrip for a full second before he caught one, checking his fall with a jerk hard enough to make his eyeballs bounce in their sockets.

Hanging by one arm, he conducted a quick internal survey. The sudden stop hadn't done any additional damage; maybe he should count that as another lucky break.

"Not bad for an artificial person," he said aloud, remembering Ripley struggling out of the airlock after she'd sent the queen from LV-426 into the void. In the silence that followed, Newt had called her *Mommy*. Bishop hadn't experienced the moment as a human would have, but he understood its nature and profundity in the abstract, and he'd saved the memory onboard as critical data.

He began climbing down, quickly but not hurriedly, trying to minimize the time each leg had to bear his weight. Every fifth rung or so, his knees would wobble, the left more so than the right; he estimated they would fail completely within the next eight hours, and eight might be too optimistic.

But that was okay. He'd settle for one.

The air quality was getting worse, and a lot more quickly than Hicks had anticipated. The thickening smoke combined with the rough stink of chemicals stung their eyes, made them cough, and occasionally, they had to stop and wait for someone to throw up. Hicks was the only one who hadn't needed a puke break. He'd come close a few times, but managed to keep his stomach contents to himself. He had to; the group needed him to be stronger than they were.

Now a tightness was gathering at the base of his skull, faint as yet but ready to blossom into the kind of headache that would make history if he let his guard down. The only way to hold it off was to do his job, to concentrate on getting everyone into a lifeboat, and off this station. Occasionally they passed through areas where the air wasn't so bad, but he wouldn't let them linger more than a couple of minutes, telling them the air would be clearer up ahead. So far, they seemed to believe him. He hoped he wasn't lying. Some of the areas they passed through were especially bad, with more wreckage, more human bloodstains, much of it still wet on the cratered and scorched walls. In some places, acid-blood had eaten through half a dozen levels before it had petered out. Several times, Jackson had had to reroute them around collapsed tunnels and passageways. It made everything seem even more bleakly overwhelming, and the way Halliday kept blubbering didn't help.

Hicks was on the verge of losing it and telling Halliday she had to shut up or they'd leave her behind when Martinez came up with the idea of a scavenger hunt in motion. Looking for water bottles, thermoses, edibles in sealed packaging, and any other useful items would get their minds working so they weren't thinking only about bad air, aliens, and how tired they were.

Initially, Hicks had been skeptical—he was trying to distance them from death and destruction, not get them closer to it by pawing through debris. But to his surprise, the group's energy level rose and even Halliday stopped crying to join in.

Rosetti's participation was limited to pointing at things and telling one of the techs fetch it, although he did spare a moment to nod at Hicks approvingly. It only made Hicks want to punch him.

Jackson found a couple of empty courier bags large enough to hold a fair amount of whatever they found. Hicks told the techs to take turns carrying them for the group. They didn't object; Anchorpoint lab techs seemed to be the civilian equivalent of grunts. Except for Spence, he thought. Spence was more like a sergeant on the officer track.

The concourse took a wide curve to the left and started gradually sloping upward, much to Hicks's dismay; the last thing they needed now was more physical effort. Then he realized the air was better and less smoky. The burning smell was still there but they weren't coughing as much and the puking had stopped.

Even the small victories count, Marine. Apone grinned at him in his mind's eye. *Every meal a banquet, every paycheck a fortune, remember?*

It seemed like forever before the passageway leveled off into an open area Jackson said was a transport and traffic control sub-station. Tatsumi perked up at the word "transport" and suggested that Jackson activate a railcar for them, routing it to the nearest lifeboat bay. Everyone, including Martinez, was enthusiastically in favor of the idea, but all Hicks could think of was the last transport he'd seen, where he'd found Spence.

"That's the worst thing we could do." Spence's voice cut through the clamoring, and they all shut up. Hicks knew she remembered the same thing and he distracted the group with a short break before herding them into a tunnel marked MAINTENANCE.

The tunnel was large and mercifully empty of any sort of wreckage, with weird acoustics that amplified every sound they made. Hicks didn't know whether this had actually triggered Halliday to begin another cycle of weeping, or whether she had simply decided it was too quiet. As always, it was soft at first but grew steadily louder, building to a crescendo of uncontrollable sobbing, and Hicks called a break so Spence and Jackson could talk her down.

He had to be extra patient, he told himself. Halliday wasn't the first traumatized civilian he'd dealt with. She wasn't even the most difficult, nor was he stuck having to take care of her all by himself.

It wasn't much of a pep talk; he was too tired to be mature. No, he was beyond tired. He was running on fumes, and not very strong fumes—more like fumes of fumes, ghosts of fumes. Driving the group so hard, refusing to let them rest for very long was the only way he could keep himself going. Because if he sat down for more than a minute or two, he'd never get up again.

He dropped back a few meters as the group approached the next bend in the tunnel. Better to lag behind for a few deep breaths. Otherwise he might lose it and start shouting at Halliday to stop sniveling and get her fucking shit together.

The group rounded the turn and he heard gasps and cries of terror before Halliday's hysterical sobs drowned them out. Then they were all rushing back toward him, and for a moment he thought they were going to run over him like stampeding cattle.

"Oh man, oh sweet Jesus, this is bad." Martinez's gold-toned complexion was almost ashen and the grip she had on his bicep was going to leave bruises. "It's so bad, it's… it's *real* bad."

Suddenly, absurdly, finally, Hicks recognized her as the Marine he'd passed on his way to meet Tully, a lifetime ago, the one who had punched his arm. Apone had been right: the damnedest things crossed your mind at the damnedest times.

He unslung his rifle and told all of them, including Martinez, to stay behind him. Whatever it was, he might be able to hold it off long enough for Martinez to get them out of there. Raising his weapon, he strode around the corner, and stopped.

"Everybody stay back!" Hicks yelled when he could finally speak. "I mean it—*stay back!*"

Instead, they bunched up behind him, not exactly obeying but not disobeying too much. After some unmeasured time, Martinez said, "Corporal Hicks, what the *fuck* is that?"

That was the Question of the Day, Hicks thought, and he hadn't had an answer anyone would like. And now he had no answer at all.

As an artifact, the pearlescent black wall sealing off the tunnel in front of him was remarkable, truly astonishing. Not because it was so large or complex—the aliens had covered over much larger spaces on LV-426. But this was the first time Hicks had known them to deliberately construct a barricade. It was also the first time he had seen human remains mixed into the stuff—flesh, bones, even body parts—in a way that was practically artful.

Maybe it is art, Hicks thought, momentarily lightheaded. *Maybe they really are artists—malevolent, violent, and lethal, but artists nonetheless. And they call this piece,* Dead End for Humanity. *From their* Extinction *series.*

"Okay, road's closed, everyone. We gotta take a detour." He herded the group back around the corner, refusing to let anyone stop for another look. Martinez took point again and led them into an area off the passageway Hicks had barely noticed before. Now he saw it was a break-lounge—Anchorpoint seemed to have more of those than any other space station he'd been to—which meant he'd have to let everyone rest again. Assuming they *could* rest while they were anywhere near that thing; Hicks would have preferred being a lot farther away.

He looked around. As large as the lounge was, it had no vending machines, but it did have its own parking area. A couple of one- and two-seater carts lay on their sides amid a scatter of broken electronics, while against the wall on Hicks's left a bloodstained tarp had been thrown over something large and lumpy. Hicks wasn't keen to take a closer took, but Martinez went over to it before he could stop her and, using the tip of her rifle, lifted a section of tarp a few centimeters to reveal a tire.

Hicks let out a surprised laugh. Martinez went to pull

the tarp back but this time he moved quickly enough to stop her.

"Oh… right," she said, frowning a little. "You want to shoot first?"

He shook his head. "If there's something nasty under there, let me flush it out so you can put it down. Hopefully where it won't splash anyone. Jackson, move everybody back to the far wall."

No one argued, although they all looked dubious, even after Jackson told them they could sit down.

Hicks slung his rifle and started running his hands over the tarp while Martinez watched him with wide dark eyes, her expression a mix of uncertainty and apprehension. The wall was a bad omen to them, he realized. If things kept going downhill, he'd have trouble keeping them together and pointed in the right direction.

He shoved the thought away. Even if the six-wheeler looked intact, that didn't mean it would run. If the battery wasn't flat, the engine might be damaged. Or maybe acid had eaten into the dashboard—

And then again, maybe not. It *felt* pretty solid, and at this point, he knew nothing was lying in wait under the tarp. The aliens could be surprisingly stealthy, even cunning, but whenever prey got close they couldn't help going into a frenzy. He poked the area covering the seats. Nothing happened.

"I'm pretty sure it's clear," he said to Martinez. "Let's see what we've got."

They pulled the tarp back. The transport was bloodstained, dented, and scraped, and there were chunks gouged out of the worn upholstery, but overall it looked okay. Martinez hopped into the driver's seat and pressed the starter on the dashboard. The vehicle came to life immediately. Martinez slumped in the seat and let out a long, relieved breath.

Hicks felt a little emotional himself. "Every so often, something good happens," he told Martinez, chuckling. "Now let's get rolling."

Martinez took another deep breath before she sat up and climbed out. "Okay, guys, our ride's here," she said. "All aboard—*now!*"

She didn't have to tell them twice, but to Hicks's surprise, Rosetti hung back, looking uncertain. Jackson took his arm but he pulled away from her.

"They don't want us to get out," he said. "They want to trap us. You saw it. Blue Concourse is completely blocked—"

"Then *fuck* Blue Concourse," Hicks snapped, "and *fuck* the fucking bugs that blocked it. This bus is *leaving*, Colonel. You and Martinez take our six. Jackson, you're shotgun."

"Copy that, Corporal." Martinez sounded matter-of-fact despite a fleeting look of unease. Rosetti started to say something but Martinez distracted him with a question about pulse-rifles vs. smart rifles. Hicks smiled inwardly; what she lacked in experience, she made up for in savvy.

Getting everyone situated turned out to be a bit tricky.

It was a tight squeeze, and Quill ended up in the backward-facing seat with Rosetti and Martinez. When they were all settled, Jackson jumped into the seat beside Hicks. "Hit it."

Hicks chuckled a little. "Which way, Ops?"

"Back the way we came," she said, "unless you know something I don't."

Hicks shifted into drive, made a wide turn into the passageway, then stamped on the accelerator.

The motion roused Halliday from her weepy fugue. "What did he mean, 'bugs'? *What* bugs? And what *was* that thing we saw back there?" Hicks could hear her squirming around between Spence and Talisa. "Where's Tom? Where'd he go and *what was that thing back there*?"

"It's nothing, it's okay," Spence said soothingly. "It was just an experiment that spilled—"

"An experiment?" Now Tatsumi was on the alert. "I know of no such experiment. Why was I not informed?"

Jackson turned around in her seat and patted him on the knee reassuringly. "Hey, don't worry, Dr. T., we'll explain later."

Hicks tightened his grip on the steering wheel, although his knuckles couldn't get any whiter. They were civilians, he told himself, just civilians, yanked out of their oblivious civilian existence by an alien shitstorm. No one had ever told them that in this life everyone was fair game, and now it was their turn. It wasn't their fault, there was nothing wrong with them—it was the universe that was fucked up.

"Take the left coming up, marked B33," Jackson said,

consulting the map on her flexi. "There isn't as much wreckage and it goes most of the way to Aquaculture, but we'll have to get out and walk the last bit—sorry," she added, glancing at Hicks apologetically. "From there, we go up a level to Aeroponics, which puts us close to Residential. Then we climb the service tunnel behind the mainframe for this sector—"

"Sounds complicated," Hicks said, dubious.

"Quickest route to a lifeboat bay," Jackson replied. "And by 'quickest,' I mean I'm pretty sure there'll be more air than smoke and less dead ends made out of dried alien phlegm and severed human limbs."

"Works for me," Hicks said. Behind him, Halliday was asking about Tom again while Tatsumi grumbled that people were failing to notify him about experiments.

The development of artificial persons like Bishop had involved extensive research into human psychology in general, and the phenomenon of the uncanny valley in particular. When it came to making AIs in the image and likeness of humans, scientists found God and the Devil slugging it out in the details, and it wasn't always clear which was which.

A great deal of painstaking research and experimentation revealed humans had less trouble accepting artificial lifeforms that blinked, breathed, and swallowed, and if at all possible ate and drank. The first three behaviors turned out to be the most crucial. They were also fairly easy to build in, although the rates for each had to be carefully calibrated.

Bishop's simulated respiration continued on its programmed loop even though the air in the elevator shaft was now practically unbreathable for a human. Fortunately, the concentration of toxins was well below levels that would adversely affect the more delicate components of his neural net. A lot less fortunately, his legs were more at risk than his brain; trousers weren't much protection for cheap polycarbon.

He stepped sideways on each rung in an effort to distribute his weight along the length of his foot. It meant he couldn't move as quickly as he'd have liked but hand-under-hand would have been even slower.

Four levels down he stopped on a small ledge beside a set of double doors, where the heat from the fire was more intense. As he felt around on the wall for the emergency lever, he ran a quick status check. Heat damage wasn't imminent, but it advised him to move to a cooler environment with fewer airborne toxins.

"To quote Corporal Hicks, no shit," he muttered and discovered the air tasted even worse than it smelled. After a few seconds, he found the lever; the metal was warm but not hot enough to damage his skin.

It wouldn't budge.

Bishop shifted position, tried again; it loosened, but only a tiny bit. Moving up a couple of rungs, he pushed down on the thing with all his weight. Metal scraped sharply against metal as the lever finally gave. The doors slid apart and he dived through them head-first, as air rushed past him into the shaft.

There was a distant *whomp* from the conflagration below. For a moment, he thought the influx of air would cause a vertical flashover and bring the fire up to where he was. But when he looked over his shoulder, he saw only a puff of tiny sparks dancing madly in the dark shaft.

He sat up and scanned his surroundings, taking a note of all the plastic crates, some in stacks, some scattered all over the deck. There had to be another lever to close the doors from this side but he didn't see anything on the wall or in his reference data.

The call panel beside the doors lit up with a message:

Danger: Empty Shaft.
Call Maintenance.

A couple of seconds later, the doors closed by themselves and a new message appeared:

Out of Service for Maintenance.
Use Alternative.

"If there is one," Bishop said under his breath. Talking to himself aloud every so often was a behavior he had deliberately cultivated after discovering that for some reason, it put people around him at ease. Even the Colonial Marines—no, *especially* the Marines—and he wouldn't have thought little behaviors would affect them.

He piled a couple of upside-down crates on top of each other and used them to push himself to his feet. In one direction, the passageway narrowed into darkness. Fortunately, he was going the other way, where the lights were still on, and even with the stacks of crates there was enough room for a small vehicle. Or there had been, before so many had been knocked down and scattered all over. Given the destruction and chaos he'd already seen, Bishop supposed it would have been surprising if he'd found them all still in neat stacks.

On the other hand, perhaps the total absence of blood and human remains and acid damage was stranger. Whatever had happened here hadn't killed anyone. Then he came to the six-wheeled transport stalled atop a small heap of crates.

Definitely an argument in favor of luck being a real thing, Bishop thought, climbing into the driver's seat.

And the blinking **Battery Recharge** light on the dashboard to let him know his luck had run out was another. Only real things ran out.

He tried the I/O button anyway, just in case, but there was only a click. Well, now he knew for certain, he thought, and decided to rest his legs in the hope it would make them feel less precarious. Although with so few nerve connections, his physical sensation was barely more reliable than luck.

Bishop gave it a full minute, then headed for the fusion chamber. If the map on his flexi wasn't too much off scale, he was fairly close. Setting the package to blow on the original schedule or—he checked the time—something close to it was still possible. The chances of having enough time to get to a lifeboat afterward, however, were slim to none and, as Hudson would have put it, slim had already evacuated.

His left leg wobbled, reminding him there was a set order to the things he was concerned about. If there was a medical clinic near the fusion chamber, it might have a supply of nanos he could transfuse, as well as splints and pressure bandages. Although he'd have settled for duct tape and reinforcing rods from a construction site.

Checking the time again only told him what he already knew—he was going to have to run. Maybe he could run faster than his legs were deteriorating.

3 5

As soon as they reached the fish farm, Martinez signaled Hicks for a break, then announced it before she got his okay. Hicks let it go. It had been a tough hike from where they'd had to abandon the six-wheeler, and the scenery hadn't been pretty. But at least the air was still pretty good, if you didn't count the all-pervasive smell of fish.

By some miracle the place was untouched—no blood and guts, no acid damage. The unrelenting fish aroma—Eau de Pisces, Spence called it—wasn't exactly pleasant but at least it wasn't the heavy copper smell of blood or the stench of human decomposition, or the stink of fear mixed with all the other unhappy odors of violent death.

The group sat down on the wooden walkway that ran between several enormous vats, some with rotors sweeping through the water in slow circles, others standing stagnant with green mossy-looking stuff growing on the surface. Hicks wasn't an expert but he doubted this was good practice, unless they were deliberately growing algae. Dietrich had made a lot of claims for blue-green algae as a miracle food but this stuff looked like plain old pond scum.

Pond scum builds strong bodies and keeps hearts healthy. In a better world, Hicks thought as he leaned against a vat, it would have been funny.

The walkway looked like a weathered pier, although the absence of water around it ruined the illusion. The fish farmers probably hadn't cared one way or the other—most of them had probably never even been on a real pier.

Jackson materialized at his elbow to show him the map. "We're actually doing pretty well." She tapped the flexi to his, giving him a copy.

"Martinez should have this, too," Hicks said.

"Already done." Jackson nodded at Martinez, who gave her a thumbs-up. "And so does Spence." She lowered her voice. "I gave Halliday's flexi to Abellera."

Hicks nodded. "Good." As he shifted position, his rifle bumped against the side of the tank. Immediately, the water erupted with frenzied movement, churning and splashing. He stepped back in alarm, raising his weapon. Martinez was already on her feet, taking aim at the tank.

"Stand down, Marines," Spence said, laughing a little. "It's just a lot of hungry bass that should've been harvested already. They don't usually use firearms for that." She laughed again. "But if you *want* to shoot fish in a barrel, go right ahead."

"Nah." Hicks smiled with half his mouth. "We gotta shoot our way out of our own barrel."

Halliday, who had been quiet for a while, suddenly perked up. "Where's Tom? What is this place?"

"That's our cue," Hicks said, sighing heavily. "Time to go." There was a chorus of groans but they all stood up.

"Couldn't we give it just a couple more minutes?" Abellera asked unhappily.

Hicks shook his head. "Gotta meet Tom," he said, jerking his head at Halliday. "And we don't want to miss him."

The aeroponics farm on the next level up was a lot bigger than the last one Hicks had visited, just before going to LV-426. Better yet, it was redolent with the scent of green things, not fish, or blood, or anything eaten away by acid.

Standing on the top rung of the ladder with the rest of the group hanging on below him, Hicks scanned the area for signs of danger.

"Well?" Rosetti called impatiently. The physical strain was really getting to him now.

"Come ahead," Hicks said, stepping up out of the hatch. "But stay alert, everyone. Heads on swivels."

Jackson emerged first and stood by to help the others. Tatsumi looked tired and his little covey of lab techs were also sagging badly. Spence shoved Halliday up to Jackson, who dragged her off to the side so she could go on weeping silently without getting in the way, then helped Spence up onto the deck.

Martinez was next, then Rosetti, who was clutching his weapon and looking around bug-eyed like a boot on his first mission. Hicks knew he had to get him smoothed out before the jumpiness spread to the others. He was about to tell Martinez to get them moving when his gaze fell on Tatsumi's drawn, weary face and decided they could sit a minute longer while he checked their surroundings for anything that didn't seem right.

The aeroponics landscape was a mixture of spare lines and lush green vegetation. The pathway ahead of them was lined on both sides with A-frame structures alternating with even taller columns, all covered with green plants badly in need of pruning. Behind those were vegetable gardens laid out in large rectangles, also overgrown, and farther back, an apiary amid flowering plants. Like everyone else, the beekeepers had had to bail, but Hicks was surprised at how much it bothered him.

"Something?" Jackson was suddenly at his elbow again. Hicks was starting to think she could teleport. She looked from him to the hives and back.

"The bees," Hicks replied. "They didn't sign up for this." Which he was sure had to be the strangest thing that had ever occurred to him while he was sober.

He turned to the group. "Okay, everybody on your feet," he said. They gave the usual groans but did as they were told. Hicks motioned for the tall, black tech—her name was Talisa Nkosi, he remembered—to help Spence with Halliday, then went to Rosetti.

"Unclench, Colonel," he said, keeping his voice casual but low. "And maybe keep the safety on for now. You don't want to hurt any good guys. Right?"

Rosetti's pupils were pinpoints; he stared for a moment then let out a long breath and nodded. He moved to follow the group but stopped when he saw Hicks kneel beside the open hatch.

"What are you doing?" Rosetti asked, crouching beside him.

"Just a precaution," Hicks said absently as he made sure the plastique was securely in place. This chunk was larger than the last little surprise he'd left to discourage pursuit. It was the best he could do until they took off and watched them implode from orbit.

He closed the hatch, locked it, and got to his feet.

Rosetti stood up with him. "A precaution?"

"They may still be following us—"

Hicks cut off. He'd answered reflexively, without thinking because he'd been focused on how much explosive to use and his carelessness had put Rosetti right back in jumpy mode. He should have distracted the colonel with a task, or tried to—the man was so drugged-up, Hicks wasn't sure anything would help.

Abruptly, Halliday burst into loud sobs again.

Spence tried to comfort her but this time, the woman wasn't having any. She swatted Spence's hands away, fell to her knees, then toppled over onto her side and curled up into the fetal position. Jackson and Talisa moved to help Spence with her but somehow Rosetti was faster. He grabbed Halliday's arm and yanked her roughly back up on her knees, brushed her hands away, and tried to force her to stand up.

Halliday just sobbed even harder.

"*Shut up!*" Rosetti roared into her face. "They'll hear you, you'll give away our position!"

Our position? Hicks blinked. If Rosetti was having some kind of druggy combat flashback, his timing sucked.

Spence kept trying to comfort her but Halliday shook her off, determined to sob her heart out. Hicks hurried toward them to tell them to run when Rosetti decided to use shock therapy and backhanded Halliday.

Halliday's sobs cut off as her head snapped back. But instead of falling over, Halliday jumped to her feet and backed away with a mix of shock and terror on her tattooed face, blood trickling from the corner of her open mouth.

Spence was the first to react; she stepped in front of Rosetti and punched him in the face.

The colonel lost his weapon as he went down heavily on his back, looking even more shocked than Halliday. Before he could move to get up, Jackson was standing over him, with Hicks's service automatic pointed at his head.

"Try it." Her voice was soft, like she was offering him an hors d'oeuvre.

Hicks finally found his own voice. "*Two-minute fuse!*"

he yelled. "Everybody haul ass *thataway*!" He pushed the group into motion ahead of him. Rosetti rolled to his feet and took off just as Talisa flipped Halliday over her shoulder and ran with her as if she weighed nothing. Hicks caught up to Spence, who looked utterly calm, as if she hadn't just punched a Marine Colonel in the face.

They'd gone past the A-frames and columns into an area Hicks thought must have been modeled on the hanging gardens of Babylon, but there was no time to appreciate the terraced arrangements of lush greenery and colorful flowers. He shouted for everyone to take cover as he hit the deck behind the nearest large structure, curling into a ball and sticking his fingers in his ears. A second later, the deck shuddered as the bomb went off.

Hicks felt the shockwave rolling through him, giving each and every part of his body a very hard, very *thorough* shake. The explosion was bigger than he'd expected for the amount of plastique he'd used; good thing they'd all been able to take cover. His first close-proximity explosion had caught him in the open during combat, which had been worse. He hadn't been able to think straight or eat solid food for days.

After a while—seconds or minutes, he couldn't tell— Hicks raised his head and unplugged his ears, which were ringing like alarms; fingers weren't much protection against a shockwave. His head was a spinning merry-go-round tipping sideways and his eyes couldn't focus. More seconds or minutes passed before the merry-go-round began to slow, allowing his vision to settle. He sat up against the wall and the merry-go-round finally came to a stop, but he had to wait a little longer before attempting to get to his feet.

When he didn't topple over, Hicks took a step toward the path, and then another, keeping one hand on the wall just in case the merry-go-round started up again. But all he felt were aches from the blast. It would be worse tomorrow. If there was a tomorrow.

Everybody else would be feeling it, too, but none more than Rosetti. A second explosion would have him gobbling a double dose of painkillers, maybe more, guaranteeing his supply would run out well before they reached the lifeboats. And if the colonel thought he felt bad now, he'd find himself suffering on a whole new level when withdrawal kicked in.

Still holding onto the wall, Hicks peered around the front of the terraced garden structure. Some of the terraces had cracked and fallen, dumping plants and growth medium into a messy pile. Farther back, he saw scattered debris all over the pathway, but little else through the thickening smoke from the burning A-frames and columns. The growth medium, whatever it was, burned more readily than the vegetation; it smelled like a combination of burning chicken feathers and scorched manure. If fire suppression hadn't kicked in by now, it probably wasn't going to. They had to get gone.

"Ow," he grunted, feeling a sudden, sharp poke in the

ribs, and turned to find Spence beside him. Jackson must have taught her the teleportation trick.

"Keep doing this and people're gonna think you *like* blowing shit up." Her voice was barely audible.

"Can you hear me?" Hicks asked, unsure how loud his voice was.

Spence nodded. "You sound far away, but yeah."

"Let me see your ears." He made a quick inspection and was relieved when he saw no blood. "Any dizziness?" he asked, checking her eyes. There were only a few broken blood vessels. "Can you walk without throwing up or falling down?"

"Not dizzy, not puking," she assured him. "I'm okay."

"Yeah, you are," Hicks said, hoping he sounded like he knew for sure. Sometimes traumatic brain injuries didn't show for a day or even longer, but if she said she was okay, Hicks had to take her word for it and hope for the best. "Good. Help me round up the others. Anybody dies now, Rosetti'll have me dishonorably discharged."

"Not if I *discharge* him first," Spence replied.

The group was dazed and not hearing too well, but somehow he and Spence managed to gather them back together and get them moving again. Halliday had stopped crying but she looked like a sleepwalker and Hicks wasn't optimistic. Everyone else, however, was more cooperative now, even Rosetti. Maybe the explosion had knocked the bullshit out of him, at least for the moment. No doubt it was already growing back.

"Hicks!" Jackson pulled him farther along the path, past the terraces to another area of plants bedded in rectangular sections. These were more heavily overgrown than anything else they'd seen. Hicks half-expected them to start grappling each other for space.

Or maybe they were trying to escape, Hicks thought, looking at the enormous gray mass in one of the beds beside the path. He might have assumed it was blight, except the shiny black patches on the misshapen leaves and the veined gray sacs growing like tumors on the thickened, crooked stems told a different story. It took a moment before he saw that it was actually more than one plant, and if he stared long enough, he could see the shiny black patches grow while acquiring a pearlescent sheen.

"What do you think that is?" Jackson asked as the rest of the group joined them.

"Nothing good," Quill said unhappily.

Hicks looked down at the nearest plants. They were still mostly green, but starting to turn brown at the edges.

"Jesus," he said. "This is a cabbage patch. A goddamn cabbage patch."

"Excuse me, please?" Tatsumi said, raising his hand tentatively. "Does anyone know where we go next?"

Jackson leaned close to Hicks, putting her lips to his ear. "Spence said the aliens got to the lemurs in pocket-Madagascar—right down to the rings on their tails. Versatile fuckers." She stepped away from him and waved her arms to get the group's attention.

"Can everybody hear me at least a little? Okay, great," Jackson went on, not waiting for an answer. "Now, straight ahead—" She pointed to the road and then to the rectangles on either side, containing only growth medium. "—past those empty beds, the pathway divides into three. We're taking the wide one on the right, okay?"

Tatsumi raised his hand again. "Where does that take us, please?"

"Somewhere else." Hicks barely managed not to snap at him. "Martinez, how's your hearing?" Martinez gave him a thumbs-up. "You're on point, I'm on our six.

"Let's move—*now*, people!"

3 6

The rhythmic lope Bishop had adopted suited his legs. As long as he rolled heel to toe on each step, they felt stable. The pace was still slower than he'd have liked—sprinting would have been optimal—but he was moving quickly enough that there was a chance of getting away before Anchorpoint blew after all. It was an extremely slim chance, but he could work with that.

He slowed to make the next turn, then stopped short. Suddenly and without warning, he had arrived at the fusion chamber. The 3D schematics in his database weren't merely out of scale, they were just plain wrong. There was no time to consider how such an egregious mistake had been left uncorrected, and very shortly, it wouldn't matter. He filed it away to revisit later, while keeping it current. There was never just one of anything, especially errors; for every one you saw, there were ten more waiting in ambush.

As soon as his shadow fell across the door to the chamber, it whispered open and the lights inside went on, without asking for an entry code. Maybe procedures had been streamlined here. Or maybe in an emergency, artificial persons had fewer restrictions. At least the aliens hadn't found it. The chamber was clean, untouched by the havoc everywhere else in the station—or, indeed, by anything or anyone, for quite some time, judging by the slight canned-air smell.

The fusion package itself sat in a spotless transparent case in the center of the room, a collection of wires and modules contained in a shallow metal bowl on a platform. He thought it looked like conceptual art made by a technophile: *Still Life for Robots in 3D and Visible Light.*

If he got out of this intact, Bishop thought, he should create something with that name, just to see how the humans reacted.

His enhanced senses perceived no definite pattern in the arrangement in the bowl. Some wires were copper braids while others were plastic-coated in every color except red (probably an inside joke, Bishop thought; fusion engineers were a clubby bunch). All the wires were connected to boxes of various shapes and sizes. The largest he could see was ten centimeters long and shaped like a teardrop— no doubt another inside joke—while the smallest was a trapezoid the size of his thumbnail.

He looked past the case to the opposite wall, where stairs led up to an enclosed balcony overhanging the case. That would be the control room, where the air would be even staler.

On the fifth step up, Bishop's left knee slipped sideways. There wasn't any pain-equivalent signal, just an odd sensation as if the joint had loosened. A quick scan told him it might hold for an hour or two more if he were careful. He gripped the railing on his left and tested its stability with human-level strength. It was solid. Maybe when he was finished, he could slide down the bannister—head-first, so his upper body took the impact. Quite inelegant, but nobody would be watching.

A panel next to the control room door lit up, displaying a mirrored disk slightly larger than the palm of his hand and—above it at eye level—a retina scanner. Bishop pressed his hand to the disk and looked into the scanner with his right eye.

"Thank you," said an artificial female voice. *"Please insert hardcopy ID."*

Bishop drew back from the scanner, momentarily at a loss, before he spotted the slot below the disk. He unclipped one of his dog-tags and slipped it in.

"Please confirm identification," said the voice.

"Bishop, Lance, AP," he said. "Science Officer Hyperdyne A-slash-5, Mark 3. Serial number PL3348172438. Permission to inspect software safety protocols."

The response was immediate. *"Permission denied. Inadequate rank and security clearance. Please refer request to your immediate supervisor."*

"Emergency protocols Code Theta 3, 5, alpha, Authority Rosetti comma Shuman."

"Permission denied," the voice said, almost before he got the last word out. *"Inadequate rank and security clearance. Refer request to your immediate supervisor."* Pause. *"Please remove hardcopy identification,"* it added, ejecting his dog-tag.

Bishop took it out of the slot, wiped both sides on his shirt, checked to make sure he hadn't accidentally added any foreign matter, and reinserted it.

"Please confirm identification," said the voice, just like the first time. Peter Pan software—it performed every operation as if it were the first time. Bishop went through the routine again, ending with his request to inspect the safety and emergency protocols.

"Permission denied," the voice said promptly. *"Inadequate rank and security clearance. Refer request to your immediate supervisor."*

It tried to eject his dog-tag again but he pushed it back in and covered the slot with his thumb. "Emergency protocols Code Theta 5, 3, alpha-omega, Authority Welles comma Fox."

Canned air wafted into his face as the door slid open. The control room had remained untouched by human hands since day minus one. And it still was, he thought as he took the chair at the console, feeling the stiff, never-used cushion resist briefly before it gave under his weight.

Adjusting the chair's height, he moved it closer to the console, which lit up as soon as he touched it. On the window in front of him, three separate sections at eye level suddenly opaqued, showing him blank white rectangles. Integrated monitors; very convenient.

"Protocols, safety," Bishop said.

The system had to think that over for half a second before an elaborate menu melted into existence on the center screen. Bishop could imagine Jackson's head bobbing up and down as she used the light-pen on her cap.

"List overload failsafes," he said.

A shorter menu popped up on the left side.

"Display routines to bypass overload failsafes." Anticipating the response, Bishop turned to the display on the right; nothing happened.

"Permission denied. Inadequate rank and security clearance. Refer request—"

"Cancel request," he said. "Display overload failsafe software."

"Request denied," said the voice, and went on to tell him why.

Bishop was unperturbed, although he understood how this could make a human want to pick up a blunt object.

"Authority Welles comma Fox," he said, talking over the voice, which fell silent as an extremely technical diagram came up on the right. It was heavily annotated with characters borrowed from several different sets of symbols and languages, just to make blowing up the space station as difficult as possible.

"Because if it were easy, everyone would do it," he

muttered, which wasn't exactly true but not absolutely false.

There was a flash of green and the graphic of a keyboard appeared on the worksurface in front of him. Now this was something he'd never anticipated. Back in his early days, he'd used something similar to sharpen his manual dexterity, but the interface had never caught on with humans. Maybe it was meant to be the final hurdle before destruction. Anyone who couldn't get past a difficult interface to destroy the space station was a dilettante, not a true nihilist. Or just off their meds.

Hicks would have laughed, Bishop thought, his fingers moving in a quick, precise dance.

The display on the righthand screen was shifting and changing, but he could tell by the rate of its responses that his input was ahead of the software by several dozen commands. The diagram began to dim, then faded out altogether.

A small square appeared in the center of the screen area and slowly grew larger. Bishop's fingers moved faster while he kept track of the box, careful to keep his input ahead of the software.

When he finished, the square was eight centimeters on a side, a simple line drawing and nothing else. Bishop sat back and waited to find out if he'd succeeded on the first try or gotten so far ahead of the program, it had crashed.

Seconds crawled past, eight in total, before all the

screens went white. Two remained blank; the center
screen displayed a simple message, without annotations
or menus:

OVERLOAD OPTION RESET

3 7

By the time the group got to the residential area, smoke was drifting in. Jackson steered them into the large communal kitchen so they could find something to eat while she put on the extractor fans. These were nerve-wrackingly loud but, to Hicks's surprise, the air quality improved right away.

"It won't last," Jackson said in a low voice. "But for now, we'll be able to breathe without choking."

Hicks shrugged. "'For now' always beats 'never.'"

Jackson grinned at him wryly. "You're a real glass-half-full kind of guy, aren't you? Didn't think Marines were like that."

"If the glass weren't half-full, they wouldn't send us out on rescue missions. It'd all just be wars and bughunts. And anyway—" Hicks chuckled as he opened a refrigerated cabinet and surveyed the contents. "—you're missing the point. The glass is refillable."

"Yeah? Refill this." Jackson tossed him a cloth tote bag from the stash she'd found hanging on a hook and started handing out the others. "Pack a lunch for later." She handed out a few more.

Hicks frowned, unsure if it was a good idea to let the group carry more stuff. They were practically carrying Halliday as it was.

Fuck it, he thought. They could take whatever they wanted, and if they had to drop ballast later, well, that was later. Right now, Hicks realized, he was so ravenously hungry he could have eaten the entire contents of the delicatessen cabinet, wrappers and all. He pulled out a selection of sliced meats and cheeses and lined them up on the counter, then looked around for bread. Jackson tossed him a couple of sourdough rolls, obviously amused.

"You saw nothing," he said.

She gave him the "Okay" sign as he opened a jar of large-grain mustard. He made two pastrami sandwiches, wrapped one in a napkin and stuffed it into the largest pocket of his vest, then saw that Quill had been watching him.

"Never go hungry," he told them. "Blood sugar gets out of whack, your head explodes."

They held up the large bowl of potato salad they'd been eating with a serving spoon. "I don't judge."

Hicks discovered the group had bypassed the dining room and gone into the lounge. He didn't blame them. The residents seemed to have dropped everything and bugged out; the odor of spoiling food combined with the smell of smoke made for lousy ambience.

On the other hand, there were no bloodstains, cocooned bodies, acid damage, or any of the other horrors they'd had to look at today. The aliens hadn't dropped by yet but they'd be along shortly, which meant Hicks had to get the group moving again soon. They weren't going to like that much, but they'd like meeting an alien even less.

He went into the lounge and was glad to see that everyone had eaten something. His comment to Quill about blood sugar hadn't been a joke, especially for civilians who didn't have training to fall back on.

Spence and Halliday were sitting together on a long, curved couch. Banana peels were piled up on a low coffee table in front of them; Halliday was hugging herself as she rocked back and forth slightly with her eyes closed. Spence was perched on the edge of the sofa, elbows on her knees and head drooping as if it were too heavy to hold up.

She brightened when Hicks sat down beside her, smiled when she saw his sandwich. He tore it in two and offered her half but she shook her head.

"You sure?" he asked. "I don't want you fainting when I need you to save my ass."

Spence laughed a little. "Nah, I'll be fine. I just ate half of Anchorpoint's banana crop. Did you know—" She held up an unpeeled fruit. "—when you suddenly get a terrible feeling of impending disaster, it's because your potassium is too low? All you have to do to make it go away is eat a banana. Two, if they're small."

"Yeah, I think I remember hearing that somewhere." Hicks took another bite of his sandwich. No banana was this good.

"Unfortunately," Spence went on, "sometimes a feeling of impending doom *is* impending doom, and bananas can't save you. Bananas can't cure aliens." Her gaze wandered to Rosetti, who was leaning against a cabinet housing an elaborate media system, including a holographic projector. He stared back at her with no expression as he dabbed at his mouth. His split lip had reopened.

Spence turned back to Hicks. "Funny story, and absolutely true, I swear—" She raised one hand, oath-style. "—I won a contest for the great privilege of going through this. Well, a series of contests, actually. Most people can't tell just by looking at me that at thirteen, I was the number one student in biology in the entire state of Nebraska." She stared past him into the middle distance. "And I owe it all to monoclonal antibodies—they put me over the top. Without them, I'd be nothing."

In a world that made sense, Hicks thought, he'd have been chuckling at her wit and wondering if she'd ask him out, or if he should ask first. But the world didn't make sense, so he was listening closely and hoping she wouldn't lose her shit before they got to the lifeboats.

Or before Anchorpoint blew, depending on Bishop.

"Then I got into Cornell. Advanced placement," Spence went on, her voice somehow both bleak and matter-of-fact. In his peripheral vision, Hicks saw the rest of the group were actually listening and noted it as something that could be useful later. "That was another contest, and then *another* one just to be considered for a position on a space station. It wasn't easy, getting out here. All of us who did—well, the ones like me, anyway—we're a whole generation who just wanted it that much."

Rosetti let out a breath. "Idealists." Most Marine officers didn't consider that a good thing but the colonel hadn't made it sound like an insult.

Spence laughed a little. "Yeah, I guess so. We wanted to build new worlds and find better ways to live in them— and you know what? It actually could've turned out that way. For a minute there, I really thought it would. But now…" She ran a hand through her thick dark curls, digging her fingers in for a moment as if she were about to tear her hair out. "I never thought it was going to be easy, but it sure wasn't supposed to be like *this.*"

She straightened up, turning to Halliday beside her, as if she'd suddenly just remembered the other woman was there. Spence touched her shoulder, then put one arm around her and squeezed. Halliday didn't react except to stop rocking.

"One thing I'd really like to know." Spence turned to Rosetti, just as he was taking a pill. He washed it down with a swig from a water bottle and tucked a small vial into his back pocket. "Why the hell did we have to bring *you*?" she said.

Rosetti didn't even blink. "Funding." His tone was

utterly unemotional but he was gazing at Spence with a weary, knowing expression that said she wasn't the first thorny idealist he'd ever had in his side.

Spence laughed again. "Yeah, I guess. You buy it, you break it. Right?"

That was enough thoughtful debate for now, Hicks thought as he stood up and crammed the rest of his sandwich into a vest pocket. "Okay, break's over, time to shag it, people." He turned to Spence. "Can you get her up and moving?" he asked, jerking his chin at Halliday.

Spence nodded as Talisa came to help her. Jackson showed him the route they'd be taking on her flexi and transferred it to his. Martinez herded them together and took point with Jackson navigating. Hicks brought up the rear to make sure nothing sneaked up on them and nobody went astray. He doubted Halliday would last much longer—despite the break, she didn't look any better—but when he gave the order to move, she obeyed. If luck was with them, they might clear the residential section before her next crying jag kicked in.

Much to Hicks's dismay, however, luck *wasn't* with them. Jackson had routed them a corridor that would exit onto the main thoroughfare. Except the corridor shown on the map no longer existed—the walls had been rearranged and it was now a large open area. But at least they were headed in the right direction, Hicks thought, just before Halliday stopped short and wailed, "Oh, *God!*"

Hicks barely managed not to grab her by the arm

and tell her, with more profanity than necessary, to stop sniveling. Talisa put herself between him and Halliday while Spence tried to calm the woman down.

"This is *bad*." Talisa looked at him over her shoulder. "We're in a *crèche*."

"Aw, Christ." Hicks pulled Jackson aside. "What the *fuck*, Ops?"

"The *fuck* is, the residents reconfigured the space for their kids," Jackson said angrily, "and didn't get around to telling us about the new layout so we could update the map. If this weren't the Alien Apocalypse, I'd fine them a million different ways for negligence, zoning violations, and endangering minors by placing them in an uninspected enclosure."

"Just go back to Martinez and keep navigating," Hicks said wearily.

"If I meet any of the fuckers that did this, I'm gonna *kill* them," Jackson promised and hurried back to Martinez.

At least the exit was still where it was supposed to be. Just as they reached it, Hicks saw Halliday grab a ragdoll off an empty shelf. Maybe it would help calm her, he thought.

But probably not.

3 8

The semi-gentle lope Bishop had taken on his way to the fusion package didn't work nearly as well now that he'd completed his task, and he was forced to downgrade to a brisk walk. So much for the UPP's goodwill gesture— the good had run out, leaving him to keep going by sheer will.

He'd hoped he wouldn't have to stress his legs even more by climbing back up the elevator shaft. But he had scanned all the other possible escape routes from the fusion chamber, and he couldn't reach the lifeboats—*any* lifeboats—unless he retraced his wobbly, unstable steps. Every other route was impassible, either too damaged, blocked off, or overrun with aliens.

When he finally made it to the elevators, he found the doors still shut though not hot to the touch, which meant the fire was weaker than before and hadn't crept up the shaft. He could open the doors without getting fried by flashover.

If he could open the doors, that was. Prying them apart

by hand was out of the question—his legs weren't strong enough for leverage. He had to find the controls or camp out among the crates until the fusion package blew.

Standing back, he enhanced his vision to survey the frame around the door, centimeter by centimeter, looking for the tiniest disruption in the surface.

And there it was, at waist level on the right, a barely-there seam in the metal that he'd overlooked earlier when he'd been more hurried. He tapped it lightly and it popped open to reveal a lever with alternating black and danger-yellow stripes. It was as stubborn as the one inside the shaft. He had to stand on a plastic crate and bear down with all his weight again to shift it from *Closed* to *Open*.

This time the alarm didn't go off. As he slipped around the side of the doorway onto the ladder, he expected the doors to close again, but they didn't, most likely because the levers on both sides were now set on *Open*.

The fire at the bottom of the shaft had died down quite a bit. There was far less heat and smoke, although the stink of burning plastic, melting insulation, and scorched metal was still strong. Hanging by his arms to spare his legs for the moment, he looked up. The elevator car seemed to be miles away.

Bishop took hold of the next rung up and carefully placed his foot sideways on the lower one to distribute his weight along its length. *As humans always say at a time like this, "Here goes nothin'," he thought, and slowly straightened his leg.

There was a loud ripping noise and suddenly he was hanging by his hands again. He felt his right leg bump against the ladder but there was no feeling at all in his left, as if the whole thing had broken off, although he knew it hadn't; his weight was unchanged.

Leading with his right leg, he swung himself back through the open doorway, hit the floor on his left side, and rolled over a couple of times, without triggering the alarm again. Another lucky break, he supposed, although it didn't count for much next to the *un*lucky break.

He sat up to assess the damage. His left leg was twisted and bent the wrong way, and still completely devoid of all sensation as he repositioned it. The artificial tibia had broken off at the knee, its jagged end ripping through the trouser material. There was no fibula—either it had broken off completely or it had never been there because the UPP didn't waste their resources giving robots silly frills.

Apparently, a self-sealing circulatory system was another silly frill—milky-white fluid was seeping from his thigh onto the floor. But he hadn't lost very much; his upper body had detected the breach in physical integrity and shut down all the feeds to his left leg. Working quickly, he tied off all the exposed broken vessels at the jagged end of his thigh.

He was doing the same to his lower leg when he discovered that despite the lack of sensation, not all the feeds to his central nervous system had been severed. After a moment of consideration, he decided to leave them intact. If he could find material for a splint and something to serve as a crutch, he might be able to keep himself mobile.

Once he was finished, he examined his tibia again, putting a careful fingertip to one of the jagged breaks. It crumbled under his touch. The UPP must have cut their polycarbon with baby powder. No, too wasteful—cornstarch, perhaps.

"Polycarbon," he said aloud, just to back up his neural net archive with more audio. Not that anyone would access it if he didn't make it off the station before it blew, and that was looking less likely by the second. Abruptly, he remembered something Hicks had said.

Hey, we win some, we lose some, the rest get rained out. But we always *dress for the game.*

3 9

The group had barely cleared the residential area before their collective energy started to flag again, due in no small part to the wearing effect of Halliday's constant weeping. Hicks couldn't understand how she still had enough moisture in her body for tears.

He managed to get them all the way to the mainframe service shaft before letting them rest again. Not because he'd planned to, but because they'd all just sat down spontaneously. Martinez signaled he should go along with it but he had almost told them to get moving. Letting the group call the shots was risky. If they were going to survive, he had to maintain his authority…

Then his gaze fell on Rosetti, sitting a few meters away from the rest of the group, holding tight to his pulse-rifle and looking lost—out of his depth, out of options, and probably almost out of painkillers—and felt a sudden, intense rush of compassion for him. Rosetti had been a real Marine once but he'd been so busy maintaining his hothouse authority that he'd lost the real thing.

Hicks set his flexi for three minutes and sat down beside Spence.

"We gotta climb all the way up, don't we?" She sighed, looking up at the ladders and platforms, some with catwalks strung between them. At this distance, they looked like strings.

"Nah." Jackson leaned forward from where she was sitting on Spence's other side so she could address Hicks as well. "Only up to the first platform above that ladder over there." She pointed at the one nearest Rosetti. "It's more than two standard levels but it's not *too* bad."

Spence sighed again. "I should be relieved about that, right?"

Jackson laughed. "The only way *I'd* be relieved is if I heard an announcement that all this was a test of the emergency alien-attack system and it's finished, and even though we flunked so bad we gotta go to night school for three years, we get to go home anyway. That's all *I* wanna hear right now."

"And that's all *I* wanna say," Hicks replied, "but I can't." Raising his voice, he added, "Thirty-second warning, people, so get ready. Jackson, you lead." He turned to Martinez. "You're behind her, then everybody else, and me on our six."

There were a few groans but they all nodded, except for Halliday, who was weeping into the ragdoll with her eyes closed. Hicks looked around at them and then at the ladder and the platform Jackson had pointed to, thinking it might take a goddam miracle just to get them that far.

Out of the corner of his eye, he saw Rosetti sneak two more pills, and swallow them dry.

They'd want another rest after this climb, Hicks knew, and he would give it to them. But after that, he had to make them haul serious ass. He hadn't told any of them when Bishop was setting the station to blow, not even Martinez. As tough and steady as she was, he wasn't sure how she'd handle knowing how much time they had—or rather, how little—and he needed her too much to risk her having a breakdown.

But the good news was, this was his last CO gig, Hicks reminded himself, giving Abellera immediately above him a nudge to climb faster. After this, he could go all outlaw, all the time.

"Corporal Hicks? Sir?" Abellera looked down at him. "Jackson and Martinez are on the platform."

"Copy that." Hicks leaned to one side to see how the rest of them were doing and bumped against a long thick loop of cable dangling beside him. Holding onto it, Hicks leaned a bit farther out for a better view and saw Jackson open the hatch. Martinez motioned her to one side so she could go through first.

Jackson went to help Spence with Halliday. They

had just pulled her up when the alien came through the hatch.

Martinez's pulse-rifle skidded across the platform. Still holding onto Halliday, Spence grabbed for it with her free hand. Her fingertips brushed the metal stock before it fell away into the shadows.

Confused, she turned to ask Jackson *what the fuck* and a warm, salty liquid hit her in the face like a slap. Then the loud, furious hissing registered on her and she realized what kind of trouble they were in.

Spence wiped Martinez's blood out of her eyes and saw the alien holding the Marine in its talons. It had torn off one arm and had the other between its steely teeth. She tried to blink away the blood dripping into her eyes and could only see in one-second snapshots.

Blink

Jackson lying face-down in front of the hatch.

Blink

Halliday on the platform in the fetal position, shuddering and sobbing.

Blink

Tatsumi on the ladder with only his head poking through, yelling for everyone to go back down.

Blink

Hicks shinnying up a cable hanging beside the platform, grabbing the platform's edge.

Blink

The hissing alien tossing away the last pieces of Martinez.

Blink

Viscous strings of saliva mixed with blood, dripping on Halliday.

Blink

A thick spool of cable left hanging on a post in front of a catwalk, then the spool in her hands.

Blink

The alien bending over Halliday, jaws open.

Blink

Spence screamed and hurled the spool of cable at the creature with all her strength.

Blink

The spool bouncing off the side of its ugly, malformed head.

Blink

The alien coming toward her, talons raised.

Blink

Her hand on the railing of a catwalk that stretched all the way across the shaft to an open doorway on the other side.

Blink

The narrow catwalk bouncing and swaying under her and the alien screaming, screaming, screaming behind her—

* * *

I really didn't think this through.

Spence hadn't been sure she could fit into the small recess at the base of the mainframe but the fucking alien had made it across the catwalk much too quickly, which had pushed her past desperate measures into the realm of last resorts. And now, here she was, barely able to breathe. But at least she now knew for a fact that she could wrap one leg around her own neck.

And if she didn't move soon, she'd be stuck in that position for the rest of her life, which wouldn't be very long maybe not even long enough for Martinez's blood to finish drying on her face, she'd still be smelling it when she died—

Shut up! she ordered herself. Shifting slightly, she tried to peek out from her hiding place, but her head was at an angle that made it impossible to see anything.

She had fled across the swinging, swaying catwalk to find herself in a place where the only light came from glowing, multicolored cables twisted or braided into discrete bundles as thick as trees and secured with heavy-duty black bands. Everyone called this area the enchanted techno-forest. It certainly was pretty, but the screaming alien spoiled the effect.

Practically on cue, the creature screamed again. Dammit, did this fucking species do anything other than kill, scream, hiss, and drool? Oh, yeah—they also snapped their extensible teeth. Take away that relentless drive to kill, and what were they? The most boring species in existence. Paramecia were more interesting.

Tully was right—the god*damned*est shit ran through your mind at the weirdest moments.

Tears threatened at the thought of him but she held them in. She could cry after she dealt with her failure to consider the consequences of bouncing a spool of cable off an alien's head.

Spence squirmed out of the cubbyhole, mostly to keep herself distracted with the physical discomfort. If she fell apart now, she was dead for sure. Either the aliens would get her or she'd go out with a bang when the fusion package blew. Although she had seriously considered finding a place to hide out till the end came. There were worse ways to die than instantly in a big, painless blast; much worse.

In the space of a few days, the universe had gone from indifferent and uncaring to a killing ground for living murder-machines, and humans had only themselves to blame for that. Because only humans could be so stupid and arrogant as to believe they could take control of creatures like that. Now the writing was on the wall and it said, *Here lies humanity: too stupid and arrogant to live.*

Spence flexed her arms and legs, then got to her feet and looked around, trying to figure out where the nearest exit might be, or at least where she was relative to the door she had come in through. She'd seen the layout for this area but she didn't have Tully's eidetic memory or his sense of direction, or his quick-witted inventiveness.

And then again, Tully's intellectual gifts hadn't been enough to save him. He'd been the first to die here, leaving her all alone with the only questions of existence that mattered now.

She didn't know much about the aliens, but no one did. What she *did* know: the thing chasing her was big, vicious, and hellbent on killing her. It had no eyes, but whatever it had instead worked just fine in the dark. Maybe the creature had the same senses as humans, but they were combined and amped-up into one big mega-sense.

Without making a sound, she sidled over to the nearest glowing cable-tree and listened for any noises that might tell her where the creature was. All she could hear, however, was a mix of ventilation and a hum pitched so low that she wasn't sure it was real. Either way, she couldn't hang around here wondering.

Taking a deep breath, Spence peered around the tree-trunk of cables just as the alien melted out of the semi-dark not five meters in front of her, multicolored light glinting off its teeth as it screamed. She turned and ran, weaving in and out among the cable-trees, hoping to slow the monster down.

But it seemed to have learned her movements well enough to anticipate them almost as quickly as she could make them. It had mastered both the art and science of hunting prey, any prey, all prey, and she wasn't much of a challenge, especially after spending too much time twisted up like a pretzel in a space barely bigger than a word balloon in one of Tully's comic books.

Graphic novel, Spence. I can't believe you still *don't know the difference.*

In spite of everything, she felt tears threaten again; a moment later, something solid and fixed slammed against her entire body from head to foot, knocking the urge to cry right out of her. Falling backward, she reached out blindly and felt her right hand close on a rounded metal tube. She clenched her teeth and her fist both and jerked to a stop before she hit the deck.

Somehow she got her other hand on the thing and pulled herself upright. It was a ladder—*another* goddam ladder. Her vision hadn't cleared but she practically flew up the rungs, hoping it would take her to a way out, back to the maintenance shaft, or into a tunnel or an airduct too small for a screaming, raging alien.

At the top of the ladder there was a walkway—not a catwalk, and no guard rail, but solid—leading to a doorway and into some place filled with glowing blue light. Shaking off her daze, she dashed through it. No door to slam, she'd have to keep running—

This time, she managed to stop *before* hitting the wall.

Spence ran her hands all over it in a frantic search for anything that might have been a hidden latch for an emergency exit. Finding nothing, she moved to the wall on her right, shoving a flimsy cot aside to get at the baseboard before she stood on the cot to reach the ceiling. It, too, was solid—no ceiling panels, no crawlspace, no airducts, and there was nothing on the floor except what had to be a year's worth of empty takeout boxes, mostly for pizza. All the while, she could hear the inhuman screams growing louder as the alien got closer.

It wouldn't be long before it picked up on her again—her scent or her heartbeat or the volume of air displaced by her movements or Martinez's blood on her face. She had made it easy for the thing by running into a dead end. Here in this lovely little break room where AI maintenance engineers had taken catnaps and gossiped over lunch, the creature would have the Queen of Failing-to-Think-Things-Through for *its* lunch.

She heard talons scraping on the metal and turned to see it stepping from the ladder onto the walkway. Screaming in furious triumph, the monster stalked toward her, claws up and ready, the sharp point of its raised tail aimed at her chest. There was no hurry now; it knew she was trapped.

Desperate, she began rummaging through the food containers on the floor again, searching for something, anything that might make even a half-assed weapon. If it was going to kill her, maybe she could give it something to remember her by.

Her hands landed on a metal box and she jumped, startled. *Please don't be some cartoon character lunch box*, she prayed as she pulled it out of the pile of containers.

The words on the top of the box glowed in bright purple and yellow.

COLONIAL TRANS. AP-49 FLARE SIGNAL
OXY-ATMOSPHERIC 20MM

Ripping the box open, she yanked the flare gun out of its foam mold, whirled to face the alien. It sprang at her and she fired.

The world disappeared in a blinding flash of light.

For a couple of seconds, she thought the fusion package had blown at the exact same moment. But then her vision started to clear, letting her see the alien clutching either side of the doorway so hard cracks had appeared in the wall. There was a nova in its guts growing brighter by the second, the color lightening from orange to yellow.

Its screams only registered on Spence when they stopped and it crossed her mind that she would be happy never hearing that sound for the rest of her life. Or what was left of it.

Blink

The edges of the doorway broke off completely.

Blink

The creature staggered backward, jaws opening and closing as it tried to scream, and only produced a frying sound.

Blink

It fell heavily onto its back, limbs flailing.

Blink

It rolled off the walkway and hit the deck below.

Blink

Spence collapsed amid the food containers on the floor, shaking with reaction.

Had *she* really just done that?

Had she really?

Just done *that*?

She looked down and saw the flare gun in her trembling hand. Yes. She had really, she thought, hugging it to herself. Just done that. *Really.*

"Okay, that happened," she said aloud, just to see if she *could* speak. "That *really* fucking *happened*. To *me*. No, *I* happened to *it*."

A wave of intense emotion swept through her as she looked down at the gun again, and before she realized what she was doing, she held it up and kissed it. Immediately, her face was hot with embarrassment despite there being no one else to see.

"Yeah, that just happened, too," she told the flare gun. "But I won't tell if you won't."

Still holding it tightly, she pulled the metal box onto her lap to see what else it contained. Finding the flare gun here had to be the most improbable stroke of good luck she'd ever had in her young life. Flare guns didn't go with mainframes. But all engineers loved playing practical jokes, especially on new hires. Whatever this crew had planned must have been a doozy.

Crazy damned engineer-pranksters had saved her life.

The thought made Spence tremble even more. If she

lived through this, she was going to kiss the first engineer she met—male, female, or other—right on the mouth.

"Spence! Yo, Spence! You still alive?"

Hicks's voice, distant but clear, snapped her back into focus. There was one more charge in the metal case. She reloaded the gun, clipped it to a lanyard, and hung it around her neck before going out onto the walkway, marveling that the alien hadn't bled there. Down below, however, the alien was sinking into the hole its acid-blood was eating into the deck. The flare in its guts had died but it had burned long enough.

Hicks called her name again, closer now.

"Yeah, I'm here!" Spence said, laughing a little. She decided to try sliding down the ladder instead of climbing and was surprised when she landed without falling. Apparently this was her day. She wasn't even shaking now—more like vibrating with electric triumph. Score: Spence, one; alien, big fat *ZERO*!

"Don't worry about the alien!" she called to Hicks. "It's dead! I *killed* that bitch! I did—*me!*"

Silhouettes appeared among the glowing cable-trees and turned into Hicks and Talisa Nkosi. They had come to save her from the alien, and instead *she* had saved *them*! Before they even *knew* it!

"Really, I *killed* that fucker! It's dead and *I* did it!"

She went on telling them about it as they led her to the hatch and brought her back across the catwalk. Talisa actually walked sideways, watching her carefully while

Hicks kept a tight hold on the back of her shirt. Spence didn't mind. Had the catwalk swayed and swung this much when she had run across it before with the alien chasing her? She couldn't remember now, and for some reason that made her laugh.

"I'm sorry," she said to Talisa, then glanced over her shoulder at Hicks, who told her to look straight ahead. "You guys must think I'm nuts-a-rama. I don't know why I'm laughing."

"It's reaction," Hicks said, sounding brisk and businesslike. "Deep, slow breaths and keep looking straight ahead."

Breathing deeply reduced her giddiness and quelled the urge to laugh; it also made her feel shaky again, and the motion of the catwalk didn't help. It seemed to take forever to reach the platform where the group waited for her in a huddle, their faces pinched and unhappy. They'd probably feel better when she told them how she'd killed the alien with the flare gun hanging around her neck.

But before she could say anything at all, Jackson was talking, and Spence was so relieved the chief of Operations wasn't dead after all that she was happy to wait till the woman had finished.

"Okay, we're heading up to the next level," Jackson told everyone, and Spence was also relieved to see she had shut off the damned light-pen so it wasn't making trails in the air every time she moved. "It's not ideal but it actually puts us closer to the lifeboat bay. So c'mon, get climbing, guys—*right now!*"

"Okay, Chief, copy that loud and clear," Spence said with a show of enthusiasm as she looked around for Halliday. "I just need a little help with—" She cut off; the ragdoll lay on the platform where Halliday had been.

"No! No, *goddammit, no!*" she shouted, looking from the group to the ladders and catwalks and cables, and finally to Hicks. "I *killed* that fucker, I *killed it*—"

Hicks moved her back from the edge of the platform but she lunged for the ragdoll. The feel of cold, thick slime made her cry out in horror and she hurled it away as hard as she could. Talisa took hold of her arm, and with surprising strength forced it straight while Hicks produced an aerosol can from a medi-kit. He sprayed her arm from elbow to shoulder with something that smelled medicinally minty, over and over until the can was empty. Tossing it over his shoulder, he turned to the group. "Okay, guys, you heard the chief—get climbing."

Rosetti was already ten feet up and moving as fast as he could.

Jackson blew out a contemptuous breath. "Look on the bright side," she said to Hicks. "If anything's up there, it eats *him* first."

Hicks motioned for Spence to follow Jackson and she obeyed, focusing her attention on the physical task and nothing else. She was no longer all souped-up with energy but she wasn't crashing yet. The urge to cry over

Halliday had subsided though it wasn't completely gone; it was more like her mind had set it aside for later consideration. For now, she was steady, stable. Good old self-preservation—it overrode even the craziest, most fucked-up shit.

And that was all it was, Spence told herself. It was *only* self-preservation, *not* selfish relief that she no longer had to hold Halliday up while she *whimpered* and *sniveled*. And more than anything, she absolutely *wasn't* furious at Halliday for getting herself killed so that all the effort Spence had put into keeping her alive, all the physical, mental, and emotional strain had been for nothing. Nope, nothing like that.

Later, when this was over, she'd have time to get her head together, come to terms with everything. But that was later, much later. Right now, she had to climb this ladder.

Martinez's blood was dry on her face. Some of it cracked and fell away in little flakes; some of it stayed under her nails when she scratched it off.

4 0

Bishop finished cinching his belt around his left leg and gave it an experimental shake; everything stayed in place. He still couldn't put any weight on it, but at least it wouldn't be swinging around and throwing him off-balance. After he got up the ladder, he could try to find something more useful in the mall wreckage. Maybe something with wheels.

But that was assuming the place wasn't wall-to-wall aliens, of course.

Pulling himself upright on a short stack of crates, he kept most of his weight on his hands then gradually and carefully let his right leg bear some. His posture was a little off but his right leg held—it had always felt a bit sturdier than the left. But it wouldn't last; Sergeant Apone would have said it was within spitting distance of failure. Although as he remembered it, Apone could spit farther than most people. Too bad the sergeant wasn't here, Bishop thought as he swung himself around the open elevator doors onto the ladder again.

His right knee sent out a signal that a human would have felt as a twinge. The reduced volume of artificial blood meant he had fewer nanos in circulation for micro-maintenance. Eventually, all his artificial muscle tissue would need downtime to recover, unless he could find a clinic and transfuse himself with more nanos to boost his kinetics.

As he reached for the next rung, he caught sight of the time on his flexi: 2139 hours. As he'd overheard Vasquez say to Drake more than once: *Shake it, vato—it's always later than you think.*

"There's no hatch here, just an air vent," Rosetti said, anxiously. The group were bunched up around him equally uneasy. This platform was slightly smaller than the last one. "Why isn't there a hatch? Are you sure this is the right way?"

"Yeah, stop asking, already," Jackson snapped, pulling a telescoping power-screwdriver out of her pocket. "Hatches are off the menu now. The last time we opened one, it didn't go well." She extended the screwdriver to its full length and went to work on the vent cover. "You got an issue, tell the corporal. Better yet, tell yourself."

She had the cover off in seconds, then stood back while Hicks shone his flashlight into the duct.

"Okay, people, it's hands-and-knees time," he said. "You got anything that doesn't fit in your pocket or anything that feels heavy, leave it. This time, I'm first, then Jackson, then Spence, and then everyone else. Colonel, you're on our six. Everybody got that?"

They all nodded except Rosetti, who looked dubious as well as apprehensive. Deciding he didn't care, Hicks clipped the flashlight to the barrel of his weapon and slung it across his front, shortening the strap so it hugged his chest, then climbed into the vent.

"Right behind you," Jackson called after him. The beam from her light-pen swooped away as she turned her cap around. A chorus of protests told her to shut it off again. After that, there were only grunts of effort, muttered curses, and loud panting from Rosetti.

The man had pushed ahead of the civilians, Hicks realized with a brief but intense surge of anger. Not that he could do anything about that now, but later he was going to make sure Rosetti got a rip for that one, even if it were posthumous.

After several minutes, the incline started to become steeper, harder to climb. Everyone was breathing heavily now, struggling just to keep themselves from sliding back down. Worse, the growing heaviness in Hicks's eyes warned him carbon dioxide was building up the way it always did in close quarters.

Hicks paused, wedging himself in place. "Everybody keeping up?" he called. "Sound off!" To his relief, they were all present and still alert.

"Barely ten more meters, folks." Jackson's breathlessness

made her voice reverberate more strongly than Hicks's had. "Then we're into area K-58-A, and from there it's a straight shot to the lifeboat bays. No more ladders or airducts. Unless we have to walk through the walls."

Rosetti's head popped up behind Jackson. "Yeah, that's great," he said, even more breathless. "Now could we get moving?"

"Yes, *sir*." Hicks looked up to see light coming through the vent cover at the other end of the duct. Not the proverbial oncoming train, he thought; that would have been too easy.

The surface went from bare metal to a smooth enamel coating; probably an anti-static overlay to resist dust building up. Why it was only on the last few meters he had no idea. Maybe they'd run out. Typical—the Company shorted everyone on everything.

He reached the vent and peered through the narrow slits at the area beyond. "Hey, Jackson, any ideas on how I get this thing off?"

Jackson gave a single, breathless laugh. "It's just crappy plastic—one punch oughta do it."

And not a particularly hard punch at that. Hicks slid out of the duct and broke off the sharp edges before he reached in for Jackson.

"They use metal covers in the maintenance shafts and conduits," she added as he helped her out. Her front was covered with dust and grime, and so was his, he realized. They had cleaned out decades of build-up with their bodies. "But the common areas don't see heavy industrial activity, so they don't make anything better than it has to be. They'd probably make the fucking *walls* out of paper if they could get away with it."

Hicks couldn't even look at Rosetti as he and Jackson tugged him out of the duct by his arms. Spence came next, followed by Talisa. Behind her, Tatsumi was gasping raggedly, trying to catch his breath as he held out both hands.

Suddenly, everyone behind him in the duct was shouting and screaming. Something else was in there, something very large and very strong, hissing and banging around in a vicious frenzy that didn't drown out terrified voices begging for help they already knew couldn't come.

Tatsumi cried out in pain as something tried to pull him back into the duct. Keeping a tight grip on him, Hicks braced one foot against the wall and pulled as hard as he could with Spence yanking on his other arm and Jackson tugging on fistfuls of his shirt. The three of them managed to haul Tatsumi farther out of the duct and the alien came with him, slimy with human blood and festooned with ragged pieces of flesh and clothing, its jaws still clamped on the man's lower leg, too kill-crazy to let go.

In one swift movement, Hicks unslung his rifle and slammed the butt down on the creature's head. The thing gave a nasty wet hiss but hung on until Hicks hit it again. Tatsumi screamed in agony as acid-blood splashed onto his leg. Hicks finally pulled him all the way out of the duct and told Spence and Jackson to drag him a few meters farther away, then bent to peer through the opening.

He was hoping the creature would jump out to attack him, so he could kill it giving anyone behind it an acid shower. For the briefest of seconds he saw the ugly, eyeless monster, baring its teeth and hissing furiously as it slithered back toward the three horrified faces behind it. Then something slammed into him hard, knocking him sideways. Hicks staggered and recovered his balance just as Rosetti thrust his pulse-rifle into the duct and fired on full automatic until the magazine was empty.

Hicks's reaction was reflexive yet completely mindful. He could feel himself twist to drive the punch with his body; the impact of his fist on Rosetti's face registered on every nerve. He saw every moment of the man hitting the wall behind him in preternaturally high definition, heard with utter clarity the sharp rap of his head against it and the rustle of his uniform as he slid down to the floor.

Instantly, Jackson was standing over the colonel, pointing his own pulse-rifle at his head. "You know, I think some part of me has wanted to kill you for quite a while, motherfucker," she said in that quiet, have-a-canapé voice. "Maybe since the day you got here."

Rosetti looked up at her. "Go ahead." As if offering hors d'oeuvres of his own.

Hicks shone his flashlight into the duct and saw only the ragged edges where acid-blood was still eating through the metal. The rest of the duct had fallen away, taking the alien and the other three lab techs with it. No more screams, no hissing, no more cries of pain and terror. He hoped the fall had killed them.

He became aware of Tatsumi whimpering in pain but he turned first to Jackson, who was still standing over Rosetti with the pulse-rifle.

"Forget it, Ops," he told her. "It's empty anyway." He pulled a fresh clip out of a vest pocket and tossed it to her. Jackson ejected the empty one and reloaded, then slung the weapon over her shoulder, giving Rosetti a defiant glare as she took ownership.

"Hicks." Spence was kneeling beside Tatsumi with Talisa. "We could use some light over here."

He obliged, watching as Talisa carefully slit Tatsumi's pant leg while a wisp of smoke rose up from where the alien's blood was still burning through the cloth.

"Watch out," Spence said as a drop of acid landed on Talisa's flexi. The tech ripped it off her arm and hurled it away, then went back to Tatsumi's trouser leg without missing a beat. Hicks stared in amazement. She had the steadiest hands he'd ever seen. Spence reached up to reposition his flashlight slightly as the other woman bent over Tatsumi's leg.

"My God." Talisa's face went ashen.

A good chunk of Tatsumi's calf muscle was gone, and the remaining flesh was black around the edges. The acid-blood had lost some potency before it could reach the bone, maybe because the alien was so new. Hicks had seen worse in combat, but this poor guy was a lab rat, not a soldier. He'd probably never been in so much pain. Hicks could see it was more than a few of Rosetti's precious pills could handle. Not that the colonel would be inclined to share.

Hicks pulled a small medical kit from a zippered compartment in the lining of his vest and removed a single-use syringe.

Spence frowned at it, puzzled. "What's *that*?"

"It only *looks* like a kid's squirt gun." Hicks pressed the business end against Tatsumi's leg just above the wound and squeezed the handle. "Only one dose, but it's the good stuff—the *real* good stuff. Can't get *this* at Happy Hour on the Ginza. Do they even have Happy Hour on the Ginza?" he added to Tatsumi, watching the man for signs of an allergic reaction. Tatsumi's whole body relaxed, his face going from agonized to composed. Good thing; there was no epinephrine injector in the kit, which Hicks thought was one hell of an oversight.

"That was fast," Spence marveled. "And it's not even intravenous."

"Told you, it's the good shit." Hicks chuckled a little. "Six times stronger than Heroin 3.0, plus eight additional ingredients to keep you up and rockin' the house. We get caught just *holding* one of these without a good reason, and it's a year in the brig."

Tatsumi looked around at them with a mildly bewildered expression and said something in Japanese.

"What'd he say?" Talisa asked Jackson.

Jackson consulted her flexi. "Translator says he wants to know if he's late for his shift." She looked past her to Tatsumi. "No, you're right on time. We're doing something different today."

Hicks passed the single dressing from the first-aid kit to Spence and tossed the empty case aside. "We'll have to carry him."

"Then we carry him," Talisa said simply, as if it went without saying.

Tatsumi raised himself up on his elbows to watch Spence winding the dressing around his calf, a bit dismayed but still calm. If the meds worked on lab rats like they did on Marines, Hicks estimated he'd be cruising for another eight hours.

Then he turned to see how his other problem child was doing.

One side of Rosetti's face was swelling but other than that he hadn't moved a muscle, not even to top up from the vial in his pocket. Maybe he was afraid Hicks would take his pills away and give them to Tatsumi. Or maybe he was running low.

"Get up, Colonel, it's time to move." Hicks turned back to Jackson and nodded at the pulse-rifle slung over her shoulder. "I think you'd better hang onto that for now. Okay by you?"

Jackson nodded.

4 1

It wasn't until Bishop was nearly at the elevator that he remembered the distance between the ladder and trapdoor, which surprised and disturbed him. The memory lapse was a phenomenon of organic brains. It rarely occurred in artificial persons while they were active, although it wasn't impossible.

Perhaps it was a glitch caused by the loss of artificial hemoglobin. He hadn't lost enough to affect the functioning of his central nervous system, so his cognition shouldn't have been impaired. But brains could be tricky, even the artificial kind. Under normal circumstances, he'd have set a diagnostic to run continuously in the background. As things were, however, he couldn't afford to use onboard resources for anything other than the immediate situation.

As he got closer to the bottom of the elevator, he saw the section of floor closest to the doors was badly cracked and broken. The alien queen had been trying to punch another hole in the floor, then stopped, probably to go after easier prey.

It wasn't hard to finish what the queen had started— as soon as he pulled at the damaged floor, it came away in chunks. Another argument for luck, he thought as he squeezed through the gap to clamber up into the mall.

For a few seconds, he lay quietly with his cheek against the floor to catch vibrations from anything large and dangerous moving around nearby, but there was nothing. Even the artificial waterfall had finally shut down. It wouldn't stay this quiet, but for the moment he could hunt undisturbed through the detritus for something he could use to improve his mobility.

His gaze fell on a long strip of metal on the floor, part of the frame around the elevator doors, and he picked it up. The alloy was light but very strong—not strong enough to withstand an enraged alien but strong enough for an artificial person with a bum leg.

Working with it took longer than usual—he could feel the strain in the artificial muscles in his arms, shoulders, and upper back. He'd lost nanos along with hemoglobin and the remaining quantity couldn't fortify or repair overworked tissue as quickly as usual. Couldn't be helped; time was growing short and he had furlongs to go before anyone could sleep.

Not as graceful as Frost's original, he knew, but it was humans who had a way with words, not artificial persons.

* * *

Hicks felt like the only thing he'd ever done was slog through smoky passageways, wheezing and coughing as he and Talisa half-dragged Tatsumi between them. Spence and Jackson led the way, also wheezing and coughing, with Rosetti stumbling along at the rear, all of them heading toward a destination that Hicks wasn't sure existed anymore.

Rosetti was having a harder time than the rest of them—the painkillers depressed his breathing. Tatsumi was coughing least, his respiration even more depressed by what Hicks had given him. The sedative effect of the painkiller seemed to have overridden all the other ingredients in the good shit; rockin' the house was off the agenda.

Well, medication was tricky. As Dietrich had often said, injuries never read the instructions on the container. Hicks had given Tatsumi something formulated for an active, physically fit Marine badly injured in combat. It had *not* been made for a middle-aged scientist whose natural habitat was a laboratory where he did a lot of strenuous thinking. Hicks imagined Tatsumi was tripping comets, but at least he wasn't in pain.

After a bit, he noticed Talisa kept glancing behind them. At first he thought she was keeping track of Rosetti, then realized she wasn't actually looking at him.

"Hey," he said, keeping his voice low. "Something I should know about?"

"I'm afraid we're leaving a trail." She jerked her chin at Tatsumi's leg. "Not breadcrumbs."

Hicks saw she was right; something thick and yellowish was leaking from the dressing on Tatsumi's wound, which in his experience was never a good sign.

He was about to call a break so he could see how bad Tatsumi's leg was when Jackson suddenly stopped short and pointed Rosetti's pulse-rifle at a shiny sign on the wall to their right:

LIFEBOAT BAY 20 METERS

"See that? We made it!" she said with a faint laugh that became a coughing fit.

"Damn." Hicks blinked at the sign. "You're right. We did."

"Don't sound so surprised," she said, and coughed some more. "Have I ever steered you wrong?"

"The day is young." Hicks wiped his stinging eyes, noting absently that he'd been doing that for quite some time.

"Not as young as it used to be," Jackson said and the grim note in her voice gave Hicks a sudden chill. Hudson smirked at him in his mind's eye. *Goose didn't just walk over your grave, son*, he said. *Goose walked over everybody's grave.*

Hicks shut him down as Jackson took them around a corner into a large circular area with a reception desk. The entrance to the lifeboat bay was to the left but the door itself was featureless. A large sign on the front of the desk declared:

LIFEBOAT & LAUNCH ASSEMBLY POINT
CHECK IN • HEAD-COUNT • ALLOCATION

Hicks felt surreal. The reception desk made boarding a lifeboat seem as mundane as a dental appointment or a job interview. *Go in when they call your number, proceed directly to your assigned bay, and don't forget to fill out the customer satisfaction survey. Thank you for your cooperation, bon voyage and have a nice life. Next.*

"I thought we were meeting groups from other areas of Anchorpoint," Spence said, concern large on her face. "It *can't* be just us. Where *is* everyone?"

"Probably launched already," Hicks said, hoping he didn't sound as uneasy as he felt.

"Guess again," said Jackson from behind the reception desk. She'd turned her cap around to use the light-pen on the countertop screen. "All lifeboats are still docked and prepped."

"But—but that would mean we're the only ones who made it." Talisa went over to Jackson, dragging Tatsumi and Hicks with her. "Could that really be—that we're the only ones?" She looked at the others; no one said anything.

"There are other lifeboat bays," Hicks said gruffly. He gave Jackson a warning look and mouthed, *Shut up.* Some questions had one answer, some had several, and some didn't have any. And when you only had answers nobody wanted to hear, you shut the hell up.

Abruptly, Rosetti came out of his painkiller fog, went

to the door, and pressed his thumb to a spot at eye level. The door slid up, revealing a long hallway with soft blue indirect lighting. Hicks wondered what the hell was it with the blue lighting as he and the others watched Rosetti march toward the very wide door at the end of the hall.

"I really shoulda greased him," Jackson said wistfully.

"Nah," Hicks said. "What'd be the point?"

"The point?" Jackson looked at him, her still-grimy face incredulous. "In case you forgot, the *point* is he let those bastards run their fucking experiments. He coulda said no but he didn't. You and Bishop tried to stop it, but not him. Rosetti *let* them do whatever the fuck they wanted."

"No, he didn't," Hicks said, realizing he really did feel sorry for the man. No Marine deserved to have their military career end in a state of total and absolute FUBAR. The only thing worse than getting wiped out with your command was being the only survivor.

And the only thing worse than *that* was being the only survivor *twice*.

But then, it wasn't over yet, Hicks reminded himself. There was still a strong chance he wouldn't live to regret this one.

"Rosetti's rank didn't mean shit to the bastards who brought this down on Anchorpoint," he went on. "He was nothing but a buffer to keep the rest of us away from them. And it wouldn't do any good to grease *them*, either."

"Bullshit," Jackson snapped. "Why the fuck not?"

Hicks gave a short, humorless laugh. "Because what

you really want to grease is the Company, and I'm not sure that's even possible." As they moved down the corridor after Rosetti, he gave Talisa a questioning look—Tatsumi was getting heavier. She gave a small shrug.

"Why not?" Jackson sounded slightly less belligerent.

"Because Weyland-Yutani's an octopus with a thousand arms," Hicks told her, "and at the end of each one is another thousand arms. Grease one and it'll just grow back. I doubt anyone could destroy them."

"No *human* could," Spence piped up from behind him. "But there are some *non*-humans I wouldn't bet against."

Her words gave him another chill, more intense and apparently too real to rate a wisecrack from Hudson. He wouldn't have bet against the aliens, either, Hicks thought, and they wouldn't stop at Weyland-Yutani.

Rosetti had reached the door and was entering a code into a small keypad on the wall beside it, or trying to. Instead of the door opening, a buzzer would sound and an electronic voice would tell him to try again. It took him half a dozen tries before the door finally slid open.

Hicks blinked at the brightly lit room, unaware that he and the rest of the group had stopped halfway down the hall. Rosetti had picked one hell of a big lifeboat—he could see racks and racks of vacuum suits, all immaculate white except for rings of color at the elbow and knee. Each had a matching, solid-color helmet. Like solid-colored billiard balls, Hicks thought, or Anchorpoint's favorite brand of plastic crates.

The idea dug into Hicks's brain and stuck there while he stared at the grotesque tangle of shiny black aliens amid the mess of overturned racks and crumpled vacuum suits in the center of the room. Bodies and limbs and heads protruded from the snarl at absurd angles, making it impossible for Hicks to tell how many aliens he was looking at. It was revolting, monstrous, but worst of all, unprecedented—he'd never seen them do anything like this—and still his mind held onto the matching crates.

Rosetti let out a terrified bellow and fled back up the corridor.

4 2

Hicks pushed Tatsumi into Talisa's arms and put himself in front of Jackson and Spence. Blind with panic, Rosetti shoved past them, tripped over his own feet, and fell face-down. Spence stepped over him as he lay on his side gasping for air to stand next to Hicks as if she belonged there. Before he could yell at her to run, she raised her arm and a bright red streak flew down the hallway, hitting the squirming alien mass dead center.

The tangle of aliens burst into flame and broke apart, screaming and raging while the now too-familiar chemical stink of burning alien flesh and acid-blood overwhelmed the smell of smoke. Hicks's stomach gave a warning lurch as he herded everyone back up the hallway, helping Talisa drag Tatsumi while turning to shoot at the fiery mess behind them.

"*Rosetti!*" Hicks yelled as they hit the reception area. "Dammit, where are you?"

Out on the main thoroughfare, Jackson beckoned to them frantically. "This way—*hurry!*"

Twenty feet farther on, Hicks saw Rosetti punching an entry code into another door; this one took him only one try.

"Good going, Colonel!" Hicks called as he and Talisa dragged Tatsumi faster.

Rosetti looked over his shoulder and his expression said it all. Hicks shouted at him to stop but Jackson was already there. She gave the colonel a hard shove into the room and stood guard to make sure the rest of them got inside before she slammed the door and locked it. A second later, something big slammed into it, making them all jump.

Lights flickered, almost came on, and failed. Hicks swept the flashlight on his rifle around the room. Jackson had Rosetti backed up against the wall, shining her own flashlight directly into his eyes.

"The son of a bitch was gonna lock us out." Jackson drew the service pistol and pressed the barrel hard against the swollen side of Rosetti's face. "I oughta *kill* you for that, you fucking *bastard*—"

"*Don't*," Hicks ordered her. Pulling her away took a great deal of effort. "You'd just be doing him a favor."

Jackson's expression said she thought Hicks was out of his mind. "*How?*"

"I've seen it before," he told her. "In combat."

It took a moment for Jackson to get it. Disgusted, she turned her back on Rosetti and he sidled away from her, keeping close to the wall and giving Hicks a resentful look. Tough shit; if the son of a bitch wanted to die, he could grow some balls and do it himself, Hicks thought as he continued shining the flashlight over the floor and walls. Amazingly, there wasn't any smoke in here but the smell was in the air, along with a hint of something worse.

"What is this, an office?" he asked.

"Yeah. I found a desk," Jackson said. "And a lamp, if it works…"

It did, and Hicks was amused to see it was a reproduction of an antique banker's lamp with a green shade. Over half the offices he'd ever been in had one of these. The warm, golden light was supposed to eliminate eyestrain. Hicks had no idea if it really helped tired eyes but it was definitely better at throwing shadows than dispersing them.

There was another hard slam against the door and they all jumped again. Things were getting more absurd by the moment, Hicks thought. Monsters were running loose out there, but in here everyone was safe from eyestrain.

Another hard bang on the door, followed by an enraged scream. Hicks motioned for all of them to stand back and put a hand on the door, to see if he could tell how long it would hold. It was surprisingly solid and he realized this was also a safe room, large enough to shelter maybe a dozen people along with whoever sat behind the desk. It was a great idea, with one major problem: now that they were in, they weren't getting out.

It figured. Life-support for a dozen people in here would last for only so long. The Company designed space stations with the assumption that in an emergency, rescue had to arrive in a timely fashion or not at all. You didn't rescue the dead, you mourned them.

Hudson popped into his head, grinning more smugly than ever. *Don't be so morbid, jarhead. Wait till you're really dead, like me.* In spite of everything, Hicks chuckled inwardly.

The door would hold for a while. How long depended on how many aliens threw themselves against it trying to get at the soft human filling inside. Hell, the surrounding wall might go before the door gave—not that it would matter either way if the air went first.

Sitting on the edge of the desk, Hicks let out a long breath. Unlike certain very young Marines he knew of, he'd never had grandiose dreams of dying heroically in combat, but after everything he'd been through with the group, sitting around in a safe room and waiting to suffocate was a real letdown.

"Hicks?" Spence said in a small, unhappy voice. She was standing next to a room divider. He frowned; it was a large office but this seemed pretentious.

Going over to her, he discovered the divider had been put up to sequester a workstation. He was looking at it from the back but he could tell it was an elaborate custom-job with multiple screens and industrial-strength processors that ran at light-speed, all built into a compact desk. Apparently, whoever worked here felt putting up an extra barrier within the office would enhance concentration. It probably did but Hicks still thought it was a bit pretentious.

The heavy copper smell hit him just as his torch beam found the dark stain on the carpet, most of it around the left side of the chair behind the workstation. It would be an ergonomic chair, very comfortable for someone who spent long hours at a workstation, although the person sitting there would be past caring about good lumbar support. Motioning for Spence and the others to stay back, Hicks moved around to the other side of the workstation, weapon raised in case something less dead was lying in wait.

The dead woman slumped in the fancy ergonomic chair was wearing a lab coat. A quarter of her head was gone, blown off by the automatic in the hand now at rest on her thigh. Hicks estimated it hadn't been even an hour since she had opted out. But first she had smashed all three workstation screens.

"That's Dr. Trent," Spence said, standing a few meters away on the other side. "Dr. Adele Persephone Trent, MD, PhD times three. Or four, I keep forgetting. Head of the Exobiology Department."

From where Spence stood, Hicks knew she could see only the undamaged part of the woman's face. Sadly, she had an unobstructed view of the blood, brain, and bone splattered on the workstation, the walls, even the ceiling. Whatever Dr. Adele Persephone, MD, Ph.D., etc. had seen on her monitors had been so awful that she had smashed all of them before using the automatic on herself.

The state of her body told Hicks she had pressed the

barrel under her chin and almost chickened out. Not unusual—lots of aspiring suicides ended up with a faceful of flash-burns after pulling the gun away at the last moment. In Adele Trent's case, however, her trigger finger had been faster than her change of heart. Hicks was sure she'd never imagined that this would be how she'd quit her job; no one ever did. He felt a lot sorrier for her than he ever had for Rosetti.

The thought of the colonel was a sudden hot surge of anger. "Hey, Rosetti! Come here!" he yelled.

Rosetti's gray face appeared over the top of the partition on Hicks's left and became even grayer when he saw Trent's body.

"See that? *Do* you?" Hicks demanded.

Rosetti glanced at him warily but didn't move.

"That was Adele Trent," Hicks went on. "She did herself. And if you don't chill out quick, somebody's gonna do likewise to *you*."

"She was brilliant," Rosetti said bleakly. "Dedicated to her work. And to the Company. Very ambitious."

Spence gave a hard, scornful laugh. "Thanks for the testimonial! I'm sure it makes her feel *a lot better* about *being dead*." She turned to Hicks. "Dr. Trent was a devoted *scientist—not* a Company meat puppet."

"Yeah, I get it." Hicks played the flashlight around the partitioned area, looking for something useful without knowing what it might be. There were two heavy thumps against the door, followed by two more.

"Hicks!" Spence gave the corpse a wide berth as she ran to him and grabbed his arm with both hands. "Look at the back wall!"

The flashlight showed a neat arrangement of shadow-box frames containing hardcopy certificates with shiny gold seals. Some were academic degrees, others looked like awards, or maybe that was just the one that kept flipping between a certificate and a 3D double helix. In the very center of the row, a white lab coat hung on a hook; there was a bit of Dr. Trent's blood and brain tissue on one sleeve.

"Don't you see it?" Spence said, even more excited.

Hicks blinked. "Gimme a hint—what am I supposed to see?" he asked.

Spence darted forward and ripped the lab coat down, revealing it had actually been hanging from a bright red handle. Hicks felt his jaw drop. Stunned, he watched as she knocked the box frames down and stood back. Block letters faded into existence on the wall, seemingly triggered by the flashlight beam:

**EMERGENCY AIRLOCK
EXIT TO HULL SECTOR 308**

"*Now* do you see it?" she shouted joyfully while another alien smashed against the door, hissing and screeching. "It's an airlock—it's *a goddam airlock!*"

For a moment, Hicks couldn't move, couldn't even

speak. The seams of the hatch were all but invisible, but now that he knew, he could make them out even in the lousy light.

"It's the only chance we've got," Spence was saying. "If we get out on the hull, we can get into a lifeboat from the outside!"

Everyone was looking at him, waiting for the go-ahead. Hicks slung his rifle and sneaked a glance at his watch. 21:46. They'd get out of the airlock, but if Bishop had succeeded, they didn't have a hope in hell of getting to a lifeboat in time. He could tell them that and watch them melt down to the soundtrack of aliens trying to smash down the door until whatever end finally came.

Or he could let them have purpose for the rest of their lives—all fourteen minutes of it. He hated to admit it, but Rosetti had been right about how people needed something to do more than they needed the truth.

"Okay," he said, hoping the heartiness in his voice didn't sound forced. "Saddle up, folks, it's go time. Let's *do* this thing!"

Spence used both hands to pull the red handle from upright to horizontal. There was a soft whisper as the door unsealed and slowly swung open. Inside, bright lights went on immediately.

"*Inner door open,*" a synthetic female voice announced. "*This is a five-person emergency exit to hull sector 308. It is equipped with five Mark 12 emergency vacuum suits, suitable for a single use in an evacuation procedure.*"

A safe room big enough for twelve people and only five vacuum suits in the airlock—typical Company math, Hicks thought. Although considering how well they'd camouflaged the escape hatch, he supposed it was a miracle there were any vacuum suits.

Talisa caught Hicks's eye and nodded almost imperceptibly at Tatsumi, lying on the carpet. He put up a finger, telling her to wait. It was the only reply he could think of.

"Each Mark 12 suit is equipped with an automatic locator beacon, inter-suit communications, and adjustable-strength magnetic soles," the synthetic voice continued. *"Each is charged with an air supply set to last for approximately two hours of ordinary physical activity. Users are cautioned that elevated respiration and heartbeat consume air more quickly. By contrast, sedation can extend the air supply somewhat, though not indefinitely. If you experience difficulty with O-rings or if you have concerns about seal integrity, please activate the help file for additional advice."*

Jackson looked around at the group. "How to fit six people into five vacuum suits wasn't on the engineering curriculum when I was in school," she said. Her gaze landed on Rosetti, who had moved closer to the open airlock, ready to jump in. "If anyone has to stay behind, I nominate *him*."

"Corporal Hicks!" Talisa said urgently. "Bring the light, something's happening—"

Tatsumi was writhing on the carpet, eyes rolled back in his head and mouth gaping while something squirmed and twisted under the stained bandage on his leg. The poison-yellow fluid had saturated the dressing and was now soaking into the carpet. Suddenly the swelling bulged and there was an ugly ripping sound as a small chest-burster tore itself out of Tatsumi's leg. Everyone jumped back as it scuttled off into the shadows.

Now they're leg-*bursters?* Hicks thought, feeling surreal again. He started to track it with the flashlight but Talisa grabbed his hand and made him put the torch back on Tatsumi. Two spots of red had bloomed on his shirt; a second later, two more creatures broke through his chest but somehow couldn't get more than halfway out, while a third emerged twisting and squirming from his mouth.

A strong hand yanked him backward roughly, putting him out of range when Tatsumi's head exploded. The air was filled with the stench of acid-blood eating through walls and carpeting and flesh, and Hicks felt his stomach preparing to jettison everything in it. Then Jackson shoved him farther back from Tatsumi and shot the last two aliens before they could free themselves from his chest.

Hicks returned the favor by pushing her ahead of him toward the back wall. "Everybody into the airlock *now*!"

Rosetti dived through the open door like a swimmer. Hicks gathered Talisa and Spence into a clumsy huddle with Jackson, shoved them all into the airlock, and pulled the door closed behind him.

"Suit up!" Hicks ordered.

Everyone stripped quickly down to their underwear.

Talisa reached for the one hanging nearest to her and then screamed as one of the things that had burst out of Tatsumi flopped out of the open front and fell at her feet.

"*Nobody shoot!*" Hicks threw himself against the hatch to force it open again before the seal activated. He managed to push it back about a third of a meter, where it stuck.

"*Get that thing outta here!*" he shouted, hoping someone would figure out how to do that before his strength failed. Jackson was reaching for something on a shelf when Rosetti stepped in front of her. In a single, smooth motion, he grabbed a yellow helmet and swung it underhand, as if he were bowling, and knocked the alien squarely through the gap. Hicks let go of the door. It slammed shut and the seals activated while everyone stared at Rosetti in stunned silence.

Abruptly, Spence raised both arms straight up. "Field goal—score! *It's good!*"

There was nervous laughter from everyone except Rosetti, who was busy examining the helmet for damage.

"Hey, Colonel, that was *great*," Spence said after a bit. "It really was. Thank you."

Rosetti looked at her, then at the rest of the group, seemingly puzzled by their reaction. "I used to be a soldier," he said, as if that was supposed to explain everything. Maybe it did.

Hicks hit *pause* on the evacuation procedure so they could all put on the vac-suits. Like the ones they'd seen earlier in less fortunate circumstances, each was white, with bands of color on the arms and legs that matched to a helmet. Rosetti stuck with yellow, Spence chose blue, and Jackson took green. Talisa picked orange after making sure there were no more nasty surprises in either the suit or the helmet, leaving Hicks with red. Appropriate that he should have the color of blood and guts, he thought. Well, it wouldn't be much longer now.

He removed his watch, careful not to look at the time, intending to toss it aside but some impulse made him strap it to his wrist on the outside of his suit, although he still refused to look at the face.

After checking that everyone's seals were secure, Hicks unpaused the airlock procedure. "*The final stage of evacuation is confirmed*," said the artificial voice politely. "*Please be seated and fasten your safety harnesses.*"

Padded seats folded down on either side of the airlock at right angles to the hatch. Hicks and Jackson sat on one side facing Talisa, Rosetti, and Spence. "*Comms test*," Hicks said. "*Sound off with your name.*"

They all obeyed, except for Rosetti, who said, "*Jackson.*"

Unbelievable, Hicks thought; they couldn't even get through a simple comms test without Rosetti fucking it up.

Jackson groaned. "*What kinda shit are you trying to pull now, Rosetti?*"

"*You were right, Jackson,*" Rosetti said. "*I should have tried to stop this. It wouldn't have done any good—they'd have gone ahead anyway. But I should have tried, just for the record if nothing else.*"

Hicks had a dreadful falling sensation in the pit of his stomach, as if it were somehow plummeting from a great height without the rest of his body. Jackson looked from Rosetti to him and back again.

On Rosetti's left, Spence touched his arm gently. *"When we get to Gateway, there'll be a board of inquiry,"* she said, her filtered voice compassionate. *"Then you can tell them what happened here. We'll back you up. We can make them find the ones responsible for this and—"*

"Ten second warning," said the artificial voice. *"All air has been expelled. Preparing outer hatch."*

Rosetti bowed his head as if he were momentarily overcome with emotion. Then he looked up and Hicks saw the blood inside his faceplate, heard his labored breathing as he began twisting and jerking in the harness.

At the same moment, the outer hatch door was slowly swinging open. Loose items of clothing drifted toward it and slipped out into the void. Hicks reached for his pulse-rifle and discovered he had locked it down just out of reach, a dumb rookie mistake he hoped wouldn't cost them their lives.

He could hear nothing on comms now except hissing and screeching as the alien fought its way out of Rosetti's body. Not a chest-burster but Hicks could tell it wasn't quite fully grown yet. Its second set of teeth bashed against the inside of the faceplate; the helmet was too small for that ugly elongated head.

Hicks motioned frantically for Spence and Talisa to

move away from the thing that had been Rosetti, but before Spence could undo her harness, it lunged at her. Under the alien's furious hissing, he heard a cracking sound and Spence crying out in horror.

"*No!*" he shouted, struggling with his harness, unable to make it let go of him. On Rosetti's faceplate, fracture lines radiated in a lopsided star shape from the spot where his blood streamed out, separated into bubbles, and floated away in all directions.

Spence twisted around in her harness, trying to fight the monster off. Hicks kept hitting the release on his own harness but it still wouldn't let go.

"*Unlock, goddammit!*" he growled, feeling the strap for a kill switch.

A message appeared on the lower left area of his faceplate advising him that harnesses would not release until the outer door was completely open.

"*Emergency override!*" he yelled. He had no idea whether that would work but it did, and much better than he'd intended. As he leaped for his rifle, he discovered his command had unlocked *all* the harnesses.

Talisa threw herself on the alien from behind, struggling to pull it away from Spence. The creature whirled on her, leaving a larger trail of blood bubbles, and gave her a hard kick with both feet. The woman tumbled backward out of the airlock into space and the alien launched itself after her.

"*I'm okay, I'm okay,*" Spence was saying to Jackson, who was checking her suit for damage. "*Get Talisa—*"

Steadying himself in the doorway, Hicks raised the pulse-rifle. Alien-Rosetti had caught up with Talisa—these fuckers never gave up on a kill. Its long black talons had ripped through the ends of the gloves now, but that didn't seem to bother the monster at all. It had Talisa by the neck and was trying to wrap its legs around her body while she struggled and twisted and squirmed in its grip.

Hicks knew from experience that close-up fighting in zero-g was extremely difficult, even in a contained area where you had walls to help you maneuver, or at least to bang your opponent's head against. But in open, unbounded space, it was a clumsy, out-of-control grapple usually won by whomever had more air and an intact suit.

Unless you were fighting an alien—then all bets were off, Hicks thought, wishing mightily that he'd thought to grab a smart gun. Then he could have just set the target and let fly. Where was Weapons Division when you really needed them? Oh, right, the aliens had gotten them first. Apparently all bets were off for everything, everywhere, until further notice.

He was still trying to line up a shot that wouldn't hit Talisa as well when the alien finally got both legs wrapped around her body. Her arms flailed but she was definitely weakening. *Hang on, Talisa*, Hicks begged her silently.

And then he *did* have the shot, dead-on perfect, as if the sniper gods had smiled on him. He fired and kept firing, again and again and again.

Empty clip.

The alien tore Talisa's head off.

For a fraction of a second, Hicks thought he saw her shocked face before ice crystals covered the inside of the faceplate. The alien kicked off from her body, propelling itself back toward the airlock. The orange helmet sailed up and out of sight while the headless white vac-suit tumbled away in a different direction, arms and legs spread wide as if to embrace the void.

Jackson shoved a full clip at him. He ejected the empty one and reloaded, wishing it hadn't been too late for Talisa as he raised the weapon to his shoulder. But then, even if he'd made the shot, she'd have been hit with acid-blood. As it was, her death had been more merciful than Rosetti's, which, in spite of everything, Hicks wouldn't have wished on anyone.

Sure, vato, you keep tellin' yourself that till you believe it, Vasquez whispered.

This shot was an easy one. Rosetti's ripped vacuum suit blew apart soundlessly, almost gracefully in a cloud of red and acid-blood. Hicks was a bit surprised there had been any human blood left. He wondered what the analysts would make of the record from Rosetti's suit, which would already have been uploaded to the local military relay. From there it would be transmitted directly to the Colonial Marines headquarters, not the Company. The Marines would archive it, uncut and unedited, unlike Weyland-Yutani, where all data was doctored as a matter of course.

It occurred to Hicks then, apropos of nothing, or maybe of everything that had happened to him in the last four years, that even if he did quit the Marines, he'd never get away from the Company.

Jackson moved into the open doorway beside him, looking at him with nervous expectation. And now there were three, but he was still in charge. Behind Jackson, Spence was hanging onto a harness and staring past him. She was still seeing Talisa, he knew, even though her body was gone.

"*I didn't know her name until yesterday,*" Spence said, her eyes bright with tears. "*Jesus, Hicks, are we gonna make it? Do we even have a chance?*"

Of course she'd ask him that. He was in charge. It was his job to give her the right answer. It was also his job to know when the right answer wasn't the correct answer. He shifted position and finally let himself sneak a look at his watch.

21:59.

"*Yeah, sure, we've got a chance,*" he said, hoping he sounded encouraging, not insane. "*No doubt in my mind.*" Shifting again, he put his hand on the doorframe so he could see the time in his peripheral vision. "*Let's all just take a breath now, get the heart and respiration down to save air, okay?*"

Jackson and Spence murmured agreement.

The watch-face flickered.

22:00.

Hicks squeezed his eyes shut and braced himself.

4 3

"Hicks?"

Spence's heart skipped a beat; she looked at Jackson. Jackson shrugged and pushed back into the airlock, where she grabbed a flat black square stuck to the ceiling. A hard shake turned it into a duffel bag; looping one handle over her arm, Jackson began opening cabinets. Looking for more ammunition or whatever, Spence supposed. Maybe she should help.

Instead, she hung onto a handle near the door and leaned over to get a better look at Hicks's face. Her heart skipped another beat.

For the last twenty-four hours, she had been in continuous red alert. She had lost Tully to alien monsters that had ruined—no, *desecrated* his work. They'd ripped people apart right before her eyes, and she'd been within seconds of the same horrible death before she'd managed to kill one herself, and that had been pure stupid luck. All told, she'd been shocked, horrified, terrorized, and crazed with fear, and it *still wasn't fucking over.*

But this—Hicks wasn't *a* Marine, he was *the* Marine, the only one who'd ever fought the aliens and lived to tell the tale. And then he'd kept on fighting them here—all but singlehandedly—for authorities that were at best ungrateful and at worst corrupt, while staying honest himself. He'd been honest enough with the group not to promise them that everything would be okay and they'd all survive. Hell, he'd never promised that *anyone* would survive, yet he'd gone on fighting—

Until now? After they'd escaped from what they'd all thought was a dead end—*that* was his cue to give up?

She blinked. Nothing changed. The thought came to her unbidden: maybe he knew something she didn't.

Her mouth went dry and she had to swallow a few times before she could speak. *"Hicks?"* she said softly. *"What is it you're not telling me?"*

He didn't move.

"Hicks?" she said again, louder. *"Can you even hear me?"* When he didn't respond, she grabbed his arm and squeezed as hard as she could, although she couldn't feel much through the thick padding. *"Come on, man, say something."*

Still no response.

"Hicks, goddammit, *you're* fucking scaring me!"

Finally, he opened his eyes and turned to her with a broad smile of utter delight. No, relief—happy relief. Her jaw dropped.

"Do you know what time it is, Spence?" he asked, sounding as happy as he looked.

"Uh... sure." She blinked at the lower righthand corner of her faceplate to wake the helmet clock. Maybe his didn't work? *"It's 22:01. No, make that 22:02. Why?"* She laughed nervously. *"You got someplace else to be?"*

Hicks laughed as if she'd said something hilarious. *"I thought I did,"* he chuckled. *"Guess I'm gonna be late."*

"I'll write you a note." Jackson materialized on Spence's left, holding a rucksack. *"Everybody breathing normally? Heartbeats down? Either way, we gotta go.* Now.*"*

Laughing again, Hicks pulled a black band off his wrist and hurled it away.

"What was that?" Spence asked.

"Tell you later. When there's more time.*"* Still laughing a little, he turned to Jackson. *"Okay, Chief, which way to the lifeboats?"*

Jackson pointed at a slender mast off to her right. *"See that comms tower? The bay's just below—not the one where we saw aliens,"* she added quickly, *"so we should find at least one undamaged lifeboat."* She held the rucksack out to him. *"Let's get tethered."*

Spence stood on the hull, wavering a little in her magnetic boots, unused to the effort it took to stand still in zero-g. By the time Hicks had connected tethers to loops at their waists, she was already feeling the strain in her ankles and calf muscles. Hicks had put her between himself and Jackson, saying the least experienced always went in the middle.

"But what if you and Jackson have to trade places?" she asked. *"Or am I overthinking this?"*

"Not a bit," Hicks said, showing her how to unlock the loop and slide it around to a new position.

"Most of this stuff is based on climbing equipment," Jackson told her, showing her something that looked like a kid-size pickaxe, but with one side of the head a lot longer than the other. Jackson passed it to Hicks and strapped another to her outer thigh.

"It'll pierce pretty much anything," Hicks said, showing her how the handle telescoped before securing it to his own leg. *"Makes a good grappling hook, especially if you start drifting away."*

"Shouldn't I have one, too?" Spence asked. *"Just in case you guys drop yours or something?"*

"Yeah, there should have been one for each suit," Jackson said sourly. *"But they ran out of inventory. Restock'll be in next week for sure."* She gave a grim chuckle. *"Frankly, we're lucky all the suits had air."*

"Really?" Spence felt her heart-rate jump.

"No, that's what passes for funny in Operations," Hicks said. *"Don't tease the civilians, Jackson, they don't know better."*

"I'm *a civilian,*" Jackson said defensively.

"Not today, you're not," Hicks said sharply. *"Spence, just remember Newton's Law, the one about equal and opposite reactions, and don't make any sudden moves. Got it?"*

"Got it," Spence said. The way they'd tethered her between them, she didn't think she *could* make any sudden moves. Her own outside experience was limited to a single

guided group trek around Anchorpoint's upstairs pole, one of several Dr. Trent had chartered for the lab techs.

Had Talisa been on that one? She tried to remember and couldn't.

"*Spence.*" Jackson tapped her green helmet lightly against her blue one. "*You still with us?*"

"*Yeah, I'm fine,*" she said, her face hot with embarrassment.

"*Good,*" Hicks said, "*because I was telling you, if you get dizzy or feel panicky, just look down and watch your feet.*"

"*I'll be all right,*" she said. "*I'm not agoraphobic.*"

"*Okay, good talk, guys,*" Jackson said impatiently. "*Now let's go.*"

To Spence's dismay, walking in magnetic boots wasn't any easier than standing still. The effort of deliberately pulling her foot up at every step had her panting before they'd gone more than a few meters. Hicks called a halt and squatted down to examine her boots.

"*The magnetic setting is over twice what it needs to be,*" he told her, standing up again. He told her how to access the setting via her helmet display and talked her through the process of adjusting the magnetic strength with eye movements. Once she did, it was easier, although it still felt weird; each foot came down on the surface all at once in a stylized stomp march. All she needed was the right music so she could keep time.

Gimme some crazy John Philip Sousa beats, Spence thought, and had to press her lips together so she wouldn't use up her air laughing.

Some impulse made her look up at the black sky and the steady, unblinking points of light. Even if she spent a hundred years in places like Anchorpoint, she was never going to get used to stars that didn't twinkle. They'd always make her uneasy, maybe because it was a reminder of how inflexible and unforgiving conditions were in space.

Looking down at her feet, she tried to imagine how the three of them must look stomp-marching across the hull toward the comms tower. Three tiny lifeforms wearing tiny helmets the color of tiny billiard balls. No, more like pushpins that had unstuck themselves to escape monsters overrunning their tiny space station. Which Hicks wanted to blow up in the hope of preventing said monsters from spreading to all the other tiny pushpins and tiny space stations on the bulletin board...

Was that still the plan? Hicks hadn't mentioned it since Bishop had left. Did he know whether Bishop had reached the fusion package?

Would Hicks tell her if she asked? Would he say he didn't know, even if he did?

For that matter, did she really want to know?

She tried to distract herself by watching her feet and concentrating on her breathing, listening to the way it went in and out of rhythm with Hicks's and Jackson's.

"*Stopping,*" Hicks said suddenly, startling her so that she brought her left foot down on her right. Jackson steadied her as she wobbled.

"*What happened? What's wrong?*" Spence asked. Her

inner ear was making everything tilt to one side. She looked down at her feet again but they were tilted, too.

"*We're here,*" Hicks said cheerfully. "*Lifeboats ahoy.*"

She looked up to see a neat row of nautical-style prows, none of them tilting. "*They actually made them look like boats?*" she said incredulously.

The other two laughed, but not unkindly. "*Those things that look like prows are actually part of the docking cradles,*" Jackson said. "*Probably designed by a squid.*"

"Squids *can design docking cradles?*" Spence asked, feeling surreal.

"*Put it on the list of stuff I'll explain later,*" Hicks said, chuckling.

"*Or you coulda just told her a squid's a sailor,*" Jackson added, with a slight edge in her voice. "*Wouldn't've taken any longer.*"

"*Thanks for that, Chief.*" Hicks's cheerful tone had an edge of its own. "*You two wait here. I want to do some recon before we commit ourselves.*" He detached his tether from Spence and walked up the side of the cradle to shine his flashlight though a porthole, then moved to the one beside it.

"*How's it looking up there?*" Jackson asked as he checked a third porthole.

"*It's looking like we can move in right away.*" He walked back down to them. "*As long as you've got the keys to let us in.*"

"*Gimme a* break," Jackson said and Spence could practically hear her eyes rolling. "*I ran a real operation here, not a clearinghouse for stupid. Now everybody keep quiet while I do this, okay?"* She cleared her throat. *"Emergency Code 1143, Jackson comma Mandala, access lifeboat 16 at Bay 63-7."*

A synthetic female voice came over the general comm channel. *"Transmission from Jackson comma Mandala verified as authentic and acknowledged. Remote unlock function has not been installed for any lifeboats at 63-7."*

"What the fuck?" Jackson shouted. "Explain! *Why isn't remote unlock installed?"*

"Software is out of date and incompatible with general operations. Updated software has been requisitioned. Original delivery date has been revised. Transmission of new software scheduled for—"

"Oh, shut the fuck up!" Jackson snapped. *"Are there any lifeboats available with remote unlock, and which ones are closest to my current position?"*

"Lifeboat Bay 17-4 is closest to you at approximately 1.571 radians—"

"Shut up, thanks for nothing, Jackson out." She turned to Hicks. *"I take it back. I have been running a clearinghouse for stupid. Not just stupid—totally fucking stupid."*

Unable to help herself, Spence burst out laughing. They were going to die because they were locked out. They'd gone from apocalyptic horror to farce.

Two hands gripped her shoulders and she found herself looking at Hicks in extreme closeup. *"Spence."* He made it sound like an order.

Her laughter cut off. *"Sorry,"* she sighed. *"I forgot getting hysterical uses up air faster. But I'm okay now."*

"*If you'd let me finish,*" Jackson said, sounding oddly amused, "*I'd've told you I can still get us in. All I need is a hotwire.*"

Immediately, Spence was back in focus. "*I can help with that,*" she told Jackson brightly. "*I can strip some cable off the starlight collector cells on the cradle. They'd be on the part that looks like a prow.*" As she turned to point at it, she caught sight of Hicks's surprised expression. "*What?*" she asked him. "*I told you about the science fair back in Nebraska, didn't I?*"

"*Sure,*" Hicks said, chuckling a little. "*But I thought you were biotech, not hardware.*"

"*Not all matter is hardware, but all hardware is matter,*" Spence informed him. "*You just have to know its properties. Come on, walk me up there.*"

Leaving Jackson on the hull, she and Hicks stomp-marched up onto the prow-shaped part of the cradle, where he anchored them while she used the shorter side of his pickaxe to pry out one of the starlight collectors to get at the wiring. Which, she discovered, was the easy part; undoing a tangle of skinny wires with sausage fingers was much trickier.

"*How do you guys do any kind of fine work in a space suit?*" she asked, fumbling with wires that kept trying to float away.

Hicks moved closer to her, straddling the prow. "*There's a couple of small screwdrivers in your left front pocket.*"

She looked up from the wires. "What *left front pocket?*"

"*Allow me.*" Hicks leaned forward, uncovered the hidden pocket, and removed what looked like watchmaking tools. His sausage fingers moved much more deftly than hers. Sensing her embarrassment, he added, "*It takes practice.*" He pressed a tool to each of her index fingers and they stayed. "*Better living through sticky shit. Without it, we'd have never left Earth.*"

"*Okay, Jackson,*" she said as Hicks helped her keep the wires from re-tangling. "*I got every color there is up here. Any preference, or should I just yank them all out?*"

"*Two strands, one red, one green, each twenty centimeters,*" Jackson replied.

"*Thickish or thin?*" Spence asked.

Jackson chuckled. "*Surprise me.*"

"*You haven't had enough surprises for one day?*" Hicks said dryly.

Spence laughed again as she finally pulled out three twenty-centimeter lengths from the tangle, one red, one green, and one red-and-green braid. Hicks used the axe to cut them for her. "*Anything else while I'm up here?*"

"*Cheese Danish and a large coffee,*" Jackson said. "*Black, no sugar—I'm sweet enough.*"

"*Sorry, they're all out,*" Spence said as she and Hicks walked down the side of the cradle to the hull. "*You'll have to settle for hotwire, no sugar, we're all sweet enou—*"

She cut off, staring at the aliens crawling toward them on the hull, about a dozen of them, their shiny black bodies unprotected from vacuum and radiation. Of course.

They could adapt themselves to any environment, every environment, even no environment at all.

This is it. We're finished, Spence thought. *Not with a bang or a whimper, but in silence. Because in space, no one can hear the world end.*

Then Jackson was up on the cradle with her; she grabbed the hotwires and sidled toward an airlock. Spence started to follow but Hicks dragged her back, taking her up over the top of the lifeboat with him. Her mouth went dry as she saw how much larger the group of aliens advancing on them had become, as more appeared and scuttled across the metal surface to join them.

Crouching with his feet wide apart and flat against the lifeboat, Hicks steadied his rifle atop the hull and gestured for her to move behind him. Instead, she stayed beside him, watching as Hicks fired in short bursts, picking off half a dozen aliens at a time. Her gaze fell on the clip of Hicks's pulse-rifle: 55.

He saw her looking and put one hand over the counter as he fired another short burst at the center of the front line.

This time, the mob scattered in all directions.

Spence looked at Hicks in bewilderment. He made his usual stay-back gesture just as a square waste-duct panel on the roof in front of them flipped open and a yellow helmet popped up.

"*Rosetti?*" Spence and Hicks said together.

The yellow helmet turned to reveal Bishop looking out

at them through the faceplate, as cool, calm, and composed as ever.

Spence burst into tears.

4 4

For a moment, Hicks thought he was having a wish-fulfilment hallucination. It wasn't uncommon in combat, although it would have been a first for him. Then he saw how Bishop was struggling to get through the narrow opening and slung his rifle to help him out of the waste duct. The jerry-rigged metal brace taped to the left leg of Bishop's vac-suit proved he wasn't seeing things. Wish-fulfilment fantasies were always perfect.

"*What happened?*" Hicks asked.

"*Molecular fatigue,*" Bishop replied.

"*Cheap polycarbon garbage,*" Spence sniffled, glancing at Hicks apologetically as she pulled herself together. "*Nobody in their right mind would replace a bone with that. I wouldn't use it for a stapes in a* baby's *ear—*"

"*Me, either,*" Hicks said, talking over her and pointed at the airlock. "*Go help Jackson, I think the hatch is stuck.*" Spence untethered herself from Hicks and walked down to where Jackson was pulling mightily on the outer door, which had opened only a few centimeters and now refused to budge.

He turned back to Bishop. *"What happened?"* he asked in a low voice, hoping neither Jackson nor Spence were paying attention. *"22:00 came and went. No, uh, fireworks."*

"I set the 'fireworks' for 22:35," Bishop told him. *"I was running late, so I figured we could all use some extra time."* He pulled a fresh clip of ammo out of a front pocket and gave it to Hicks. *"Figured you might need this, too."*

Hicks was glad they were in vac-suits; otherwise he might have kissed him.

"Hey, guys!" Jackson called. Hicks looked over the side to see her grinning up at him from the inner side of the open door, and Spence holding onto the outside. *"All aboard, let's go while—"*

Her voice cut off with a harsh, wet, strangled noise as the sharp end of a queen's tail burst through her back. Spence cried out in horror as she reached for Jackson, but the other woman hit her with one flailing arm. Too hard to be accidental—Jackson's last thought had been for Spence, who was soaring up into open space as the tail pulled back into the airlock, taking Jackson's body with it.

Hicks bent his knees, intending to launch himself toward Spence, but Bishop gripped his arm so tightly he winced despite the padding. *"Better idea,"* he said, pulling a long length of cord from an auto-spooler at his waist. *"Anchor me, just in case."*

He tethered Bishop to himself, watched him make a perfect loop and lasso Spence with it on one try.

"*Good work*," Hicks said, as Bishop dragged Spence back to the lifeboat.

"*Not my first rodeo*," Bishop replied.

Hicks blinked. Had Bishop *really* just made a joke— *now*?

The question would have to wait. "*We came out an emergency exit from Adele Trent's office*," he said. Bishop looked a question at him as Spence's boots hit the lifeboat, making a tiny vibration. "*She didn't make it.*"

"*That's too bad*," Bishop said, and Hicks was certain he meant it.

The memory of Adele Trent in her office was replaced by Jackson impaled on the sharp tip of a queen alien's tail and Hicks's stomach gave another lurch. Damn, that was all he needed; being the poor sap who puked in his vac-suit wasn't how he wanted to spend the last minutes of his life.

He felt the lifeboat vibrate under him as the queen threw itself against the airlock door; without Jackson and Spence holding it open, it had resealed. Something else occurred to him, and he lunged for the trapdoor Bishop had emerged from to slam it shut.

"*Jackson*," Spence said tearfully.

"*Nothing we could have done*," Bishop told her.

"*I know.*" She sniffed. "*I just wanted to say her name. Mandala Jackson.*"

"*It's going to be okay*," Hicks lied.

Bishop caught his eye and pointed. The aliens were

starting to regroup now, and there were a lot more of them than before. The sight sent a white-hot surge of fury through Hicks and he bypassed the pulse charges for the grenade launcher.

Too late, he realized his feet were in the wrong position. The recoil knocked him backward and he felt his boots lift away from the hull. Something caught him by the ankles and his inner ear lost all sense of position.

A moment later, his helmet slammed into the back of his head and everything went as black as space without stars.

Spence tethered the unconscious Hicks to herself and grabbed his pulse-rifle before it flew away without having to be told. She was a quick study, Bishop thought, which was no mean feat under these circumstances.

Keeping low, Bishop fired short bursts at the approaching alien swarm, noting they'd begun shifting positions among themselves, many of them pushing up to the front line so it was wider than the mob behind it. They were also coming more slowly. This wasn't a kill-crazy rush; their movements seemed more deliberate, as if they were responding to commands. They slowed even more and then stopped altogether.

This couldn't be good, Bishop thought, but he didn't have enough data to estimate how bad it was going to get. Or rather, how much worse. He stood up to get a better look at the mob.

Nearby, Spence crouched on the lifeboat hull with Hicks in her arms. Bishop heard her in the comm, speaking softly to him, urging him to please wake up, they needed him. Any time a human took a hit to the head hard enough to cause unconsciousness was never good. Making a quick field-scan would tell him how much he'd have to lie to Spence, but there wasn't time. The aliens were stirring; something was moving among them, keeping low as it made its way to the head of the mob.

Bishop saw the talons first, pushing aside the creatures at the front. Those immediately behind fell back into their neighbors, making them give ground. Long, jointed limbs, black and shiny, widened the gap in the front line to let the rest of the creature emerge and unfold to its full height.

A queen.

Or rather, another queen, Bishop thought, wondering why there seemed to be so many of them. The aliens didn't serve a queen in the way bees did, and the latest generation didn't need a queen's eggs to reproduce. But apparently when a queen was present, it could take charge.

Was its control absolute? If the queen in the lifeboat came out, would it fight this one? Or would they divide the swarm between them?

The queen took up a position in front of the mob. It was at least two meters taller than the others, and definitely larger than the one he'd met in the mall. The horny growth on its head was also larger and more elaborate.

Ripley had said the queen reminded her of a rhinoceros beetle, but without the gentle whimsy, a description that had made Newt giggle. Good thing they couldn't see this one, Bishop thought, watching the queen's enormous crest swivel from one side to the other as it surveyed the assembled mass before it turned around and fixed its eyeless gaze on the human prey in front of it.

Although it gave no signal or command that Bishop could discern, the aliens began moving forward again, slowly and deliberately, their formation becoming wider as their numbers increased. No need to hurry now; they could see their prey had nowhere to go. It was the first time Bishop had ever seen them cooperate and, like everything else about them, it didn't bode well.

The number on his rifle's clip counter didn't bode well, either. But he knew that even with *all* the Colonial Marines and an endless supply of ammo, there was no hope of wiping them out. There were more aliens now than could have come from Anchorpoint's original population. He had no idea how they could be reproducing and it seemed certain now that he'd never find out.

When the counter read 01, he stopped and waited.

The queen extended its second set of teeth, snapping them in his direction. Maybe it was screaming at him, unaware that in space, no one could hear aliens scream.

He didn't bother with the sight as he raised the weapon; he knew exactly what position and angle he needed to take. The swarm kept coming, parting around the queen as it opened its arms and spread its talons. Bishop saw its leg muscles flex as it prepared to leap and he set his sequential perception to micro-intervals. The moment the queen rose away from the hull, he fired his last shot straight into its open jaws.

The grotesque head exploded in a cloud of acid-blood, which crystallized in the vacuum. The tiny particles left no damage as they ricocheted off the hull in all directions, sparkling prettily. Bishop logged this development with great interest, for the record and for later speculation as to how the next generation might adapt to maintain their blood's lethal properties in a vacuum.

As this ran in Bishop's secondary awareness, the queen's headless body flew backward into the creatures coming up behind it, who hurled it toward him. Their aim was lousy; pretty crystals streamed from the gash in its torso as it slammed into the lifeboat, well below where Bishop was standing but hard enough to make it vibrate.

The swarm came to a stop again, this time only a few meters away, talons digging into the metal hull to keep them in place. Their long heads swung back and forth, as though they were confused by the sudden absence of the queen. If so, Bishop was sure that was temporary; they'd probably revert to their kill-frenzy in a minute or two.

"Bishop!" Spence yelled. *"Over here! This way!"* He turned to see her moving in slow-motion bounds toward the comms tower with Hicks tethered behind her.

"Hicks?" Bishop asked. He tossed the empty rifle away

and moved along the top of the lifeboat, then reduced the magnetic setting on his boots so he could hop one-legged onto the cradle.

"Yeah, I'm back." Hicks laughed weakly. *"Looks like we're climbing Anchorpoint's Eiffel Tower."* He gave another weak laugh. *"What the hell, why make it easy for them?"*

Bishop measured the distance from where he was to the base of the tower. Even with only one good leg, he could get there in a single leap. And he'd better do it before the aliens remembered they could kill without a queen.

Bending his good leg, he started to push off, and suddenly realized he'd failed to control his other leg properly. Something caught the metal brace around his left boot and instead of flying up, his body swung forward and down, smashed into the cradle, and rebounded with his foot still caught so that he hit the cradle backward.

As he popped up again, he saw his jerry-rigged brace was hooked on part of a starlight collector that someone had pried out of the docking cradle and then just left floating loose. This was what humans called adding insult to injury, he thought, arms swinging wildly as he tried to grab something. He had killed a queen and thrown the aliens into momentary confusion, but thanks to one clumsy movement, he was going to bob around like a silly toy until the aliens realized he was helpless and tore him apart.

* * *

"*Go*," Hicks told Spence, pointing at the handholds running the length of the comms tower. Without waiting for an answer or a protest, he untethered himself from her and leaped back toward Bishop.

One jump took him halfway; he caught himself on Anchorpoint's hull with the pickaxe. The second jump took him straight to Bishop, or rather straight into him. The impact rattled his eyeballs in their sockets, as if to remind him he'd just taken a hard blow to the head, but he and Bishop managed to hang onto each other, letting Hicks slam his boots down on the lifeboat and bring both of them to a stop.

"*Hang on while I figure this out*," Hicks said, mildly surprised at how calm he sounded; almost as calm as Bishop. Anyone hearing him would never have guessed the swarm of aliens were now surrounding the docking cradle and already digging their claws into the metal as they climbed toward the last juicy humans available for light-years.

"*I'm going to have to ruin your masterpiece here*," Hicks added.

"*My what?*" Bishop asked, sounding so genuinely puzzled that Hicks couldn't help laughing as he hacked away at the tape holding the metal frame to the android's leg, careful not to pierce the vac-suit.

As soon as he cut away the last bit of tape, he put one arm around Bishop's waist, intending to jump them both back toward the tower.

"*Wait,*" Bishop said, and pulled a long length of cord from the spooler at his waist and made another lasso. "*Spence?*"

"*Right here!*" The white figure with the royal-blue head was up near the top of the tower, legs locked around the metal framework. "*Swing it, cowboy!*"

Bishop let fly and she caught the loop with ease, then pulled them in hand over hand.

"*That was almost like fun,*" she said wistfully as they reached her. "*Maybe in some alternate universe somewhere, fun's still real.*"

Hicks motioned for her and Bishop to get moving. The aliens were swarming over the lifeboat now but many of them seemed tentative, like they didn't understand why the humans weren't there. Others were already moving toward the comms tower.

"*It shouldn't be much longer,*" Bishop said, as if they were waiting for transport to Gateway rather than the next life.

They reached the tip of the tower and held on, gazing down at the first wave of aliens clambering up the metal framework after them. Not great climbers even in zero-g, Hicks noted. They seemed physically impaired, like they were having trouble with perception and coordination.

Maybe because they were weightless in a vacuum, he thought. Adapting to an environment without either air or gravity was a far more drastic change than finding faster ways to reproduce. A lifeform that could live unprotected in space called for major alterations. It might take them a while to produce the perfect mutation, maybe as many as half a dozen generations. Although considering how quickly they'd been reproducing, that would probably take a couple of days.

Hicks began shooting at the creatures, picking off the closest ones. *What can you do when there's nothing you can do?* Apone grinned around his cigar at him. *Target practice—till you run out.*

He smiled to himself. Of all the damnedest things that had crossed his mind lately, this was the least absurd.

When the counter on his clip read 04, Hicks stopped and looked at Spence beside him. They were stretched out, flying like flags.

"Four minutes to overload," Bishop said, as if someone had asked.

"What a coincidence—I've got four shots left," Hicks chuckled. *"Think it means something?"*

If Bishop replied, it was lost in a painfully loud burst of static in the comms. Before Hicks could ask what the hell, there was another, even louder burst. Damage to the comms tower? Then Spence punched his arm hard and pointed up.

Or, more precisely, UPP, Hicks thought, almost giddy as the interceptor slowly descended on them. The vessel was much the worse for wear—the hull was pitted and badly scorched, although the two IDs on its belly, one in Cyrillic, were still readable. Which meant this couldn't be a dying wish-fulfilment hallucination either; he didn't know Cyrillic well enough.

The airlock opened and soft golden light shone down on all three of them.

And then again… Hicks thought, blinking in wonder.

4 5

"*Spence, you first,*" Hicks said. "*I'll give you a boost.*" She moved up so she was standing with one foot on the very tip of the tower. "*And turn off the magnetism!*" he added.

She obeyed and Hicks shoved her at the open airlock of the interceptor still slowly coming down. Whoever was on the stick was a goddamn good pilot, he thought. "*You next,*" he told Bishop. "*Don't argue, I outrank you.*"

"Yes, sir," Bishop said as Hicks boosted him up by his good leg. Above them, Spence was leaning out of the airlock, arms reaching for them. Bishop took her hands and Hicks kept hold of Bishop's good leg, firing one last shot at the aliens on the tower.

It was like that old game, Hicks thought, Barrel of Monkeys, and he couldn't help laughing as Spence hauled him and Bishop into the airlock. Just before the outer door closed, he caught a glimpse of a pulse-cannon descending from a panel two meters to the right. Then the hatch shut and the *thump-thump-thump* of the weapon firing on the aliens made them bounce all over each other in the tiny space while air rushed in.

The inner door opened and a skinny, tattooed arm reached down, grabbed Spence by the back of her vac-suit, and dragged her into the cabin. As Hicks helped Bishop up after her, he heard scratching noises, first on the hatch, then moving up the sides of the interceptor.

"Come! Come *now!*" a woman's voice shouted at him, and added something else in Vietnamese; Hicks wasn't fluent but he knew enough to understand she was telling them to haul ass unless they wanted to get violated to death. As soon as he hoisted himself into the cabin, Spence slammed the inner door behind him and locked it. Hicks removed his helmet and looked around.

The woman with the tattooed arms was in the pilot's seat. She yelled something else then cut off sharply, listening to the sound of claws moving up to the roof.

Bishop called to the pilot in Vietnamese; she swiveled around to the control panel and tapped a series of buttons quickly. All at once, Hicks found himself tumbling backward along with Spence and Bishop, to fetch up against some cabinets in the storage area.

They all heard claws scraping the length of the spacecraft as the creatures tried to hang on. Hicks estimated they were at three-gs before the aliens finally let go.

"Tell her to fire on them," Hicks said to Bishop, straining

to get the words out. Bishop obeyed and they heard the *thump-thump-thump* of the pulse-cannon again as the acceleration began to ease off.

"I don't think we have to worry about them surviving," Bishop said. "They'll get pulled into the implosion."

"We can't leave even one of those bastards floating around," Hicks said. "If it gets picked up by someone looking for salvage—" He saw Spence looking up at him. "Ripley told me what happened when just one of them got aboard her ship. The *Nostromo*. And that was *before* they could survive in a vacuum."

Spence nodded. "Yeah, I know." She got to her feet and unzipped her suit a few centimeters, fanning herself with one hand. "But if it's okay with you, I need a break from saving the human race from extinction. Not long, anywhere from fifteen minutes to, oh, say, five years?"

"Me, too," Bishop said. Hicks and Spence both turned to him in surprise. "As I said back on LV-426, I may be synthetic but I'm not stupid." He looked at his left leg, where it lay in a bizarre zigzag. "Could someone help me to a chair?"

Spence spotted a wheeled stool locked to the wall, pulled it out, and helped Hicks get Bishop situated on it. Then they rolled him across the cabin and parked him next to the pilot.

A quick look at the console told Hicks the interceptor was a model he was familiar with, albeit out-of-date. He moved around to the pilot's other side and pressed a panel. A small flatscreen popped up from the console, displaying a view of the starry black space behind them.

"Increase magnification?" he asked the woman.

Her glare said she didn't appreciate his taking liberties with her console, but she did as he asked. One of the stars in the center of the screen suddenly swelled and became Anchorpoint.

"What are you looking for?" Spence asked.

She had barely finished speaking when the entire screen went white.

"That," said Hicks. A wave of intense relief washed over him and suddenly he had to sit down on the padded bench against the wall.

"Good work, Bishop," he said, his voice shaky.

Bishop dipped his head noncommittally. "I try."

Sitting on the floor to one side of the console, Luc Hai watched the robot as it bent over the open control panel. Occasionally, it would pull up a small circuit board embedded in a tangle of wires and carefully disconnect each one, then reconnect them in a different order.

The robot had told her the problems she was having in the navigation had been caused by the destruction of Rodina Station, or rather, by being too close to it. Yesterday she would already have fixed the problems herself. Now she couldn't muster enough energy to think about them.

Just keeping the interceptor on course with the glitchy navigation had worn her out.

She'd gone to Anchorpoint hoping for help. Instead, she'd ended up rescuing the last two capitalists left alive, and their robot—the same damned machine she had delivered to them only a couple of days before. Merely an astounding, against-all-odds coincidence? Or a karmic wake-up call?

The UPP disdained things like karma as superstition, but Rodina Station was gone, leaving her alone in a universe dominated by capitalists. If there was some significance to this, she didn't know what it was. Maybe significance came later, in retrospect.

Either way, it wasn't her concern. She wasn't going to last long enough for hindsight, or even to tell her part of the story.

Maybe they would do her the honor of commemorating her along with their own people, while Boris and Ashok and all the others sacrificed on the altar of Suslov's ego would pass into obscurity, their lives unacknowledged and their deaths untold. History was written by the victors—i.e. the survivors—and she wouldn't be among them. She had no history anymore, and no future, only the here and now, for however long it lasted.

Her gaze drifted back to the robot still at work on the console. She trusted it completely. Machines knew machines, and whatever was wrong, the robot would fix it, if only because it was programmed to keep the man and woman safe, acting as their servant and guardian. Capitalists. Did they have any idea what this arrangement looked like from the outside?

They had built these so-called intelligent machines, insisting they were equivalent to humans, *citizens* even, and then made them into a permanent servant underclass. And yet they claimed to adhere to the principles of justice, equality, and freedom. But any society that had masters and servants could never be just, or equal, or free. Not even if the servants were machines.

Well, if these two expected her to treat the robot like a human, they'd be disappointed. They could indulge themselves in any way they chose—she couldn't stop them even if she wanted to. But she wasn't going to validate their master-and-servant mentality by anthropomorphizing a machine.

The man, Hicks, sat on the bench against the opposite wall, close to where the robot was working. Spence, the woman, was stretched out with her head pillowed on his lap. She had lain down right after Anchorpoint had disappeared and was still deeply asleep, her face relaxed and peaceful. Luc Hai wondered how she'd take it when she woke up and found herself back in the same bad dream.

Considering the woman had stayed alive long enough to be rescued, Luc Hai thought she would eventually recover—she just had to let herself, which was the tricky part, so much easier said than done. When this was over, she'd have her whole life ahead of her to figure it out.

Except it wasn't over, not yet. They hadn't reached a safe place and there was no guarantee that they would; shit happened, even without aliens. Still, she envied both Spence and Hicks anyway, wishing she could have faced the end with someone she cared about instead of dying among strangers. *Capitalist* strangers. Her eyes fell shut.

"Bishop?" Hicks's voice sounded far away. "Are Spence and I—are we…" There was a long pause. "Are we infected?"

The question pulled her back from her oncoming doze. She opened her eyes to see the robot had put down its tools to fish something small out of an inner pocket of its spacesuit. It held the object under the high-intensity lamp and Luc Hai heard a pleasant bell-chime. Setting the item down on the console, the robot shook its head. "No."

"Are you sure?" The man's face was wary.

"I am," the robot said. "I used all available data to calculate a solid set of parameters on the incubation periods for the various forms. Neither you nor Spence is a carrier." It tilted its head toward her. "Nor is she."

Luc Hai could see Hicks un-tense. "You set an alarm?" he asked.

"Yes," said the robot. "My internal chronometer confirms it, but I knew you'd feel better if I gave you something concrete. Like a watch."

Hicks laughed a little. "Can't beat a watch for the right time."

The robot reached into another pocket in its vac-suit

and came up with an automatic. Luc Hai recognized it as a standard Colonial Marines weapon. To her surprise, the robot offered it to her, handle first.

"Giữ nó. Nó không có ích với tôi," she said. *Keep it. I've got no use for it.*

A powerful wave of fatigue swept over her and she let her eyes fall closed again. The voices faded away.

4 6

Hicks looked from the Vietnamese woman to the gun on the console and then to Bishop.

"Was that for us?" he asked. "If we were…"

"Yes." Bishop picked up his tools and adjusted the lamp slightly before he bent over the console again. Most of the time, Hicks found Bishop's unshakable composure reassuring, and once in a while, maddening. At the moment, however, it was disturbingly cold-blooded.

But then, an artificial person *was* cold-blooded, ruled by their programming—a series of orders to follow. It was just that Bishop's orders were factory-installed; he had no choice but to obey.

Hicks had never imagined any artificial person would be capable of *interpreting* these orders. Yet somehow, Bishop had learned to read between the lines of his programming, to find deeper meaning. As a result, he had extended the original command to protect individual humans to include *all* humans, as a species. It made him wonder if even the most brilliant AI experts really understood what they had created.

A memory from his early days in the Marines popped into his head, of a course he'd been required to take after he was out of basic, something called *Challenges in Emergency Martial Actions.* He'd braced himself for a series of jargon-filled lectures on how to CYA after a FUBAR, and then discovered the title actually translated as *Whom You Should Fuck Over, When, & How Badly.*

One of the scenarios the instructor had hammered away at was The Trolley Problem. Hicks had already known that one: you're driving a train and the brakes give out. If you stay on course, you kill five people, but if you switch tracks, you kill only one person. Whom should you fuck over?

He'd always been resistant to The Trolley Problem, partly because of all the incessant arguing it inspired, but mostly because it sanitized the situation so much that it stripped all the truth out of it. Life wasn't a neat series of discrete events—it was messy and dirty and chaotic. In an emergency, you didn't have time to argue about the ethics of a situation or whether your moral compass could find true moral north, or anything other than *What the fuck, what the fuck, what the fuck?!*

Finding out he was right about that had been no consolation.

And yet, after everything that had happened to him, here he was thinking about that fucking trolley. Well, there was always time *after* the fact to think, rethink, and overthink all the aspects and permutations and implications of a situation. He sneaked a look at Bishop, wondering if anyone realized the trolley problem was running for real now, and an artificial person was driving.

"She's dying," Bishop said.

The sudden break in the silence made Hicks jump.

"Radiation poisoning," Bishop added, nodding at the Vietnamese woman.

"Is there anything we can do?" Hicks asked, even though he knew better.

"Unfortunately, no," Bishop replied. "The interceptor's anti-radiation system neutralized the ship itself and made it safe for passengers, although I'd recommend regular decontam treatments until we dock somewhere, just to be on the safe side. If she'd had a vac-suit on when they nuked Rodina, she might have a chance of pulling through. Although she was so close to the explosion, I'm not sure a suit would have given her much protection. All we can do is make her comfortable. If she lets us."

Hicks nodded; he had a feeling she'd resist any kindness for as long as she could.

"You're going to have to start thinking of yourselves as a species as well as a civilization," Bishop went on. "'You' meaning humanity as a whole. You're faced with something you've never had before—a natural enemy."

Moving carefully so he wouldn't wake Spence, Hicks got up and slipped a folded jacket under her head. He was about to join Bishop at the console when his gaze fell on the Vietnamese woman, and he brought her a thermos of water. She shook her head and turned away from him. He left the thermos beside her and sat down in the pilot's seat.

"Humans as a species spent a few thousand years running and hiding from things that wanted to eat us," Hicks said. "Then we figured out how to make weapons to protect ourselves."

Bishop shook his head. "Those predators just went in search of easier prey, which allowed humanity to ascend to the top of the food chain. You've been there ever since, not simply undefeated, but also unchallenged." He put down his tools. "These aliens aren't wild animals you can drive away with a few warning shots. Weapons don't scare them off—they're dedicated to killing. Humans as a species have never faced this kind of threat."

"I'm pretty sure the aliens kill *all* living things," Hicks said, remembering pocket-Madagascar. "Not just us."

"They're still your natural enemy, Corporal, as relentless in killing as humans are at surviving. Think about it. They don't kill for food, dominance, resources—they don't even kill for sport."

Hicks shifted uncomfortably in the pilot's seat.

"They have no discernible language," Bishop went on. "They don't group in families or communities for mutual benefit or even protection—in fact, they seem completely unaware that they can be hurt or killed. Until I saw the queen assert itself as their leader, I'd have said they were barely aware of each other." He paused, frowning a little. "They may be an enemy to all forms of life, but none more so than human beings."

"You're a real glass-half-full kind of artificial person, aren't you?" Hicks said with a faint laugh. "Humans'll just have to stay out of their way."

"You can't." Bishop's calm voice now had a hint of urgency. "The universe isn't big enough for the both of you."

Hicks gave him a skeptical look. "What's *that* supposed to mean?"

"You have to figure out where they came from—where they're *still* coming from—and put an end to them right there, at the source." Bishop leaned forward a little. "This isn't merely interspecies competition. These creatures are to biological life as antimatter is to matter. You have to track them down to their place of origin and wipe them out. Obliterate them. Nothing less than total extinction. Scorch the earth and salt it so that nothing can ever grow there again."

The trolley was picking up speed, Hicks thought. "You know, I've heard that kind of thing before," he said. "But only from crazy extremists."

Bishop shook his head again. "You need to understand this is war and it's a fight to the death—to *complete* death. To extinction. The enemy doesn't have any other mode."

"I've been fighting in wars for most of my adult life," Hicks said. "The entirety of human history is pretty much one war after another—"

"Those were wars between humans," Bishop said. "Humans always thought they were their own worst enemy. But that isn't true anymore. You have met the enemy, and for the first time, it *isn't* you."

Hicks had no answer for that.

"It's a Darwinist universe," Bishop said after a moment. "Will humanity be the ultimate survivor? Or will it be the aliens?"

The question hung in the air. Hicks glanced at Spence, still peacefully asleep, then turned to the Vietnamese pilot, now stretched out on the floor. Bishop had gone back to work on the console, so for the time being, there was nothing for him to do. Except maybe get started on the existential crisis.

Bishop, you're good but you're not quite right about this one, Hicks thought. *We have met the enemy, and we've mistaken it for something our plowshares can beat into a weapon.*

Not that it really made any difference.

Some unmeasured time later, the proximity alarm roused Hicks out of a semi-doze. He popped up another screen on the control panel and ran through the feeds from the external cameras. All but one of the surveillance devices on the roof had been damaged by the aliens in their desperation to hang on, but one was all he needed to see the enormous letters on the belly of the spacecraft above them:

USS KANSAS CITY

Bay doors opened, revealing a brightly lit hold.

We're going to Kansas City, Hicks thought, limp with relief. *Kansas City, here we come.*

Ripley and Newt appeared fleetingly in his mind's eye. They were replaced by Hudson, Apone, Vasquez, Gorman, and the rest of the squad from LV-426. Tully, Charles A. joined them, along with Jackson, wearing her baseball cap with the light-pen, and Martinez and Rosetti, and then Anchorpoint itself just before it faded to white.

Understanding bloomed in his mind, complete and fully formed: it still wasn't over.

The horrors that he and Ripley and Newt and Spence and Bishop had survived, that had killed the LV-426 colony, a squad of good Marines, and two entire space stations—it was on him to make sure it all hadn't been for nothing.

Dammit, he just *couldn't* get a break.

ACKNOWLEDGEMENTS

Many, many, *many* thanks to:

Steve Saffel, who was brave enough to offer this opportunity and saw it through all the slings and arrows and other vagaries of outrageous fortune and misfortune, including (but not limited to) my undying devotion to the semi-colon and the unintentional installation of a sunroof in our bathroom ceiling;

Amanda Hemingway, aka Jan Siegel, who has listened to me wax rhapsodic about semi-colons, among other things, and also makes a great rum-based quarantini, and just generally rocks the house anyway;

Ellen Datlow, for teaching me how to write real good in the first place and for hanging out with me on Skype because friends don't let a quarantine spoil the party;

Caroline Oakley, fellow-traveler and fellow-Skyper, good company, good and wise friend;

Mic Cheetham, my agent, defender of the faith, and truly A Force For Good In Our Time;

My son Rob Fenner and his girlfriend Justyna Burzynska, who are always the best bright lights in our lives;

And always to my husband, the Original Chris Fowler, always the most interesting person in the room, whose unfailing and unselfish support has kept me going even when I wasn't sure I could.

(And a shout-out to whomever invented the semi-colon. Not to be confused with the colon, it's subtler and more discreet than the em-dash for sentence fragments but works equally well as a connector for two complete thoughts; sometimes more!)

ABOUT THE AUTHOR

Pat Cadigan has won the Locus Award three times (so far), the Arthur C. Clarke Award twice (so far), and the Hugo Award, Japan's Seiun Award, and the Scribe Award for best movie novelization, for *Alita: Battle Angel* (once each, so far). She's optimistic. She lives in London with her husband, the Original Chris Fowler, and Gentleman Jynx, Coolest Black Cat On The Planet. She has written twenty-one books in total, including several originals, one YA, two nonfiction, and a few movie novelizations/ media tie-ins. Most are available as eBooks.

In late December 2014, Cadigan was diagnosed with terminal cancer and given two years to live. Although normally conscientious about deadlines, she missed that one. Cadigan believes she was put here to accomplish a certain number of things and she is now so far behind, she can never die.

For more fantastic fiction, author events, exclusive
excerpts, competitions, limited editions and more

VISIT OUR WEBSITE
titanbooks.com

LIKE US ON FACEBOOK
facebook.com/titanbooks

FOLLOW US ON TWITTER
@TitanBooks

EMAIL US
readerfeedback@titanemail.com